Suitable for Framing

Suitable for Framing

EDNA
BUCHANAN

HYPERION

NEW YORK

The individuals and incidents portrayed in this novel are fictitious.
Any resemblance to actual incidents, or individuals living or dead,
is purely coincidental.

ISBN 0-7868-6047-2

Design and Illustration by Holly McNeely

For retired Miami Police Lieutenant Bob Murphy,
Sergeant Jerry Green,
and all the other heroes

I will speak daggers to her, but use none.
—William Shakespeare

Suitable for Framing

Chapter One

I knew what it was when I heard the shots.''

The witness had been pumping self-serve gas at an Amoco station across the street. I sidled up with my notebook, virtually ignored by uniformed cops accustomed to my presence.

"I knew it wasn't firecrackers,'' he told them, nervously smoking a cigarette. His face was flushed, and a slight paunch hung over his khakis. "I hit the ground. I was in Saigon, the Tet offensive in 'sixty-eight. I know gunfire when I hear it.

"Never thought I'd see something like this, right in broad daylight.'' He shook his head.

A middle-aged French Canadian in a rented red Cadillac had objected when a Latino kid jumped out of the car behind him at a traffic light and stuck a gun in his face. He had stomped the gas pedal. In street-speak he "bucked the jack,'' trying to escape—a mistake in this case.

The young gunner fired three shots in rapid succession, blasting out two windows. Showered by broken glass, the driver swerved, slamming into a nearby light pole.

The 'Nam vet had sneaked a peek from the ground as the shooter scampered up to the damaged car. "He looked like a little kid, but he had a big gun. I'll be damned if he didn't open the driver's door, calm as you please, and shoot the man point-blank in the leg.'' He winced. "Musta hurt like hell. I heard the guy screaming all the way across four lanes. The kid just yanked him out of the car by the back of the neck, threw him down on the street, and took his Caddy.''

A yellow Nissan Pathfinder, a four-by-four, had followed the Caddy at high speed. Probably an accomplice. That became certain moments later, when the occupants of the second car were described as three Hispanic teenagers. The thieves had all been wearing Raiders caps over dark scarves tied around their heads.

The midday sun heated my skin, right through the fabric of my white cotton dress. Covering stories like this one, not long languid days on the beach, reinforces the sun streaks in my dark-blonde hair and the tan on my legs. Sweaty cops were all over the place, and they weren't smiling. The chief and an assistant city manager were on the way. Mugged residents may be left waiting on hold, but violence against tourists creates high anxiety, hand-wringing, and paranoia at city hall, the Chamber of Commerce, the Convention Bureau, and the Hotel Association.

As I took notes, a red-faced woman pulled over in a pickup and hailed the cops. She had seen the carjacker jump out of the Pathfinder and draw a gun from his belt as he approached the rental car. Frightened, she drove on but then doubled back to see what he'd done and tell what she'd seen. She had jotted down the tag number for the cops. The car was stolen, taken from a North Miami man an hour earlier.

A high-pitched three signal interrupted conversation with the woman. The dispatcher's cool, disembodied words followed the emergency tone bleated in stereo from half a dozen police radios.

"A three-thirty. White male taken from his vehicle and shot in the leg. Four-oh-oh-three Ponce de Leon Boulevard."

Twenty blocks south, in the Gables. Cops exchanged glances. "What the hell?" muttered a husky sergeant.

"Somebody out on a spree," said a black officer.

Where will it end? I wondered, dashing for my borrowed car.

The shooter in the Gables had arrived in a red Caddy and fled in the new victim's white BMW, according to my portable police scanner.

Traffic was clogged by Gables police cars, now joined by two from Miami. I edged between bystanders after parking on a side street. The reek of traffic mingled with the acrid smell of gunpowder that hung in the still air. A well-built dark-haired man in obvious pain half sprawled, half sat, on the curb. He ignored staring strangers, one hand shading his eyes from the merciless sun. A tourniquet on his leg stanched the flow of blood that had puddled in the gutter. A pale band of skin circled his tanned wrist, signaling where his Rolex used to be.

This victim, now moaning aloud, had not even tried to buck the jack. Sharp-eyed urban hunters had spotted his Rolex and his white BMW 540i sedan across four lanes of traffic. Their stolen Caddy swung into a U-turn, falling into traffic behind the Beemer, witnesses said. At the first stoplight, a teenage passenger stepped out, trotted up, and almost nonchalantly shoved a nine-millimeter Beretta in the man's face. He removed the driver's watch, shot him in the leg, then dragged him out of the car, which he took. The Caddy followed. Two motorists had stopped to help the wounded man in the street; others just veered around him.

I gazed down busy Coral Way as though trying to pick up the scent of the predators. "Wonder where they're headed with all these flashy cars?" I said aloud.

"We know where one just was," a Gables sergeant said, listening to his radio.

A twenty-nine, a robbery: an elderly couple in the parking lot of a South Miami Kmart. The young thief never even got out of the car. A passenger in a yellow four-by-four, he had simply plucked the woman's purse from her arm as the driver floored it. When I arrived, the victims still stood dazed, alone in the middle of the vast lot. He leaned shakily on a cane. She clung to his arm. No crowd had gathered. Bustling shoppers paid scant attention. He was eighty-one. She was seventy-seven.

Luckily the purse had not been attached to her by a strap, so she had escaped being knocked down or dragged. She had no money inside but had lost valuable items. "My prescription glasses are in my pocketbook. They cost three hundred dollars," she told me in a trembling voice. "My Social Security card and my medication . . . they're gone."

Her husband's frail body quaked and she patted his arm.

They lived in a nearby apartment. Occasionally they strolled across the parking lot to the Kmart. Must have looked like easy targets from U.S. 1. The kids had veered into the lot and nailed them on the first pass.

I tried to comfort them. "They'll throw your purse away once they go through it. Whoever finds it will probably call."

"You really think they might?" Hope lit her brimming eyes.

"Sure." At least no one was shot, I thought. The boy with the gun must still be driving the BMW.

I wanted to stay, but after twenty minutes there were no new developments. A familiar voice tersely advised on one of the police channels that he was responding to the scene of the last shooting. My stomach did loop the loops. Lieutenant Kendall McDonald. I was tempted to return to the scene for more information and to look with feigned surprise into his silvery-blue eyes. Common sense prevailed. I had to get back to the newspaper, and there was no point. One of the cops promised to call me if the cars were recovered or the bandits captured. As I drove, I scanned the traffic flow for the missing cars and the roadside for the stolen purse. The thieves must have discarded it by now. I fought the urge to stop and start checking dumpsters. It would be like searching for a contact lens lost in the surf, but I wanted somebody to do it.

I sighed, thinking of the old couple, preyed upon by the young in the winter of their lives. What would McDonald and I have been like after so many years together, if circumstances had been different, if career choices, pride, and ethics hadn't stood in our way?

Back in the newsroom I rolled my chair up to the terminal at my desk, picked up the phone, and dialed the library as I began work on the story.

An unfamiliar voice answered. I asked for Onnie.

"She's off today," the stranger said.

"Tuesdays? Since when?" I asked impatiently.

"Since I got hired this week," the voice snapped back. "This is Trish."

A new hire who knows nothing, I thought irritably. A savvy friend in the library comes in handy. Where was Onnie when I needed her? I nearly hung up.

"This is Britt Montero," I said. "I cover the police beat and need to know if we have any carjacking stats for this year and the latest figures on crimes against tourists. You may be able to find—"

"I know who you are," she said quickly. "I'll get them out to you."

"Thanks. I'm on deadline," I added.

"Right."

I skimmed through my notes, thumbing through scribbled pages, then began to write a lead.

"Here you go, Ms. Montero."

Startled, I looked up at a slender young woman hovering at my elbow, a stack of papers clutched to the front of her prim, crisply starched blouse. "A press release issued by Miami P.D. last week breaks down class-one crimes for the first six months of this year. The carjacking stats are listed."

She peeled off the sheet and placed it on my desk. Her hands were small and graceful, nails neatly trimmed and coated with clear polish.

"Here's a wire piece on the national epidemic of similar crimes." Her voice was husky and all business, the accent midwestern. A mane of silky dark hair, cut short and sassy, framed her fresh-scrubbed face.

"A safety bulletin issued by Triple A." She whisked another paper from the sheaf.

Her only jewelry was a school ring with a blue stone and a wrist-watch with a no-nonsense black leather band. A final printout hit my desk with a flourish. "I thought you might be interested in a new bill pending in the state legislature. Here's a copy. It's aimed at increasing the penalties for carjacking."

My jaw must have dropped. "You running a game on me?"

"I beg your pardon?"

"Usually this place does not run like a well-oiled machine. Thanks for your help. . . . What's your name again?"

"Trish Tierney."

"Well, I'm Britt. Thanks."

She grinned and gave a smart little salute, and I turned back to the story.

"Who *was* that, Britt?" Ryan Battle asked moments later. He is the general assignment reporter whose desk sits just behind mine.

"Trish," I said.

"Trish," he repeated softly, his spaniel eyes following the direction she had taken. Ryan falls in love at the flick of an eyelash. "She work here?"

"The library. Make your move fast," I said over my shoulder. "She's too good to stay there long."

I finished the story and made one last phone check. The French Canadian was undergoing surgery to remove the bullet; the slug that hit the other victim went through his leg completely. No arrests. I added a tag line and hit the SEND button.

Chapter Two

The next afternoon was golden. The dealership had called. In a giddy mood, high on the aroma of my new T-Bird that had arrived at last, I picked up my friend Lottie at the paper and chauffeured her on a lighthearted drive.

It was a steamy late-September day with a flamboyantly brilliant sky full of fast-moving clouds and heat lightning that sizzled on the horizon. We parked at the mall, where my new set of wheels stood out, glistening like a polished gem, and strolled inside to snack on frozen yogurt. I like strawberry, smothered in wet walnuts. Lottie ordered chocolate with multicolor sprinkles.

I studied aerobic shoes in the window of a sports store as Lottie cooed at an adorable baby in a bright yellow stroller. The young mother held a second child by the hand, a big-eyed curly-haired toddler. He wore a Barney T-shirt, shorts, and red sneakers that looked brand new, but his baby sister was clearly the star. Her bib said SPIT HAPPENS, and she was strapped into a car seat in the stroller. Aware she was being admired, she chortled, babbled, and reached chubby hands for Lottie's frizzy red hair.

Lottie Dane was born in Gun Barrel, Texas. She always wears cowboy boots and is a top-flight photographer who shot major news around the world before settling in Miami. Eight years older than I am, she is close to forty now, is crazy about babies, and has craved her own for years. Long divorced with no kids, her search for Mr. Right has accelerated to a feverish manhunt as her biological clock winds down. If the man is out there, he remains at large. Love and marriage often elude people caught up in the whirlwind of daily journalism. Nine-to-fivers don't understand.

The lifestyle of this young mother with whom we briefly chatted seemed as foreign to us as that of an alien from outer space, but it agreed with her. She glowed.

"Come on, Jason," she murmured fondly. "Time to go meet Daddy."

The child waved bye-bye as his mom pushed his little sister's stroller toward the parking lot. Lottie waggled her fingers at him.

"Lordy." She sighed. "Some women hog all the luck."

"Bet she's thinking the same thing about us. Probably yearns to be a highly paid professional instead of listening to baby talk all day."

"Highly paid?" Lottie cut her eyes at me. "Hell-all-Friday, Britt. Is there something you haven't told me?" Her freckles screwed into a pout. "I swear I wouldn't mind walking in her shoes. Wonder what the daddy's like."

She looked wistful as we ambled toward the parking lot, window-shopping along the way. A new look called deconstructionism dominated fashion displays. Did consumers actually buy garments with ragged exposed seams and unfinished hems? I'd have to ask my mother, the fashion authority in the family, for an explanation.

A mannequin flaunted an ensemble with stitches and buttons sewn on in weird places, stirring unpleasant memories of my only attempt at dressmaking. The more I had sewed, the more I ripped. Today my sorry original would have been haute couture.

I started to tell Lottie that I had missed my true calling. A man's shouts interrupted our conversation, breathless and indecipherable, except for the expletives. The disturbance was in the parking lot, beyond our range of vision. We exchanged startled glances, then broke into a trot, along with others around us. Miamians never shy away from trouble, they run headlong to greet it. Like journalists, they all want to be there first. Ground zero, that's where the story is.

Glass shattered as we breathlessly emerged into the warm moist air. Rubber shrieked on blacktop. Thuds, like sacks of potatoes hurled to the pavement. A baby wailing.

"My car!" I blurted, picturing its pristine opal frost finish. I thought I would never love a set of wheels again after my beloved old T-Bird wound up at the silty bottom of an Everglades drainage canal, nearly taking me with it, but that was before inhaling that heady new-car smell.

It was not my car skidding, hurtling in reverse. It was a flame-red Trans Am with dark tinted glass and a broken windshield on the passenger side. The young mother who had been pushing the stroller was sailing across its roof, arms extended like a sky diver in free fall. She flipped face first onto the windshield, glanced off the hood, and dangled for an instant before slamming to the asphalt.

The driver ground into gear, brakes smoking. The car exploded forward, tumbling the woman like a rag doll, dragging her for at least thirty feet, as it roared flat out toward the exit. From beneath the speeding car came a chilling scraping sound, like metallic fingernails gouging a blackboard. As the red car freewheeled out onto the main thoroughfare, tires screaming, I glimpsed what was caught in the undercarriage: a crumpled yellow baby stroller.

"Oh, no. Oh, no!" I murmured aloud.

A muscular young man in gym shorts and a cutoff T-shirt charged after the Trans Am like a maddened bull, then wrenched a rock from the landscaping and hurled it like a football. The car easily outdistanced it, as he cursed in frustration, turned, and punched a parked Pontiac, setting off its alarm.

He winced, shaking bruised knuckles as the siren and a baby's cry keened in a chorus of high-pitched wails. Something lay broken in the traffic lane. It wore little red sneakers.

Shoppers poured from the mall. Horrified drivers had stopped, but impatient motorists to the rear leaned on their horns in a mind-numbing cacophony. I ran to move the child to safety but saw his head as I approached. Shuddering, I knelt, touched one of his new shoes, then backed away. The back bumper had been level with his skull. He was dead.

Eyes blurring, I looked wildly around, focusing on the cries in the confusion. The center's lone attempt at landscaping was flowering hibiscus in the narrow median. The baby, still strapped into her padded car seat, had been thrown into the hedge by the impact.

"It's all right, it's all right." I dropped to my knees, crooning. "Don't cry. Please don't cry." Her thin blanket was scorched and a tiny flailing arm was red and blistered, probably by the car's muffler or catalytic converter. No bleeding, no obviously broken bones. She was wailing loudly, a good sign. Afraid to pick her up, I tried to make her comfortable in her seat.

Her mother was lying silent on the pavement, legs splayed in a terribly twisted position, bones obviously broken. Lottie and an older woman hovered over her. I searched faces in the growing, babbling crowd and shouted.

"Did anybody call Nine-one-one?" Blank, shocked expressions.

"They're on the way! On the way!" A young black security guard was barking into his radio. Waving his arms, demanding that people stand back, he averted his eyes from the dreadful sight on the pavement, trying to direct traffic around the scene and clear a path for rescue.

Lottie gripped my elbow. "She's got a pulse," she muttered, her face white. "The mother's still alive, but I don't know for how long. Your keys," she demanded, twangy voice flat.

"The keys? We can't follow them, they're long gone."

"Your keys," she repeated, her outstretched hand remarkably steady. "My cameras."

Of course. I tossed her the car keys and she took off at a dead run.

Swallowing hard, I fished a notebook from my purse. There was a fire station just a mile away, and I prayed that rescue was not tied up elsewhere. I enlisted a motherly middle-aged woman to keep anyone from touching the screaming baby until help arrived.

The scene was a mess. A plastic baby bottle crushed on the pavement next to the mother's scuffed left tennis shoe, laces still neatly tied. Her purse spilled, contents scattered over a wide area. Her right shoe, fifty feet from its mate, between a diaper bag with tire tracks and a Raiders cap.

Cops and paramedics arrived fast, though the wait seemed like forever. It always does in real emergencies. The mother's right arm was also fractured, white bone protruding. Blood trickled from her mouth. Air rescue had been dispatched. She and the baby would be airlifted to the county hospital trauma center. No rush to move the toddler. No hurry when the next stop is the morgue.

"They took my fucking Trans Am," the agitated young man in the muscle shirt blustered to the first cop on the scene. "They took my fucking car! Look what the hell they did!" He gestured angrily toward the chaos. "I can't believe this. I can't fucking believe this!"

His name was Arturo, and he noisily complained that he had just put fifteen hundred dollars' worth of work into the car. The cops took his car's description and plate number, then issued a BOLO: Be on the lookout.

"They went west on One hundred sixty-third Street," I offered. "They could be on the I by now." The Interstate and the Palmetto Expressway were nearby, with Broward County and downtown Miami just minutes away. They could be anywhere.

"Street punks. Stinking little bastards," Arturo was saying. "Son of a bitch! They got my Trans Am. There's his hat!" He pointed at the Raiders cap. "That hat belongs to one of them."

After a workout at a mall exercise club, Arturo explained, he had stepped outside and seen a trio of street kids, no more than sixteen or seventeen years old, breaking into his car. He shouted as they piled inside and hot-wired the car as he bore down on them. He was fast, but they were faster.

We had seen only two shadowy silhouettes behind the dark-tinted front windows. But Arturo said there was a third; a skinny kid had scrambled into the backseat.

The car's engine had sprung to life with Arturo only a few strides away. In a last desperate effort to stop them, he had heaved his gym bag containing a set of ten-pound weights. The windshield broke and the driver reacted by slamming the car into reverse, into the woman and her children.

"They gonna be okay?" Arturo had simmered down, voice subdued, suddenly comprehending something much more tragic than a stolen car. "Look at them." He stared wide-eyed at the victims. "They just left them, like roadkill. You don't drive off and leave an animal in the street like that."

The woman, now surrounded by medics, must have heard Arturo's shouts and tried to steer her kids out of harm's way.

"You a witness?" the cop asked me.

"To part of it." The young mother replayed her airborne acrobatics slowly in my mind, churning my stomach. "She went over the top of the car, and they hit her. Dragged her."

"Accounts for the road rash." His stolid face remained impassive. "She alone with the two kids?"

I nodded. "We had just seen them in the mall."

The lot could not be cleared because many of the cars belonged to moviegoers inside the mall's triplex theater. Police blocked 163rd Street instead, so the chopper could touch down in the roadway.

With a mounting sense of dread, I studied new faces in the still-growing crowd. What had she said? "Time to go meet Daddy."

He must be on the way or waiting somewhere, checking his watch, expecting his family. My stomach knotted in sympathy for this stranger whose life was about to change forever.

Detective Bill Rakestraw had arrived and was removing his Rola-tape, a digital tape measure on wheels, from the trunk of his unmarked car. He wore a grim expression and department-issue coveralls, navy blue, with MIAMI POLICE on the back.

"Britt. How'd you get here so fast?"

"I didn't. I was here when it happened. Lottie too. We just stopped for some yogurt, saw this woman and her—"

"Is this what they say it is?" His thin, sharp face was somber behind the bristly mustache.

"Yeah," I said miserably. "Kids."

I know how he reacts to fatalities involving children. A tough cop, he is also a family man and nearly quit traffic homicide after handling the hit-and-run death of a nine-year-old bicyclist the same week that a three-year-old swung open the back door of the family car and tumbled into an expressway fast lane. Two so close together seemed overwhelming.

There are many sad jobs in police work. Rakestraw has one of them. He investigates fatal accidents. Whenever his beeper chirps, somebody is dead.

My own beeper, clipped to my purse, began to sound and I darted into the mall to call the city desk.

It was my day off, but that never stopped Gretchen Platt, the editor from hell.

"Britt, we have a report of some kind of hit-and-run involving pedestrians at the—wait a minute, let me see here—the Hundred and sixty-third Street Mall. Can you check it out? See if it amounts to anything."

"It does. I'm here, at the mall. A mother and her two babies. Some kids backed a stolen car over them at about forty-five miles an hour. They got away. It's awful, Gretchen. They're working on the woman now."

"How many dead?" Bright and officious, her voice had a distant quality.

"One little kid, maybe the mother."

"I'll send photo." Her businesslike tone never changed. Did this woman have a clue as to what was happening?

"No, Lottie's here too. She's shooting a lot of stuff."

"Excellent. We'll need you to write for the state edition."

Rakestraw had talked to witnesses and was now on hands and knees inspecting the asphalt where the stroller had gouged the pavement. That would help determine the point of impact.

"Got anything?"

"Just starting to document the physical evidence," he said slowly. "A busted tail light."

"How did they get into the car? The owner said he locked it."

"Looks like they busted a window. Probably used a spark plug."

Spark plugs are convenient tools for thieves. Their porcelain tops will crack car windows, which can be easily pushed in without the shatter of broken glass. Kids wear them on leather shoestrings dangling from their necks or belts. Some pride themselves on spitting spark plugs with enough force to smash a window. Whatever happened to innocent times when kids were content to see who could spit seeds the farthest?

"And it was a GM." The detective shook his head. "The GM steering column is the lifeblood of thieves."

A patrolman sent to follow the stroller scratches in the roadway reported back, his words tinny on Rakestraw's walkie. The driver had pulled up on a curb three blocks west of the center. The front-seat passenger had jumped out and yanked the stroller from beneath the car, witnesses said. It was still there where they had left it.

Rakestraw instructed him to hold the scene until he got there. "If we're lucky we may get a print off it," he said. "That baby was saved because her mother kept her strapped in her car seat. It absorbed the impact, exactly what it was designed to do."

His job was to painstakingly reconstruct exactly what happened in those terrible split seconds. The physical evidence, witnesses' stories, and information gleaned from injuries would all fit together like the pieces of a jigsaw puzzle. He measured skid marks, the width of the road, and the location of the driveway, meticulously stepping off paces as he rolled the tape to the closest cross street. Scene diagrams drawn to scale, site sketches, and photographs would be provided to the state attorney's office for use in a prosecution—if the guilty parties were ever caught.

I retrieved my keys from Lottie, who was shooting the medics' feverish work, and drove the three blocks to where the stroller had been found.

A lone police officer guarded the mangled bit of evidence, left in the gutter in front of a small dry-cleaning establishment. In the traffic on his walkie, I heard the mother referred to as a "possible forty-five." A dead body.

Cops and medics are sometimes wrong, I thought. Our new trauma center literally plucks patients back from the dead. I thought of the young police officer shot in the head by a deranged army deserter. All but the trauma team presumed him dead. No way he could survive, a weeping colleague told me at the crime scene. Wrong. He will never be a policeman again, or the man he once was, but he is alive.

She's young, I told myself, unlocking my car to return to the mall. Young bodies are astonishingly resilient, and she has lots to live for. A white Buick stopped alongside. A man about thirty, wearing a white shirt, his tie loosened, rolled down his window. "What happened?" he asked, staring past me at the patrol car and the tattered strip of yellow canvas caught in the crumpled metal framework.

"An accident," I said lightly. I am usually impatient with gawkers who stop to eyeball the misery of others. I have an excuse to be there; it's my job. But something about his voice, or maybe his big eyes and curly hair, suggested he might be more than just a curious passerby.

"What kind of accident?" His tone became more urgent.

I stepped away from my car and approached his. If he was who I suspected he was, I didn't want to be the one to tell him.

"My little daughter has a stroller like that one," he said.

Fear had begun to grow in his eyes. He gripped the steering wheel.

"There's been an accident over at the mall," I said.

"At the mall?" He looked confused. "How did that get here?"

"It was dragged under a car. But I think the baby is fine," I quickly added.

"My God! How could she be?"

"She flew out, in her car seat," I said gently.

He looked numb.

"There are a lot of baby strollers. This one probably isn't yours." I tried to sound reassuring.

He didn't seem to hear. A car honked behind him. He didn't seem to hear that either.

"I was supposed to meet them at the mall exit by the bus stop." His voice was controlled, as though trying not to panic. "They weren't there yet, so I came to pick up the dry cleaning. I'm going back for them now."

"Who were you picking up?"

He glanced sharply at me, as if wondering who I was. "Britt Montero," I said, "from the *Miami News*. I'm covering the accident."

"My wife, my little boy, and my baby girl. They're at the mall," he repeated.

It was him. Cringing inwardly, I dug in my pocket for a business card and handed it over.

"I saw a lot of flashing lights inside the parking lot when I went by." He stared past me, at the policeman. "I kept going." A terrible awareness was overtaking him.

"They may have been involved," I said quietly. "If there is anything I can do to help, please call me. Stay here, and I'll ask the officer to notify Detective Rakestraw. He can give you all the details."

"No," he said, suddenly moved to action. "I'm going back there. My wife must be scared to death. The baby, and Jason—"

"No, wait," I said, as he shifted into reverse. "Don't. It's better if you stay here and—" But he was gone.

Tires squealing, the Buick shot across two lanes of traffic to turn east, back toward the mall.

"He doesn't know," I told the patrolman, who had left his car and joined me. "That's the husband and father of the victims." He radioed Rakestraw that next of kin was on the way, scared and unaware.

Traffic had snarled into a worse tangle back at the mall as heavy chopper blades beat against the growing dusk, rising slowly, hovering noisily over the roadway. The man who had been driving the Buick sat in the passenger seat of Rakestraw's unmarked. The car had been repositioned so the occupant could not see the accident scene. When Rakestraw emerged, clipboard in hand, I approached him. "He's the husband?"

The detective nodded and asked an older policeman to join the man in the car. "I don't want to leave him sitting there alone," he said, turning to me. His deep-set eyes, shadowed and weary, flicked to his notes. "Name is Jason Carey."

"What did you tell him?"

"He wanted to know where his wife was." Rakestraw glanced toward the darkening sky, which had swallowed the flashing lights of the chopper. "They were just taking off when he got here. I feel so sorry for the guy. Gave him what I could. Told him his boy had expired. That his wife is critical and on the way to the trauma center with the baby. I think the little one will go to the ER and be admitted. She looks like she'll be all right."

"Think the father will?"

Rakestraw shook his head. "He's totally lost. It takes them awhile to comprehend what you're saying."

We stood wordless in the gloom.

The detective left to resume his work. Only in his thirties, his shoulders looked stooped.

A huge fire engine rumbled up, slowly angling into place, back-up signal bleating, to light the area for the investigator and hose away the blood. The medical examiner's wagon followed. The routines that attend violent death were beginning to be carried out.

The Trans Am was still missing, along with the occupants. Had yesterday's carjackers added death to their crime spree? If so, what could they be thinking now?

Arturo was waiting for a girlfriend he had called to drive him home. "What do you need my insurance information for?" I heard him ask a cop, his voice aggrieved. "It wasn't my fault."

Rakestraw was rewalking the entire lighted scene to be sure he hadn't missed anything.

Jason Carey sat in the detective's car, head in his hands. His partner in a small water purification company was en route to take him to the hospital, Rakestraw told me. I approached and tapped on the window. The officer in the driver's seat rolled it down. The chill from the air-conditioning spilled across my bare arms, making me tremble.

"May I speak to Mr. Carey?"

The officer indicated that it was up to his companion.

Carey raised his head, eyes drowning.

"Remember?" I said gently. "We met in front of the dry cleaners?"

He nodded.

"I wanted to ask a few questions about your wife."

"Why?" It was more a sob than a question. "Have you heard anything from the hospital?" he said fearfully.

"Not yet, she's still en route. I'm writing a story."

"Why?" he repeated.

"This is a tragedy. People care. It may help find the ones who did this."

He nodded again. "Okay."

The patrolman climbed out, leaving the door open, and went to assist Rakestraw. Breathing again, stomach still clenched, I slipped behind the wheel. "How old is she?" I asked carefully.

"Jennifer is twenty-seven; her birthday was last month, the sixteenth," he said, choking on the words.

"Is she a Miami native?" I handed him a tissue from my purse.

He pressed it to his eyes for a long moment. "No. Her parents moved here from Lexington, Kentucky, when she was eleven."

High school sweethearts, they met when she was a freshman and he was a junior. He played basketball. She was a cheerleader. They married after college, almost five years ago.

Jason and Jennifer had been discussing moving, finding a better place to raise their children because of the crime in Miami. They weren't fast enough.

"And how old is your son?" I kept it present tense. No victim will hear a loved one referred to for the first time in past tense from me. Death is so final. The realization comes soon enough.

"If I lose her, I'll have nothing left," he said, weeping. His raw pain permeated the air around us. "Nothing left to live for."

"She's hanging in there," I told him. "And your daughter, your little girl needs you." My own eyes tearing, I forged on, asking to borrow a family photo and waiting as he fumbled in his wallet.

If I did this story right, the killer's own mother might be moved to surrender him. Hearts would be touched, readers outraged. One of the thieves might even feel remorseful enough to turn himself in, though that possibility seemed remote. The teenage criminals I'd encountered lately were scary creatures. Sometimes I suspect they were born with a birth defect, like a cleft palate or an absent limb. But what they lacked was conscience. Look in their eyes. All you can see are MTV, rap music, and violent movie fantasies.

A public outcry would fuel the investigation and assure justice. The family would not stand alone in its grief. Someday a little girl would read about this violent afternoon from a yellowed news clipping with my byline on it and understand exactly what happened to her and her mother and the brother she never knew. So why did I feel like such a ghoul?

He stared at the photo through watery eyes, then handed it to me. Jennifer Carey's hair, tied back today, had been carefully curled. She wore blue and a warm smile as she held the baby, all ruffles and satin ribbons. Her husband, Jason on his knee, rested a protective hand on his son's shoulder, the other arm around his wife. Perfect.

"We had it taken for her parents' anniversary in July. . . ." His voice trailed off. The baby's name was Eileen.

I promised to return it.

"How could anybody just drive away and leave them?" he burst out. "They must be animals!"

"They'll catch them. The police put out a BOLO, and tomorrow half a million readers will want them in jail. I'll do the best I can," I promised.

I did not mention that if they were juveniles, too young for adult court, punishment would probably be no more than a minor inconvenience.

I went back to find Lottie. Rakestraw, wrapping up his work, echoed my unspoken thoughts. "Hope to hell they're not juveniles," he muttered.

Lottie and I drove back to the office in a far more quiet and subdued mood than when we had set out. "Remember," she whispered, "just before it happened? I was wanting to trade places with her."

The lighthearted spirit and the golden afternoon were gone.

I worked late on the story for the final, long after Lottie had delivered her photos to the city desk and gone home. Luckily, Trish was on duty in the library. She printed out hit-and-run statistics and even unearthed sports clips from Jason Carey's high school record as a forward on the all-city team.

She watched over my shoulder as I worked. I object vociferously when editors do that, but I didn't mind Trish at all.

"Think you could use a breakdown on crime in that shopping center?" She sounded thoughtful. "You know there's a push now to ban juveniles from some malls until after six P.M. on school days."

"If you could dig up some stax on the mall—especially auto theft figures—it would be great. You think like a reporter, Trish."

"I know," she murmured, her tone curious. I looked up, but she was on her way back to the library.

I wrote about Jennifer Carey's career as a speech therapist, put on hold until her children were older; the irony of her only sister's work as a counselor for troubled teens; and the young couple's plans for a future, now uncertain. She was still in surgery when I checked with the hospital.

Gretchen wouldn't be able to edit my story for another twenty minutes and I wouldn't go home without watching the process, so I returned the clips to the library. Trish sprang up from a desk where she'd been nibbling a sandwich.

"Need something else?"

"Nah, just bringing these back." I dropped them in the in-basket and leaned across the counter.

She seemed to want to say something but just stood there. The latest economy kick at the paper is to use as few lights as possible at night, when the building is largely unoccupied. The features section, on the other side of the library's glass wall, was dark. Her perfect skin luminous, she looked young and vulnerable in the chilly cavernous room filled with looming shelves and shadows. It was probably safe, but it sure looked spooky.

"You're all alone back here?"

"Yep, the only one working tonight. But I don't mind. In fact I'm learning local history, reading some old stories."

I opened the half door and slipped behind the counter. A number of clips were spread out on the desk: The topless dancer saved by her silicone breast implant, which deflected a bullet. The hapless firefighter who forgot to engage the stabilizers before sending an aerial ladder nearly a hundred feet into the air. (When the $750,000 fire truck tipped over, the ten-story aerial ladder and bucket crashed into a busy intersection at rush hour. Half a dozen motorists were injured, along with three firefighters, who fell off the truck as it toppled.) The saga of "Crime Boy," age thirteen, with a rap sheet of sixty-six felonies. Federal officials took immediate action when his record was publicized, authorizing HUD to relocate him and his family from the sweltering projects into a three-bedroom waterfront home. Crime pays.

A fat file lay open: that of Linda Snell, a serial killer whose crimes I had covered. The sweet churchgoing Snell had been widowed three times. No one suspected more than bad luck until the lonely widow took to picking up men at truck stops across the state. When next seen they were dead bodies at the side of the road.

A bad woman, but a welcome change from the usual serial killers—

men who stalk women like animals. Solved a lot faster, too. The cops took quick action.

"I remember these stories," I said fondly, sitting down at the desk and glancing through the stack of neatly folded clips. "She's still on death row."

"You haven't done a folo in some time." Trish took a seat opposite me. Her eyes were soft gray and glowing, with striking dark rims around the iris, and her body language was intimate, as though eager for the company.

"There you go again, sounding like a reporter."

"You're one of the reasons I'm in this business," she blurted.

"The library?"

"No. Please." She lightly dismissed her surroundings with a small wave of the hand. "Journalism." She smiled, pronouncing the word with reverence. "I'm a reporter. I interned on a small paper in Oklahoma, and when your stories crossed the wire we would fight over who got to read them first. Now"—she glanced warmly around her—"here I am."

"So if you're a reporter, what are you doing in the library? How come you're not out in the newsroom?"

"That's what I keep asking myself—and your editors." She pulled a shapeless cardigan tightly around her small frame. If they are so intent on saving energy, I wondered, why don't they turn down the confounded air-conditioning at night?

"Would you like half my sandwich—it's only peanut butter and jelly—and some tea?" Her thermos was red and yellow plastic.

I had forgotten how hungry I was. The yogurt, long ago at the mall, was all I had eaten all day.

"I wouldn't dream of eating your lunch, but I'd love some tea."

She found another mug and poured a steaming lemony brew.

"Some of the stories you file are odder than fiction," she said as we sipped. "We'd post them on our newsroom bulletin board back in Black Mesa. Not much action there," she said ruefully.

Trish had gone on to work general assignment for the *Shelbyville Post Gazette* in Oklahoma and the larger *Star-Courier* in Kansas City.

"Will you transfer into the newsroom when there's an opening?"

"You know of one?" Her eager eyes locked on mine.

"Not at the moment. But that means nothing. You know how it is."

Most reporters are gypsies. Why any writer would leave this great news town, the city I love, where I was born and belong, remains a mystery to me. But they do, every day. Little newsroom farewell soirees seem to take place every other Friday, with punch and cookies rolled out after deadline for the bulldog edition.

Restless colleagues yearn for bigger markets in Washington, New York, or Chicago or dream of covering exotic wars in foreign lands. Those whose dreams come true never experience anything that does not break out in Miami at one time or another. Every major national scandal has a Miami angle. As for action, why dodge bombs or bullets on some godforsaken strip of real estate thousands of miles away when you can do it right here? We have it all: war, murderous weather, foreign intrigue, spies, refugees, and hand-to-hand combat in the streets. What more could a writer want?

"I thought hiring on as a reporter would be easier," Trish was saying, "especially after I won first place for deadline reporting in the annual Oklahoma Press Association awards last year. I applied for reporting jobs here three times, but they never called me." She shook her head, face pinched. "I guess I should have had a job before I quit the old one, but I just had to get out of there and I was sure this was the right move. This"—she lifted her eyes, shadowed in the gloom, to the broad picture window framing Miami's sweeping nightscape of glittering city lights—"is the place for me. I just know it."

I could relate. I never take it for granted. I am always thrilled by the lacy shadows of palm fronds on stone, the warm caress of soft moist air, the roar of the sea.

"And it's always easier to get a job when you're in the same city," Trish went on. "Right?"

"I thought it was always easier to get a job when you had one."

She sighed. "I never dreamed it would take this long, and I was getting low on cash. . . . Maybe I shouldn't have settled for the library, but I needed work and thought it would be a foot in the door, that I could more easily move into the newsroom from here."

"I knew you were too good to be true. You're great to have back here on deadline—but I'll let you know the minute I hear about anybody leaving."

She scooped up a bleating phone. Somebody from the national desk wanted a recent photo of Boris Yeltsin. "What's he done now?" she asked. "Is he dead?"

A reporter's curiosity. I smiled. She looked up and winked.

"Pissed off the Latvians again. Okay, I'll bring it right out."

Back at the city desk, I saw that Gretchen was editing my story and had inserted the word *alleged* in front of the phrase "hit-and-run car."

"Gretchen, Gretchen," I argued impatiently. "It really happened. I saw the car hit her and speed away." Then I saw that she had also added an *alleged* in front of the word *victim*, referring to Jennifer Carey.

"Well, if we don't qualify it you should attribute it to the police," she argued stubbornly, pursing her lips. "Whose word do we have on this?"

I suddenly felt very tired. "Take my word for it. The woman was a victim. She did not crush her little boy's skull and then fling herself across the parking lot; they were run over. That is fact. We don't have to qualify it or attribute it to anybody. All that does is slow down the story and make me look silly. It happened, Gretchen. Believe it."

She grudgingly deleted the offending words. I should have been more diplomatic. She would make me pay for this, but I felt fresh out of patience.

Before escaping the cold and nearly empty building into the heat of the night, I made final phone checks with the cops, the hospital, and the intern who mans our police desk in a noisy little nook off the newsroom. No new developments. Jennifer Carey clung to life. The thieves and the Trans Am had vanished without a trace.

I drove across the causeway, half listening to the crackle of the new police scanner in my dashboard and the rumble of thunder across the Everglades. While fighting deadline and the desk there had been little time to think. Now I felt drained.

Bitsy yapped, running in circles as I unlocked the door to my apartment, while Billy Boots meowed in agitation from atop a bookcase. Several volumes lay scattered on the floor, evidence of rough play or a serious skirmish.

"What's been going on?" I scolded. "Can't you two just get along?" Ignoring the winking red light on my message machine and the cat purring against my ankles, I foraged in the fridge. Pickings were sparse. I hungered for real food, *salteado de camarones,* shrimp sautéed in onions and garlic with chopped plum tomatoes, or *ropa vieja,* which translates as old clothes but is shredded beef in savory wine sauce. All I could find in the depths of the freezer was a frozen breakfast bearded by frost an inch thick. Eleven P.M. was no time for breakfast, but my stomach wouldn't know the difference. I scraped ice off the package, popped the little tray in the oven, fed the animals, then took Bitsy for a stroll. Jennifer Carey's little son and her struggle to survive haunted my thoughts. Would she ever go home again?

The night was starless and hot, the temperature holding at 88 and the air thick with humidity that dampened my clothes and curled my hair in wispy tendrils. The moon, a faint glimmer, burst free from the dense overcast for just a fleeting moment as we returned. Full, lustrous, and ripe, it took a bow, then sailed again into its cover of clouds.

I picked at my midnight supper, juicy little sausages oozing sodium phosphate atop pancakes bursting with goodies like calcium caseinate and sodium aluminum phosphate, all listed in tiny print on the side of the carton. My stimulated taste buds cried out for an accompaniment of orange juice and strong coffee. I drank a glass of wine instead and went to bed.

Usually I sleep well, but this night something disturbing, a prescient sense of trouble, hung in the air. Must be the full moon, I thought.

Chapter Three

B reakfast at midnight had been a mistake. At 6 A.M. I awoke
hungering for a Cuban sandwich, my body clock convinced
that it was lunchtime. Jennifer Carey was in surgical intensive
care. The Trans Am had not been spotted, said the cop who answered
my call, which meant that by now it was most likely at the bottom of a
canal, totally dismantled in a chop shop, or on the high seas aboard a
southbound freighter.

I skipped my usual run on the boardwalk. Sluggish and out of sorts,
all I could manage was a slow jog around the block with Bitsy. Even
her short legs were able to keep up with me. I showered, dressed in
lettuce-green cotton, drank some black coffee, and headed out, thrilled
at the sight of my new car waiting, its finish as smooth and lustrous as
the inside of a seashell. The beat was relatively quiet and driving sheer
luxury in an automobile with a functioning air conditioner.

I visited the cop shops, scrutinized the logs of overnight check-ins
at the morgue and the county jail, and arrived at the office armed with
several stories.

An offshore storm had driven a school of sharks in toward the
beach, where one had mistaken a surfer's foot for lunch. The surfer
had been sewed up at Mount Sinai while the Beach Patrol hastily
hoisted warning flags for swimmers, who ignored them anyway.

A bolt from the same storm killed a thirty-two-year-old Sunny Isles
bicyclist as he pedaled north on Collins Avenue. Struck by lightning,
he crashed into a tree, fell off his bike, and was hit by a cement truck.

And a Miami family had called police to report their dead mother missing. Her body, shipped to New York for burial, had been mistakenly sent to Aruba. The mistake was discovered when an empty casket, intended for Aruba, arrived at the funeral home in Brooklyn. Now services were postponed indefinitely because customs officials were refusing to return the body from Aruba without proper identification, certification, and other necessary paperwork.

I wrote all three for the early edition. Before returning my messages, I checked the Careys' conditions—baby Eileen was fair and her mother critical—retrieved the borrowed family picture from photo, slipped it into an envelope addressed to the father, and dropped it into a wire room out-basket.

Then I opened my own mail.

The first piece was neatly typewritten, on good stationery:

Dear newswriter Britt Montero,

You are the second to share my discovery of an Inspector Deity, a new deity. U.S. Senator John Glenn was first. Enclosed is a copy of his letter to me. The following news is for immediate release.

The subjects are quasi-stellar radio sources and the universe's new type-M red stars. Scientists believed that stars were created by clouds of cosmic dust condensed from stellar supernova explosions. If not otherwise informed by our Inspector Deity, I would have thought that myself.

However, more than ninety percent of the red type-M stars in the universe are formed by golden G-type stars like our sun and Alpha Centauri.

Terrible infrared light and heat make it necessary for planets around golden G stars to be moved to an icy glacial distance when a type-M red star is being created.

Please report this to the world at once.

Best regards,
Emmett R. Merrill, M.D.

He thoughtfully included his telephone number and a copy of a letter to him, under a U.S. Senate letterhead.

Thank you for your letter concerning the discovery of an Inspector Deity. I have forwarded the information to NASA for their comments. You should be hearing from them in a few weeks. Feel free to contact me again if I can be of further assistance.

Best regards.

John Glenn, United States Senator

I opened the next envelope, a friendly invitation, handwritten on lined paper:

Ms. Montero,

Next time you find yourself in the neighborhood of South Florida State Hospital, please stop by for a chat and a cup of tea.

Sincerely,

Perwin Thompson

The return address was a forensic unit that houses the criminally insane. Thompson was confined years ago after police found parts of his wife and his mother in his septic tank.

The next letter was also handwritten, on lined paper torn from a yellow legal pad.

Dear Ms. Montero,

With all sincere hopes these few lines find you in good health and relaxation. I am illegally incarcerated in the Dade County Women's Jail. The bastards lied! I did not assault those police officers. They harassed and followed me and planted the knife! My only desire is to entertain and to touch the hearts of people with the sound of my voice. God has gifted me with a solo lead voice. I sing from the stomach. I began singing after my drug experience so I am confident that I don't have significant brain damage. Please investigate the lying bastards on the police department at once.

I was familiar with this one too: the Singer.

Was my name scrawled on a bathroom wall somewhere? Other reporters receive fan letters, notes of gratitude, commendation, and praise. I get mail from the jail.

I sighed. The editors of this reader-friendly newspaper instruct reporters to answer all correspondence.

Taking a cue from John Glenn, I typed a brief response to Dr. Merrill.

Thank you for your letter on the Inspector Deity. Since I only cover the police beat, I have forwarded your letter to the news desk. Their correspondents cover the entire planet and beyond. You will hear from them soon.

Yours truly,
Britt Montero.

I wondered what the news desk would do to get back at me and swept the other letters into the trash. I will not become pen pal to people in cages and padded cells, I told myself. They are there for a reason and have more time to write letters. Management could not have had them in mind when they issued the reader-friendly edict.

Rakestraw should be in by now, I thought, so I drove to the station and dropped by AIU, the Accident Investigation Unit. He looked agitated, not surprising for someone whose office is decorated with grisly color art of crash victims. He had news, major headway in the Carey case.

"Got a line on the thieves," he said grimly. "Don't know the backseat passenger for sure, but we've got a positive ID on the driver and a street name on his front-seat buddy. Same guys who did the carjacks and kneecaps the day before."

"Great," I said, pen poised. "Who are they?"

"Can't tell you. They're all puppies."

"Puppies! No way. Puppies are cute. You mean the killers are juveniles?"

"You've got it. Junior scumbags. The driver won't be eighteen until October fourteenth, so we can't release names." He rifled clumsily through his desk for something, didn't find it, and slammed a drawer irritably.

"Does the driver have a past? Was he the shooter the day before?"

"Is the pope Catholic? Do bears shit in the woods? Will you keep asking questions?"

"What kind of record? How long? How bad?"

"You know I'm not allowed—"

"Well, if you won't tell me his name, at least you can let me see his past."

"All I can say is that it's extensive, okay?"

"How'd you find out who he was?"

"Got his name from 'nother kid, the one brought in on that trailer fire that burned up his little sister."

"His past include violence?"

Rakestraw nodded.

"Has he done any time?"

"Our boy's a dropout. Last time he hurt somebody the judge punished him by ordering him to go back to high school."

"How nice for his teacher and the kids who want to learn. Sounds like he's overdue for his name in the paper, just to warn his neighbors that he's living next door."

"Can't do it, Britt. Much as I'd like to."

"You know I would never say how I got it."

"It's against the law." His words were clipped, his mouth a tight line. "We have to protect these misunderstood children."

"Swell," I said sharply. "You'd rather wait until he maims and kills a few more women and little kids."

Rakestraw's jaw tightened and his eyes flashed. Hell, I thought, I've pushed too far. He stood up, glaring. "Look, Britt, you know I can't give you the information in this file, but I can't prevent you from printing it—or anything else you find out on your own."

"Right," I said sullenly, wondering how in hell I could do that.

He stretched his lean body and arms, then sighed as though stifling a yawn. "I'm going for a cup of coffee."

Dismissed, I angrily snapped my notebook closed and was about to tuck away my pen when he added, "I'd ask you to join me, but I'm sure you'll find other things to do here while you're waiting for me to come back."

He checked his watch. "I should be gone at least ten minutes." He stepped to the door of his small office, eyes lingering, along with mine, on the open file atop his desk blotter. "The captain is prowling around the building somewhere like a homicidal maniac, so be cool." He strolled out and closed the door, leaving me alone.

This is illegal, I thought, feeling giddy as I spun the folder around to scan the contents. The adrenaline gave me a rush. No wonder some people find crime fun.

Gilberto Sanchez, street name Peanut, 2475 Northwest 27th Avenue, parents Ileana and Mario. Habitual offender, a busy boy. His juvenile record began at age seven, its roots apparently planted even earlier. Shoplifting, chronic truancy, fighting in school, burglary by age nine, armed robbery with a knife by eleven. He didn't miss much. Everything from lewd and lascivious conduct at twelve to grand theft auto at thirteen. Loitering and prowling, aggravated assault, destroying public property, arson, and carrying a concealed weapon. Not much left but murder, and this creature wasn't even eighteen yet. But he would be soon. Had his mother given birth just a few weeks earlier, he would be facing these charges as an adult. Even then, of course, he would be treated as a first offender, his juvenile crimes not even considered. No wonder these kids share a common contempt for the system.

When Rakestraw returned, a half-full coffee cup in his hand and doughnut dust on his whiskers, I was primly leafing through a Fraternal Order of Police magazine.

"Feel better?" I smiled.

"You still here?" He took his seat, put the cup down, and slipped the file folder into a drawer.

"I need the street name of the passenger."

"J-Boy."

I gave him a questioning look.

"Because he likes to smoke joints."

"That sure narrows it down."

"Probably only ten thousand or so running around out there," he agreed amiably.

"Anything at all on the backseat passenger?"

"Black kid."

"American, Latino, or from the islands?"

"Don't know. These gangs of kid car thieves are pretty well integrated."

"Nice to see the younger generation overcoming prejudice."

"Yeah. Now if they'd just quit robbing, raping, and shooting—"

"Think they stole the Trans Am 'cause they liked it or for some other reason?"

"Coulda been to cannibalize for parts, maybe on order from some adult who repairs them, or to export, or to use in some other crime." He shrugged. "A lot of adult criminals are using juveniles. If they're arrested, it's no big deal. The kids aren't afraid of the system. We've had twelve- and thirteen-year-olds delivering expensive late-model cars to these guys for as little as a hundred and fifty bucks apiece. It's tough for auto theft to nail them because we don't have any undercover cops who can pose as juveniles in a reverse sting. We're getting hit hard, averaging a hundred and ten stolen cars a day.

"One other thing," he added. "Arturo neglected to mention something until after you left the other night."

"What's that?"

"When they stole his Trans Am?"

"Yeah?"

"He had a loaded nine-millimeter Glock in the glove compartment."

Swell, I thought. As if Peanut and J-Boy weren't menace enough out there in high-speed 3,000-pound machines, now they had another gun, a rapid-fire model with a clip that holds fifteen rounds.

I left Rakestraw, locked my purse in the trunk, and went off to Northwest 27th Avenue to find the home of Peanut Sanchez. I disliked leaving my new T-Bird unprotected on his turf, in front of the dingy apartment house. I would feel more comfortable and less defensive after the first dreaded dent or ding.

The dusty hallway walls were decorated with mindless graffiti and scribbled vulgarities, marking off turf like stray cats do. Cooking smells mingled with mildew and the acrid scent of urine. It was nearly 10:30 A.M. on a weekday, but TVs and radios blared in both Spanish and English from behind closed doors.

A pregnant teenager answered my knock. Dark hair fell in curly ringlets around her oval madonna face, marred only by a smattering of teenage pimples. She wore gold hoops in her ears and a maternity smock over black short shorts. Wads of crumpled tissue separated her naked toes. A blood-red sheen glistened on eight toenails; two remained untouched by the tiny brush in her right hand. The small red bottle was in the left. Formaldehyde and alcohol, the odor of wet nail polish, permeated the air.

Her pudgy fingers were encrusted with rings. Some gold, some silver, some plain, others ornate and decorated with stones or tiny chains that linked them together.

"*¿Cómo está usted?*" I began.

"I speak English." She eyed me and my notebook suspiciously.

"Hi, is Peanut home?" I asked, wondering what I would say if he was. It would not be the first time I had chatted with somebody wanted by the police. Criminals are so eager to convince journalists of how unjustly accused and terribly misunderstood they are that it rarely occurs to them to do bodily harm to reporters. They are usually on their best behavior. However, the memory of bloodstained pavement was still too fresh for me to take Peanut's explanation seriously, if indeed he had one.

"Ma!" the young mother-to-be yelled, her voice startlingly shrill.

From behind her, a woman emerged from what had to be a bedroom. Skinny beneath the housecoat, she had thin-edged features under big pale-blue curlers in bangs of blond frizz that showed an inch and a half of dark roots. The toenails protruding from her cotton scuffs had been painted the same shade of blood red.

"She's looking for Peanut."

The woman regarded me from behind sleepy eyes, plucked a coffee mug from the drainboard next to the sink, plodded to the coffeepot on the four-burner stove, and poured herself a cup without heating it first.

She slumped into a kitchen chair, downed the coffee like it was whiskey, then fished what looked like the last cigarette out of a crumpled pack of menthols, lit it, inhaled, and blew out a cloud of smoke.

"The police have already been here. They were here when I got home from work." Her voice was husky from sleep; the slight accent sounded Cuban.

"I think she's from the state," the girl offered, as though I wasn't there. "Probation or HRS."

"No," I said, offering my card, "I'm a reporter, Britt Montero from the *Miami News*." I looked around, disappointed. "He's not here?"

The mother shook her head, trying without success to pat into submission the blond frizz that stuck out on one side. The other was mashed flat as though she had slept on it.

"I don't know why everybody's bothering me about him now," she said, annoyed. "I told 'em. I warned 'em. Nothing I can do for him anymore. I done all I could for him."

"Who?" I asked. "Who'd you tell?"

"Everybody—the cops, the school, social workers, the juvenile court. I told 'em all. I called the police on 'im myself, a coupla times. They never did anything!" she said accusingly.

The hand holding the cigarette toyed with her coffee cup. "I raised these two alone. My daughter here, never any trouble; but him—"

The teenager couldn't help but look pleased, bent head hiding a smug smile, though from the looks of things she was no potential Mother Teresa herself. She was now seated, her unfinished foot propped on a kitchen chair, bending with some effort as she concentrated on painting the last pale nail.

"Boys are nothing but trouble," her mother said bitterly. "Boys and men. He's messed up in the head. Won't take his medication. Did good in computers in school for a while, but then . . . I moved here to get 'im away from the neighborhood where he always got in trouble. So what's the first thing he did? Got in trouble again."

"What about his dad?"

"What about 'im?"

"Does he help, did he try to straighten out your son?"

She glared, eyes narrowing. "First time I see his ass in this neighborhood, I call the police. Look, I work on my feet, long hours, cocktail waitress at the Velvet Swing. I did the best I knew how, went everywhere I could for help. You wanna know how many times I sat in juvenile court after working all night? He was warned it was his last chance three times by the same judge. I begged 'em not to let him come home. But no, it's out of my hands now. They say he's in big trouble this time. Well, what took 'em so long to get excited? I coulda told 'em. Hell, I *did* tell 'em. Bastards never did a thing."

"Does he know the police are looking for him?"

She and the girl exchanged glances. "He saw the TV news Tuesday night and took off with some of his friends," the mother said.

"Did you see the car he was driving?"

Another exchange. "Hah." She snorted. "There's always a car. I don't know what this one was, but I heard rubber burning." Her voice sounded hollow.

"Have you heard from him since?"

"He was here," she said, "while I was at work. He came by for some clothes."

"He said I could have his stereo." The girl's face was eager. "He took his laptop."

"His computer?"

She nodded brightly.

"It *is* serious this time," I told the mother.

"It was serious every time," she said. "Just because nobody dies doesn't mean it's not serious. But it took this to get their attention.

Don't know what he'll do now. But he ain't out joining the Boy Scouts.'' She stared at me accusingly. ''I didn't see no newspaper reporters interested before. Where were you when I was trying to get help?''

''It can't be easy,'' I acknowledged, ''raising children alone.''

''Tell me about it.'' Cigarette smoke wreathed her sallow face.

I took notes, shocked to learn she was only thirty-six, four years older than I am. She looked ten years older, and brittle.

''If you hear from Peanut, ask him to call me,'' I said. ''I'd really like to talk to him about what happened.''

''He don't want to be called that anymore,'' the girl sang out in a warning tone.

Her mother and I both turned to stare.

''He tol' me last night,'' she chanted, looking coy from under long eyelashes. ''Nobody's supposed to call him that anymore. He got a new name.''

''What is it?'' I asked.

She concentrated, the effort curling one corner of her mouth and narrowing her eyes. ''F,'' she said slowly, ''M, J.''

I glanced at the mother, puzzled. ''Somebody's initials?''

She shook her head, face resigned.

''Must stand for something.''

''Yeah,'' the girl said, smiling. ''Like my name is Rings.'' She waggled her weighted fingers.

''Mirta,'' her mother mouthed. ''Mirta.''

''Rings!'' the girl said peevishly. ''He tol' me what it meant.'' The teenager screwed up her face. ''Then I forgot, but that's what he wants to be called from now on, FMJ.''

''Was he with J-Boy?''

She glanced at her mother, saw no warning, and nodded.

''Where does J-Boy live?''

She shrugged. ''Somewheres over on Forty-seventh Street.''

''What's his real name?'' I held my breath. It would be neat to ID the front-seat passenger before the cops did. I love that.

''Don't know, but I know his girlfriend. They call her Gangsta Bitch.''

Delightful, I thought, sighing. The woman had her eyes closed and a fresh cigarette between her teeth. Lottie should be here, I thought, to glimpse the joys of motherhood. I felt blessed at being spared.

"Who else was he with?"

"Dinky, Little Willie, Cat Eye." She ticked them off on her fingers.

"Is he the black guy?"

"Cat Eye? No. You must mean Cornflake. He's a black dude."

"Where does *he* hang out?" I asked, thinking of the backseat passenger.

She shrugged. "Maybe at the Edgewater."

"Cat Eye has green eyes," she trilled, seeing me to the door. "They call Little Willie that 'cause his daddy is Big Willie."

"And Cornflake, he likes cereal?"

"You got it." I was catching on.

I stepped into the hall.

About to close the door, she hesitated. "I remember," she said, face alight. "FMJ, I remember what it stands for: Full Metal Jacket."

I swung by the Edgewater, the vertical mall that rises just north of downtown. The towering monolith draws kids like a magnet to its game rooms, eleven movie theaters, and food courts. Because it is near the paper, Lottie and I used to see movies there, but the audience has become younger and rowdy, with kids shouting out rude advice to the actors and cheering the villains.

The floors of the video game room are carpeted to absorb the explosions of intergalactic warfare and the ceilings mirrored to monitor the pumped-up participants. The intense body language of kids playing the sophisticated games, mostly violence-oriented and involving guns, suggests that to them it is more than a game. They are rock-and-roll without the music, most wearing au courant garments that baffle me. Are they pants that are too short or shorts that are too long? A number of youngsters seemed to know Cornflake, but all agreed they hadn't seen him for a few days.

"Why you looking for him when you can have a real man like me?" Flashing a gold-toothed grin and swaggering, he couldn't have been more than sixteen.

They fielded my questions with typical teenage macho and curiosity. "You his probation officer?" somebody demanded, as a metallic voice from the machine he was playing instructed, *Destroy all buildings to move to next level.*

"Nope," I said, "just a reporter."

"What channel?"

"Yeah, I seen her before," bragged a boy wearing a purple rubber baby pacifier on a cord around his neck, another hard-to-fathom new fad. "On TV."

"*Eyewitness News*," cackled his sidekick in baggy hip-hop shorts. "Eye in the Sky."

"No, I work for the newspaper, the *Miami News*."

The hip-hopper's stare was blank. "What channel?"

The future of my chosen profession looked bleak.

A skinny shy-looking kid in a Marlins T-shirt lingered on the fringe.

"Maybe *you've* seen him," I said, trying to draw him out.

He shook his head slowly. Something sly shone in his eyes. Was he lying?

The boy who had been sucking noisily on his pacifier removed it to ask, "Why you want Cornflake?"

"I write stories and thought he might have one to tell."

That brought choruses of, "I tell you a story, baby," "I got a story for you," as they preened and postured and tried hard to look bad. "How about a nice *bedtime* story?" asked a kid wearing a Malcolm X T-shirt and a fade haircut.

"When you see Cornflake, ask him to give me a call," I said briskly, ignoring their hoots. "I need to find out if some things I heard about him are true."

They eagerly snatched the business cards I offered, exhausting the supply in my skirt pocket. A rash of obscene phone calls would probably be the only result. Who cares? I thought. Let them talk dirty to the newsroom voice mail. That curse on mankind deserves it.

"Bitt?" said one, scrutinizing my name.

"Brrritt," I said, entertaining ugly thoughts about the Dade County school system.

"Staff writer?" asked the shy kid, reading off the card I had given him. "What's that?"

My reply—"I cover the police beat"—elicited cries, guffaws, laughter, and mock trigger pulling. *"Pow! Pa-pow! Pow!"*

"Right," I said serenely, as the laughter died down. "I need to talk to Cornflake because he may be getting blamed for something that wasn't his fault." Seed planted, I took off.

When I opened the trunk of my car to retrieve my purse, it buzzed like a swarm of killer bees. I flicked off my pager and it immediately began to beep again.

I drove across the street to the paper and called the city desk from the security phone in the lobby. "Where *are* you, Britt?" Gretchen's voice could shatter contact lenses.

"On my way in to the office."

"Where have you been?"

"Out on the police beat, Gretchen, where I go every day." I should have known better.

"I had a question, and since you couldn't be reached we had to pull one of your stories out of the early edition. I've warned you to stay in touch. You didn't answer your page." Her tone was the one most people reserve for misbehaving ten-year-olds.

"I had it locked in the car so it wouldn't get snatched." I sighed. "Give me a break. Remember? It was my day off yesterday, yet when you paged me I was already at the scene and on top of the story."

"What have you done for me today, Britt? You're not off now."

The lobby security guard whose phone I had promised not to tie up for more than a moment began to pout. I turned away to avoid his scowl. "I'll be right in, Gretchen, as soon as I can," I promised. "Hope traffic isn't too bad."

I sprinted for the elevator and moments later, when Gretchen glanced up from the city desk, I was working diligently at my terminal. She looked puzzled and narrowed her eyes. "Britt, when did you get back?"

I shrugged innocently. " 'Bout half an hour ago, I guess."

She glanced at the clock and gave me a murderous look.

Gloria, the city desk clerk, promised to tell me right away if Peanut or Cornflake called.

"You working on something with teenage gangs?" asked Ryan. His rumpled shirts hide the heart of a poet. He is much too gentle to be in this business.

"I don't think they're an organized gang, like the Thirty-fourth Avenue Players, just freelance carjackers who may have escalated to murder."

He waxed bitter about the story he was working on, a feature on the Miami Design Preservation League, one of Gretchen's pet projects.

"That again?" I commiserated. "If anybody can make it interesting, you can."

"Luckily I never get bored," he said, "with you around, Britt."

I offered to bring back coffee, headed for the third-floor cafeteria, and encountered Trish on the elevator. She wore a neat navy blue suit and a white cotton shirt with a little red string tie. The uniform of a job seeker, I thought. "You're in early," I said.

"Thought I'd make another pass at personnel. Guess our talk last night gave me the heart to try again."

I looked in her hopeful face and saw myself seven years ago. "I was just taking a break. You have time for coffee?"

"Sure." She beamed at the invitation. "Great story this morning by the way, stripped on local. That poor mother and her children."

She reached for a teabag as we passed through the cafeteria line but switched to Cuban coffee when she saw it was what I was having. "Never tried it before," she said, grinning.

"If you want to stay wired for a week, it's great."

We settled at a table with a postcard-perfect view of the bay, the eastern sky, and the shimmery Miami Beach skyline. Her big eyes drank it all in.

"You talked to the husband, right?"

I nodded, thinking of Jason Carey.

"How'd you ever get him to open up like that? How they met, the last thing she had said to him that day, all the details about their lives together. It made it so real, the readers must feel like they know them." She bravely sipped her coffee, barely wincing. I imagined how the cafeteria's muddy brew would taste to a tea drinker who had never tried it.

"Did he know his son was dead when you talked to him?"

"Yeah, the detective had told him."

"Whew!" She leaned forward, intense. "Did you see the little boy's body? How did he look?"

"Bad." I stared into my cup. "I knew he was dead. Killed instantly. We were there before the police. In fact, we were there when it happened."

"How in hell did you manage that?"

"Coincidence, bad luck, timing." I shrugged and thought about all the stories where nothing more than poor timing cost a life. Minor mistakes, like losing your way or a wrong turn become major when a young man with a gun is waiting on the next corner. Oversights as trivial as leaving your car window down, or setting your door ajar as you carry in packages, or walking to a window after mistaking the noises outside for firecrackers—all can prove fatal.

Some risk takers survive life on the edge and achieve ripe old age. Others lead cautious lives but make a single small mistake and die. Some make no mistake at all. What did Jennifer Carey do wrong?

"The detail," Trish was saying. "How do you ever get all that detail? Like your story about the librarian who had his landlady's head in his freezer with the chicken potpies. You mentioned the icicles hanging from her nose!"

"I talked to the policewoman who opened the freezer for some ice for her Coke."

"What a surprise." Her expression was mock gruesome.

"Sure was," I said nostalgically. "She was killed not long after, but I often wonder if anybody asked how her day had gone when she went home that night. What did she say? What could she say? How can any of them ever explain to normal people what it's like being a cop in Miami?"

"Or a reporter," Trish said, eyes bright.

I told her about the Swiss tourists who witnessed fifteen crashes and a bank robbery during a ten-day Miami vacation. *Miami Vice* fans, they were never alarmed. The city was exactly what they had expected. "I like it," the wife told me, pleased that her husband captured the bank robber on film as he was being captured by police.

I went back to the Cuban coffee machine for a refill. Trish passed, remaining seated, hungry eyes slowly surveying the cafeteria. "What do I have to do to get on the reporting staff at this newspaper?"

"Speaking Spanish would help." My hire was a mistake. They simply assumed, because of my last name, that I wrote and spoke fluent Spanish. When the mistake became obvious, I was assigned the police beat, which no one else coveted. A lucky break for me.

"I'm taking lessons."

"Good. Don't forget to emphasize that to them, and don't give up. Editors love persistence."

Her eyes never left my face.

"Which ones have you met?" I asked.

"Fred Douglas. And I met a Murphy and an Anson."

"They've all got clout, but Fred is the best. Watch out for a guy named Fellows, a real womanizer. He'd make a move on you for sure."

She took a small clothbound notebook from her purse and uncapped her pen.

"Abel Fellows," I said, lowering my voice. "Never be alone with him. But keep calling the others or dropping by, since you're in the building anyway. Editors love enterprise. Send them notes and memos but keep it tight; they love brevity, too. Timing is important. I'll put in a good word for you and let you know if I hear of anything."

"You'd really do that for me?" She looked perked up—probably flying on caffeine. "I don't know how to thank you, Britt."

I went back to the newsroom with Ryan's coffee, feeling good about our talk. Women don't reach out to one another enough, especially in this business. Those who make it become one of the boys, turning their backs on their sisters. Like Gretchen. We have seen the enemy and she is us.

When Fred Douglas stopped by my desk before the afternoon news meeting, I seized the moment.

"Hear you interviewed Trish Tierney. Gonna hire her?"

"The gal from Oklahoma? Isn't she working in the library now?"

"Sure, but that's not where she wants to be."

"Didn't know you knew her."

"Not real well, but she's super eager and smart as hell. Probably be a good hire."

"She's young, without much experience." He looked doubtful.

"How will she get any if nobody gives her a chance? She's already won statewide prizes."

"In Oklahoma," he pointed out.

"You always say we need more women in the newsroom." I stood up and looked him right in the eye.

"You may be right," he said, his tone noncommittal, before escaping to his meeting.

Chapter Four

Victims, cops, car-alarm salesmen, and my mother had left a long printout of messages in response to my carjacking and auto-theft stories. They all wanted me to call them.

One couple had driven in separate cars to Dadeland Mall to see their interior decorator. They met again later, wandering aimlessly through a sea of parked cars. Both of theirs, similar sports jobs, had vanished. Did the same thieves steal both? If so, were they aware that out of thousands of cars they had selected two, parked an acre apart, belonging to the same couple? Do browsing auto thieves make up most of the people milling about in mall parking lots?

A small boy aboard a sightseeing boat in Biscayne Bay pointed out an automobile just like the family car on the deck of a passing Liberian freighter bound for Haiti. "Look, Daddy, there's our car!" he cried. His parents laughed. When they returned to port at Bayside hours later, their car was missing from the parking garage.

"Have I got a story for you!" a Hialeah detective promised. I love it when a man says that to me. I love it when anybody says that to me. "We've got a guy and his wife had their car stolen from a shopping center parking lot last week."

"Yeah? Old news, isn't it?"

"Wait, wait." He paused for effect. "They file a police report and rent a car. Three days later they come home in the rental. What do they find in their driveway? Their missing car."

"The thief returned it?"

"Right, and leaves a handwritten note on the windshield. Listen to this." I heard the sound of paper rustling. "It says, *I'm sorry, but if you knew the circumstances under which I was forced to take your car, you would know that it was a real emergency. Please accept my apology and these theater tickets.* Attached are two tickets to the Grove Playhouse. For Friday night."

"You're kidding! A remorseful thief. Cool. I wonder what the emergency was. Maybe it was—"

"Wait."

"Uh-oh. The tickets were stolen? They got busted at the box office?"

"Nope. They use the tickets, enjoy the show, but get home and find their house cleaned out. Empty, wall to wall. The thieves must have backed up a truck. Hey, they knew they had plenty of time, at least three hours."

What a scam. I love Miami, but sometimes I suspect Rod Serling is the mayor.

The victims agreed to a picture. Lottie was the only photographer in house at the moment, so I walked the assignment back to photo. She was hunched over a light table. The illumination from within made her red hair glow, as she squinted through a loupe at long strips of color negatives.

Photo was shorthanded, and she grumbled as usual. "I don't even have time to wind my watch or scratch my ass."

"It's no big deal," I said. "Maybe they could just stand next to their car, in front of the house."

"No, no, no! That'd be as stiff as a pair of leather britches on the fridge!" She snatched the card from my hand and read my brief description of the story. "I'll shoot 'em in a room where their furniture used to be. With a wide-angle lens, maybe an eighteen; that'll make the room look big and empty, and they'll look small and pitiful. Maybe they could hold up their ticket stubs. Poor babies. Were they insured?"

That's one of the things I love about Lottie. She may bitch and moan, but she is all pro at heart and gets right into the spirit of a story.

I told her about Trish and her efforts to transfer to the newsroom.

"Maybe they're doing her a favor," she said glumly, scowling up at an overhead vent. "She probably ought to quit the library and bail outa here while she still can. I swear this place will kill us all. Something poisonous is spewing outa the air-circulation system at this very moment."

"Lottie, this building is only ten years old."

"I don't care if they built it last Saturday. I tell you if I had to work in here every day, my life expectancy would be something short of six months. We're lucky we spend a lot of time out in the field."

"Sure, on the streets of Miami where it's much safer."

"You heard about the PCBs, right?"

"I heard the pressmen were complaining." I trailed her back to the photo-pool equipment room, wondering where FMJ was holed up, while she searched impatiently for a 500-millimeter long lens for a Dolphins game assignment at Joe Robbie Stadium that night. "Anything to it?"

She turned, hands on her hips, hair in her eyes. "Only that polychlorinated biphenyls were discovered in one of the ink tanks in 'concentrations higher than the acceptable level.' They're claiming it's not dangerous, but I asked Miriam, the medical writer, to look it up." She leaned forward, eyes narrowing. "That stuff apparently causes everything from cancer to two-headed babies and nerve disorders."

She saw my skepticism.

"You know how Ryan's always whining that he feels sick." Her tone was growing argumentative.

"He's a hypochondriac. Always has been."

"Maybe not," she said, finding the lens she wanted. "Maybe he's just more sensitive to his environment than most of us. You know, like the canaries they send down in the mine shafts."

I sighed. "PCBs or not, Trish would gladly change places with anybody out in the newsroom."

"You want some young smart-ass female nipping at your heels, lusting after your job?"

"For God's sake, Lottie! That's the attitude that makes it so tough for women to get anywhere. We have to help each other."

"Try suggesting that to Gretchen."

"Right," I said. "But Gretchen's an aberration. You'll like Trish. She'll fit right in. Let's go to La Esquina de Tejas some night next week and bring her along. It'll cheer her up. She needs to meet people. I'll see if Ryan can join us."

She grudgingly agreed.

My phone was ringing when I got back to my desk.

"I got your message."

"Who is this?"

There was a pause. "Cornflake."

Startled, I slid into my chair and snatched up a pen. "I'm glad you called."

"The information was inseminated that you wished to discuss some matter with me." He was trying his best to sound mature and businesslike.

"You mean disseminated?"

"Whatever. What is the nature of your requisition?"

I couldn't help but smile. "Let's get together and talk," I said, "just you and me."

"We are conversing at the present time." His voice sounded wary and faintly familiar. "How may I assist you?"

"Let's meet. How about the Japanese Garden, on Watson Island?" He hesitated.

I had forgotten. This kid was only fifteen or sixteen. "Do you have a car?"

"No, but I can acquire the necessary transportation."

"Never mind," I said quickly, "I'll come to where you are."

"Edgewater complex, level two. Park in section pink or orange, proceed straight south, and board the elevator to level two. Stop at the merry-go-round first, then proceed to the food court. Purchase a Coke and sit at a table for two."

"I'll wear a white carnation." I couldn't resist.

"Say what?"

"Never mind. How will I know you?"

"I know you."

"Why do I have to go to the carousel first?"

"So I can ascertain that you are alone."

I sighed. "Okay, how about twenty minutes?"

"Fifteen."

I got there in ten.

The pastel painted horses rose and fell in rhythm with the music. A few mothers stood on the revolving platform next to their squealing tots. I had not been instructed on how long I was to watch the carousel ponies, so I waited until the happy music slowed and began grinding to a stop. Then I strolled past book, luggage, and smoke shops to the food court, nearly empty at this time of day. I ordered a soft drink. Did it really have to be a Coke? I wondered. The cooking smells made my mouth water. Would the entire rendezvous abort if I ordered a hot dog? I have little patience with people determined to transform life into *Mission Impossible*. Everything is already too complicated.

Boys will be boys, I thought, sipping my soda and wondering if this one would show at all.

He stepped up and turned the chair facing me around, straddling it. "What's up?" he said, mimicking the moves of some suave movie hero.

He was the shy, skinny kid among the raucous group from the video parlor.

"So we meet again," I said. "I thought it might be you."

He lifted an eyebrow and looked nonchalant, trying hard to be very grown-up. I flipped open my notebook.

"I wrote the story about Jennifer Carey and her little boy."

The confidence faded from his shiny dark face.

"She and her children were hit by the red Trans Am."

"I know who she is." His voice was somber. "How is the lady?"

"If she lives, she'll probably never be the same. The police know that FMJ—Peanut—was driving. I understand he's a friend of yours."

"I might know the dude, I wouldn't call him a friend. I might know the dude," he repeated regretfully.

"Seen him today?"

"No way. I don't run with that crew."

"Oh? You and FMJ have a falling out?"

"Look that motherfu—that dude's crazy. I got no business with him, nothing to do with him."

We watched each other in edgy silence for a moment.

"You said somebody was hanging some shit on me for something I didn't do?"

"You understand the felony murder rule?"

"I'm familiar with that aspect of the law." He licked his lips, looking beyond me into the mall. "But you could refresh my memory about it."

"Under Florida law, when somebody dies during a felony, like auto theft for instance, then all the people who were involved in that crime are guilty of murder. Even if they didn't mean to kill anybody. An old lady has a fatal heart attack during a robbery, she's been murdered. Somebody gets run over by a stolen car, it's murder. Everybody involved shares equal responsibility."

He shifted uncomfortably in his chair. "Even if it's an accident?" His voice was low, without bravado.

"There are no accidents if a crime was in progress."

"Sheesh." He sat motionless, digesting what I had said.

"Everybody in the Trans Am could be charged with felony murder, even if they were just along for the ride."

His eyes looked hollow. "The big one," he muttered softly.

"The cops say J-Boy was the front-seat passenger."

He looked startled. "They know that?"

I nodded. Suddenly he scrambled to his feet. I thought he was leaving.

Instead he fished in his pocket. "You want another Coke? I'll buy." Though rail thin, he looked clean and neat. Somebody's son. Why is nothing ever simple? He took my empty paper cup, dropped it in a trash can, and returned with two ice-filled soft drinks, plastic straws protruding from the top. This time he sat rigid in his chair, like a child in the principal's office, a child in trouble.

He spoke softly now, voice worried. "Peanut—FMJ—he bad news, he crazy, man; the dude is dangerous. I got nothing to do with him. Never should've."

"Why did he take the name FMJ?"

His twisted smile was ironic. "Full metal jacket, the bullet he like to use. Hits hard, punch a hole right through a car. Don't mushroom out."

I stirred my icy drink with the straw. "Why does he shoot people in the leg?"

"He say he likes it. Nobody he shoots can chase him on one leg. He want everybody to remember his name. Bullet in the leg, it take a long time to heal, makes them remember him, and they don't die." His eyes inched up toward mine with a cynical expression. "He didn't want no murder rap."

"I'd like to talk to him. Would you give him my number?"

"I tol' you, I ain't gonna be seeing him. Count on that. And you don't want to find him either. He's cold. He likes to put a hurt on people."

"There was another passenger, in the backseat."

His stare was steady.

"The police say there were three people in the car."

"Shouldn't have happened, man. Shouldn't never have happened.

You don't have to hurt nobody to take a car. Nobody has to get hurt. He don't care, he'll do anything.''

"Was it you in the backseat?"

His eyes darted around the mall. "Somebody say it was? I never said that."

Afraid he would bolt, I backed off. "Think FMJ is worried about Jennifer Carey, sorry about her little boy?"

"Naw, shit! He think he cool. That's why he FMJ now. Thinks he really bad. I told you, he's cold. He's cold." He rubbed his hands together vigorously as though they, too, were cold. "Ain't no need to take cars away from people," he muttered. "You wait till they park it and gone. No muss, no fuss. No need to hurt nobody. But FMJ, he don't care. He got nothing to lose now."

"How do you know it's so easy to steal somebody's car?"

"Experience." He puffed up a bit. "I can take me any car in no time—sixty seconds, less."

"Congratulations," I said, unimpressed by his braggadocio. "What do they do with all these cars?"

"Must have somebody somewhere who wants 'em for something," he said vaguely, his expression suddenly that of a person late for an appointment. "Got to get going now."

"Isn't your mom worried that you know FMJ?"

He snorted a derisive laugh, stood as if to go, and I got up with him.

"So how do I reach you?"

"For what?"

"I'd like to talk some more about what happened."

"Let me think about it. I still gotcher card, I'll establish communication," he said, hands jammed into his pockets as we rode the elevator.

We had reached the pink parking level. "One more thing," I said, as he turned to go.

He stopped, apprehension in his eyes. "What's that?"

"You just don't look like a Cornflake to me. What's your real name?"

"Howard," he said. "You can call me Howie."

"That's better. Thanks for the soda, Howie. Let's stay in touch."

We shook hands. His felt moist and the motion was awkward. I went to my T-Bird without looking back, hoping he wasn't still watching

and wouldn't see its new-car finish. Why am I so paranoid? I thought.
He didn't seem like such a bad kid.

Back at the office there was news, and I quickly dialed Trish in the
library.

"Debbie Weston got a job at the *Washington Post,*" I told her.
"She gave two weeks' notice this morning. Move fast."

"I'm on it! I'm on it! Thanks, Britt! Thanks a million."

One more call and I could go home.

"Hi, Mom."

"Where have you *been,* Britt?"

"Working on a story."

She sniffed. "That's why I called, Britt. A story." She sounded
peevish.

"Oh? What kind of story?"

"A positive one. Why are you always so absorbed by bad news?"

I rolled my eyes and began clearing my desk, the receiver tucked
under my chin.

"You never want to hear any good news."

"Yes, I do, Mom. I love happy endings. They just don't happen
often enough."

"Maybe it's because when somebody wants to tell you one, you
don't bother to return the call."

I pressed a thumb and middle finger against my closed eyes, gently
massaging the lids. "What kind of story, Mom? Is it a fashion—"

"Not exactly."

Why me? I wondered.

"Unlike the kind of stories that you always—"

"What is it?" I interrupted. "I was about to go home. If I hang
around here too long something will happen and I'll wind up working
all night."

"You never have time to listen."

"It's not that, Mom, it's just that I need to get out of here." I stared
at the air vents in the ceiling, envisioning poisonous PCBs raining
down upon me. "I'll call you from home."

"It's about Heidi," she blurted, "the new stylist who worked the
fashion show yesterday. I may have mentioned to you that her car was
stolen when she and her husband went out to dinner."

"And she got it back?"

"Yes! When they arrived home the night before last it was in the driveway. Not only that—"

"Oh, no." I straightened up in my chair. "There was a note?"

"How did you guess? From the thief, and it was so sweet. He left theater tickets. They went to the playhouse tonight—"

"Mom! Call the police."

"What? Are you joking?"

"Mom, I'm dead serious. Call the police. Do you know where Heidi lives?"

"Why, no. What *are* you talking about?"

I snatched the phone book. "What's her last name?"

"Britt, I have no idea. Wait, is it English, or is it Irish? I *think* it starts with an A. I'll ask at our staff meeting tomorrow."

My head began to ache. I quickly explained. "Mom, try to remember! We can't page her at the theater if we don't know her name. And without her address, we don't even know which police department to call, much less where to send them."

"Well," she said comfortingly, "we don't know that they'll do it again. Maybe they were sincere this time."

I glanced at the clock. Most likely it was already too late. "Mom, you don't understand. They're being ripped off at this very minute."

"Well, dear." The tone was chastising. "You really should have returned my call sooner."

Chapter Five

Despite my frustration, I did sleep that night—for three hours. I was dreaming of fire, leaping flames, in blazing color and CinemaScope, when the claxons faded and the sirens stopped, forced out by a sound more persistent. So real was my dream that I groped for the phone, convinced that the call was a tip on some major out-of-control inferno and wondering whether I had remembered to stash my fire boots in the new T-Bird's trunk.

I expected the raspy voice of a fire department source or an editor. It was Rakestraw.

"Britt, you awake?"

The digital clock glowed in the dark: 3:15 A.M. I blinked.

"Sure," I mumbled. "I'm always up by now."

"Sorry, but you said you wanted to be in on any new developments."

"You got Peanut?"

"You mean FMJ?"

"Whichever." I felt groggy. "You've got 'im?"

"Nope. He's pulled another Casper on us. But get used to seeing people on crutches."

"What?"

"Two more carjackings tonight, drivers shot in the leg."

"So it was him. Why do you think he keeps doing that?" I croaked irritably, groping over Billy Boots for my notebook on the nightstand.

"Maybe he aims for their heads but he's a lousy shot. Could be he's making a statement. Maybe he's just a mean little bastard. Who the hell knows? But that ain't all."

"What?" I switched on the reading lamp, squinting in the light.

"The cars they took tonight. They're using 'em."

"For . . . ?"

"I wondered why one was an old battering ram of an Olds, not like the hot new models they've been taking. That was it—battering ram. They hit the Jordan Marsh department store downtown. Backed it right through the glass front doors."

"Didn't the alarm go off?"

"Sure, but they're not stupid. They know that after breaking glass activates the sonic alarm, it takes the security company three or four minutes to process it and notify the police. They also know that since alarm calls are ninety percent false, cops aren't impressed. Hell, they'll finish their coffee or whatever and take their time. Depending on where they're at, it takes them five to fifteen minutes or longer to respond. These kids know they've got a window of eight to twenty minutes. They're fast. They ran in and cleaned off the high-ticket racks. Loaded up all the most expensive shirts, pants, and jackets they could carry and hauled buggy, three carloads full. We got 'em in action on store security tape."

"Think you can round them up by morning?"

"Hope to. Everybody's looking, even the chopper. They shouldn't be too hard to spot. We're watching the warehouse districts and their neighborhoods. Want to come out and play?"

I hate to turn down an invite from a source, especially a cop. Their love-hate relationship with the press runs hot and cold. Say no and he might invite somebody else, maybe a TV crew, and with my luck the big one would break.

"Sure, I wasn't doing anything anyway."

"Meet me at the station. If I have to leave, they'll know where I'm at."

"Be there in twenty."

I hit the floor and snatched my trusty navy blue jumpsuit off the closet door where I keep it for middle-of-the-night emergencies. Of course, now that I was up, Bitsy pranced to go out and Billy Boots howled for breakfast, circling his empty dish like a shark.

Too rushed to open a can, I shook dry cat food into a dish, debating whether to call Lottie. Why drag her out at the cost of a night's sleep for something that might not be major? I decided.

Bitsy whimpered at the door, excited and ready for adventure. She yelped and whined as I tried to slip out without her. I sighed and opened the door. "Come on." We bounded out into the dark of night together.

Rakestraw stood next to his unmarked in the eerily lit station parking lot, talking to a detective from juvenile. "What the hell is that?" asked the other cop, smirking down at the white toy poodle with a red ribbon in her hair.

"As good a police dog as you've ever seen," Rakestraw said. The other detective shook his head and walked off. "I used to work midnights with Francie," Rakestraw said quietly. "I wondered if you still had her sidekick."

I had never wanted a small yappy dog, but her owner was my friend. Francie used to smuggle Bitsy onto the midnight shift in her patrol car. When she died in the line of duty, I inherited Bitsy. After action-filled nights spent chasing bad guys and taking prisoners, she probably finds her life with me boring, but if she can cope, so can I.

"She's no trouble," I said. "It would have broken her heart not to come. If there's a problem, we can follow you in my car."

"Wouldn't want to break her heart now, would we? Come on." I signed the ubiquitous release form, absolving the taxpayers from liability should I be killed or maimed, and we settled into the unmarked. Bitsy crouched on the floorboard, ears cocked to the police radio chatter, like old times.

"She never forgot," I said. "She's still a police dog at heart."

Rakestraw didn't answer. His eyes were sweeping alleyways and dead ends as we cruised the dark past the Edgewater, then past the apartment house where I had met Gilberto's mother and sister.

The warm, soft night blurred the city's hard edges. I never cease to be fascinated by Miami's mysterious netherworld.

"Your story was all right," Rakestraw said, the closest he has ever come to a compliment.

My quotes from the mother and sister of Gilberto, aka Peanut, aka FMJ, made it unclear who had divulged his name to me. The woman's only outrage was directed at the system that had failed so miserably when she sought help for a son who scared even her.

"It's good," Rakestraw said. "The publicity will put heat on that judge who kept sending him home, and on the state attorney's office to try him as an adult."

"Can't try him till you catch him."

"Something's gonna catch up with him—we will or lead will," Rakestraw predicted. "If we don't find him first, he'll pick the wrong victim and get his brains blown out." He threw me a sidelong glance as we turned a corner. "The public defender's office called the captain to ask if we had released his name to the media."

"They should know you wouldn't do that," I said. Jennifer Carey remained alive but unconscious. I hoped she would survive and testify against him. FMJ was growing into a bigger story. I couldn't wait to interview him. I hoped it would be tonight.

We cruised for an hour listening to the activity on the police radio. Bitsy snoozed, probably dreaming she was back on patrol with Francie. I yawned, glad I hadn't awakened Lottie to wander the city aimlessly with us when she could be sleeping.

"Where do you think they took the stuff?" I stifled another yawn. "Think they stole it on order or spur-of-the-moment?"

"Some is probably for personal use, but they've obviously got connections, somebody with a store or space at a flea market. None of the cars they took have turned up. They're not driving them, they're stealing more. Somebody's in business." He squinted sideways. "Want to stop for a hit of coffee? You look like you could use some."

He must have read my mind. I did not look forward to work later. I knew I would run out of gas by late afternoon.

This evening appeared to be a dud, but it gave me a chance to know Rakestraw better and develop him as a source. He swung east, toward the boulevard and an all-night coffee shop.

The intercity frequency burst to life as we got out of the car: Miami Beach units involved in the high-speed pursuit of several westbound vehicles on the MacArthur Causeway. We froze, listening. The dispatcher reported about ten subjects in three cars fleeing a smash-and-grab at the Jordan Marsh on the Beach.

"Son of a bitch, it's them! They hit another one!" We piled back into the car and Rakestraw turned the key. "And they're headed this way!"

"That's *my* Jordan Marsh," I protested, rebuckling my seat belt. "It's only a few blocks from where I live."

Rakestraw stomped the gas and the car jumped the curb back out onto the boulevard. A Beach unit had been run off the road near the Coast Guard base and rescue had been summoned.

"Damn, they'll kill a cop before they're through!" Rakestraw snatched up the mike, took a deep breath, and drawled in an unnaturally calm and casual voice, "Unit Seven-twenty-four. Think I'm gonna swing by and have a look-see in case the Beach needs assistance."

Then he floored it; the car leaped forward with such power that I was glad we'd skipped the coffee.

"The chase policy," he explained.

"Right." Now I understood his oddly passive voice to the dispatcher.

Talking on the air is like speaking on the record. Taped radio transmissions are the only official documentation of what happens out on the street.

Miami Beach officers can pursue fleeing felons at high speeds. Miami cops, however, are forbidden to do so in crimes against property. Cops hate it when bad guys get away. The unpopular policy was established after four teenagers ran from police in a stolen car and wiped out in a fiery crash. Instead of reflecting on how they managed to spawn car thieves, the irate parents filed wrongful death actions against the city. They charged that the youngsters would not have crashed if the police hadn't chased them. They also sued the hapless owner of the stolen car and his insurance company.

Now Miami cops can engage in hot pursuit only when lives are threatened, such as by shots being fired.

We raced south on the boulevard, the staccato adrenaline-charged voices of the Beach officers reporting their progress by radio.

One had to stop and investigate what appeared to be several dozen Haitian boat people wading ashore near Palm Island. At the sight of flashing lights, they had run in all directions.

The remaining cops were chasing the fleeing cars across the straightaway at speeds exceeding one hundred miles an hour, past Watson Island, still coming west.

"They're exiting onto the boulevard, into the city!" a Beach officer shouted.

"He's not gonna make it. He's gonna lose it!" one cried as the fleeing cars hit the exit ramp.

"He made it! But we lost unit two-fourteen; he hit the barrier! He's got right-side damage. There goes a tire! Oncoming units use caution, there's a tire rolling down the westbound right lane!"

How could teenagers, probably still unlicensed, outmaneuver cops trained in pursuit and combat driving?

The exit ramp loomed ahead. The oncoming wails of distant sirens merged into stereo with the same sounds on the radio frequency.

Sirens converged from other directions now, and radio traffic increased: Miami officers advising circumspectly about plans to mosey on by, then jamming pedals to the metal.

We saw them now, three blocks distant, headlights out. The battering ram, a black 1981 Olds, roared down the ramp, closely followed by a new Grand Marquis that took the curve on two wheels and a skidding Toyota.

"Here they come!" yelled Rakestraw.

I braced and held on. Wide awake, Bitsy crouched on the floorboard, ears at full alert, tail wagging. I failed to share her elation. If we crash head-on, I thought, my poor mother, whose calls I neglect to return, will not collect a cent. But had I stolen a car, run from the cops, and crashed, she would be able to sue for enough to retire to Barbados.

The suspects never slowed down. All three cars blew a red stoplight at 13th Street at seventy miles an hour. The Toyota whined like a jet engine as it hurtled straight into Overtown. The battering ram turned north, toward us, and the Grand Marquis fled south. Blue and red lightning flashed, beams bouncing and whirling through the night as half a dozen Beach units careened down the exit ramp, sirens screaming.

"You hear something?" Rakestraw barked.

"What?"

He snatched the mike. "Seven-twenty-four. I believe I just heard gunshots in the vicinity of the Beach's chase. I'm in pursuit."

"Affirmative," radioed another city officer. "I heard the shots."

Rakestraw smiled wickedly and slid the blue flasher onto the dash. Another siren came up fast behind us. The driver of the oncoming Olds saw us and skidded into a U-turn, sliding sideways for half a block as Rakestraw stood on the brakes. So did the cop behind us as I braced for an impact that did not come.

The Olds' tires gained purchase on the pavement, and the car shot across the boulevard like a bullet. I thought I heard shouts and saw a backseat passenger perched high atop what had to be Jordan Marsh merchandise stacked all around him.

"We've got 'em boxed in now!" I saw Rakestraw's eyes and did not want to be any of those kids.

The Olds bounced across a sidewalk, ran two stop signs at a flat-out sixty, and accelerated the wrong way on a one-way street, aiming at an expressway entrance ramp. A tire blew and the driver lost it. They crashed into an expressway piling under the overpass, near the homeless encampment. A hubcap soared high into the air, bounced, then clattered across the roadway.

Smoke rose lazily from the wreck as both doors burst open and three skinny figures hurtled out into the haze. They hit the ground running in three different directions.

"They bailed!" Rakestraw shouted into his mike. "I'll take the one in the T-shirt and baseball cap, headed toward Second Avenue." Police cars skidded to stops all around us, with cops taking up the foot chase.

"Stay here."

"I'll go with you," I said.

"No way. You can't keep up and you can't run around out here alone. I can't watch out for you."

I watched him dart up the embankment, scale a fence halfway up, and run surefooted across sloping concrete at a 90-degree angle.

I hated this part. If I stayed with the car, I'd miss the action. Had FMJ been driving the Olds? Where was he now?

The busy radio was my only link. Breathless patrolmen reported their locations as they pounded down alleys and checked abandoned buildings. The Grand Marquis had ignored warning signals and roared across the Miami Avenue Bridge as it was about to open for a boat. The pursuing police cars didn't make it, and the Marquis had vanished on the other side of the river. Overtown, scene of Miami's last riot, seemed to have swallowed up the Toyota. The suspects on foot had eluded pursuers so far. Nobody can outrun a scared teenager. One patrol unit was called away to check a report of dehydrated Cuban rafters beached at Dinner Key near City Hall. The remaining searchers called for K-9 units and set up a perimeter. The harsh glare of powerful spotlights exposed the barren postapocalyptic nightmarescape of predawn downtown Miami. Chopper blades rent the air, hovering low, as the search focused on an area about four blocks away. Where is the Miami of my memories, the clean and gentle city where I grew up? I wondered. How did this happen?

Bitsy began to whimper and I stroked her head. Then I saw it. Furtive movement near the still-smoking wreck. Heart pounding, I caught my breath.

Shadows had come alive. Dark shapes, skittering figures emerged from everywhere, swarming over the Olds.

Homeless people rousted in the night by the commotion, they were looting the stolen merchandise in the smashed car.

I scrambled out, leaving the door of the unmarked open. Bitsy stood growling under her breath, eyes watching me expectantly. What would Francie have done? "Hey," I yelled indignantly. "Hey, you!"

Nobody paid attention. A wraith in ragged clothes glanced up dismissively, then continued to load his shopping cart.

I kept shouting until one turned and took a short menacing step in my direction, the way someone would stomp to scare off an annoying cat or dog. Oh, for Pete's sake, I thought, got back in the car, and slammed the door. This is insane.

In daylight, I could reason with them face-to-face, but in the dark it's different. I am only a reporter, I told myself, not a cop.

When the cops straggled back, breathless, sweating, and empty-handed, the stolen car had been stripped clean by the homeless. Even the battery was gone. Rakestraw was mad as hell, sorry he had invited me. This had turned into the Chernobyl of local police work. The Beach had lost two cars in the chase, one patrolman was hospitalized with a neck injury, another was being checked out at the emergency room, and a city cop searching an abandoned building had plunged through a rotted floor. He too went to the hospital, for shots and stitches.

More than twenty thousand dollars in loot was gone, as were the culprits, at least ten kids, three of whom had eluded the cops on foot.

We drove to the Beach to see the tape from the store security camera. After the Olds exploded through the glass double doors, the kids swarmed inside like a mob of looters. I did not see Howie among them. Maybe he was telling the truth, I thought. The thieves, organized and fast, seized armloads of the most expensive merchandise. They took nothing cheap.

Rakestraw pointed out FMJ: wiry, slightly built, and short, clearly in charge and enjoying himself. The kid looked younger than his age, with a mop of wavy hair, the fuzz of a thin mustache, and a grin that would have been engaging had there not been a handgun stuck in his waistband, right next to his digital beeper. A few others wore dark glasses or scarves across their faces like the highwaymen from the bad old days of the Wild West, but FMJ did not. He mugged and swaggered, rolled his tongue at the camera, and mouthed obscenities.

Like Howie had said, he was cold. He didn't care.

The ill-fated chase had been launched when a Miami Beach patrolman arrived at the store on a routine alarm call and three cars sped away. The wrecked Olds wore a fresh license tag stolen from an apartment house parking lot during the night. In the trunk the cops found a piece of luggage belonging to a wounded Chicago tourist, shot in the knee. He had been driving the Toyota.

The amount of paperwork required by both departments was staggering. It was nearly sunrise when Rakestraw drove me back to the station for my car. The city looked innocent, like a watercolor, soft-edged in the dawn light, or maybe my eyes were bleary. As we rolled west on Northeast Sixth, a homeless man shuffled across the street in front of us dragging a large piece of cardboard. He wore a brand-new Ralph Lauren shirt, price tag still dangling. Rakestraw slowed for a better look, and the man gave us a toothless grin.

Too late to catch a nap, I showered, dressed, and ate breakfast at the Villa Deli. I ordered fuel for my body engine, the special: two eggs over easy, grits, bacon, and a toasted bagel slathered in cream cheese. I had the waitress wrap a cheese Danish to go. When lack of sleep caught up with me, chewing would keep me awake. The upside about staying out all night is that I can eat anything and never gain an ounce.

I wrote the story, turned it in, then plodded out to check my beat, tired and irritable. Only Bitsy had had fun. Now she would expect to ride in police cars again every night. Even Lottie was mad as hell.

We met for coffee after the first edition. "Did you notice on the way in today that all the windshield washers downtown looked well dressed?" she said. "I could have sworn that one who jumped on my hood was wearing an Armani jacket."

"Probably was." I told her why.

"You and the cops were out chasing those little rodents all night and didn't call me?"

"I swear I thought about it but figured it wouldn't pan out, so I let you sleep."

"Are you crazy? I could've shot some great stuff."

"Who knew?"

"You should have called me." She pouted.

My mother called when I got back to my desk. The home of Heidi, the stylist, had been cleaned out while she and her husband attended the play.

"I didn't tell her it could have been prevented if you had only called me back," she said.

"Thanks, Mom."

Too weary to argue, I answered the next call with feelings of foreboding and resignation. It was good news.

"Is that you, Britt? Finally! We did it! We did it!" It was Trish Tierney. "I start in the newsroom Monday, general assignment. Thank you!"

There is some justice in the world after all, I thought.

Chapter Six

I want you to come by for dinner. To celebrate,'' Trish said.

"Tonight?''

"Right, when you get off.''

"Well, I've got a couple of stories I'll be working on for a while, and then I'm probably gonna go round and round with the city desk. And I'm really tired, so I don't think I can, but it's great news. It'll be fun having you in the newsroom.''

"Britt!'' Her hearty tone was positive and persuasive. "No excuses. You are my best and only friend in Miami. I owe you a lot. And you have to eat sometime. Remember, I'm a reporter. I know. It doesn't matter how late. Sounds like you could use a nice little dinner. Nothing fancy, for God's sake. Nothing that won't keep warm. Just some good nourishing food.''

"You wanna meet somewhere?'' I said uncertainly.

"No. I'm cooking,'' she said firmly. "Look, call me as you leave the paper, I'll pop dinner in the oven, and it'll be hot and ready to eat when you walk in the door.''

The woman would not take no for an answer, and her offer was tempting and convenient. She lived on the Beach, she said, not far from me. The frozen wasteland in my freezer influenced my thinking. "You're on,'' I said. "Shall I bring something?''

"Not a thing. Just yourself.''

Nice. I called my wonderful landlady, Helen Goldstein, to ask if she would take Bitsy out for a few minutes so I could go straight to Trish's.

Mrs. Goldstein, married to the same man for sixty years and sold on the concept, agreed as usual, sounding pleased. "So," she said optimistically. "You have a date. Your lieutenant? The skipper? Or somebody new?"

"I'm just going to grab a bite with another reporter. A woman," I added, dashing her hopes.

The skipper, Curt Norske, was the dashing captain of the *Sea Dancer,* a sightseeing boat that catered to tourists and cruised Biscayne Bay. Sparks flew when our eyes met over a submerged body. So far, that relationship had been intermittent and casual, but "my" lieutenant, Kendall McDonald, was a longer story. I dismissed his image and focused on work, the prospect of warm food a tantalizing incentive. Living on coffee, adrenaline, and headlines gets old. One of these days, I thought, I have got to go to the supermarket and stock up. My problem is time; I am either too busy, too late, or too impatient for endless checkout lines. My pantry is well stocked only with pet food and my aging hurricane supplies, untouched for years, mostly outdated canned tuna and bottled water.

Trish's address was on a neon stretch of Collins Avenue hotels and high-rises. Somehow I had pictured her in an efficiency with a hot plate. I double-checked my notebook. This was it, I thought, if I took it down right.

The building was a condo conversion, the latest trend, Miami Beach's new look, wrought by enterprising developers. Older oceanfront hotels from the city's glory days are renovated, updated, and converted into condominiums. The lucrative market appeals to young local professionals, wealthy Europeans, Asians, and Latins, and anyone looking for a part-time Miami Beach residence.

The phenomenon is another metamorphosis in a city that has evolved in less than forty years from world-class resort to shabby retirement community to the new playground of the rich and famous. Trendy New Yorkers find it simpler to jet to Miami for the weekend than fight traffic to Connecticut, the Jersey shore, or upstate New York.

This pink and lavender building had been the Star Light Hotel, designed by one of the most prominent Art Deco–era architects. In the forties it was *the* place for celebrities and nightlife; in the sixties it hosted international beauty pageants. Encroaching shabbiness overtook it in the seventies and eighties. The glamour, the history, and the excitement faded into ghosts. But now the Star Light was back, restored to splendor, with all-new windows, a remodeled lobby, new cabanas, security, and renovated corridors.

My heels clicked across the mirrored and marbled lobby. The security guard took my name and said I was expected.

He must have telephoned my arrival. When I emerged on the fifth floor Trish was standing in the spill of light from her open doorway.

She wore shorts, a blue silk blouse, and sandals, a wisp of a girl with a contagious smile.

"It's been the most wonderful day. I just can't tell you." She was nearly giddy with excitement. "I've been jumping up and down all afternoon! Of course, I'm also scared to death." She looked closer at my face. "You look exhausted. Poor thing!" She drew me inside to rosy lighting, good music, and comforting aromas from the kitchen.

Sliding glass doors stood open to the terrace, sheers billowing in the breeze off the ocean, vast night sky and sea beyond. The apartment was gorgeous, including a crystal chandelier, plush carpet, and glass brick. My jaw must have dropped. This poor jobless reporter's apartment put mine to shame.

"What a nifty place!"

"Terrific, isn't it?" she said, smiling. "Let me get you a drink."

The bar was built-in and well stocked, with crystal wine goblets suspended overhead. I opted for Dubonnet over ice. She pressed the glass into my hands. "Here, relax, make yourself at home and I'll be right back. I think I smell something burning." She declined my offer of help and disappeared behind the glass brick.

I wandered out onto the terrace with my drink, my hair blowing in the evening breeze. The dark Atlantic was one with the midnight-blue horizon; the only lights twinkled from ships at sea. The music made the atmosphere instantly inviting and relaxing. There were breakers on the beach below and laughter from people in the outdoor pool.

I drank in the view and stepped back inside the magazine-perfect apartment, uncluttered, scarcely lived in, no cats, no dogs, no confusion. The only personal touch was a photo in a silver frame on the mahogany breakfront, a child that must have been Trish and a frail-looking boy who resembled her enough to be a brother or a cousin. Wearing jeans and plaid shirts, they sat on ponies.

I settled on a brocade love seat, sipping my Dubonnet and still gazing out toward the sea. Beautiful nights like this one always made me think of McDonald, wondering where he was, who he was with, and if he ever thought of me.

Trish emerged, pink-faced, wearing oven mitts and carrying a long dish covered by a pink linen napkin.

"Told you it would be ready in a jiff."

"Sure you don't need help?"

"Absolutely. The kitchen's only big enough for one." She placed the dish on the table, covered in rosy linen and set with bone china.

"How long have you had this apartment? It's perfect."

"Isn't it?" She poured herself a club soda, perched gracefully on a settee, and gazed around the room. "If only it *was* my apartment. But no such luck. A friend back in Tulsa knows the owners and I'm house-sitting. Once they arrive for the season, I'll be out on the street."

"Too bad, you must hate to give this up."

"You know it, but I've sure enjoyed staying here. And"—she grinned and raised her glass—"now that I have a reporting job, maybe I'll be able to afford something as nice."

"Well, it may take awhile," I warned.

"Oops, I almost forgot." She reached into the pocket of her shorts for something wrapped in a fold of white tissue paper. "This is for you."

Startled, I unfolded the paper, and a delicate pendant on a silver chain dropped into my lap. "What's this?"

I held it up. A spider web had been spun through a circular silver rim, leaving a small opening in the center. Caught in the web was a tiny turquoise chip. Hanging from the bottom was a perfect little silver feather.

"I've never seen anything like it."

"That's because it's one of a kind, handmade by a Native American friend, a Comanche I did a favor for, back in Oklahoma. It's a dream catcher."

"A what?"

"Good dreams are caught in the web, trickle down the feather, and bring you good fortune. Bad dreams pass right through that hole in the middle. The turquoise is for protection. It worked for me. I wore it for a long time. No bad dreams. I want you to have it, Britt."

"I couldn't possibly, Trish. It's fascinating, but it was a gift to you from a friend."

I held it out, silver glinting in the palm of my hand. She shook her head and closed her fingers over mine. "And now it's a gift to another friend. You've done so much for me, Britt. I want you to have it."

"If you're sure," I said hesitantly. I fastened the chain around my neck. I loved it, but I felt a little guilty. All I had done was encourage her. She probably would have landed the job anyway, with her determination.

"Why were you so set on Miami?"

She looked surprised at the question. "You don't win Pulitzers working in Oklahoma."

"That'll take awhile too." I smiled at her enthusiasm. "But seriously, there are lots of good news towns. Why Miami?"

"For the same reasons you love it, Britt. The people back home are glued to their TV sets, watching *Geraldo* and *Oprah*. The people in Miami *appear* on *Geraldo* and *Oprah*."

We both laughed.

"Sit down and I'll feed you."

She unfurled the pink napkin, exposing a loaf of golden brown bread, sliced it, and I nearly swooned.

"I thought you said this would be something simple!" A crisp crust stuffed with cheese, pepper, and onion. "You made this?"

Her two-handed gesture was breezy, as though it was nothing. "It's a lot easier than it looks, an old family recipe."

Tiny roasted potatoes and crisp green beans nestled around the perfect chicken. She opened a bottle of Chardonnay. "To Pulitzers," she said exuberantly, as our glasses clinked.

"If reporting doesn't work out, you can always break into the bread business. You could sell a ton of this stuff and make a fortune. It's out of this world."

"Don't even suggest that this job won't work out." Her smile faded. "I'm scared to death and it's no joke. If I don't make it I'm in big trouble. I can't go back home."

"Why?" I sipped my wine. "Your old paper'd take you back in a New York minute. Probably even pay you more money. Sometimes you have to quit and go back to be appreciated."

"No." She shook her head, luminous gray eyes fixed on her plate. "I can't go back. There's something you don't know. I had a bad experience, and I'm afraid. . . . ."

"Afraid? What happened?"

She took a deep breath. "You see—"

Sudden shouts and pounding cut off her words.

The commotion came from the corridor outside. A man's quavering cries, murmuring voices. A door slammed.

Our startled eyes met. "Jesus, what's going on?" She rose, turned off the stereo to hear better, and darted to the door.

"Wait, Trish," I cautioned, following. "I wouldn't open it until you're sure."

On tiptoe, she peered through the peephole. "What in tarnation?" She threw off the safety chain and swung the door open.

Right behind her, I glanced around the room for the telephone, in case we needed it.

The shouts were louder now. "Ellie, Ellie! Where are you? Come out. Come back. Ellie!"

Trish stepped into the hallway and I followed. Breathless and agitated, an elderly man in yellow Bermuda shorts was shouting and pounding on doors. A gaggle of perplexed tenants trailed in his wake.

"Did you see her? My Ellie. Where is she?" A child must be missing, I thought. In a manner of speaking, that turned out to be the case. Trish took command. She intercepted him, grasping his wavering hands in hers.

"What's wrong?" she said. "How can we help you?"

"My Ellie." His eyes were wild. "She's not there. She wandered out again. This time she's gone. I can't find her."

"She has Alzheimer's," somebody said. "She doesn't know where she is sometimes."

"Don't worry," Trish said reassuringly. "We'll find her."

"She's not herself. She could be down on the beach. The ocean!" He groaned. "She was taking a nap, so I went to the card room. She must have woke up and come down to find me . . . lost her way."

The security guard emerged from the elevator. "She's not in the lobby, but she might have gotten by. I checked the pool."

Tears streaked the old man's mottled cheeks.

"What was she wearing?" I asked.

He looked bewildered, then bit his lip. "A blue dress, pale blue, and house slippers."

"How old is she?"

"Seventy-one."

"Somebody check the roof," I suggested, "and the stairwells."

"She's confused." He started to cry, his sobs ragged. "She doesn't

know where she is, who she is. I never leave her alone. But I needed
. . . I went out for a card game, for just a little while.''

"Of course," Trish crooned. Her arms circled his thin shoulders.
"You need a break once in a while. We all do. We'll find her."

I ran back through the apartment to the terrace. No elderly woman
in a blue dress below. But the beach was dark and full of shadows; she
could be anywhere. Traffic is heavy on Collins.

"Call the police," I told the security guard.

He rolled his eyes and looked reluctant. "Last time they didn't
show up for forty-five minutes and we'd already found her."

"Right," I said. "But if she's a wanderer they may have already
picked her up. If so, they won't know where she belongs."

He called from Trish's phone. Ellie hadn't been picked up, but her
description was broadcast to the zone cars. Short gray hair, five feet
four inches, 125 pounds, with a slight limp. Most neighbors had returned to their apartments, though a young couple did offer to check
the beach. The guard said he would search the roof. "Is there any way
she could have gotten the elevator door open?" I asked quietly, remembering a missing octogenarian found at the bottom of an elevator
shaft.

The guard said no.

No sign of Ellie in the laundry room. Nothing.

While Trish comforted Ellie's husband, whose name was Ben, I decided to do a floor-by-floor down to the street.

"Wait." Trish took me aside, her face intent. "Let's brainstorm,
Britt. Her husband says she has a bad hip and tires easily, but didn't
take her cane. You know"—light gleamed in her gray eyes—"little
children missing from home are usually found much closer than anybody expects."

True. I had covered my share of stories where searchers beat the
bushes miles away for a tot who was home all along, hiding in a closet
or at the bottom of a murky family pool.

"Let's remember that advanced Alzheimer's patients are like little
kids." She turned calmly to the husband. "What's your apartment
number, Ben?"

He gestured to an open door halfway down the hall. "Five-four-
teen." His voice trembled.

"Let's start there."

Made sense to me. Neat apartment, drapes drawn, television still blaring to an empty room, prescription medicine neatly arranged on a kitchen counter. We checked beneath the bed and in every closet and cabinet, as Ben flailed his arms frantically, insisting, "I looked! I looked! She's not here. Ellie. She could be in the ocean. Ellie," he moaned. "It's my fault."

We found a stack of adult diapers in the bathroom, more evidence that late-stage Alzheimer's patients are like helpless children. She was not in the apartment.

Undaunted, Trish led us back out into the hall. "I want to check the storage bins under the stairs," she said, moving quickly toward the fire exit.

She propped open the fire door and we descended a flight. Beneath the stairwell were numbered and padlocked storage lockers for residents. "These padlocks all seem intact." Trish's voice echoed in the poorly lit stillness. I held Ben's arm tightly on the stairs. This was a bad idea, I realized. What if he falls? What if somebody closes the fire door, trapping us? Most victims of geriatric dementia wander away in search of their primary caretaker. She wouldn't look for Ben down here.

"Here's one without a lock." Trish's voice came from below. The hinges of a wooden door protested loudly.

"Omigod, omigod, she's here! Britt! She's here!"

I clung to Ben as we scrambled down the last few steps. Trish was on all fours, reaching into the tiny space, no more than 22 inches wide, by about 28 inches high and not quite 24 inches deep. The missing woman filled the cubicle, curled into a fetal position, knees beneath her chin.

"Ellie!" Ben sat down hard on the stairs, out of breath and panting.

I rushed to help Trish, who had tugged the woman's arm and now grasped her beneath the shoulders, trying to free her from her small prison.

"She must have shut herself in there and couldn't get out," Trish said, grunting. "There's no latch on the inside."

"It had to be stifling," I said. "There's no ventilation."

The woman lay supine, her blue dress rumpled and soaked by sweat and urine, bare feet still inside the enclosure. "Jesus, she's not breathing!" Trish's face was white.

I slipped my fingers into the groove at the woman's neck. Her skin felt clammy, her lips looked blue. "I don't feel a pulse!"

Trish knelt and turned the woman's face to one side to clear her airway in case it was blocked. Her fingers explored the slack mouth and gingerly removed a set of false teeth.

I shivered and turned to Ben, trying to sound calm. "Go upstairs now and dial Nine-one-one. Be careful and don't fall, but hurry." I helped him to his feet and propelled him up the stairs. Thank God it was only one flight.

Trish pinched the woman's nose, took a deep breath, and began mouth-to-mouth, covering the bluish lips with her own, forcing air into the woman's lungs. I straddled the still body and began closed heart massage.

"One-one hundred, two-two hundred, three-three hundred, four-four hundred, five-five hundred. Breathe!"

I felt her breastbone and fragile rib cage, like that of a delicate bird, beneath the heel of my hand as I tried not to press too hard. I had heard horror stories about overzealous rescuers breaking bones, crushing ribs.

"One-one hundred, two-two hundred, three-three hundred, four-four hundred, five-five hundred. Breathe!" Trish lifted her face, inhaled a deep breath, then began again as I counted. "One-one hundred, two-two hundred . . ."

Once when Trish came up for air, she gasped, "Is he calling rescue?"

"Yes, response time should be only a few minutes."

We kept on. It seemed surreal, this almost mechanical teamwork in the shadows of a musty stairwell. The food, music, and camaraderie shared minutes ago seemed like a distant dream.

"Getting anything?" Trish gasped.

I searched for a pulse. Nothing.

"Keep going," I said. "Keep going. At least till they get here."

It went on forever. Slowly I began to realize that we were alone in the semidarkness with a corpse. This wasn't working. She was lost. We were going to fail.

"One-one hundred, two-two hundred . . ." I forced myself to think only of the counting.

Somebody gasped and gagged. I thought it was Trish.

"She's breathing! Britt, she's breathing!"

Right then, as I found a thin, reedy pulse, there was a clatter at the top of the stairs. Voices, a beam of light from above.

"They're here," I said. "Thank God."

By the time the medics loaded up Ellie for the ride to the hospital she was thrashing, muttering, "No, no, don't, don't."

"Good job," the rescue lieutenant said. "What the hell were you doing here anyway, Britt?"

"Visiting," I said, grinning. "If not for Trish here, we never would have found her."

Trish and I high-fived and climbed the stairs arm in arm, both weak-kneed and shaky.

Our food remained on the table precisely as we had left it, which never would have been the case with the bold cat and the ravenous little dog at my place. We both reached for our wineglasses.

Trish wiped her lips with her napkin. "Whooh!" she said, and shuddered.

"You were great. What a gutsy thing to do, Trish. Even medics won't use mouth-to-mouth anymore with everything that's out there."

Her eyes were solemn. "A life is a life, Britt; you can't just watch it slip away."

We drank to that.

"I'm sorry our dinner is spoiled," she said. "We'll have to do it again."

"The next one's on me. But don't expect me to cook. We'll go to my favorite Cuban restaurant."

"Can't wait. But there's still dessert. We've earned it."

We nibbled poached Bosc pears, buttery and elegant on pink paper doilies, and sipped a fragrant tea from delicate porcelain cups.

It was over tea that I remembered. "Before everything happened you were about to tell me why you're afraid to go back home."

"It was a man," she whispered.

"A bad romance?"

"This was no romance. Except in his mind." She put down her cup. "A stalker situation. The man had a fixation. I felt flattered at first, but when I turned him down he wouldn't stop, wouldn't leave me alone."

"But they have stalker laws now." My voice rose in indignation.

"Try telling that to small-town cops when the suspect is the only son in a socially prominent, politically influential family. They wouldn't, couldn't, do a thing, they said, as long as he committed no crime. The man was obsessed." Her eyes looked haunted. "Middle-of-the-night phone calls, driving by my place, pulling into my driveway at all hours. I'd look up in a restaurant or a store—and there he'd be, staring, big as life, an odd smile on his face. I couldn't go out. I was scared to death of him,'' she said bitterly. ''My only option was to run.''

A not-so-old fear scorched my soul. This time, the fear and indignation was for her, not me. ''God, Trish, I know what you went through. Only people who live through it know what it's like.'' I touched the dream catcher suspended from the chain around my throat. ''It happened to me. It was horrible. He was a rapist. Thank God he's in prison and will be for a long, long time, God and the parole commission willing. Even though I know where he is, I still have trouble walking into a public rest room alone. That was his MO; he cornered me in one. I'll never forget it.''

She leaned forward intently. ''We're so much alike, Britt, it's eerie. My stalker is capable of something just as scary, or worse.'' Tears glittered in her eyes. ''Before I left he was writing ugly, obscene letters—and I found out he had bought a gun.

''However.'' She smiled, chin up. ''Yours will grow gray behind bars, and mine's more than a thousand miles away. His name is Clayton Daniels. He doesn't know where I am, and I aim to keep it that way. That's why I can't go back. I've got to make it here.''

''You will, Trish, for sure.''

''From your lips to God's ears.''

As I left the building I met Ben returning from the hospital, accompanied by a married daughter who lived in Surfside. Ellie was going to be all right, or at least as all right as she would ever be.

The drive home took only five minutes. A storm was brewing over the Everglades, dark clouds mounting. The distant thunder sounded like cannons in a war that was drawing closer. I ignored it. Exhausted, well fed, and righteous, I slept like the dead.

Chapter Seven

Islowed down to a crawl every time I passed the Edgewater, scanning the streets for Howie. Slim chance in a fat city, but two nights later there he was. I wasn't sure it was him at first. He stood at the front door of an elderly woman who was the last holdout against the big-time developers. She had lived there all her life, but her small wooden frame house now resembled a toy, dwarfed by the looming walls of the towering shopping center and high-rise hotel complex surrounding it. Miami pioneer Margaret Mayberry resisted when developers planned the project more than two decades ago. They bought up the necessary properties. Everybody had a price. Then they approached Margaret Mayberry. When she declared she would never sell, they assumed she was simply a shrewd negotiator.

Condescending at first, they humored her. Eventually patience wore thin, they got tough, played hardball, and threatened to have her house condemned. She didn't cave; she simply dug in, so they redoubled their efforts. They sweetened the pot, offering $1 million and the lot of her choice, to which they would move her cottage at their expense. She took a broomstick to the lawyer who brought the offer.

Eventually they came to realize that she was not only serious but as tough as the indestructible Dade County pine her father had used to construct the only home she had known. Bleeding cash, their project stalled. They redesigned the north end of the complex around her property, with the parking garage entrance next to the porch where she loved to sit in the evening, sipping iced tea. She continued to live there, but instead of bay breezes, a steady stream of traffic now flows by her door and the scent of star jasmine has been replaced by exhaust fumes.

Howie stood on the front porch, speaking through the screen to Margaret Mayberry. She opened the door and handed him a small package. Eagerly he took it, bounded down the stairs, and trotted into the parking garage without a look back. My antenna rose. What was this street-wise little jitterbug from Overtown up to with this octogenarian Miami pioneer? Was he ripping her off? Shaking her down? Intimidating her? I swung the T-Bird into a U-turn and trailed him into the garage. The computerized time clock spit out a cardboard ticket and the mechanical arm lifted. The center's north side was nearly deserted at that hour, and he was easy to spot once my eyes grew accustomed to the light.

He had stepped onto an elevator. I parked nearby, punched the button, and the twin elevator promptly arrived. At the lower mall level I leaned out, didn't see him, and continued on to the upper mall. It wasn't even Halloween yet, but many stores were already decorated for Christmas. As the door slid open, I glimpsed him stepping into a stairwell, still carrying the package. I called out his name too late.

I hurried across the mall, pushed the door open, and heard his footsteps on the stairs above. I closed the heavy door behind me, slipped off my shoes, and padded up the stairs after him. He quickly outdistanced me, ascending flight after flight. Eventually another door creaked open, then clanged shut. I got there breathing hard. The door was marked NO EXIT. A crumpled fold of cardboard kept it from locking. I hesitated for a moment, then cracked it open. Night sky glowed above, scattered stars awash in moonlight. This was the roof of the mall-garage-hotel complex. The top tier of the eight-story parking garage was to the south, empty and vacant. The mall is never that full. Downtown did not rebound the way the developers had hoped. The hotel draws mostly conventions, some South American tourists, and local business meetings and banquets.

I opened the door wider. No one in sight. I stepped out. The air was cool and the surroundings quiet, a silent world above the chaos and crowds below. Lights to the north seemed to be the hotel laundry, which opened out onto the roof. The view was superb. The Julia Tuttle Causeway, a beaded string of glittering lights, stretched across Biscayne Bay to the east. The blue-and-white Bacardi building stood sentinel at the northwest. To the immediate southeast lay my home away from home, the Miami News building. I could see the lights of the fifth-floor newsroom I had just left. Downtown, to the southwest, the Centrust Tower stood bathed in brilliance, gleaming against the night sky. The complex beneath my feet stretched for an entire block and its vast roof seemed to be a connected labyrinth of small stairwells, all sorts of structures, and vents, sheds, and rooms for maintenance of air conditioners and utilities. Most were obviously no longer used, lots of little staircases to nowhere. Bordering this city block in the sky was an eleven-foot fence. The top three feet of wire angled inward. This fence was not designed to keep intruders out; it had been constructed to deter jumpers, people intent on suicide leaps. How many ways can people be protected against themselves? I wondered. Where had Howie gone? I slipped my shoes back on and walked across the roof to a metal door, which I opened. The narrow staircase inside led to a huge, unused, and rusty exhaust fan. I backed out and the door thudded closed behind me. Glancing about, I began to feel uncomfortable at being alone. But I wasn't, was I? Howie had to be here somewhere.

A small structure stood in what appeared to be a seldom-used rooftop corner. It had apparently housed an air-conditioning system at one time. The door stood slightly ajar. For a split second I thought I glimpsed a light. Perhaps it was metal reflecting light from the outside. The interior was in total darkness as I pulled open the heavy door and leaned in for a better look.

An earsplitting cry pierced the dark, and a blade flashed as a shadowy figure lunged toward me.

"Howie!" I cried out, stumbling backward, heart pounding. Off balance, I fell, sprawling flat on my bottom as my attacker loomed over me.

Legs apart, he stood poised like a warrior, a spear grasped in his right hand. Moonlight glistened off the blade.

"Who . . . Britt? Is that you? What are you doing here?"

"Howie?" I gasped, heart palpitating. "You scared the hell out of me! What is that thing?"

His left hand reached out and helped me to my feet. No longer menacing, he looked sheepish and embarrassed. Though my knees were shaky, I sensed that I had scared him as much as he had scared me.

"Whatcha doing here? Man." He shook his head. "I don't believe this, man. I coulda hurt you."

He leaned the weapon against the wall.

"What *is* that thing?"

"My protection," he mumbled, trying to regain his usual attitude. The weapon was a stick about three and a half feet long with a wicked-looking knife taped and wired to the tip. The makeshift spear appeared to be fashioned from a broom handle. I wondered if it was the same one Margaret Mayberry had used on the developers' lawyer.

"How the hell you get up here? Whatcha doing here anyway?"

"Looking for you," I snapped, brushing off my skirt. "You promised to stay in touch, remember? But you never called, you never wrote."

"You followed me," he said accusingly.

"You got it. Now what are you doing up here?"

He gazed past me at the purple haze hovering over the neon-lit city. "This is my pad, man. This is where I stay."

"You live here?"

"What's wrong with that?" he said arrogantly, arms crossed, legs apart. His voice thinned. "You ain't gonna tell anybody, are you?"

"I guess I've got no reason to, but how do you . . . how can you . . . ?" At a loss for words, I gestured at the small cubicle behind him.

"Come on in. I'll show you."

He acted house-proud. As I followed him inside, he snatched up something he didn't want me to see and shoved it behind a small shelf. An army-surplus sleeping bag lined one wall of the cell-size cubicle. An electrical outlet accommodated a small lamp and a hot plate. A small stock of supplies sat on a makeshift shelf. There was a plastic water jug, instant coffee, and crackers. T-shirts, sweatshirts, and jeans were neatly folded. Socks rolled into little bundles. A milk crate to sit on. A stack of paperbacks, mostly science fiction, and a battered well-used *American Heritage Dictionary*.

"Not bad," I said. "My first apartment was an efficiency."

"The price is right."

"How long have you been up here?"

He paused. " 'Bout a year and a half. Came here when I was fourteen."

"That long! Oh, Howie. You mean you haven't been going to school? It must get hot as hell up here."

"It ain't too bad. 'Fore that I stayed in a car for a while and in an empty house. Want some coffee?"

"Sure." I sat on the milk crate and watched. He filled a small metal pan with water from the jug and set it on the hot plate.

"It ain't bad at all." He measured instant coffee into two plastic mugs. "It's not the heat, it's the humility. That door face the bay. When I prop it open there's always enough breeze to make sleeping tolerable." He opened a jar crammed with paper packets of sugar and powdered cream, probably from the food court in the mall. "Sometimes storms come barreling across the bay shooting big bolts of lightning. Sound like a war in outer space. The rain sprays in on my bedroll. I thought it would be a bitch up here when it was hot, but ain't nothing. Winter be something else. When I first moved up here it got real cold one night, bad-ass cold. Down to the thirties. Shoulda seen me shivering and shaking up against that wall."

"You could freeze up here." The indignation in my voice reminded me of my mother.

"Freeze to death in Miami?" He lifted a skeptical eyebrow.

"Not literally, but we do have one of the highest death rates from hypothermia in the United States. That's when your body temperature drops enough to kill you." The burner in the hot plate glowed red in the semidarkness. He had had to unplug the lamp to use it. "Up north, people know enough to seek shelter when it's cold. But in Florida, homeless people stay out on nights when the temperature drops to the thirties or forties. People can easily die of hypothermia, especially if they're in poor physical condition."

He did not seem alarmed.

"You like the pink ones, the blue ones, or the real sugar?" He sifted through paper packets, the perfect host.

"The real stuff," I said. "I think those others are bad for you."

While he was busy with the coffee, I snaked my hand behind the shelf to see what he had stashed there. His secret was odd-shaped and plastic: a battered replica of the U.S.S. *Enterprise* from the original *Star Trek* movie. One of the two warp nacelles was broken off.

I slipped it back into place and focused on the boxy bluish package taken from the old woman. "I saw you with Margaret Mayberry," I said casually.

He turned, a steaming cup in his hand.

"You're not running some scam on her, are you?"

"Gimme a little credit." He shook his head, offended at my foolishness. "No way. She a stand-up old lady. All alone. Like, I help her out sometimes, clean around her yard, fix anything she need around her house. Make sure nobody mess with her. She's my cover. I used to get hassled by security down in the mall sometime. Now the man stop me, ask what I'm doing here all the time, I say I work for Miss Mayberry. Everybody know her.''

Tenderly, he placed the bluish box between us, his face eager. Up close, I saw what it was: Tupperware.

''I don't 'cept no money from her, but sometimes . . .'' He opened the box with a greedy flourish of anticipation. Half a dozen homemade brownies nestled on napkins inside.

He passed me one, along with a mug of coffee.

''Mmmmm.'' I savored the first bite.

''You should try her banana bread,'' he said, mouth full. ''That's real bad.''

It felt cozy up here atop Miami in the evening breeze with steaming coffee and rich chocolate treats. Almost like camping out.

''What is it with that thing you almost impaled me on?'' I said.

''As you can see''—he gestured with a half-eaten brownie—''I'm not real big. One night some dude grabbed me by my shirt collar, took me by the throat, and pulled a blade on me.'' He paused and sighed. ''No way to win a knife fight,'' he said softly. ''Too damn close. It don't pay. Only place anybody win a knife fight is in a Hollywood movie. Make-believe. So I put together my protection. You do whatcha gotta do.''

''You'd be better off living with your own folks. What about your mom?''

''She don't worry about nothing 'cept where to score 'nother hit of crack. I ain't seen her in six months.''

I sighed. ''What about your grandparents?''

''The big dirt sleep. They dead, man.''

''Your father?''

''Dead too.'' He tossed it out casually, almost too casually. ''Got blowed away by a shotgun. I was six years old, sitting on my front steps. Seen the whole thing. Cut right in half. DOA.''

''Robbery?''

He shook his head. ''They was arguing over drugs.''

''My dad got shot too.''

His head came up. ''No sh. . . .''

I licked the chocolate off my lips. ''Yeah, I was three years old. I didn't see it like you did. He was Cuban, a freedom fighter. Went down there on a mission and got caught. Castro had him executed by a firing squad.''

"What about your mother?''

"She's still pissed off at him for getting killed—and at me too, because I remind her of him. We have a lot in common, Howie.'' I glanced at his library. "I love reading too.''

"You got a good job?'' he said curiously, more a question than a statement.

I nodded. "You still taking cars?''

He stirred restlessly and looked uncomfortable. "Sometimes I need the bread, but I don't get greedy. If I need transportation I can borrow a car from here''—his head angled toward the parking garage—"but then I just leave it parked somewhere, I don't sell it. Sometimes''—he grinned wickedly—"I take one, bring it back, park it on a different level.''

"I hate parking garages,'' I said, thinking of all those times I was sure my car had been stolen, then found it, parked elsewhere. Maybe I wasn't forgetful after all; maybe it *had* been stolen.

"I don't do too much round here, you know,'' he said solemnly, "'cause I live here. Don't wanna make trouble where you live.''

"Yeah, the mob has a phrase for it.'' He offered another brownie. Tempted, I declined. "You're so skinny,'' I said.

"You got nothing to worry about.'' I took his sidelong glance as a compliment.

"So where do you get them if you don't take 'em from here?'' I asked, worrying vaguely about the *News* parking lot just a block and a half away.

He shrugged. "The church and the hotels across the street. Pick a set of keys off the valet board over there.'' He shrugged. "Or go up the boulevard to one of those gas stations by Bay Point.''

The publisher of the *News* lives in Bay Point, an affluent, walled-in waterfront community. Private security officers man a guardhouse and screen visitors. Lawns are green and homes lavish, with flower beds and landscaping and cookie-baking mommies who attend garden club meetings. It is *Leave It to Beaver* land, with children at play on safe, shady streets, while outside the walls, in gritty real life on the boulevard, prostitutes flag down traffic, the homeless hunker in doorways, and crime plagues small businesses.

"When they go pay for their gas and leave the keys,'' Howie was saying. "Tha's when you jump in and be gone with the car 'fore they turn around. But I quit that game." He frowned. "Too many people carrying guns these days. Kill you over a car."

"You mean the police?"

"Hell, no, I ain't worried about no police. They won't shoot at a kid, tha's against official procedure. It's the damn civilians." He stopped chewing his second brownie to wax indignant. "Too many of 'em got guns! They'll kill you! Some guy shot at a friend of mine. Damn near smoked 'im. The crazy fool was shooting holes in his own car! Almost killed somebody over a car!"

"Odd you should say that," I said mildly, "because that's what FMJ is doing, shooting people over cars."

Howie's face was half masked in shadow. "He shoots people he don't have to shoot. He say his gun want to get blood on itself. He cold crazy. He ain't shooting 'cause of the car, he's shooting 'cause he likes it; the dude likes hurting people."

A sudden shudder tickled my spine. Must have been the caffeine and the chocolate cavorting through my system.

"You can't go on living like this, Howie. You've got to straighten out your life, get your act together, get back into school and make something of yourself. You're smart, you're a survivor. Jesus, Howie, you can *be* somebody." I leaned forward. "Do it now. You have your whole life ahead of you."

His gaze stayed steady. His expression didn't change; he didn't say a word.

"Sure," I went on, "all this may seem swell now, but you don't wanna be living up here when you're twenty or thirty years old. Sooner or later some security or maintenance man is gonna catch on to you, or they'll do major renovations, a little urban renewal up here on the roof, and knock your house down."

He stared at the floor.

"Maybe things are better with your mom now, and you can live with her."

He sighed. "Once a junkie, always a junkie."

"You sound like the parent instead of the child."

"That's how it was sometimes."

"Is that why you left?"

"I couldn't stay because of her boyfriend."

"Maybe she isn't seeing him anymore."

"She always seeing somebody."

"Maybe you can learn to get along with him."

He looked up at me, eyes shiny. "He was the dude I tol' you about, with the blade."

It was my turn to sigh. "But this isn't it, Howie." I gestured at his small abode. "This is no place to live."

"I thought it wasn't *where* you live but *how* you live." His voice rose angrily. "I do the best I can."

"I know." I was contrite.

"It's better than being locked up."

"What makes you think you'd go to jail?" I thought again of Jennifer Carey and her son, hoping that Howie was not the backseat passenger.

"I was on probation," he said warily.

"If it was for auto theft, you won't go to jail. You have to kill somebody to go to jail these days."

He stared between his knees at the floor, arms clutched to his chest as though afraid of letting something escape.

"Even if you've done something more serious, deals can be worked out."

"How?" His voice was small, with a trace of hope.

"You're still a juvenile. If you weren't the main player, maybe you're more a witness than a guilty party. Maybe they would need your testimony."

"You mean be a rat." His eyes burned.

"It's more like being a hero," I said, "to help get FMJ and the adults who are dealing with him off the street. He's dangerous. You say that yourself. He's about to have a big birthday. The big one-eight makes him an adult, which means state prison. You don't want to wind up like that. There have to be other options. Maybe I can find out something. Then we can talk about it."

"You won't send anybody else here or hand me up?"

"Hell, no. I'll find out, then you can decide the right thing to do."

He nodded.

I thanked him for the coffee. He walked me as far as the door to the stairwell. I left him standing alone, surrounded by the vast night sky. Two minutes later I emerged into a world of bright lights and canned music, a mall full of families and children, and happy shoppers and holiday decorations.

Chapter Eight

I felt like a mother hen. "The city can be treacherous," I warned Trish. "This ain't Kansas—or Oklahoma."

She stood at my desk, more color than I remembered in her face, holding her new *Miami News* ID card, just issued by security. Unlike most, her postage-stamp-size Polaroid was a good one. It was the megawatt smile that did it.

"I know what it's like out there," she protested. Her eyes reflected the heady excitement of the newsroom, the nerve center of this big-city paper, with its spectacular view from massive bayfront windows, reporters at their word processors, editors clustered around the city desk, executives in their glass offices, and big overhead clocks ticking down to deadline after deadline, day after day.

I knew how she felt. I regularly realize how lucky I am to have this job.

"Traffic is a bitch," I told her. "Miamians are a hostile breed. They floor it to be first at a red light. Most are unfamiliar with North American driving habits. They've got guns, baseball bats, and short fuses. Sometimes it's easier to bail out and hoof it. Leave press ID on the windshield and *maybe* the cops won't tow it. Metro Rail would have been handy, if it went to the airport, the seaport, or the Beach— the places with the most serious parking problems. But it doesn't. Thank our elected officials for that."

I pressed a good road map into her hands.

"It's easy to get lost," I said in my most helpful schoolmarm mode, "so remember St. Louis."

"St. Louis?" She looked impatient, in a hurry to go out and tackle the world. I didn't want her tackled first.

"Streets, terraces, and lanes: S T L," I explained. "In Miami they all run east–west. Everything else runs north–south."

She nodded solemnly.

"Stay alert. Hey, we've had a couple of reporters robbed, one stabbed, another winged during the last riot. Ryan here almost got his head bashed in."

Ryan looked up from his desk behind us, as though on cue, obligingly sweeping his chestnut hair off his forehead to proudly display his scar.

"When a man gets hurt, the powers that be get over it. It's an occupational hazard," I told her. "But when a woman gets hurt, everybody looks bad. Her editor catches heat for sending her out there, and we risk being told that there are certain stories or assignments we shouldn't handle."

Ryan smiled sweetly. I stared him down, and he turned back to his terminal. Socializing could come later. This spiel was important.

"As you drive," I told her, "watch the guys loitering on street corners. Especially the one with the paper bag in his hand. It could be a sandwich, a can of Coors, a brick, a rock, or a Molotov cocktail. Somebody sitting on the top of a bus bench is probably there to see inside passing cars, looking for a purse or something worth stealing.

"Remember—"

"I know, I know." She grinned. "This ain't Kansas."

Trish went to orientation and I drove to headquarters to see Rakestraw. A man on crutches lurched painfully out of the office, his face purple. "This is where our tax money goes?" he bellowed. He was mad as hell. So was Rakestraw.

The wounded victim's car and personal possessions were still missing, along with the gunman who had shot him. No wonder the man was irate.

Rakestraw's sour mood had another reason, a setback in the Carey case. Arturo, owner of the red Trans Am, had been unable to pick FMJ out of photo lineups as the driver.

"Think you'll still be able to make a case?" I asked, settling into a chair.

"I'm hoping that when we finally pick them up, one of the other subjects in the car will flip and testify against him," Rakestraw said.

"So you'd make a deal?"

"To nail FMJ, sure. We've got plenty of other robbery and agg assault charges against him, but the felony murder is the biggie."

"Have you ID'd the backseat passenger yet?" I thought I sounded casual, but Rakestraw was nobody's fool.

"Nope." His shrewd eyes rose slowly from the reports on his desk to check me out. "You know something, Britt?"

"I'm not sure, but I'll let you know as soon as I am."

We then danced around a debate on where an unnamed hypothetical, salvageable street kid on probation could reside while finishing school. The Crossing was the best choice. A halfway house for troubled kids committed to straightening out their lives; for most it's a last chance before being locked up.

As I left the station, I was accosted by a tall grim man in the lobby. I answered his question before he asked it.

"You want Detective Rakestraw," I told him. "Second door on the right." I am not psychic; his crutches were a clue.

He hobbled in that direction.

I was about to pull out of the parking lot when the driver of a rented Buick in the next space carelessly pushed open his door, bouncing it off the side of my brand-new T-Bird. I hate that and furiously rolled down the window to tell him so. Before I could, I saw the crutches he was awkwardly maneuvering, struggling to get out. I sighed, rolled up the window, and took off.

I thought about Howie and the Crossing and discussed it later in a phone chat with Lottie.

"How you gonna get him to go? You can't just throw a net over him like a stray tomcat. That's you, Britt, always picking up strays. It don't work with bad-ass teenagers."

"That's just it. He might be redeemable. He's never had a chance, but he's so self-reliant, living on his own the way he does. He reads the dictionary, for God's sake. If he'd only read the definitions too, he might sound educated. But he tries. You haven't met him."

"But I've seen his work."

"He probably was in that car," I conceded, "but he wasn't driving. Listen, we've all been in bad company once or twice, or in the wrong place at the wrong time."

.   .   .

Trish was assigned a desk in the last row, in the far back corner of the newsroom, but she was usually up front, near mine. "Where's Britt, Jr.?" Ryan would ask when she was not. She would roll up the nearest empty chair and watch me work, asking questions, absorbing like a sponge.

She wanted to know it all.

"How do you handle victims and survivors? You always get so many wonderful quotes," she said. "How do you approach them?"

"It's the toughest part of the job," I replied, trying to dig a path through the clutter of notes, mail, printouts, and clippings on my desk. I tossed aside the obvious jail mail and tore open a neatly typed envelope. "Uh-oh," I said. "Bad news from the Inspector Deity."

"Who?" Trish said.

"Listen to this. 'Please find enclosed a very important scientific announcement. The Inspector Deity regrets having to inform four billion-plus Homo sapiens that a terminal progressive planetary depletion of atmospheric oxygen is coming soon. Best regards, Emmett R. Merrill, M.D.'"

"Good gawd," Trish said. "I just got this job."

"I knew it felt close in here." I stared up at the air-conditioning vents. "Where were we?"

"Talking to victims." She dropped her small hands into her lap in feigned despair. "I once tried to interview a woman whose husband was shotgunned in a stickup. She slammed the door on me and threatened to call the sheriff."

"It happens. And the TV wolf pack doesn't make it any easier. The competition is fierce, and they usually wind up grossing out everybody you want to talk to. But it's important because the survivors are the only ones left to speak up for a victim."

"How do you get them started?"

"Well, not like the TV reporters who chase them asking, 'How does it feel?' You have to be gentle. Sometimes they start and can't stop. I think it's cathartic in many cases."

She hung on every word. "You know, Britt," she confided, "I also lost my father as a kid, grew up without a dad. We're so very much alike."

Personally, I doubted that the daughter of a Cuban freedom fighter and Miss Middle America shared much in common. But it was flattering that she thought so.

. . .

We celebrated Trish's first *Miami News* byline, a story on studies revealing that it would cost $80 to $90 million to enlarge the Miami Arena, somehow built too small just six years earlier at a cost of $53 million. Nothing like the farsighted vision of our elected leaders. The story, of course, revealed a problem to taxpayers but was a breakthrough for Trish.

We toasted the occasion at the 1800 Club a few blocks from the paper. We even talked love lives that evening at a little table in the crowded semidarkness. I spilled my sad story about Kendall McDonald and how ethics and job pressures drove us apart.

"Maybe it will all work out someday," she said sympathetically.

"It would be nice," I said wistfully, "but unlikely." A low tolerance for alcohol tends to make me feel sorry for myself after a drink on an empty stomach. "We still care about each other. In fact, when that incident with the rapist happened he was wonderful. I couldn't have gotten through it without him. Just made me miss him more. We're a perfect example of why you can't mix business with pleasure."

She looked thoughtful. "But dating a source can be super convenient. Can't hurt to have the inside track on your beat, especially when there's tough competition."

"No way." I shook my head. "Too risky. Tends to get complicated."

"So where do you draw the line?" Trish leaned forward, eyes serious.

"When a relationship with a source begins to be fun and feel good—you stop." I stared morosely into the light reflected in my glass. "The story of my life. It's a bummer because the men you deal with on the police beat understand the hours, the pressures, and the deadlines. But they're off limits. It'll be easier for you," I assured her. "You won't be dealing with the same sources daily."

She smiled mysteriously, as sly as a cat with her paw in the canary cage. She's keeping a secret, I thought. Must be a romance.

The arrival of my club sandwich and Trish's dinner salad interrupted. I would feel better after eating. "Did I tell you to watch out for Gretchen?" I asked, when the waitress had gone. "She'll pace and lurk around behind you on deadline like some psycho killer. Don't let her rattle you."

"Actually she's been pretty decent so far," Trish said. "Those clothes! She always looks gorgeous. I wonder where she has her hair done?''

"Someplace we peons can't afford," I said. "There's a beauty school on the Beach with cut-rate prices if you let the students work on you. The best part is, you don't even need an appointment. It's great. I'll give you the address."

Trish studied my hair, not at its best at the moment. "Gretchen does look terrific," was all she said.

"Packaging lies."

Appetite whetted by her first byline, Trish had little patience with stories that were not major news. The following afternoon she was assigned the daily weather story.

She peered over my shoulder at the story I was working on, human body parts found in the rubble of a downtown demolition site. The crew had failed to check the interior for vagrants before imploding the building.

"Good gawd!" she said.

"The guys on the work crews all claim they thought somebody else checked the interior," I said. "It makes you wonder if anybody pays attention to what they're doing anymore."

"And I'm stuck with the boring ol' weather. It never changes: hot and humid with afternoon thunderstorms. When will I get something juicy to work on?"

I hit the SAVE key. "Just wait. Some days weather is the biggest story in this town."

"When that happens you can bet they won't give it to me." She pouted. She wore a silky blouse that made her skin glow.

"Pay some dues," I said. "Nobody starts out a star."

"I know, you're right," she said. "Have you got the inside number for the weather service?"

"In my Rolodex," I said, returning to the demolition story.

She flipped through the cards. "God almighty, Britt, you must have the unlisted numbers of every cop, politician, and muckety-muck in this town."

"Took years to collect," I said.

She ran her weather story by me, we polished it up, and she turned it in while I finished my story.

Deadline was minutes away, and I had a few final calls to make.

Two truckloads of rubble had been removed before the remains were spotted. Detectives with cadaver-sniffing dogs were at the county dump searching for body parts. I wanted to know what they had found and whether the medical examiner had enough for an identification. Trish sat at the next desk, reading a printout of my Sunday piece about the police pistol range, closed for renovation after poor ventilation caused the rangemaster to suffer lead poisoning.

"Trish, would you check my voice mail for messages? It's nine-one-eight-two," I said, giving her my four-digit code as I dialed the ME office.

She picked up a phone, punched in the numbers, monitored my messages, printed them out, and handed them to me while I talked to an investigator at the morgue. The wrecking company owner had returned my call.

"Would you get him back for me?" I whispered, one hand over the mouthpiece. "Ask about their safety procedures."

She had already spoken to him by the time I hung up.

"No comment, on the advice of his attorney," she said.

"I figured," I said, "but it doesn't hurt to try." I wrapped up the story and got it in just under the wire.

Later, Trish picked my brain about the local suicide hot line.

"I've gotta do a feach," she complained. "Sounds like a yawner."

"Reach Out? Always good human-interest stories there."

"Here's hoping." She winked, picked up a notebook, and headed out.

I followed, minutes later. Reports of a sniper at an upper-floor window of a high-rise near county hospital, where the Interstate and the Dolphin Expressway intersect. At least ten shots fired. Police diverted motorists and closed off both highways, halting traffic for miles. The building, nearby offices, a motel, and about a square mile of city streets were being evacuated as SWAT moved in. I was halfway there when suddenly my scanner erupted. Several cops had been injured and were en route to the emergency room.

The chaos on the air sounded as though they had been shot. I fought traffic, drove on the shoulder, and burst into the ER, heart pounding. The place was crawling with brass who had heard the same exchanges on their radios.

A hospital staffer confirmed the officers' arrival, saying only that their injuries were being evaluated. Then I saw Evie Snow show up and caught my breath. Sergeant Tully Snow, her husband, had to be one of the injured. I knew them both. Attached to the public integrity squad, he vigorously pursued police and political wrongdoers with an almost religious zeal. He'd worked his way up from patrolman to detective sergeant despite personal tragedy. He and Evie had four children. The youngest, a little girl, had died of leukemia two years earlier after a long history of remissions and relapses. Police medical coverage was good, but benefits for their little girl were exhausted long before her struggle ended. I had written about some of the fund raisers held to help defray expenses. The ordeal had taken its toll on both parents. This was the first time I had seen Evie since little Lynette's funeral. Stressed and distracted, in jeans and a loose blouse, she was escorted into an emergency room cubicle. Had tragedy struck again?

Sergeant Danny Menendez, the public information officer, appeared. "How bad are they? How many hit?" I said.

He raised a hand. "It's okay. No major damage. False alarm."

"What?"

"There was no sniper. Turns out it was just medical students partying. One of them lives there. They were taking turns shooting a thirty-two caliber weapon off the balcony to celebrate passing some exam."

In the ensuing panic and confusion, two police cars had collided. Four cops suffered minor injuries, none serious enough to be admitted.

"Somebody said on the air that they'd been hit," Menendez explained. "Since they were on the sniper call, everybody assumed. . . ."

What a relief. False alarm, this time. I encountered Evie in the corridor outside the ER.

"How's he doing?" I asked, greeting her with a smile.

"Fine," she said, winking back tears. She had aged considerably in the few short years since I had last seen her. New worry lines were etched across her brow. How do police wives cope? I wondered.

Before leaving the hospital, I checked on Jennifer Carey, whose condition had been upgraded. She was out of the woods but faced extensive therapy and might never walk again. New stories unfold every day, but hers haunted me. So did the whereabouts of FMJ. I called Rakestraw from the hospital's community relations office. No arrest appeared imminent. Identical smash-and-grabs had gone down at department stores in Hollywood and Fort Lauderdale. Sounded like FMJ and crew had expanded their horizons.

Where do you start to look for a teenager? When teen robbers killed a British tourist upstate, civil rights advocates accused the cops of being discriminatory and racist because they interviewed every teenager in the area. They would prefer, I suppose, that the cops question octogenarians about teenage crime. On the way back to the paper, I stopped at the Edgewater to look for Howie, wandered both levels, but didn't see him.

At the office, I stepped off the elevator into a newsroom alive with the excitement that every journalist senses instantly, a big story breaking.

"Hear what happened to Trish?" Ryan's face was serious, eyes concerned.

"No." I held my breath. "Tell me she's all right."

"She is. But wait till you hear the story she's got. Some woman killed herself, right in front of her."

"No! She was working a story on the suicide-prevention line. What happened?"

A cluster of people at the city desk parted and I saw Trish at the epicenter, speaking intently to the editor in the slot.

Janowitz drifted away from the group and joined us. "Hell of a story," he said admiringly. "She was doing a feach on Reach Out, listened to a call from a suicidal woman, heard the volunteer slough the woman off, took down the address, and went out there. Trish spoke to her, but before she can drive away, the woman hotfoots it out of her apartment, crosses the street, and goes up to the roof of an eight-story parking garage. Trish figures it ain't kosher, especially since the woman didn't drive a car and had talked about jumping. So she goes after her. Gutsy thing to do. Finds her alone on the roof, tries to talk her down, grabs her, but the woman wrestles away and does a full gainer. Close call. The woman could have taken her down too."

I caught up with Trish as she left the city desk. Pale and slightly disheveled, she still clutched her notebook. "You okay?"

She nodded, face haunted. "It was horrible, Britt. I tried to hang on, but she was bigger than I am and so strong. . . . I'll never forget her eyes."

She brushed a hand across her face as though wicking away emotion and got down to business. "The desk wants a first-person story— with an investigative piece later on whether the Reach Out staff followed proper procedure and has adequate training and supervision."

"They're usually on the ball," I said, still stunned. "They save lives."

"They sure as hell didn't save this one. Wish I could have." Her voice cracked.

"Whatever you do," I said quietly, "don't cry in the newsroom. Can you handle it?"

She took a deep breath. "I can, if you could sort of look over my shoulder. Never did a story like this one. It's tricky and I'm still a little wobbly. Will you help me?"

"Sure thing."

The dialogue between her and the woman who died was chilling. *I will never forget a word she said as long as I live,* Trish wrote.

Life had not been kind to Magdaly Rosado, who had talked freely to Trish.

At forty, she had already been through hell without end. Her first husband was in prison. Her second abused her and fought bitterly with her only child, a son, now nineteen. She cleaned downtown offices while her husband drank and her son used drugs. The son wanted his stepfather to stop beating his mother. The stepfather wanted the son kicked out of the house.

Magdaly was caught in the crossfire. Her own mother had recently died; her ex-husband, nearing release, was writing threatening letters from prison; and the landlord had begun eviction proceedings because of noisy family fights that often involved the police.

As her world grew darker and more dangerous, Magdaly, treated for depression in the past, stopped taking her medication.

Trish said that despite a history of suicide threats both husband and son seemed stunned that she had actually done it. They were apparently among those who subscribe to the theory that people who threaten suicide don't mean it and the ones who do don't talk about it first. Wrong.

I pulled up a chair next to Trish's terminal and we worked together. "The volunteer said she was a regular; he had talked to her before," Trish said. "He had sent her literature and referrals in the past. He was busy and figured she would be okay, but there was just something in her voice, Britt." She bit her lip. "I felt scared for her, so I took the address and drove over there. Figured if she wasn't okay I'd find her some help, and if she was it would be a nice endorsement for Reach Out."

She had found Magdaly alone and depressed. They talked, heart-to-heart. Magdaly had promised to seek counseling. As Trish sat in her car jotting some notes on their conversation, Magdaly emerged from her building, crossed to the municipal garage, and boarded the elevator.

"There was no time to stop and call anybody, and I thought maybe she had a legitimate reason for going over there. But I had to follow and be sure. By the time I got up to the roof she was sitting on the edge with one leg swung over the side. Nobody else was around; only the first four levels were full.

"I told her she had a lot to live for. She didn't buy it." Trish's eyes glistened. "Too many people kept letting her down. All her life, I think. We talked for about fifteen minutes. I kept hoping somebody would come. But nobody did. That's when I grabbed her. If only I could have held on to her, Britt. I tried, but she just broke away and went. I ran all the way down eight flights. You should have seen her." She shuddered. "Head smashed open. I never saw anything like that before."

"I'm sorry you had to see it now." I put my arm around her shoulders and squeezed. "You did everything you could."

The story screamed to be read.

The copy editor even framed one of Trish's most compelling grafs inside a quote box:

"I begged her, but as I reached out, she simply stepped into space. I could see her eyes. She wanted to die. At the very last second she seemed to change her mind, but it was too late. She was gone."

A powerful story, stripped across page one with a small photo and a thumbnail sketch of Trish.

It was the story everybody talked about the next day, including the radio talk-show hosts. The Reach Out counselor was dismissed, not for failing to answer the victim's cry for help but because he had allowed Trish to monitor a call that should have been confidential. Typical.

The furor would probably cost Reach Out what little funding it had, I thought, rereading Trish's story over breakfast the next morning. At the very least, it would cause a major shakeup in administration. Too bad somebody had to die before that happened.

Chapter Nine

I can deal with crank letters from total strangers. I resent them from my editors. The interoffice envelope in my mailbox had my name scribbled on one of the neat little lines outside.

The memo was to: The Staff; Subject: New Expense Report Form.

Please discontinue using the old expense report forms. Should you have any old forms, please place them in a newsroom recycle bin. The new forms may be obtained in the wire room.

Be sure your name is clearly printed at the top, not the bottom. Please use INK, not a pencil. Be sure you attach the proper receipts for all charges. The bottom portion, the payment request detail, must be filled out by you and signed, in ink, by you and your supervisor or the designated clerical person in your department.

On and on it went, for a page and a half, in a pompous style and the cautionary attitude that a first-grade teacher would use on new recruits. "Allow approximately five weekdays for reimbursement, providing the report is not sent back to you for corrections."

Given the waste of time and trees and the insult to intelligence, Gretchen's signature at the bottom was no surprise.

"Does she lie awake at night dreaming up things like this to torment us?" I asked Ryan, who was also grumbling.

Her arrogance added to the uneasiness that had plagued me since I awoke that morning. The unrelenting heat on the streets seemed to smolder that much hotter, knowing as I did that FMJ was out there somewhere, with nothing to lose, armed, dangerous, and fresh out of Prozac.

The call from Jason Carey did nothing to lift my spirits. "The baby's home from the hospital," he informed me wearily. "She cries a lot and misses her mother, but otherwise she's doing fine. Jenny regained consciousness yesterday, but she didn't recognize me or her mom."

The ache in his voice made me think of Magdaly Rosado, who literally threw her life away, while others, like Jennifer Carey, must fight to survive. If there is a God, I thought, he has a mean sense of humor.

"How are you?" I asked Carey. "Are you taking care of yourself?"

"I'm having trouble sleeping," he confessed. "I think it's because I hate waking up, that first moment in the morning when I realize again that it's not a bad dream; it really happened. Jenny isn't here. Jason isn't going to go to kindergarten or grow up."

Oy, I thought, wishing for some Prozac or a stiff drink myself.

"There is a victims' support group you ought to contact," I said. My right eye began to twitch. It usually does that only when I am exhausted or talking to my mother. "It helps," I told him. "And what about your family?"

"There is only one thing that will help," he said quietly. "That's the reason I called. The police seem to know who is responsible but haven't arrested him. I'm afraid they've put the case on a back burner, that they'll forget."

"Not at all," I said. "The detective is good and very committed. They're working hard."

"I've heard nothing for days. There hasn't even been anything more in the paper."

"There have to be new developments," I said.

"Do you think it would help to offer a reward? I could put together ten thousand dollars. Or should I use it to hire a private detective to go after them?"

I pressed my fingers against my eyelid as it did the rumba. "I don't know what to tell you, Mr. Carey."

"Jason."

"I know it isn't easy, but I would wait a little. Money attracts a lot of fakes and charlatans and predators. They smell it and come crawling out of the woodwork and from under rocks. You don't want to expose yourself to them or waste your time. I could see doing it if the police had no name and no leads, but they know who they're looking for. Same goes for a PI. The police have far more resources. It's only a matter now of one of them spotting him or stopping him for traffic or some other offense.''

"Why don't the police put his picture in the newspaper, on TV?"

"He's protected because he's still a juvenile, a child.''

There was a silence. "Jason was a child. This creature isn't.''

"You're right. I believe he will be eighteen this week, and I think that once they arrest him the state attorney's office will move to charge him as an adult. Save your money for medical expenses and Eileen's education. Give the cops a month, tops, to wrap it up. Then you can reconsider.''

He sighed and agreed.

Providentially, the next call was from Howie.

"Nice to hear from you,'' I said. "Where are you?''

I guess he didn't like the sound of my voice. I feared for a moment that he'd hung up.

"Why?'' the voice was low and wary.

"I really need to see you. I have some information you need to know.''

"Come alone,'' he began, "and—''

"Forget the spy stuff,'' I snapped. "You have to trust me. I'm your only friend, Howie.''

We met on Bayshore, the street that runs behind the Edgewater, between the vertical mall and the bay. A frisky breeze had picked up with what might be the first hint of fall. A good omen, I thought.

I drove over and saw him standing alone, near Morningside Park, on the bay. He looked stick thin but clean and neat in jeans, a Star Trek T-shirt and, high-top sneakers. I had been afraid he wouldn't show, but his face lit up when he saw me pull to the curb. I parked and fed the meter as he came loping across the street in long easy strides.

"Don't have to do that.''

"What?''

"Spend cash money on a meter.''

I blinked in the sunlight. "Yes, I do. My expense account doesn't cover parking tickets.''

"Man, you got an expense account? Cool."

"Not so cool, twenty-two cents a mile."

"That's it?" He looked offended. "They should give you a car to drive." He fished something small out of his pocket, held it up, inserted it into the meter, and flipped the handle. It promptly registered, adding an hour to my time.

"What was that?"

"Tab off a Miller."

"A beer can tab?"

"Yeah, some meters, you don' even need that. Jus' hit 'em in the right spot, buy you some time. Wanna see?"

"Some other time," I said, glancing around to see if anyone was watching.

We walked, watching the bright sails of a Sunfish regatta bobbing out on the bay.

He seemed slightly taller than when I had first seen him. Maybe he was in a growth spurt. That happens with teenagers. His voice even registered at a somewhat lower pitch.

Though his body language was casual, his alert eyes took in everything: passing traffic, parked cars, purses, pedestrians, the wallet bulges in their pockets. Sociopaths do that. Their view of life comes from a different perspective. But so, of course, does mine. I am constantly tempted to warn careless strangers to be more cautious. Don't carry a purse in a way that asks to be dragged by a thief in a passing car. Don't leave that handbag in your shopping cart while you browse. Don't block the windows of small stores with posters that may obscure what is happening inside. Why invite trouble? It shows up often enough.

To give him the benefit of the doubt, Howie had probably picked up similar insight while surviving on the street. Maybe he was actually a budding reporter, not a predator. Many people swear they are one and the same.

"Look." Howie tilted his head toward the corner. "Thought you'd wanna see it."

Spray-painted graffiti covered the side of a vacant building that had once housed an Italian restaurant. The number ninety-nine scrawled inside a red circle with a line drawn through it. Ninety-nine is street jargon for the police. Interesting, but not as arresting as the larger display: F   M   J in gigantic black letters next to the number 784.

"Know what that means?"

"Yep." The Florida State Statute for murder is 784. "Doesn't seem to worry him," I said.

"He bragging on it. He be here last night."

"You saw him?"

"No, but this in a buncha other places round here. Wasn't there yesterday. Probably all over town."

FMJ was taunting the police. I wondered if Rakestraw had seen it. We walked back down to where we had met and sat on the seawall in the shade of a sea-grape tree. We could see Miami Beach across the bay, a distant pastel city shrouded in clouds.

"Do you know where they sell all the cars they steal?"

Howie was oddly forthright. "To whoever place the order. A dude in Hialeah'll pay a thousand for every '95 Camry XLE you can bring him. The juice man. Sweet deals on stolen wheels," he chanted softly. "Won't buy from anybody eighteen or over. I could deliver six a day myself," he bragged.

I smiled indulgently. Maybe FMJ was nearing the end of his career. Washed up at eighteen. "If you could, then why don't you?"

He shrugged. "I'm not greedy, like some dudes."

Thinking of my T-Bird, I asked the expert, "What kind of car is most likely to be stolen?"

"One that is unoccupied."

"Cute. Although not entirely true, with FMJ out there."

"He always in a hurry," Howie said. "Toyotas are easy."

"Oh?" I said dubiously.

"Master key the big thing. Ain't nothing to cop master keys for Toyotas."

"How?" I raised a skeptical eyebrow.

"A lotta guys have a contact with a dealer. But actually"—he snorted—"when the key is worn down it'll get you in any Toyota. Jus' file it down a little on the curb, no problem. A-course, the older the Toyota, the easier it is."

I cut my eyes at him.

"Want me to demonstrate?" he asked.

I laughed. "Nah. Want a hot dog?"

A street vendor with kosher red hots had set up shop half a block away. I hadn't had lunch.

He shook his head, looking a bit miffed.

"Be right back," I said, slipping off the wall. "Wait here. I've got a lot to tell you."

I trotted down the street and ordered up a hot dog with sauerkraut, relish, mustard, and pickles. I ordered two orange drinks, paid the man, grabbed a few extra napkins and straws, and glanced back toward the seawall. Howie was gone.

Shit! I thought. Did he really take off? I spilled some orange drink on my skirt as I rushed back to where we'd been sitting. He was nowhere in sight.

Then I realized my car wasn't either.

"Goddammit! Howie!"

I must have looked like the girl in *The Exorcist* the way my head swiveled around, frantic, hoping I was mistaken, that I had parked somewhere else. A car is stolen every nineteen seconds in this country. I knew that. But that car never belonged to me. Not only was my T-Bird gone, but a woman in a Chevy was backing into my space, with all that free time still on the meter.

That little bastard. What would the cops say? They'd get a big laugh out of this. I never should have dealt with Howie myself. I should have turned him in to the cops the first time I ever laid eyes on him.

How did he pull this off so fast? I checked my pocket, smearing yellow mustard on my white blouse in the process. I still had the keys.

My beautiful new T-Bird, not even five hundred miles on it. I'd never hear the end of this in the newsroom. What would my insurance company say? Especially after what happened to my last car. What would the credit union say? I had just received the payment book in the mail.

I loved that car. I left the hot dog and orange drinks on the seawall, my appetite gone, and stalked across the street to find a pay phone and call the cops. As I crossed, I scanned traffic, hoping to spot a police cruiser. Where the hell were they? Never around when you need them.

I reached the other side as a motorist leaned on the horn. Dammit. It wasn't even safe to be a pedestrian—which I was now.

The horn blared again and I spun toward the sound with murder in my heart. My car! My gleaming T-Bird rolled up to the curb. Howie grinned from behind the wheel. He lowered the window.

"Need a lift, pretty lady?"

"You little son of a bitch!" I screamed, as startled passersby stared. I dove at the driver's door, while Howie, laughing and raising his arms in mock defense, shifted over into the passenger seat.

I slid behind the wheel. "I'm gonna put your nasty little ass in jail! You . . . you . . . how the hell *could* you?"

His mouth opened in surprise, all wide-eyed innocence and righteous indignation. "You dissed me! That was a challenge! You was giving me the fish-eye like you didn't believe I could. What'd you expect me to do?"

"Look what you've done! This car is brand new!"

"All you gotta do is replace that little plastic collar round the steering column." Earnest and persuasive, he didn't seem to understand what all the fuss was about. "That ain't nothing."

I rested my forehead on the steering wheel, weak-kneed and shaky with relief.

"I didn't *take* it. I brought it back. It was jus' a little spin round the block. Come on, Britt. You know I wouldn't vic you. You challenged me." He seemed astonished that I had taken offense.

I lifted my head, resisting the urge to bang it on the dashboard over and over. "Want an orange drink?"

"Sure."

We retrieved the drinks, pulled into the cool shadow of the Edgewater parking garage, and got serious. "The cops need you to testify about what happened with the Trans Am."

He looked grim. "You want me to be a rat."

"Right. Because nothing you can do will make you a bigger rat than FMJ and those guys. No bigger rat than somebody who hurts women and babies. You're lucky the cops need you and are willing to make a deal."

"That AK?"

"AK?"

"Actual knowledge. You know they would?"

"The detective on the case said so."

He half turned in the seat. "You told 'im about me?"

I shook my head. "Not by name. Just asked a hypothetical question. You can straighten out, you can go to school. You wouldn't have a record after you turn eighteen. You can become somebody."

"I could stay here?" he jerked his head toward the top of the building.

"You know you can't. That's always been temporary at best. You've just been lucky so far."

"So where I stay while this all happens?"

"You have any other relatives?"

"Maybe an aunt some town in North Carolina. Never seen her."

"There are places here."

"Don't want no foster home."

"There's a place called the Crossing. Sort of a group home, a halfway house for teenagers, where you can stay while you finish school."

"I heard of it," he said quietly, staring at his knees. He turned and faced me. "You wrong 'bout one thing," he said gravely, as my heart sank. "You not my only friend."

I waited.

"Me and Miz Mayberry, we had a long rap the other night. She say you're right. I do wanna be somebody. Do somethin' wit' my life." He stared out the window at the wedge of sky visible from our level of the garage. Clouds were stacked up over the bay. "I been thinking. Like, I heard my cousin died the other day. We was, like, the same age. We went to school together, man. Back when my grandma was alive."

"What happened to him?"

"Sniffing from an aerosol can, that stuff you spray on frying pans. Wanted a rush. Got a rush, all right. A rush to the emergency room." He sighed, his smile bitter. "But not fast enough."

I nodded. "SSDS."

"Say what?"

"Sudden Sniffing Death Syndrome. I heard about two last week. Kids who got a killer buzz from sniffing household products. Which one was your cousin?"

He looked down. "Fat Jaw his street name. Real name Tyrone Brown. Like a bro to me when we was little. Always say, 'We here for a good time, not a lot of time.' Like he knew. Damn! He was stupid, stupid, stupid! I don' wanna be stupid anymore. I don' want my kids to have it rough someday. I want an education. I wanna be like . . ." He made a small dismissive gesture. "Miz Mayberry thinks I could do it."

"So do I, Howie. You could have a helluva future. You're smart, disciplined, self-reliant. You can do anything."

He looked almost eager.

"I'll do it," he said. "Whatever I gotta do."

"You're making the right decision," I said quickly. "You can trust Rakestraw. He's good people. And you'll have me and Miss Mayberry in your corner."

He nodded. "I'm in the car with you on this one. Won't be easy, but like they say, 'Nothing valuable comes easy.' "

"Good man."

I drove Howie to police headquarters before he could change his mind. He fidgeted in his seat as we pulled into the parking lot. I could sense his reluctance.

"You're gonna like this detective," I assured him.

Howie said nothing, his face solemn.

I was unwilling to leave him in the car while I found Rakestraw, fearing he might run—worse yet, with my car. He stuck close as we stepped inside. I plunked my purse onto the conveyor belt and stepped through the metal detector's plastic archway. Howie looked wary. Any kid going to school in Miami is acquainted with metal detectors and drive-by-shooting drills, but Howie hadn't been to school for nearly two years. The machine raised no alarm, and we proceeded into the lobby. Howie deliberately avoided the stares of cops who greeted me and eyed him curiously as they passed.

The officer at the front desk called AIU and told us that Rakestraw was unavailable, in a training class.

"It's important," I insisted.

"We can come back later." Howie glanced hopefully toward the double glass doors.

The cop at the desk looked at Howie with idle interest.

"Excuse me," he said, diverting his attention to an irate citizen with a complaint about the manners of a traffic cop encountered downtown.

Keeping Howie in tow, I wandered over to a conference room across the lobby. Training sessions—or large press conferences—were often conducted inside.

A crowded class was in progress. Through the small glass panel I spotted Rakestraw in a back row. At first I thought it was an encounter session. Everybody was shouting at a hapless officer as a seated instructor watched.

Then I realized they were all shouting in Spanish, or a reasonable facsimile.

"*¡El sospechoso! El tiene un sombrero. El es alto. El tiene un tatuaje.*"

Even I could manage a rough translation: The suspect! He has a hat. He is tall. He has a tattoo.

The officer at the front of the room, brow furrowed in concentration, did not do as well.

I opened the door a few inches. Howie gingerly backed off. A few uniforms inside glanced my way. I motioned at Rakestraw, mouthing his name. Somebody nudged him and he swiveled in his seat.

I beckoned and he gave a slight annoyed shake of his head. I beckoned more insistently. Frowning impatiently, he got to his feet and came to the door, slipping through without opening it wide.

"Britt, this damn thing is mandatory—" He saw Howie and studied him for a moment. "What the hell." He closed the door behind him.

"He with you?"

I nodded and introduced them. "He wants to talk to you. About the Carey case."

Howie, all arms, legs, and frightened eyes, looked poised for flight.

"Sure," Rakestraw said, suddenly affable. "I've got all the time in the world. Let's go get some coffee."

Behind us we heard class members shouting, *"El es un muerto."*

He is a dead man.

We went to the third-floor cafeteria. There were few people there, but we said little as we fixed our coffee. Rakestraw asked Howie if he was hungry and offered a doughnut, which the boy declined with a small twitchy smile that said he saw a certain irony in being offered something by a cop. Rakestraw casually asked Howie's age; then we followed him, carrying our cups back to a small pleasant office.

Colorful posters brightened the walls, and a few paper flowers bloomed from a vase on a small table covered with a cheerful yellow-and-white plastic cloth. "I never saw this room before," I said, following Howie inside.

"The interrogation of juveniles must take place in a nonintimidating atmosphere," Rakestraw said, sotto voce. "No police radios, a nice room with flowers and pictures on the wall. I'm doing this strictly by the book. He the backseat passenger?"

I nodded.

"Figured."

We took seats around the table and sipped coffee, watching one another warily.

"Before we begin," Rakestraw said, "I think we should notify your parents."

Howie explained about his only relative. "My mother is indisposed. In fact I don't know where she stay at right now."

"An approximate address?" Rakestraw said, pulling out a pen and a small notebook.

"Like a crack house, somewhere," Howie said vaguely.

"It's not mandatory to have consent from your parent or guardian before we talk, but if you want, Howard, you can give us a last known address and we can send somebody out to try to locate her."

"Nah." He shook his head, as though sure such efforts would be useless. "Don't think she'd 'preciate it. This is something I got to do on my own."

"Where do you want to start, Howard?" Rakestraw asked.

Howie had regained some confidence, or at least tried to give that impression. "Well, my associate here, Miss Montero"—he glanced my way and I nodded—"gave me the expression that if I can assist you in a certain matter you might be able to assist me."

"What is it that you would like us to do for you?" Rakestraw asked, looking utterly relaxed. Knowing how much he wanted to close the case, I marveled at his calm. He had to be as thrilled as I am when zeroing in on an important story.

Howie leaned forward, boyish sincerity breaking through. "I wanna go back to school, finish high school, turn eighteen with no record. I wanna be . . . I wanna start over. And I need a place to stay while I go to school. No foster homes." He glanced at me.

"A place like the Crossing," I interjected.

"And protection," he added, his dark eyes troubled. "You know how it is: snitches get stitches—or worse."

"Depends on what the whole story is here, but I don't see where any of that would be outside the realm of possibility," Rakestraw said.

I listened, fascinated, though I knew most of it, as Rakestraw led the boy through an accounting of what led up to those terrible moments at the shopping mall. FMJ had an order for a Trans Am the year, make, and model of Arturo's. FMJ, a crew chief of sorts, had a shopping list of three cars that afternoon. The Trans Am was their third. It was only the second time, Howie claimed, that he had accompanied them. FMJ wanted him along because of his speed and expertise. I could vouch for that.

The thieves were not cruising in a random search for the right model. FMJ already had Arturo's car listed. In the old days, Rakestraw said, nodding, car thieves carried little spiral notebooks. FMJ used a laptop computer to keep an inventory. They had driven by Belle Court, an apartment complex where a suitable Trans Am was usually parked, but it was not there. The man who had ordered the car wanted it right away. FMJ didn't like waiting and moved to the next prospect on his list. Arturo worked out regularly at the center, and FMJ had seen the car there before.

They were in luck. Jennifer Carey's luck was about to run out.

A teen named Skank dropped the trio off at the center. Then things went awry. After the tragedy, it was J-Boy who had jumped out and pulled the stroller from under the car. They had fled west on the Palmetto. FMJ dropped the boys off at a Burger King and went to deliver the car himself, as usual.

He was to return with $100 each for Howie and J-Boy and $50 for Skank.

Howie didn't wait. Horrified at what FMJ had done, he left, catching a bus back to downtown Miami and the Edgewater.

"Was FMJ upset about what happened?" Rakestraw asked.

"Yeah," Howie said. "Not because we hit the lady or the kids. He was steamed, in a big hurry to go drop off the car and get paid. The Man always say don't do nothing with the car, no drive-bys, no robberies, no nothing. He wants to get it and chop it before the owner even know it's gone. He don't want no heat. Say it's bad for business. So FMJ, he wanna get there and get paid before the Man seen the TV news. He figures, the lady and the kids hadda be on the news. It was."

Howie didn't know the address of the buyer, only that the chop shop was west of Miami and east of the Everglades. FMJ usually delivered the cars personally after dropping off his accomplices. He didn't want them becoming entrepreneurs. Howie said he thought the cars sold for $400 to $500.

Sounds cheap for a $20,000 car, but as Rakestraw later reminded me, "The guy is buying it from a seventeen-year-old with thirty minutes invested. The kid is happy as hell to get that much for it.

"Kids steal 'em, adults deal 'em. Juveniles work cheap," he said. "If they get caught they face no penalty and they don't flip on you. No reason to." True. Facing a prison term, an adult might well be persuaded to turn on his partners in crime. Juveniles are far tougher for cops to deal with.

Auto theft, like any other business, is conducted for maximum profit at minimum risk. Car theft and stripping is an $8 billion industry.

"They even chop up brand-new cars?"

Rakestraw nodded. "The parts are worth more than the whole."

I shuddered. Maybe I should invest in a Lojack, I thought. This auto security system is like the devices used to track panthers in the wild. It operates like a beeper in reverse. When a theft is reported, the stolen car is beeped with a special code, activating the tracker, a tiny chip hidden in the car. Police can zero in on it almost immediately by following the beep, beep, beep, like tracking a big cat.

"Why did they want that particular Trans Am?" I asked.

"Let me put it like this," Rakestraw said. "Your car needs a new front end, you take it to a body shop. They ask if you want used or new factory parts. When you hear the prices, you want used. The body shop calls a salvage yard. The operator says, 'Let me see if I can find it.' He calls another salvage yard and is told, 'Yeah, I think I can get my hands on a front end for a '91 Chevrolet Caprice.' And he puts out an order for one. It's billed through the salvage yards, with the paperwork easily convertible into legitimate channels.

"It's so prevalent that Allstate won't even authorize repairs with used parts. Factory parts cost more, but it's cheaper in the long run for the insurance company not to encourage the resale of used parts."

"So that's why more than forty thousand cars were stolen in Dade County last year," I said. Howie did a double take at the figure.

"In part," Rakestraw said. "But our biggest problem is the big surge in illegal exports."

Howie nodded. "Like, I know some dudes who drive stolen cars to the port. They got phony papers."

"We'll want to talk about that later," the detective said, "but right now we've got more pressing business."

He left briefly, returning with a photo lineup and another detective. He spread out seven or eight photos like playing cards on the pretty checkered tablecloth. The immature faces of kids who should have been posing for high school yearbooks instead of police mug shots stared up at us. Howie unhesitatingly identified FMJ and J-Boy, pointing them out as the other occupants in the car that hit Jennifer Carey and her children. They wrote the date, the case number, and Rakestraw's name on the back of the photos and had Howie initial them.

Two more detectives, from robbery and auto theft, joined us. The room was growing crowded. Howie steadfastly denied involvement in any of the carjackings, shootings, or smash-and-grabs. I believed him. They seemed to.

"I have to advise you of your rights, Howard. It's a formality," Rakestraw said. "Do you know your rights? Let me read them to you." He took the small laminated card from his billfold and read Howie his Miranda rights, then had him sign a paper stating that he understood. As he signed, Howie shot me a glance that said, Look what you got me into.

They brought in a court reporter, put Howie under oath, and interviewed him again in more detail.

Some of the other detectives appeared annoyed at my presence even though I wasn't taking notes, so I told Howie I'd be back and wandered over to public information to call the office. Howie was in good hands, I told myself; only good things would happen to him from now on.

When I went back, Howie was chowing down on a burger with fries and giving the cops a list of locations frequented by FMJ and his crew.

I asked Rakestraw about the arrangements to place Howie at the Crossing. "I'll go see what I can do," he said, and left the interrogation room to talk to his captain. He reminded me of a car salesman saying he has to run a proposed deal by his manager for approval, except that Howie had already signed the contract.

When Rakestraw returned, the other detectives cleared out as if they knew what was coming.

"Here's the problem," Rakestraw said.

"What do you mean *problem*?" My heart sank.

"Because Howard has no parent or legal guardian he will have to be declared a ward of the state. It takes a judge to do that, and we also need a court order to have him admitted to the Crossing. Before a judge will issue one he'll want a psychological evaluation to convince him that Howard is stable and not just giving us a con job."

"You can tell him that," I protested.

Howie's eyes darted back and forth between us.

"That's not the way it works, Britt. You know the system well enough to grasp how it operates. He'll have to spend a few days at Youth Hall first."

"He has to be protected. You can't just throw him into general population. If word leaks out that he's talked to you—"

Howie got to his feet. "You said—" he began angrily.

Rakestraw made a sharp motion to cut him off. "This is only temporary, Howard. Just temporary, a couple of days at the most. If you're gonna work within the system you have to let the system work, and it takes time.''

"This isn't fair," I said calmly.

"He'll be in isolation. A couple of days," Rakestraw said. "We'll press to get the formalities done ASAP.''

There was no point in arguing in front of Howie. I didn't want him to panic.

"I don't get to go home for my stuff?''

Rakestraw shook his head. "We can send a zone car by later to pick it up, if you like. How much do you have?''

"My books, my hot plate, my dictionary. My clothes, man.'' His situation was sinking in, and apprehension filled his eyes. "I don't want no police taking it. Britt?'' he implored, shaking his head.

"I'll pick everything up for you," I said. "I can store what you don't need at my place and bring whatever you want to the Crossing. I'll take care of it.''

My reassurances did not have the effect I had hoped. "What if I change my mind 'bout everything right now?''

Rakestraw looked uncomfortable. I gave him credit for that, at least. "You just confessed to a number of felonies," he said. "If you don't stick to the deal you take the fall for everybody.''

Howie's eyes locked on mine. I saw him struggle to stay calm. He kept a stiff upper lip.

"Remember," I said quietly, "nothing good is ever easy. But you want to do things right in your life from now on. This is the way to do it. AK. I'll take care of your stuff; Rakestraw will take care of everything else. You and I will stay in touch. Call me whenever you can. This won't take long.''

Rakestraw nodded in support but spoiled the moment by reaching behind him for his handcuffs.

"Empty your pockets and turn around," he told Howie. He saw my look. "We can't transport without them," he said. "Sorry.''

"How long?'' Howie said.

"No more than a week," Rakestraw said, "maybe less.''

Lower lip jutted out, Howie did as instructed and the cuffs were snapped around his wrists.

"Will you tell Miz Mayberry where I'm at? Don't want her to worry 'bout me.''

I promised, as Rakestraw steered him down the hall to booking.

Watching him go, it was hard for me to remember that he was not a man. He was just a boy. Somebody's son.

I took the elevator to the lobby, suffering mixed emotions about Howie and how I was going to lug all his worldly possessions down from the roof of the Edgewater. Once I did, where would I put them? I hadn't considered that when I blithely offered to safeguard them for him. Sometimes I am my own worst enemy, I thought. Preoccupied, I didn't even see Trish or hear her call my name.

She plucked at my elbow as I crossed the police station lobby.

"Britt!" She looked flushed and breathless. "You must be working on something major. You look so serious."

"What are you doing here?"

I must have sounded curt because she hesitated. "Picking up my police-press ID card."

Discomfort flickered in her eyes for a moment. Most likely she didn't like being asked to explain herself; I wouldn't.

"Thought I'd take the opportunity to introduce myself around," she said lightly, "since I had to be here anyway. Never know when you'll cross paths with the cops on a story."

"Good thinking," I agreed. "Right. Sorry, I'm just a little crazed. Actually I'm not even working on a story for tomorrow."

We walked together to the front desk, where I picked up a clipboard. "Guess who I met," she whispered as I scanned the entries on the twenty-four-hour log. "Your Lieutenant Kendall McDonald."

I stopped reading. "He's not my lieutenant," I said ruefully.

"Too bad," she said with feeling. "Those eyes! That hunk could make the devil sweat."

"Now you sound like Lottie." I laughed. "What did he have to say?" I hated my own prurient interest in everything the man said and did.

"We talked mostly about the Rosado suicide. I thought I should report the latest to somebody."

"The latest?"

"I've been getting phone calls from both Miguel, the husband, and Ernesto, the son. I can see how the two of them made that poor woman crazy. Each blames the other for her death, the suicide survivors from hell." She tossed her head, pushing back her hair with an impatient gesture. She was letting it grow, and the longer, wavy look was becoming. She has really blossomed since being hired, I thought.

"There's always been bad blood between them," she was saying. "She was the peacekeeper. Now she's gone, it could very well lead to violence. Did I tell you about the brawl at the funeral home?"

"No, what happened?" Our heels clicked in unison as we crossed the cavernous lobby.

"The two of them really got into it, chairs broken, women screaming, the whole nine yards. The police were called to break it up."

"How'd you hear about it?"

"I was there." Her eyes softened. "Went to pay my respects. You know, since I was the last . . ." Her voice trailed off.

"What a nice thing for you to do," I said, mildly surprised.

"Next day at the cemetery, relatives and the priest had to restrain them from attacking each other. I tell you, Britt, grief does strange things to people. I've been trying to talk some horse sense into them."

"Maybe you shouldn't get too involved. If they call again, suggest grief counseling."

"I doubt those macho types would go for it. But I'll give it a try."

"Yeah, no point in them compounding the tragedy."

A sudden thought struck me as I pushed open the lobby door and I smiled.

"What's funny?"

"Me, warning you not to get involved. You busy later, Trish? I need some help and some cardboard boxes."

She looked at me questioningly.

"So, okay," I said. "I got involved."

I itched to call McDonald when I got back to the office. The mere mention of the man's name did that to me. I wanted to ask him to run interference for Howie, to assure that things moved along smoothly the way they should. For Howie, as well as for justice in the Carey case. A phone call would be safer than seeing him in person. Grow up, I told myself. Did I want to call because justice is so rare and people sometimes slip through the cracks, or was it an excuse to hear his voice?

Instead, I recruited Trish, Ryan, and Lottie and made a run to a liquor store for some cardboard boxes.

Lottie came with me in the T-Bird, and Ryan brought Trish in his car. We parked up on the roof near Howie's lair. Better than trying to haul cartons of household possessions down flights of stairs past security.

Lottie was in a sour mood. "What the hell is that?" She peered at the damaged plastic sleeve on my steering wheel. "Did you hot-wire this car?"

"I have to get that fixed," I mumbled.

"This is a new car." She eyed me suspiciously. "You did buy it, didn't you, Britt?"

"Of course!" I told her about Howie.

"You let him demonstrate on your brand-new car?"

"Not exactly."

Then she asked about Ellie, the neighbor Trish had saved.

"She's about the same, I guess. Trish said the family has hired a part-time companion to give the husband a break."

"I can't see why you were so impressed and bragging on her. Call that a good deed? Sure, Trish was a real Girl Scout, but hell-all-Friday, I wouldn't thank her if I was that poor old woman. What about quality of life? If you were in her shoes, would you want to be saved?"

"A life is a life," I said, quoting Trish. "You can't let it slip away. Her husband was nowhere ready to give her up. He would have blamed himself."

"If it was me," Lottie muttered, "I'd be asking Dr. Kevorkian to make a house call."

She was getting on my nerves, unusual for Lottie. She seemed to be pouting about something. "Well, don't say that in front of Trish," I told her. "I hope you're in a better mood when we go to dinner."

Ryan pulled up behind us, looking over his shoulder, fearful that we'd be arrested. He stayed with the cars to act as lookout. Heat waves rose from the rooftop pavement baked by the blinding late-afternoon sun.

"I can't believe the kid lived up here," Lottie said as we entered Howie's little cubicle. It didn't seem so cozy in broad daylight.

"It's not a bad view." I folded Howie's three pairs of socks and three pairs of underwear into his three T-shirts and packed them in a box.

There wasn't much to take. His paperbacks, a book titled *How to Increase Your Word Power,* his dictionary, and the hot plate filled one box. His clothes, toiletries, and meager cooking utensils went in another. Trish carried the bedroll. I even packed the jar with the little packets of sugar and coffee creamer.

"Should we toss this out?" Trish wrinkled her pert nose as she held up the plastic model of the U.S.S. *Enterprise.* "It's broken."

"No," I said, and packed it with his clothes.

"What in blue blazes is this mean-looking contraption?" Lottie brandished Howie's "protection."

"Was he practicing for the javelin toss?" Trish asked.

I didn't mention I had almost been the target. "I guess we can leave that behind," I told them, checking to see if we had missed anything.

Everything fit in my car. When Howie called from Youth Hall I could truthfully tell him that his place was packed up, his belongings safe.

When we got back to the newsroom, no one had even missed us. I typed up my notes for an eventual story on FMJ and company. Trish parked at the desk next to me, as usual. When I finished, I rolled my chair around to face her. She always looked so bright and eager.

"What do you really want to do, Trish?" I asked casually. "What's your ambition?"

"To be famous," she replied softly, without hesitation, "and rich."

"Get serious." I leaned my chin on my hand, elbow on my desk. "You work for the *News,* remember? I meant what's your goal here, at the paper?"

"I want to do what you do, Britt."

I smiled. "If you do what I do, Trish, then what am *I* going to do?"

"I don't know." She shrugged and casually turned back to her reading, a *Corrections Magazine* that had arrived in my mail.

Funny, I thought. I didn't know if she was serious or joking. We had all planned to go to South Beach later for a drink and a bite to eat. Ryan was between his usual brief and intense romances and was obviously hoping Trish would succumb to his charms.

My luck ran true to form. We planned to leave at seven-thirty. Gunfire erupted at seven-twenty. I promised to join them as soon as I could. "Sure," Lottie said knowingly. "We'll believe it when we see you."

The scene was way up in North Dade, just south of the Broward County line. The distraught family of a despondent unemployed factory worker who had been drinking and threatening suicide had called police to come and stop him. They did. However, in order to do so, they had to shoot him. Now he was just as dead as if he'd succeeded in the first place. The hysterical family insisted that it probably would have ended better had they never called the cops. No way to know for sure, but there are few situations that a policeman can't make worse. The survivors did stop wailing and cheered up considerably, however, when it occurred to them that now they had somebody to sue. The bereaved were already consulting with one of Miami's fine legal practitioners, a specialist in wrongful death actions, before the body was removed. I finished the story at eleven-thirty, then cruised by the Edgewater and Margaret Mayberry's little wooden frame house.

I didn't intend to stop at that hour, but there were lights on. I parked on the dark, empty street and tippy-toed to a window. The house had to have been built in the 1920s, ancient for Miami. The sky was a blank slate without a star. The scent of moisture in the air felt as though a rainstorm was huddled, brooding, somewhere out over the bay. I could see the old wicker furniture in the living room and, beyond that, movement in what looked like the kitchen. She was in there. I caught sight of her, wearing a cotton dress with a bib apron over it, as she worked, quickly and efficiently.

I thought about it, then knocked. She stopped and listened.

"Miss Mayberry, it's Britt Montero from the *Miami News*. I have a message for you from Howie."

She approached the door, wiping her hands on a striped dish towel, opened it, and squinted through the screen.

I identified myself.

"Lord have mercy. I thought I heard someone."

It was the first time I had seen her close up. Taller than I expected, she was imposing, at least five feet ten in sensible shoes. Her mostly gray hair was parted in the middle, tightly pulled back, and anchored with two small plastic combs. She had to be close to eighty but carried herself with a stalwart dignity, back straight, eyes alert.

"I wouldn't have bothered you this late, but I just left the office and saw your lights."

"I do my baking at night," she explained. "Keeps the house cooler."

The heady aroma from the kitchen smelled like bananas and sugar. I told her about Howie. "He didn't want you to worry."

"I hope they do right by that young man," she said thoughtfully.

"I'm sure they will. It'll give him a chance at an education."

"Howard deserves the opportunity."

"I'm glad we agree. I think he's salvageable."

''To be sure. He's a fine young man and he certainly knows his way around tools. He's quite the handy one.''

''Definitely gifted,'' I said. I didn't say that I knew from personal experience. Maybe it was the hour, or her natural reserve, but she did not invite me inside. I couldn't blame her, though I was drooling to get closer to whatever was browning in the oven.

''Thank you for telling me,'' she said. ''Howard has been a great help to me here. He has some character. I think your advice to him was excellent. I just hope it all works out. Does he need anything?''

''Our support as friends. This will be the start of a new life. It's the best thing that could have happened to him.''

''If you plan on seeing him at any time, please let me know first. I'll have something to send him.''

I said I would and bid her good night. The wind picked up, carrying leaves and debris into little whirlwinds as I drove across the crossway. The rain began as I carried Howie's things into my apartment.

Chapter Ten

How I missed the story I'll never know.

That morning the beat seemed quiet, and I spent my afternoon in the broiling sun on the Palmetto Expressway after a sinkhole suddenly yawned open in the center lane, swallowing three trucks, two cars, and a van loaded with migrant workers. Other motorists crashed into one another to avoid it, while a motorcyclist soared over the gaping crater like Evel Knievel and kept going. No one was killed, but it was a hell of a mess. The usual suspects were blameless. The guilty parties were neither Mother Nature nor South Florida's shifting water table. They were members of a county work crew, assigned to drill through the embankment to install a water pipe under the expressway. They had miscalculated. Not bad for a slow news day.

The stretch of highway was closed off, creating a maddening afternoon rush hour. I had called Lottie but she was out, and the desk had dispatched Villanueva to shoot aerials from a chopper. Lottie loves to fly, and I knew she would hate missing it.

I innocently walked in and saw feverish activity around the city desk. No assistant city editor would care what I had. The buzz was a breaking story that hit me like a sucker punch.

"They got 'im!" yelped Ron Sadler, our usually quiet and studious political writer. "They nailed his pasty white ass!" He slammed his right fist into his left palm and spun around in the middle of the newsroom.

"What? Who?" I said, bewildered. Picking up snatches, my heart sank. The biggest damn political scandal in years was breaking—on my beat. And I had no clue.

Detectives had swooped down on Miami City Hall during a commission meeting recess and arrested the vice mayor, Zachary Linwood. Marched his honor out in handcuffs.

"City of Miami detectives?" I had been at the station a few hours earlier, as well as every day in recent memory. Hadn't heard a whisper.

How, I wondered, did the cops ever keep a lid on something so explosive? When there's a big investigation, especially a politically connected probe, rumors and whispers ride the wind like wild seeds. They take root, sprouting from nooks and crannies all over the city. Word is in the air, and reporters know something is about to break. I plow and fertilize my beat faithfully, schmoozing with sources and shooting the breeze, ever alert, ears open, antennae tuned. I hadn't been out of circulation, on vacation, or asleep at the switch. How the hell did I blow it?

"What are the charges?"

Trish strode by me, pausing to check her notebook. "Conspiracy, bribery, extortion, unlawful compensation, official corruption, and misconduct." She hurried on to the city desk.

Shoot, I thought. They sure didn't think them up on the spur of the moment right after I left the station. Where were my sources?

Fred Douglas must have picked up my thought. He looked up, a phone in one hand. "Britt, have you been working on this?"

"Uh, no," I said lamely. "I was out on the—uh, sinkhole story." His eyes dismissed me as he turned away.

"All the department will say is that the chief, city manager, and state attorney plan a joint press conference later," Janowitz yelled from his desk.

I was not alone in my humiliation. Barbara DeWitt, the city hall reporter, stood near ground zero at the city desk, face pale, arms clutched across her abdomen as though struck by a sudden stomach ailment.

"Did you know anything about this?" I asked quietly.

She shook her head. "Nothing. How come we didn't hear? I was covering the commission meeting," she said, voice tight. "When they took a break everybody went out to eat. So did I. Every reporter at the meeting, all the TV guys, missed the whole thing."

Jesus. The final edition of the afternoon paper was already on the street, out of the running. The story broke on our time, taking us totally by surprise. "At least nobody else has it. We'd look a lot worse if somebody did."

Barbara looked at me oddly. "Nobody's got arrest footage. We're the only ones with art."

"Art? We have art?"

"Yeah. Trish and Lottie were there."

I followed her hollow stare. Trish stood at the city desk, the eye of the storm, cool and in charge. Consulting her notebook, flipping through pages, she was briefing a clutch of editors who hung on her every word.

Barbara stepped back, hoping to disappear in the confusion. It made sense, but my curiosity beat out the urge to lie low. I edged up to listen as Trish spoke to a copy boy: "Pull the file on J. L. Harvey; he's a contractor." She refocused on the editors. "At least that was his front. Harvey was arrested last month, drug trafficking. He's the link. They were partners." She paused, eyes reflecting the avid expressions around her. "It's all a land scam and they were in it together."

"Ain't that something." Ron Sadler stood next to me, shaking his head, arms folded in front of him. "Guess who was sitting in his office when the cops got there, broke out the handcuffs, and read his honor his rights?" he whispered.

"Trish?"

"They were sharing a Pepsi."

What luck! Old demon envy followed hot on the heels of my surprise. What the heck was she doing there? Was she just introducing herself around to the local politicos? Never know when you'll run into one on a story.

The managing editor emerged from his office, like a bear from his cave, sleeves rolled up, intense and driven, the scent of political scandal sending the printer's ink that passes for blood pounding through his veins. Only a few stories a year lure him out of his lair and into the newsroom.

And of course Gretchen chose that moment. "Britt, where were you? How could you be so out of touch!" Her voice rose, and my face flooded with color. "We're lucky Trish was on top of this!" Out the corner of my eye I saw Barbara step behind a pillar.

Pitying eyes regarded me solemnly, then returned approvingly to the star of the show.

"The chief is mad as hell that we were there," Trish was saying, one hand resting confidently on her hip. "He pitched a fit, got all apoplectic and red in the face."

"He looks good that way," the managing editor said warmly, eliciting obligatory laughter from the troops.

"He ordered that no further details be released until the press conference at ten A.M. tomorrow," she said.

Uh-oh. On the afternoon paper's time.

"No problem," she added crisply. "I have enough to lay the whole thing out."

"We have somebody out now, picking up copies of the arrest report and the search warrants," the city editor announced to the chief.

"The cops served them simultaneously, at his office and his home," Trish added.

"The art is great," the city editor went on. "We're the only ones in town who got a thing. TV's got nothing and they're scrambling."

As if on cue, Lottie bustled into the newsroom still wearing her darkroom apron, a stack of freshly printed photos in her freckled fist. Editors flocked over to the photo desk just six feet away and the rest of us crowded around. She had it all: the vice mayor, wearing metal bracelets by Police Products, Inc., along with his usual silk tie and conservative suit. His honor marched out of city hall in disgrace, bundled into the backseat of a cage car, aristocratic features folded into something querulous. Detectives from the public integrity squad lugging boxes of seized files and documents from his office to their cars.

"Great stuff," Fred Douglas said admiringly.

There was Sergeant Tully Snow, obviously recovered from his little mishap during the bogus sniper incident. Face distorted, he was shouting at the photographer to back off. Lottie didn't often draw that sort of antagonistic response from cops. Had to be pressure from the top on this one.

Onnie delivered library photos of Zachary Linwood during various high points of his career, to run in a layout with the jump of the main story. Our eyes connected as she commiserated silently with me. She knew the score.

Lottie's pictures would run front page, in color.

They were good but sad, I thought. Zachary Linwood had always been a gentleman to me, unfailingly polite and eloquent, when I called him at home in the dead of night for his comments on breaking stories, police shootings, scandals, or a fired police chief.

Of course that didn't mean I wouldn't have been delighted to break this story myself. Linwood was a Miami institution, old establishment, last of his breed, the remaining white Anglo male on the city's governing body. A former U.S. senator, folksy and cantankerous, he had been a strong voice in South Florida politics for more than thirty years. A two-term mayor in the eighties, he was now sixty-seven and likely to be retired by the voters at the end of his term in eighteen months. Court-mandated changes in voting districts made it almost certain he would be replaced by a Hispanic.

Instead of going out in style after a long and distinguished career, he was ending it with a rap sheet and a likely new record, as convict.

"He was going to cast the deciding vote to change the zoning on a tract of environmentally sensitive land for commercial development," Trish was explaining.

"But he'd need five votes to make it work," the managing editor said skeptically.

"Exactly." She arched an eyebrow. "Each of the other four commissioners owed him a vote in exchange for his on their pet projects."

There was silence, except for ringing telephones ignored in the background.

"They bought the property," she said, referring to her notes, "for just under five hundred thousand dollars, but the zoning change will push the value to at least three million. The partnership was only on paper. Linwood never invested any money; the dope dealer put up the cash. Linwood's contribution was delivering the votes. His share was to be a third."

A third of $3 million. Not bad. Trish knew chapter and verse, all the inside details of a complex and highly secret investigation. I couldn't wait to hear how all this had come about.

"They had to move fast," Trish was saying, "because environmentalists had taken their concerns to the federal government, asking that they move in to tie up the property.

"The scheme went awry when J. L. Harvey was busted last month on drug trafficking and money laundering charges. The case against him was solid, but he had insurance in case something like that happened.

"He had recorded the entire conspiracy. He had secretly taped every meeting, documented every discussion with Linwood. Apparently he did a better job of it than most undercover cops."

I found myself nodding. Made sense. A criminal's best escape route is to deal his way out of trouble, and the most valuable bargaining chip is a dirty cop or politician. Cops and prosecutors will always deal to land one of them.

"He called Miami detectives from his jail cell and offered to give them the vice mayor. Our man," Trish said, "is pretty well nailed." She snapped her notebook closed.

"Why did he do it? He's so close to retirement." An assistant city editor shook his head.

"You've got it," Trish said, skin flushed with the color of a reporter on top of the hottest story in town. "This was his last chance to score big before being run out of office. This would have been his retirement money. The income from his small law firm has never really funded the lifestyle he likes. He was so sure this would go down without a hitch, he'd been out shopping for a second home in Vail."

The rookie reporter I had recently instructed on how to find Flagler Street had wrapped up every detail of Miami's story of the year.

"Hell of a job, Trish!" said the managing editor. His use of her name was significant; most of us in the newsroom are convinced that he has no idea who we are.

"I'd better start writing." Trish checked her watch.

"Need any help?" I offered.

She briefly broke stride. "Thanks, Britt, but Fred is going to work with me on this one."

As they settled in front of her terminal, I beelined for Lottie at the photo desk. She was seated in front of an IBM Selectric typewriter, tapping out the pink caption sheets for the backs of the photos.

"How did you two ever pull that off?"

She stopped typing and leaned back in her chair. "Hell-all-Friday, Britt, I take back whatever I said about that woman." She gave a low whistle. "You were right. I hand you that. She is damn good."

"But how . . . ?"

She winked. "She's got great sources."

"Who?" I demanded. "She doesn't even know anybody in Miami. It's my own damn beat and I had no clue."

"Lottie, I need those left-to-rights!" bawled Joe Hall, the photo editor.

Frowning, she banged out the last one, identifying the detectives escorting Linwood. She glanced up at me. "Snow is still a sergeant, ain't he?"

"Right," I said impatiently.

She handed them over to Hall. "All I know," she said, "is Trish called in, said something major was about to go down at City Hall, and we had to send a photographer. Bobby was in the slot and didn't take her too seriously, but I said I'd go."

"Everybody's taking her seriously now," I murmured.

"Betcher boots." She paused. "The other night in South Beach she said a big story was about ready to break."

"Never said a word to me."

"You weren't there, remember?"

She stopped as Hall interrupted, collar open and rushed. He hovered over her chair. "AP called. They want to take one of these. This," he said, displaying the shot of cops escorting the handcuffed politician out of City Hall, "is the page-one picture. We want to see it in color for the final. It's being played big. We need to get the black-and-whites down to engraving."

I glanced back at Trish and Fred, in deep concentration, him reading over her shoulder as she typed rapidly on the screen.

Hall wheeled and walked away.

"We met near the commission chambers and she said to stake out his office," Lottie said, hurriedly continuing our conversation. "She is so cool. The minute the meeting broke she glued herself to that man like stink on shit. Invites herself into his office and the cavalry arrives.

"Shoulda seen the looks on their faces when she answers the door and I pop up and start shooting." She grinned. "I love it."

"So the cops didn't act like they expected her?"

"Hell, no. The lead detective raised the chief on the radio, demanding to know who was responsible for the leak. Apparently the case was hush-hush; only the chief, the state attorney, and four investigators knew about it."

"How'd she get all that inside stuff?"

Lottie shrugged. "You should know, Britt. You do it all the time. Ask her. She's your friend." She headed back to the darkroom.

I smiled, but my heart wasn't in it.

Yeah, I thought. At least somebody was on top of the story. Otherwise I would have been out all night, knocking on doors, scrambling with the rest of them, trying to piece the facts together and explain myself to irate editors. Instead, I could go home, thanks to Trish. I should have been relieved, but I wasn't. Where were my sources? How the hell had I missed it? I couldn't wait to find out.

Chapter Eleven

Trish's story led the morning paper.

Police released few details. Frustrated reporters from other organizations were reduced to quoting liberally from the *News*. What a coup for us. For Trish.

I watched the press conference just because I happened to be at headquarters, the usual stop on my beat that time of day. Trish covered it; it was her story.

I stood in the back while she sat in the front row, standing out from the crowd, stunning in a white double-breasted blazer, dark slacks, and big sunglasses. The police chief glared down at her and ranted about the leak to "a certain newspaper," his ire only enhancing her reputation, of course, in the eyes of her colleagues.

I had met Danny Menendez, the PIO sergeant, on the way in, and he told me that the brass was convinced that a cop was responsible for tipping off Trish and that an internal affairs investigation had been opened to identify the culprit.

Across the nests of TV crews' coiled cords and tangled wires my searching eyes spotted Kendall McDonald amid a cluster of other brass. He wore the department's dark blue uniform, burnished leather gleaming, metal twinkling in the strobes. As a detective lieutenant he usually wore plainclothes, which meant he must be representing the department today at some official meeting or luncheon. Tall, lean, long-legged, cleft chin. *Guapísimo*. I sighed and looked away. When I glanced back, his eyes were on me. The sizzle was still there. He smiled. I returned it, then self-consciously shifted my attention back to the speaker.

Luckily I would not have to report what the chief had just said.

Later, on my rounds, when cops asked me how the *News* nailed the Linwood story, I could truthfully say I didn't know.

Blowing the story left me jittery and extra careful out on the beat. I asked for a pass to visit the office of the public integrity squad but was turned away. The desk sergeant had been instructed to say that nobody up there was talking to the press. So I went to the pay phone in the lobby and dialed the number direct.

Tully Snow had always been a straight arrow with me in the past, and we had a good working relationship.

"He's on his way back from court," the secretary said. Hoping he hadn't detoured along the way, I loitered near the elevators where I could watch each entrance. Less than five minutes later, Tully entered the lobby, stopping to stub out a cigarette in a sand-filled receptacle. He carried files under his arm and was wearing a tie, a sure sign that he'd been testifying.

He seemed to regret seeing me. Especially when I asked about the Linwood case.

"God, Britt," he said quietly, looking around to be sure we were not overheard, "the whole damn thing was so hush-hush and super-secret, only a few of us knew what the hell was going down. Everybody involved was sworn to secrecy and had their lips buttoned."

"Somebody didn't," I said, my skepticism obvious.

"Sure as hell wasn't me."

"You could at least have warned me that something was in the wind. I looked so stupid to my editors."

He punched the elevator button. "Well, you guys got the story anyway."

"Sure," I said bitterly, "but it was on my beat."

"You hear about the missing kids?" he asked in a conciliatory tone, as though trying to make it up to me.

"No, what kids?"

He paused and lowered his voice, eyes scanning the lobby. At the moment it was apparently a major offense to be seen just talking to a reporter.

"Heard it go out on c-channel a little while ago. Deep south. Two babies, twins, missing."

"Think it's a custody snatch?"

"Hell, Britt. I don't know, it's a county case, but it didn't sound it. Sounded like the mother couldn't remember where she left them."

"What?"

To his relief, the elevator doors slid open and he stepped inside.

"Thanks, Tully. Talk at you later."

This is a glorious business. Miss one story, there is always another. Every day is an adventure.

I got to a phone and called Metro-Dade. Sure enough, I heard the BOLO broadcast countywide as I drove south: Be on the lookout for five-month-old twin girls. A retarded teenager in rural South Dade had strolled to the corner store for some Marlboros and a can of soda pop the prior afternoon, taking her twins with her. She had moseyed on home almost twenty hours later, at about 10 A.M., alone. She wandered in a kitchen door and was foraging in the refrigerator when her mother asked where the twins were. Her response was a vacant stare. She seemed to have forgotten that she had taken them with her.

It had rained on and off during the night and there was cause for alarm. Cops were checking dumpsters, canals, and garbage cans. How do you retrace the footsteps of somebody who hasn't the faintest idea of where she's been and with whom? Dogs had been brought in, and Police Explorers were searching the woods.

The small wood-frame house was sparsely furnished but remarkably neat. A county policewoman I had never met had the call. Her nameplate said WATSON. Her first name was Annalee, she said. Solidly built, she looked even broader in the county's unflattering brown uniform, padded at the waist and hip with hardware, leather, handcuffs, radio, ammo, mace, keys, and all the other little accessories that make cops creak and jingle when they walk. I am always amazed when cops, burdened by that extra load, manage to win foot chases and tackle unencumbered suspects. Annalee Watson's dark hair was pulled back in a ponytail. She wore a sharpshooter's badge and a patient expression.

"You think they're alive?" I asked.

"Don't know. I've encountered Janice before and she seems to be a good enough mother. I don't think she would deliberately hurt them, but she has a short attention span and if she walked off and left them in danger, you know, anything can happen out there."

She glanced toward the scruffy neighborhood of migrant and low-income housing and the dusty strip of all-night bars and tacky stores along Homestead Avenue where it cuts through strawberry, pole bean, and tomato fields. Roughneck kids congregate in the convenience store parking lots.

Worry flickered in the cop's honest brown eyes.

"If her mother was home when Janice went out to the store, why did she take the babies along? Wouldn't it be easier to leave them at home? Babies don't travel light."

"Janice is eighteen now. Since she was twelve she's had a habit of going to the store and disappearing for a day or two. Apparently that's how she got pregnant in the first place. So the mother makes her take the babies with her. She thought it made her more likely to come home. Up to now, it's worked."

"Can I talk to her?"

"Be my guest." She shrugged. "Better do it now, because if we don't come up with something soon we're going to take her in for a statement, just in case. Can you believe it? She remembers what they were wearing but not where she left them. Sad," she said, "some people try and never can have a baby. And she has two of them. That's not for publication," she added.

"Right."

While cops and neighbors searched, Janice sat, knees apart, on a threadbare sofa watching *Oprah* on TV.

Two pink plastic barrettes held back her dishwater-blonde hair except for stringy bangs over a sloping, wedgelike forehead. The indistinct features of her pink, pudgy face were clean and makeup-free, although her short ragged fingernails had been painted orange. She looked potbellied in baggy slacks. Her worn shoes didn't match, but the socks did.

Her small blue eyes were placid, unlike those of a mother whose helpless babies were hungry and lost.

A stranger in her living room did not seem to interest her, and she kept her eyes on the flickering screen as I introduced myself.

"Remember when you went to the store yesterday, Janice?"

That got her attention. "I didn't lose the money," she said, turning to face me.

"That's good." I smiled.

"Do you remember where you saw the twins last?" Her eyes roved back to the television screen. I thought I'd start at the beginning. "You bought cigarettes and a can of soda, right?" Her eyes wandered my way again. "Did you leave the babies with anybody after you left the store?"

"I didn't lose the money."

The babies' future, if any, seemed bleak to me.

"Were they crying when you left them?"

She regarded me seriously for a moment. "If they're not wet you burp them."

"Makes sense to me."

It seemed she had taken a ride with somebody whose name she could not quite recall, in a car she could not quite describe.

We went round and round for a while until Officer Watson appeared in the doorway and motioned for me to join her. "Anything?" she said.

"She didn't lose the money."

"I could have told you that." She sighed. "We've got people canvassing. No luck so far. I'm gonna take her to the station for a statement. Come on, Janice," she said to the woman on the sofa. "Let's go for another ride."

"Should we bring a bottle for the babies?" She frowned and surveyed the room as though trying to remember something. "Where did I put the bottle?"

"Where did you put the babies?" Watson said. "That is the question. Bring a sweater, Janice, it's cold at the station."

"Am I in trouble?"

"I don't think so." Her voice was sympathetic. "We just need to find the twins. You have to try to remember."

I gave Watson my card, home number scrawled on the back, and extracted her promise to call me the minute any new information surfaced. The babies' grandmother, a heavyset middle-aged woman with a heart condition and thick glasses, gave me a good snapshot of Cindy and Mindy, two little Kewpie dolls. Then she left to knock on doors and help in the search. Too bad they don't have Lojack systems for babies, I thought.

Back at the office I spotted Trish alone at her desk, giving me the opportunity to ask what I had wondered about all day.

"Great work on Linwood," I said. "Helluva job."

Smiling, she looked up from her screen. "Thanks. That means a lot coming from you, Britt."

"How did you hear about it? I didn't have a clue."

"A good source." She pushed her hair out of her eyes and stretched her back, catlike.

"Who?"

She leaned forward. "Can you keep a secret, Britt?"

"Sure." I nodded.

"Well, so can I." She stared up into my expectant eyes, expression righteous, a note of finality in her voice.

"But you know I would never repeat—"

"Why, Britt, I was sworn to secrecy. You would never reveal a source, would you?"

"You're right," I said lamely.

She was. Her word was good and she was keeping it. No way to fault someone for that, but I felt frustrated and annoyed.

Being accosted by Janowitz on the way back to my desk didn't improve my frame of mind. "How does it feel to be scooped by the new kid on the block?" He grinned.

"Don't mind a bit," I lied jauntily. "Especially when it's a friend."

Howie had left a phone message, with no return number. My frustration mounted when I called Youth Hall and they gave me a runaround. Finally I got through to Linda Shapiro, the director.

"You know that because of confidentiality we are not even authorized to confirm that a particular individual is here," she said, in her infuriating bureaucratese.

"But this is different, goddammit," I snapped, tired of being jerked around. "I'm the one who brought him in. He just got there, and I want to make sure he's okay. I'm only returning his call."

She paused. "If, as you say, someone did call the *News* from this facility, that is something we will have to investigate internally." Her tone was officious. "You may not be aware of the fact that telephone privileges are earned here and are not extended to anyone for at least seventy-two hours after their arrival. Even then, calls are strictly limited to next of kin. Parents only. Sorry, Britt, I cannot confirm that we even have such a person here."

There was no persuading her. Seething, I slammed down the phone. Wait until she wants something, I thought viciously. I dialed Rakestraw and was told he was gone for the day. "Will you buzz him at home and ask him to give me a call?" Normally that's no problem.

"You know we can't do that," said the officer who answered.

"Come on," I coaxed. "You know it's done all the time."

"Sorry." The chief was furious at the *News*, so suddenly everybody was operating strictly by the book. I found Rakestraw's beeper number in my Rolodex and called it, punching in my own.

I sat there fuming, but he didn't call back. Poor Howie, I thought. He must feel abandoned.

"What's wrong, Britt?" Trish stopped at my desk.

"Oh, just one of those days," I muttered. "This job is enough to make you want to put on a postal uniform and pick up an automatic weapon."

"You okay? Anything I can do?"

"No, but thanks."

I called Watson at the county's south substation. The hunt for the twins was still on. She promised again to call me at once with any developments. Here I was feeling sorry for myself, and those poor helpless babies were lost out there. I wrote the story for the final and told the desk I would keep tabs on it until the local section locked up at 1 A.M. Where were they? I wondered. When would they be found? Would they be found? The mysteries I hate most are those that are never solved. They haunt you forever.

Chapter Twelve

Something had happened during the night. The subtle shift from rainy season to winter had begun. The hot, moist, south-south-west Caribbean winds that soak up even more moisture from the Atlantic, the Gulf of Mexico, and the Everglades had surrendered to northern currents, which had started to push south. Tornadoes spun up and down the coast, sinkholes opened in the far north lanes of the Interstate, and the dawn was cool and less humid.

I called Watson's south district number at 5:30 A.M. She wasn't in yet and there was no news in the search for the twins. I pulled on shorts, my Miami Heat T-shirt, and running shoes, clipped my beeper to my waistband, and trotted two blocks to the boardwalk. Jogging the 3.2-mile round-trip was easier than two days earlier, when I had returned with my hair drenched. I ran at a steady pace, as the sea evolved from green to blue to silver under low-flying, fast-moving clouds. I warmed up fast, but other locals wore sweats and one elderly early bird even toddled along swathed in a winter coat. The temperature drop had little effect on the few tourists out that early. Peeled down to their swimsuits, they were hitting the beach as though it were the Fourth of July at Coney Island. They were paying winter rates for a bronze glow and would get it, by God, even if it was really windburn.

The hush before dawn was glorious as I thudded into the home-stretch, ocean on one side, oceanfront hotels and their gleaming turquoise pools on the other. Something dark rode in the sky high over a ship on the horizon miles off the coast, perhaps a blimp tethered to the ship below.

I slowed down and another jogger, lean, in his fifties, drew abreast. "What is that out there?" We both stared.

Occasionally blimps or weather balloons escape the weather stations in the Keys.

"I don't know." He resumed his pace. "Didn't even notice it."

No one else seemed to either. Sometimes it seems like that is how I spend my life, I thought, looking for something strange on the horizon. Look hard enough, and it is always there.

I went home and took Bitsy around the block. She felt the weather change too, prancing exuberantly. Then I showered and sliced a tiny banana into my cereal. Thanks to Mrs. Goldstein's green thumb, a cluster of banana trees thrives along the east side of our building, producing hands of fruit so heavy that the trees must be propped up for support. Sweeter and more delicious then any supermarket variety, they have a single drawback. They all ripen at once. What do you do with fifty or sixty ripe bananas? She shares the bounty.

I scanned the paper while eating breakfast. Trish had made front page again with her follow on the Linwood story. She had had a good run with it. Coverage would now pass into the hands of the reporter assigned to the courts. I had to admit she had done a hell of a job. My twins story was on local and I winced. Whoever was in the slot had cropped the picture badly, trimming it just beneath their chins as if to eliminate numbers there. It looked like a police mug shot of tiny incorrigibles, as though the accompanying headline should read ESCAPED INFANTS ON RAMPAGE. I wondered where they had spent the chilly night.

I took a short cropped jacket to wear over my shirt and slacks and made Rakestraw's office my first stop. I was waiting, dander up, when he arrived, unshaven, harried, and preoccupied.

"Calm down, calm down," he said. "Everything is fine. Moving along on schedule."

"Howie tried to call me, Rakestraw. They wouldn't let me get back to him. I don't even know if he's okay."

"He's fine. Saw him yesterday. There was a hearing, and the judge ordered his evaluation. Once he gets the report he'll place him right into the Crossing. No problem."

"You should have told me. I would have come to the hearing. I don't want him to feel like I abandoned him. I wanted to tell him that I got his stuff—"

"It was unofficial, in the judge's chambers. If it makes you feel any better, Britt, I'll have them let him give you a call later today. I've got more pressing problems at the moment. Looks like FMJ shot a Brazilian tourist in the ankle last night and took his rental car."

"Where?"

"Right here in Overtown."

"What was a tourist doing there?" Overtown's desolate and often explosive inner-city streets are not included in the usual tourist itinerary.

"Claims he was lost. Maybe he was trying to score some dope. Who knows."

"The heat from city hall and the Chamber of Commerce will give you all the overtime you need."

"Yeah, but OT won't do us much good unless we can put our hands on that little street slug. This case, however, is different from all the others. FMJ turned eighteen yesterday."

"Hell of a way to celebrate."

He opened a fat folder and handed over black-and-white photos of FMJ, front and side views, from a freshly printed stack. "For you," he said, "hot off the press. This is his first felony as an adult. Put it in the paper, Britt. Run it big."

"Great! Wish we'd done this weeks ago. How come you didn't answer your beeper last night?"

"Oh, Christ, did you try to get me? I shut it off when I put in the new battery and forgot to turn the damn thing back on."

"I need your home number," I said. "The office wouldn't call you, 'cause the chief is in a snit at the media."

Reluctantly, he recited the number. "But I'd appreciate it if you'd use the beeper if you need to get in touch. My home phone is a last resort, in a real emergency. Okay? Things are tough at home. We've been having some problems, because of the hours and all. The wife wouldn't appreciate any strange women calling right now."

I promised. Cops' wives endure more than their ration of grief. I always explain who I am and why I'm calling. Sometimes that's not enough.

I checked my own beeper to be sure it was working, in case Watson had news about the twins, and called the office for messages. There were none.

Rakestraw walked out with me on his way to PIO with FMJ's pictures. "Met your friend. She's sure something else," he said admiringly.

"Who?"

"That other reporter. One that did the story on Linwood. Sure pissed off the chief. Reminds me of you. Said she's a good friend of yours."

"Well, we didn't grow up together or anything. She's from Oklahoma. Smart as hell."

"Real friendly. Ran into her in the elevator. Told her how you caught the Fly for us a coupla years ago."

I smiled fondly at the recollection. A slightly built armed robber who wore big prescription eyeglasses had terrorized small businesses. One victim swore the holdup man looked "like a fly," with his skinny neck, high-pitched voice, small chin, and those oversize thick lenses. Sure enough, when the police artist finished his sketch, the suspect did resemble a fly. The cops stood around squinting at it, expressing serious doubts as to its accuracy. My editors were equally dubious, but the victims insisted that was him.

We called him the Fly when we ran it. The paper hit the street and phones rang off the hook. Everybody who knew the man knew exactly who we were talking about. Quickly nabbed, he did, indeed, look like a fly. The headline was: SWAT TEAM CORNERS FLY. The department had actually even thanked me for my help on that one.

I laughed. "What'd she say?"

He rubbed his whiskers and thought for a moment. "Said she'd like to compete with you on the same story to see who did better. I'd like to see that myself."

I laughed uneasily, wondering if he had quoted her accurately. "Well, you won't. We're on the same team. We're out to beat the competition, not each other."

I continued my rounds, rolling into the office about 2 P.M., an hour before the street deadline. I had FMJ's mug shot and a story on his new victim and felt pretty good.

Bobby Tubbs was in the slot.

"We need to run this guy's picture as big as we can," I urged.

"Not our job, Britt," he cautioned. "We're not cops."

"I know," I said, exasperated. "But this kid is a one-man crime wave. A time bomb. He drove the hit-and-run car that killed that little boy, and he's the one who's been kneecapping drivers, including several tourists, one of them this morning."

He curiously scrutinized the picture I had handed him.

"I know it's only a mug shot, but will you try to give it the best play you can?"

"We've got some great art for the street," he said enthusiastically.

"What?" I picked up a red grease pencil and flipped FMJ's photo over to print his name, Gilberto Sanchez, clearly on the back.

"The babies. The missing twins' reunion with their mother and grandmother. Great stuff."

I did a double take.

"The twins? They found them? They're safe?"

"Yep, both okay."

"Who's doing the story?"

"Trish." His round blue eyes were serene.

"What? That's my story!" I spun around and saw Trish, briskly working at her terminal. "The cops were supposed to call me when they found them."

Tubbs stared up, bland and innocent. "Guess she got a call." He shrugged. "You weren't here. You were busy, out on something else anyway."

I stormed back to Trish's desk, slowing only long enough to check that I had no messages from Watson.

She greeted me with a smile. She wore ice blue, nearly as pale as her gray eyes. "Hi, Britt, I was looking for you. Did you get the age of the babies' grandmother?"

"Forty-two," I snapped, in spite of myself.

She tapped the numbers onto the screen.

"Trish! That was my story. I was on top of it. Watson was supposed to call me. Why wasn't I called?"

She looked from the screen to me, mouth open in an expression of wonderment. "Britt, I didn't know you had dibs on it. You weren't here." She jerked her fingertips from the keyboard as though it was hot.

"Did the desk assign you?" I thought venomously about Tubbs, unable to conceal the hostility in my voice.

"No. I just picked up the city desk phone and it was Annalee Watson. She wanted to let us know the children had been found alive and well. I told Tubbs and he said to run with it."

"She was supposed to call me, then beep me if I wasn't here."

"Maybe she lost your number and just dialed the main." Her voice was meek as she pushed her chair back, as though distancing herself from the story on her screen. "I never would have worked it if I thought you—"

"You saw my story this morning. You had to know I was following it," I said bitterly.

"I didn't even know when you'd be in."

"You should have asked!" About to stalk away, I couldn't resist, "Where were they? Who had them?"

"Oh, Britt, it's the neatest story." She hesitated, realizing those were the wrong words to use in my current state of agitation. "There are tons of kids in that neighborhood, mostly latchkey, a lot of migrant kids raising themselves—and each other."

Apparently Janice had handed the babies to two little girls, nine and ten years old, to hold. When she went off and didn't come back, the kids eventually took them home to play house. Both households were disorganized, to say the least, and so full of kids of all ages, siblings, cousins, and friends, that no adults paid much attention. The children who cared for the little ones cared for them all. Amazingly, no one had noticed an extra baby or two.

A cop canvassing that morning had asked a child near the store if she had seen the missing babies. She led him to one and pointed out the place where the other had been taken. They were well fed and wearing clean diapers, all due to the care and kindness of children old beyond their years.

A touching, happy ending. Except for me.

"Britt," Trish said firmly, "you want the story, you take it."

"Obviously that's impossible, twenty-five minutes from deadline, after you've done all the reporting," I said, voice tight. "I want you to know that I resent it."

I stomped off and wrote the FMJ story quickly, pounding the keyboard like it had offended me.

Howie called as I finished.

"Hi, guy, how you doing?" I hit the send button. "Good to hear your voice."

"I gotta get outa here, Britt."

"Rakestraw says things are moving along, your stuff is safe in my apartment, Miss Mayberry sends her love. She's baking brownies for when you get to the Crossing."

"There's a couple of dudes here who run with FMJ." He spoke so softly I had to strain to hear. "They know me."

"But they don't know you're gonna testify—"

"Oh, right. They got me all by myself instead of wid everybody else. Whatcha think that tells 'em?"

"You should be out of there and in the Crossing in the next day or two."

"I don't know, man," he fretted. "The dudes know me. It's like a telegraph system. FMJ's gotta know by now."

"What are their names?" I scrawled *Cat Eye* and *Little Willie* in my notebook. "I'll get hold of Rakestraw. Don't worry, he wants you safe and in one piece."

"Yeah, till I do what he want. What happens then?"

"You finish your education and live the good life."

"Happy ever after?"

"Sure."

"Hate being locked up. Wish I had my books." He sounded miserable. "You should see the books they got here. Nothing. *Moby Dick, The Three Mouseketeers.*"

"Try one, you might like it."

"What's the matter, Britt? You bummed?"

"The job. A bad day."

"Somebody got a beef?" He sounded indignant. "Don' let 'em push you around, Britt."

"No way. How's the food?"

"Regular. I really want outa here."

"I hear you. But hang in there. Promise me, Howie, that if you have any problems you'll talk them over with me before you do anything. I'll be here for you, I promise."

"Okay, Britt. Hope this works out."

"You're doing the right thing. Do what they tell you and it'll be soon."

"Uh-oh, gotta go now."

"Stay in touch."

He said he would.

I headed for the cafeteria. Trish followed. I punched the elevator button. "Britt?"

I turned my back on her and headed for the escalator. She followed. "Britt!"

"Would you leave me alone right now?"

She persisted. Had to give her credit for that. Great attribute for a reporter.

"You shouldn't lash out at people who care about you." She joined me on the moving metal stairs.

I didn't answer.

"You know better than anyone that there are enough hassles in this business," she said. "It's horrible to hassle with someone you consider a friend."

I couldn't shake this woman, and she was succeeding in making me feel guilty.

"I'm not dying for a byline or desperate for a story," she said, voice rising. "No story is worth a hassle with you. I'm as territorial about my job as you are. But I am not interested in stepping on toes or intruding."

We had hit the fourth floor landing. She tagged along onto the next flight of moving stairs, stepping up her little diatribe, ignoring others around us.

"Nor am I interested in having to walk on eggshells around you. If we're friends and there's something you don't like, speak up—before it gets out of hand," she snapped.

She trotted off the escalator to keep up with me at the third floor. I turned and looked her in the eye. "Okay, Trish. It was a misunderstanding, more Watson's fault and the desk's than yours. But you are right about me being territorial. Don't step on one of my stories again."

Face flushed, she nodded. "Still friends?"

"Sure," I said. "Let's go have coffee."

Chapter Thirteen

S aw you having coffee with Trish,'' Janowitz said, wearing his usual troublemaking grin. Sometimes he reminded me of a manure salesman with a mouth full of samples. "She tell you about her raise?''

"What raise?''

"Because of the Linwood story,'' he said smugly. "She got hers early. Probably unprecedented for somebody to get a merit raise so soon in this newsroom.''

New hires are not reviewed for raises until after six months on the job. He watched expectantly for my reaction.

"Nice,'' I said affably. "She didn't mention it.''

"She's the golden-haired girl around here right now. Can do no wrong. Hear they assigned her to interview Gloria Estefan on her yacht.''

"Somebody's gotta do it.'' I smiled sweetly.

"Why don't I get those kinda plums?''

Every new reporter who creates a splash with a good run of stories enjoys a honeymoon during which the desk showers him or her with the best assignments. It never lasts, and soon it's someone else's turn.

Trish was on a roll. Her touching twins story, with its great color photo, landed on the front page. Officer Annalee Watson was quoted liberally. That bitch, I thought. Why hadn't she kept her word? I called to ask, but she wasn't in.

I mined my beat diligently for the next few days but hit no mother lode. This had to be the lowest point in the cycles all reporters experience. I had the pedal to the metal and was spinning my wheels—getting nowhere. I got several tips on FMJ sightings. Even had a message purportedly from one of his crew and drove through rush hour all the way down to South Miami to meet him at a diner where I drank too much coffee and waited for hours, but he never showed. I hate waiting. It's not what I do best.

Hard to believe that a kid so bold and violent, responsible for so much pain and so many crimes, could continue to cruise South Florida, shooting strangers and thumbing his nose at law enforcement. Sooner or later a cop would stop him on a traffic violation or at the wheel of a stolen car. I hoped that man or woman would be alert and prepared when walking into his sights.

Howie didn't call again, which meant he must be doing fine. Rakestraw told me after three days that he had been moved to the Crossing, where I assumed he was being kept busy in a wholesome, structured environment. By now, I hoped, he had put a little meat on his bones, was hooked on Herman Melville, and had discovered that Alexander Dumas was not Walt Disney. In his case, no news was good news.

By the time Martin Anderson, an old buddy from J-school, called to say he was in town on a story, I was ready to relax with some good food and conversation. Marty and I had dated at Northwestern until we realized that our friendship was stronger than our physical attraction. He is on an investigative reporting team at the *Chicago Tribune*, the latest in a series of bigger and better newspaper jobs.

"Whatcha working on, Marty?"

"Between us?"

"For sure, unless it's on my beat."

"If it was on your beat I'd never tell. I know how you are; you'd ravish my body and steal my notes."

"You wish."

He was working on a piece about TV Martí and had been in town for nearly a week before we got together for dinner.

It was my day off and I pampered myself with an aerobics class in the morning, followed by a walk on the beach. Instead of a fast shower, I luxuriated in a bubbly tub as Bitsy and Billy Boots watched balefully, certain I had gone mad. For lunch, I ate half a dozen cookies, Rocky Roads studded with huge chunks of chocolate and walnuts and dunked in a glass of milk.

Lottie called at three o'clock to invite me to join her and Trish for dinner.

"Can't. I have a date."

"Who? Who? Who? You didn't tell me!" she accused. "Somebody sexy?"

"No," I said sheepishly. "No big deal. A reporter from the *Chicago Trib*. We're old friends."

I wore white with a crimson sash to show off my tan. He whistled, then hugged me, as Bitsy broke into furious barks and Billy Boots stared with silent malice from the high back of a chair.

Marty hadn't changed. Conservatively dressed, nice face, medium height, medium build, medium brown hair. A man no one would notice in a crowd, perfect for an investigative reporter.

"Blondie, you're as gorgeous as ever."

"You say that to all the girls."

"But this time I mean it. I'm serious, you do look great."

Bitsy continued to bark.

He winced. "Didn't know you had a dog."

"Don't ask," I said. "Long story."

We went to South Beach and strolled Ocean Drive dodging in-line skaters, Spandex-clad nightclubbers, and stunningly snooty models, male and female. We had drinks at the pool bar at the Carlyle Hotel, watching the full moon rise, and ate dinner at Amnesia.

"The change in this place is astonishing," he said, lighting a cigarette. "First time I saw the Beach it was Geritol Junction, God's waiting room. Now it's the world's new epicenter of cool."

"It does have everything," I said, gazing affectionately at the endless street procession. "Fun seekers, sun worshipers, serial killers, America's most wanted. We've got them all."

"I take it you haven't become bored by blue sky and ocean beach yet."

I shook my head. "I love the heat, the humidity, and the screaming." Marty had been a lifesaver at school, a blessing when I felt terminally wind-chilled and homicidally homesick for Miami in all its warmth and living color.

"No better place to be a reporter."

"Yeah, that reminds me. I saw the Gloria Estefan piece on One-A in the *News*. That Trish Tierney byline looked familiar. I wondered if she's the same one I worked with once."

"Small, real pretty, black-haired, gray eyes?"

"Sounds like her."

"From Oklahoma?"

"Bingo."

"What's the story?" I was more curious than I liked to admit, even to myself.

Marty put down his drink and seemed to be thinking. "We worked on the same little paper for a time, out west. Obsessive, ambitious overachiever? Nothing ever enough?"

"Sounds like her. She's made quite a splash."

"I wondered whatever happened to Trish. Didn't expect to see her byline here."

"Why not?"

He shrugged. "Wasn't well liked, as I recall. Thought she'd either soar right to the top or drop out of the business. I moved on not long after she was hired."

"She left her last job in fear, trouble with a stalker. It wasn't you, was it?"

He laughed, tore off a chunk of crusty roll, and slathered it with herbed butter. Marty never worried about cholesterol or major coronaries. "If you ask me, any stalker would be crazy to take her on."

"Well, this one apparently had connections and wound up running her out of town."

"Humph. Hadn't heard about that. How's the job treating you?"

"Great, except I'm going through a dry spell lately." I frowned. "You know how that can be."

"How'd you feel if you were on an investigative team and only broke into the paper every three–four months or so?"

"Very nervous. I guess I have to justify my existence every day to prove I'm worth the salary. I love breaking news, lots of stories in the paper. I like feedback. Even my crank mail. But maybe I need a project to break me out of this rut. Fred Douglas, the city editor, is always pressing me to do more takeouts, more big weekend pieces. He says I'm like a runaway freight train, trying to cover every purse snatch in Miami. My problem is I hate to miss anything."

We walked and talked, then drove over to Tobacco Road for a nightcap. The room melted with happy conversation. I learned about the current woman in his life, an entertainment writer at the *Trib,* and we joked about the sorry state of my love life. That's what's wrong, I told myself on the way home. When my personal life is great I have no trouble enduring a negative turn on the job—and vice versa. When both are on a high, it is heaven. When both run dry it was what I had now. Both were due for an upswing. Talking it out with a friend made me feel better.

I wasn't even vexed by Trish's byline on the front page next morning. By now it was routine.

A Hialeah man trying to mediate marital problems between his daughter and son-in-law lost patience and pulled a nine-millimeter Luger. In the ensuing struggle he shot them both, then turned the gun on himself. Nothing like a marriage counselor with a gun.

The story was the only thing that didn't have any holes in it. Trish had done a good job. Even Lieutenant Kendall McDonald had been quoted on the virtues of professional marriage counseling and tougher gun control. I sighed and closed the paper.

The beat was quiet so I went to the office earlier than usual, primed to start work on a project. The problem is me, not Trish, I thought. There were certainly enough stories in this town for everybody. I had a couple of ideas in mind and thought I'd bounce them off whoever was on the desk.

"Saw Trish landed another great story off your beat," Janowitz gloated as I walked into the newsroom. I had no time to answer. My phone was ringing and I snatched it up.

I didn't recognize the frantic, shouting voice at first.

"How could you, Britt!" There was a ragged sob. "I trusted you! How could you do this shit to me?"

"Howie? Is that you? What happened? Are you all right?"

"Yeah! Like you care." He snorted and sniffed, like he was wiping his nose.

Horns blared and there were traffic sounds in the background.

"Where are you?"

"You think I'm goddamn crazy? Tell you anything?"

Oh, shit, I thought.

"You're not at the Crossing," I said flatly.

"Damn straight! Why'dja do me this way, Britt? Pretend to be my friend?"

"I *am* your friend."

That only agitated him. "Don't fucking give me that shit!" he shouted. "You said you was with me."

"I am."

His bitter laugh ended in a sob.

"What the heck has happened?" I pleaded.

"This was my chance, Britt! My chance for school. To be somethin'." He was crying. "Why didn'tcha answer my calls? I needed help! Goddammit!"

"I would have if I got any, Howie." I spoke slowly and distinctly, hoping he wouldn't hang up until he told me where he was. "This is the first call I've had from you since you went to the Crossing. I thought everything was okay."

"Don't lie to me, goddammit! You said you wuz my friend! I left a dozen goddamn messages on your machine, that fucking voice-tape thing! I been calling since the first day I was here!"

"Howie, I swear, I was off yesterday, but I checked my messages and there was nothing. Today there was one from my mother. That was it. What number did you call?"

"Don't lie like that! Nobody will listen! I didn't know what to do!" The raw pain in his voice cut through me like a blade. "They knew I was here from the first day."

"Who?"

"FMJ! They say they gonna shoot Miz Mayberry if I didn't take off and go with them. I couldn't let 'em. She was the only person, the only friend I had." He gasped. "I thought you—"

"Howie, I follow you." I was on my feet now, unable to sit through this conversation. "I don't know why on earth I didn't get your messages. But I'll come meet you right now. Where are you?"

"You crazy? Fool me once, it's your fault! Fool me twice, it's mine! Think I'm that stupid?"

The line went dead. I stood there holding the phone, hoping I was wrong and would hear his voice again.

I hung up and sat down, mind racing. What the hell happened? I snatched up the phone again and punched in Rakestraw's number in a rage. I wanted to weep in frustration myself.

"Britt," Rakestraw said, "I was just gonna call you."

"What the hell happened to Howie?"

"You heard from him? He ran. The goddamn little street slug ran. The house mother at the Crossing said he went out to a utility room to do his laundry last night and kept going."

"He just called, hysterical. He claims he tried to call me a dozen times. I never got any messages."

"He called here too, six–seven times in the last couple days,"

Rakestraw said sheepishly. "Some of his messages say 'urgent'; others are asking for help. I was off. Didn't get 'em till I came in today. We drove up to Altamonte Springs for my parents' anniversary. The damn civilian they had taking messages in here is two bricks short of a load and didn't know enough to try to reach me or pass it along to somebody else."

"Howie said word leaked out, that FMJ knew where he was all the while and was threatening Miss Mayberry, the woman who lives in the little house—"

"I know who she is," he snapped. "Did he say where he was?"

"He's mad as hell at me. He blames me for getting him into this and not being there for him like I promised. At this point I'm sorry I ever brought him to the station!"

"Oh, swell, now don't *you* go crazy on me, Britt! These things happen. This is all a misunderstanding, nothing that can't be straightened out." He sounded both patronizing and impatient with me.

"Now I see how police informants get killed! Straightening out your misunderstandings doesn't make them any less dead." The venom in my voice surprised me. "I'm sorry," I said. "But I'm the one who urged him to trust you. He's just a kid. He was upset and unloading on me."

"I know," Rakestraw said quietly. "Crap seldom runs uphill, it runs down and spreads out."

"We should've taken better care of him, Rakestraw. We owed him that. He's trying to protect Margaret Mayberry, and we should too."

"I'll have a watch order put on her place; the beat people are all aware of her anyway. But chances are no kid will harm her if Howie is out there with them doing whatever it is they want him to do."

"I wouldn't count on it," I said. "You know how unpredictable FMJ is."

I knew it was probably futile, but I had to go to the Edgewater to see if Howie might have returned to his old home.

Gretchen caught my eye as I fumbled for my car keys. She waved a scrap of paper. "Britt, the police desk says there's been a boat explosion down on the river, a couple of workers injured. It's still burning. Here's the address."

"Can't go right now, I'm too busy." I took tentative steps toward the elevator.

"I don't see anything from you on the budget," she said, trailing me, her pace deliberately slow. She wore what looked like one of Oscar de la Renta's bright plaids. My mother would have loved it.

"Can't talk right now, but I really can't do it. Is there somebody else?"

"If you're too busy, I'll give it to Trish." She smiled knowingly.

I stared at her for a moment. Was this some sort of in-house joke? Was everybody in the newsroom snickering?

"Good," I said, and walked out. Let Trish's head ache and her hair smell of acrid smoke and burned flesh. Let her ruin good shoes running through a fire scene.

At the elevator, I looked back and saw them at Trish's desk, heads together. Then Trish began to gather her things. Gretchen has hit a new low, I thought, as the doors whispered open. Start manipulating reporters and encouraging professional jealousy and no one in the newsroom would trust anybody. What a delightful prospect.

Miss Mayberry stared at me through the ever-present screen.

"He stopped by last night," she said, shrewd eyes oddly veiled. "Said he wanted to be sure I was all right. Didn't like the looks of the boys he was with. Didn't seem as though he liked them much either. But he went with them. Didn't wait to take the banana bread or the brownies I baked him. What's going on with that boy?"

"I know he was worried about you." I chose my words carefully. No sense in us both taking guilt trips.

"Pshaw, I'm a tough old bird." She waved off my concerns with a casual gesture. "I can take care of myself."

"What did the boys look like?"

"Four or five of 'em, in a new . . . one of those four-wheel-drive things. A Blazer, I think. Bright yellow. They didn't come to the door, so I didn't see 'em close, but they were blowing the horn and yelling. Sounded like bad business to me. Don't know why Howard would sashay around with that bunch."

"Miss Mayberry," I said, "be careful. If any of those kids come around, don't open the door. And call the police."

"On what? I don't own a telephone. Never had one. Don't need one," she said stubbornly. "There's a pay phone right inside the mall."

.   .   .

Despite what she said, despite the reality that Howie was in the company of trouble, on the run with FMJ and his crew, I went to the roof. A short, pudgy man stepped out of what looked like the hotel laundry and stood smoking a cigarette. I waited in my car until he crushed the butt with his shoe and went back inside.

Howie's little hideaway was empty except for dust mites floating in the shaft of sunshine that fell inside when I swung open the door.

"Howie?" I called hopefully, more to myself than him. What remained of his "protection" lay near the door, the stick broken as though across someone's knee. A loose snarl of tape hung from the business end. The blade was missing. Either Howie had been here or someone else had decided not to let a perfectly good knife go to waste.

I walked around trying to think, gazing at traffic below, hoping to magically spot the yellow Blazer from this vantage point. Black smoke spiraled skyward to the south. I watched its color change to yellow, then white. Either we had a new pope or the boat fire on the river was now under control. Sirens wailed in the distance. A white car approached and parked across the street as I looked down on the east side. Rakestraw got out and crossed, apparently to see Miss Mayberry. His warnings would carry more weight than mine. My vantage point was comfortable. Instead of the frustration that had dogged me recently, I felt a sense of power: unseen, yet able to see everything. I wanted to stay where I was and never go back down to reenter the real world.

I tore a page from my notebook, scrawled a message, and left it inside Howie's little space: *Please call me. It can still be all right. It's not too late. Your friend, Britt.* I underlined *friend* and included my phone number, adding my home number as well.

Rakestraw's car was still parked as I left the complex. I expected to see him on Margaret Mayberry's front porch speaking through the screen. He wasn't there. Evidently she had let him in the house. I drove by the apartment where FMJ's mother and sister lived. No one answered my knock. I scribbled *Please call me* on the back of my card and slid it under the door.

Back at the office I stopped at the police desk to ask Jerry, the cub reporter who monitors the police radios, about carjackings the night before. "Only one that I know of," he said, adding what I expected: "A tourist who got shot. They took a yellow Blazer."

I walked preoccupied into the newsroom. Trish was dictating from the fire scene. A few people, including Gretchen, were peering over the shoulder of the intern taking the story. Two of the three victims had died, the third was at the burn center along with a fireman critically injured in a second explosion.

I wondered what had happened and wished I were covering it, but there was no time. I had to track Howie down before he got into serious trouble and wound up in prison or worse.

I left the office and just drove, listening to the police scanner in my car, checking every place I could think of—teen hangouts on the Beach, in Overtown, and around the Edgewater—willing him to be there each time I turned a corner. If the police couldn't find them, what chance did I have? But I kept looking till midnight.

The next morning I checked Howie's place again and circulated my cards among the kids at the Edgewater game rooms. They all flat out denied knowing him, even the ones I had seen him with the day we met.

Rakestraw called after I got to the office.

"Where you been? You get my messages?"

"No," I said. "I just checked my voice mail."

"Well, you better check it again."

Goddammit, I thought. Why isn't the system working? What if Howie had called?

"Guess who I've got here?" he said.

"Howie?"

"I wish. A lady I thought you might want to speak to."

"Miss Mayberry?"

"No." He quit the guessing game. "Howard's mother. Want to talk to her?"

"I'll be right over."

On the way out I confronted Gloria. "Did you call the Audix room to find out why I'm not getting my messages?"

"I did, and your line is working fine, Britt. If nobody calls, you don't get messages."

She saw my face and made a hasty suggestion.

"Why don't you change your code? It's easy to do. Somebody else might have theirs mixed up or something."

I decided to do so when I got back. Right now, I was in a hurry.

. . .

She was sprawled in a hard wooden chair in Rakestraw's office, slump-shouldered and awkward, bare legs stretched out in front of her. Rail-thin and bony, she wore skimpy short shorts, ankle-high boots, and a midriff top, sans bra. If seductive was her intended effect, it would have worked better to cover her scarred arms and legs.

She raised her head but failed to register my presence. Her eyes had the dusky, unhealthy glaze of somebody on the street too long.

Rakestraw leaned against the doorjamb, apparently finished with her. He rolled his eyes as I sat down opposite the woman, smiled cheerfully, and said, "Hi, so you're Howie's mom."

About to nod off, she made a losing effort to focus.

"Have you seen him lately?" I asked, glancing anxiously back at Rakestraw. His look told me she hadn't.

"I tol' him," she slurred, jerking her head in his direction. She winced, eyes narrowing, teeth set on edge, as though even the slightest movement created discomfort. "I ain't seen that boy fo' a coupla years." Something in her stare reminded me of the retarded mother who had mislaid her children. "I always called him my sweet boy," she muttered. "He a man now," she announced, chin skidding toward her chest.

"Not quite. We need to find him before he gets in serious trouble," I said urgently. "I'm a friend of his."

Her eyes came up again, lips pursed in an argumentative expression. "He a good boy. Always helped me."

"I know." I thought of his rooftop lair. "He's very self-sufficient."

She leaned forward then, intent on speaking. "I was never able to do nothin' for 'im. See, I been on drugs all his life. Whenever I got money I didn't do nothin fo' him, spen' it on crack. Now I never will be able to do nothin fo' 'im. I'm sick." She spat the words out. "I got the HIV." She sniffed. "You see 'im, tell my sweet boy his mama loves 'im."

Exhausted by the exertion, she slumped back in the chair with a sigh, head lolling.

"Did you ever give him a Star Trek toy, a model of the U.S.S. *Enterprise*?" I asked. I sensed an impatient movement from Rakestraw behind me.

She frowned. Her eyes lifted, though she never raised her head, giving her an odd wolflike expression. "Never bought 'im no toys." She brought up a scrawny hand and rubbed at her forehead, as though massaging a memory. Her cracked lips curled on one side. "You mean that spaceship thing?"

She nodded gingerly, a half smile on her face. "Came one Christmas. He musta been eight or nine. All wrapped up. With a food basket, Toys for Tots or some shit like that."

"He still has it," I told her, not knowing why I felt it important for her to know, "or did until just recently." Presently it sat in a box behind my sofa. She didn't seem to hear.

"She hasn't seen him. Probably wouldn't recognize him if she did," muttered Rakestraw. He had picked her up outside the same crack house where she was last busted. She belonged in a hospital but declined medical attention, so he was about to take her back where he had found her. We both urged her to have Howie turn himself in or call us if she saw him.

As she got slowly to her feet, an emergency signal, a 330, a shooting, went out on the radio. At 47th Street and Seventeenth Avenue. Rakestraw and I exchanged glances. I asked aloud what we both wondered. "Think it's them?"

We listened to the rapid-fire transmissions. "Doesn't sound like it," he said. "It's at the cemetery."

More than one victim, at least two down, at Our Lady of Victory Cemetery.

"Inside the gates?" I asked.

"Sounds like it."

We have had mourners robbed at the graves of departed loved ones, a rape or two, thieves who steal the bronze flower vases from gravesites—and the usual problems during full moon rituals—but I couldn't recall any recent shootings breaking out among the dead.

"Sounds like a smoker," he said, referring to a scene so fresh that gunsmoke still hung in the air.

I headed for my car. The cemetery was ten minutes away. By the time the ornate wrought-iron gates loomed ahead, a half dozen emergency vehicles were inside, lights flashing. No one had roped it off yet, so I followed.

Our Lady of Victory is my kind of cemetery, an old-fashioned burial ground studded with tombstones, crosses, marble angels, madonnas, and mausoleums—as opposed to one of those sterile park-like places with metal plaques set flat in the ground. I favor places like the old Key West cemetery, where one tombstone bears the message *I told you I was sick.* Another is engraved with a message from a widow: *I know where he is sleeping now.*

Whatever happened here had gone down in the interior of the grounds, along a crunchy gravel drive. I parked as close as I could without blocking emergency vehicles and grabbed my notebook.

Paramedics worked feverishly over one victim. Another lay dead among the tombstones, already covered by a yellow plastic sheet. A playful breeze lifted one corner, exposing a foot wearing a basketball shoe. At least a dozen blood-spattered white roses were scattered nearby, along with a gun lying in the grass.

The deceased would be removed from the cemetery and taken to the morgue. The natural order of events had been thrown into reverse. It would make more sense to merely roll him into an open grave. But murder is seldom efficient or sensible.

I quickly pushed open my door, before somebody official could order me to move the car. Then my stomach did a free fall.

A slender woman in blue stood under an oak tree talking intently to two cops.

Trish. What the hell was she doing here? On my beat, my story. How the hell did she hear about it and get here so fast?

I scrambled out of the car and stalked over to them.

One cop had his hand on her shoulder.

"Trish!" I exploded. "What are—"

"Oh, Britt!" She threw herself into my arms for a hug. "It was terrible. They killed each other!"

I stood frozen, then pulled away and stared at the bloodied green carpet of manicured grass. That was when I saw the small gravestone among the scattered flowers. A new one. MAGDALY ROSADO, 1954–1994.

"It's them!" Trish blurted, eyes red-rimmed. For the first time I saw the blood on her pale linen skirt.

"Trish." I nearly recoiled. "What happened?"

"The desk knows," she said breathlessly. "I called the paper right after I called Nine-one-one. Photo is on the way." Her gray eyes were huge. "It's them," she repeated. "Miguel Rosado—and Ernesto." She gestured toward the covered corpse. "I couldn't stop them. They both had guns. I'm lucky to be alive. I was nearly caught in the cross-fire trying to stop them. If I hadn't stumbled, I'd be dead." She winced, placing small polished fingertips over both ears. "They're still ringing. He was standing right next to me when he emptied the gun at Ernesto."

I still couldn't comprehend. "What were you doing here, Trish?"

"You know I'm working on a story about Reach Out's mishandling of the Rosado suicide."

I nodded, gazing at the wounded man. Two IVs dripped fluids into his body, an oxygen mask covered his face, and a medic was pressing sterile gauze over a bloody wound in his abdomen.

"I was doing a sidebar on her death's impact on the family," Trish continued. "There's been bad blood, a bitter feud, between them, so I was interviewing them separately. I arranged to meet Ernesto here today when he brought flowers to his mother's grave. Miguel suddenly showed up. They began shouting at each other and they both pulled guns. I couldn't believe it . . . I tried to stop them. I got it on tape."

She held up a miniature recorder.

"The police are taking it, but they promised to copy it for us."

Miguel was being readied for the rescue van, apparently too close to death to wait for an ambulance.

"I can't believe he's still alive," she said, her voice a husky whisper. "He was hit at least four times. I tried to stop them."

"Jesus Christ," I said. "What does the desk want us to do?"

"I'm writing a first-person account. I think I've got everything. Then I have to go down to police headquarters to give a statement." She gazed into my eyes. "What a story," she said solemnly. "What a tragedy."

Villanueva had arrived and was already shooting, using a Nikon with a 300-millimeter lens. Trish stepped over the bloodied roses and stood near the body. He worked quickly, closer than usual, firing off at least a dozen frames before the cops asked Trish to step away. They were more relaxed than if the killing had been a whodunit. The cops had both shooters—one, maybe both, dead—and an eyewitness. As the medics lifted Miguel into the rescue van, Trish motioned to the photographer, then reached out to steady the IV bottle. He caught it. So did a TV news crew that had just arrived.

Back at the office, I sort of hung around on the edge of the chaos. No one needed my help on the story. Trish had it all.

Chapter Fourteen

The tape ran everywhere, over and over and over, on radio and TV news shows, coupled with the police 911 tape of Trish's call for help.

Transcribed and published in black and white, the shooting tape didn't read like much, but listening to the gunfire and the screams was electrifying.

Trish had inadvertently pushed the record button in the excitement seconds before the shooting. Incomprehensible shouts and curses from the two men. Muffled sounds as though someone was running or had dropped the recorder. Then *pop-pop-pop,* the unmistakable rattle of gunfire. A shrill scream that had to be Trish.

"No! No!" from Trish.

"You killed me!" an anguished cry from one of the men.

More gunfire. Seven more shots. Groans, moaning.

"Oh, my God!" from Trish. "Somebody call the police!"

Gasps, fumbling sounds, then nothing, as Trish apparently turned off the recorder as she ran for help. She had a cell phone in her car.

"Nine-one-one operator."

"This is Trish Tierney. I'm a reporter for the *Miami Daily News.* I need help. Police and an ambulance, right away." Slightly out of breath, she spoke coolly and distinctly, the way parents and school officials teach bright children to do should they ever have to make an emergency call. I have always suspected that staying cool tends to encourage the cops to take it lightly. I have always been in favor of screaming your brains out. That way they know you mean business.

"What is your emergency?"

"A shooting. Two men were just shot, a number of times. I think they're both dead."

"What is your location?"

"Our Lady of Victory Cemetery. Pretty much in the center, near a grave. You'll see the cars."

"Do you have the street address?"

"It's about Forty-seventh Street and Seventeenth Avenue. But it's inside the graveyard."

"Is the person with the gun still there?"

"No. Yes! They both had guns. They're both shot. I almost got shot myself. Would you please get somebody out here?" A hint of impatience.

"We have units on the way. Where are the weapons?"

"Where are the . . . on the ground where they dropped them."

"Are the victims conscious?"

"I think I hear a siren now; tell them to pull straight into the cemetery and I'll watch for them. Thank you."

As chaotic and terrifying as the first tape was, the second was controlled, a call from a woman with inner strength and common sense who didn't panic in a crisis.

Even the rival paper ran a headline: GUTSY REPORTER CAPTURES MURDER ON TAPE.

The networks and CNN picked up the story and played the tapes. The implication was that the failure of Reach Out to save Magdaly Rosado had now very nearly succeeded in killing all three members of the family—as well as the courageous reporter who had tried to rescue them.

Miguel, rushed into surgery, hung on, in intensive care at press time.

The story was big. Bigger than I realized.

My phone rang at six-thirty next morning. It was Lottie.

"Britt, guess where Trish is?"

Oh, Lord, I thought. What now?

"Frankly, Lottie, I don't give a damn."

"Britt! The poor thang nearly got killed."

I sighed. "Okay. Where is she? Sharing an egg McMuffin with Elvis at McDonald's? Swapping secrets with Deep Throat? Reuniting the Beatles? Or has she found Amelia Earhart?"

"Britt, you're jealous!"

"I am not!"

"Ain't you the one who was always saying there's enough stories for everybody?"

"I changed my mind."

"I figured. Put your TV on. Trish is gonna be on the *Today* show."

"What?"

"They flew her up to New York last night."

"You're kidding! For what?"

"The cemetery shooting. It's only the biggest damn story in the country."

"Because the damn public gets off on listening to somebody die? Doesn't the whole thing strike you as weird, Lottie?"

"Weird?"

"How she just happened to be there with her handy-dandy tape recorder when those two guys blew each other away?"

"No," she yelped. "She was doing an interview. She had her recorder. Nothing unusual about that. Remember how we just happened to be there when Jennifer Carey and her little tyke got hit? She's got a gift for being where the action is. A natural-born reporter. Shit happens. Everybody's gotta be someplace."

I sighed. "I don't know what I mean. It's just—"

"You been into your medicine cabinet this morning?" she demanded. "Whatever you took, take the antidote. Get a grip. You're just pissed 'cause it's not you."

"Goddammit, Lottie!"

"Watch *Today*. I'm gonna tape it. Talk to you later."

Still in the jogging clothes I had planned to wear to the boardwalk, I sat on the floor in front of the TV. I decided to work off some steam and use the time efficiently by doing sit-ups. I had done thirty-five and felt red in the face by the time she was introduced.

"A unique tragedy took place in South Florida yesterday, and a brave reporter from the *Miami Daily News* was there. We have with us this morning Trish Tierney. Good morning, Trish."

Trish said good morning, looking confident and beautiful in TV makeup and a bright blue jacket I had never seen her wear before.

"You had to be terrified when bullets started flying in that Miami cemetery yesterday."

"Oh, I was never afraid—until later, when I had time to think about it.'' She nodded, smiling bravely. ''When it was happening, all I could think about was trying to stop them from hurting each other any more than they already had.'' Her expression softened. ''They'd both been through a great deal of anguish after the suicide of their wife and mother.

''When the husband pulled his gun—and then I saw that the son had one too—I was focused on trying to keep them from firing. Once a bullet leaves the muzzle of a gun, it's too late. Nobody can call it back.''

Great line, Trish, I thought. I sat there on the floor mesmerized, sit-ups forgotten, Bitsy on my lap, my coffee cooling in a cup on the end table next to the sofa.

The audio tape and the 911 call were played, of course, as well as scene footage shot by a news team from the network's Miami affiliate. In a sound bite, the homicide detective said that the tragedy could have been prevented.

Trish briefly shared a split screen with a psychiatrist, a specialist in grief counseling, and the founder of a national suicide hot line. The Miami Reach Out counselor had declined comment.

A few politicians eagerly got into the act, huffing and puffing, proposing county or state training and the testing and licensing of all employees and volunteers at suicide and drug hot lines, to ''ensure the prevention of future tragedies.''

As if the state doesn't have enough to do, I thought, when it can't even keep track of all the dependent, abused, and abandoned children in its charge.

The report was pretty well rounded. They even tossed in the easy availability of handguns as a contributing factor. True, I thought, they might simply have beaten the snot out of each other if neither had had access to a firearm.

In the few seconds that remained, the anchor asked Trish about the current state of crime in Miami, ''a city where the vice mayor has been arrested on corruption charges.'' I half expected her to stumble on that question out of left field but she did well, relating the status of the Linwood case and glibly quoting the latest FBI and Miami crime statistics. You had to hand it to her. She was good.

''That was Trish Tierney, top crime reporter for the *Miami Daily News*. Thank you, Trish, for being with us. I guess for you it's back to the hot streets of Miami.''

Top crime reporter? Shit. I stared at the commercial that followed. The woman was not a crime reporter. I covered the damn police beat. The mistake was natural, I realized. She had covered a death by suicide, the vice mayor's arrest, then a shootout. If she was not the paper's top crime reporter, she was doing a pretty damn good imitation.

For the first time I began to worry about my job. If I didn't dig in and start producing, she *would* be the crime reporter if she wanted the job. And I had no doubt that that was what she wanted.

Janowitz gloated. "How does it feel to be upstaged on national TV?"

Even my mother called. "Do you know that reporter who was on the *Today* show, dear? She was wonderful."

"I know her."

"Do you think she met Katie Couric?"

"I'm sure she did."

"Did she buy that jacket in Miami? Is it a Criscione?"

"I'll be sure to ask her." I sat with my palm over my right eye to quell the twitching in the lid.

"Would you like to come to the cocktail party for the opening of the new show at the Planetarium Friday?"

"I feel like I've just been to the Planetarium."

"What does that mean?"

"I'm under a lot of stress on the job right now, Mom. Don't count on me for anything, but I will try."

I dialed Chicago. Marty answered.

"Am I a jealous bitch?"

"I didn't know you cared."

"Seriously, Marty. You've known me since we were kids in college. Is it me? Am I all unstrung just because she's better than I am?"

"I've never known you to be anything but generous and supportive to other reporters, though you may have changed a lot since we last spent time together."

"Thanks much, Marty. This is serious."

"Yeah." I could picture him massaging the back of his neck the way he always did when thinking. "Your instincts are always on the mark. I'd say follow your gut."

"Thanks. I needed that—and a couple of *Atta girl*s."

He chuckled. Back in Chicago he had always been lavish with his *Atta girl*s when I needed a boost.

"People like her burn out fast, Britt. You built your beat out of nothing. You want to keep that job, fight for it. Nobody is tougher than you out there in the trenches."

"Nobody knows the streets of this city better than I do," I agreed.

"Atta girl."

I felt a little better, despite a slightly sore throat and a runny nose. This was no time to get sick. I stopped at Epicure on the way home. Their chicken soup will cure anything. Had I mentioned it to Mrs. Goldstein she would have whipped up a batch, but I was in no mood for company.

Epicure Market is one of the seven wonders of Miami Beach. Visiting rock stars send out for the whopping shrimp and juicy steaks. A gourmet menu hot line operates twenty-four hours a day, tempting callers with loving descriptions of delicacies such as piña colada chicken, black bean and papaya salad, and shrimp tempura.

Chocolate mousse cakes, miniature eclairs, and cranberry scones are baked on the premises. In the produce department there are Fuji apples, Yukon gold potatoes from Alaska, and mushrooms gigantic enough to be mutant strains.

I wish I could afford to shop there. With my luck, by the time I can, my metabolism will have slowed down so much I won't be able to enjoy it.

But when I'm ailing, I do indulge in Epicure's soup.

As I pushed my little shopping cart past the bakery counter something caught my eye. A mouthwatering loaf of crispy golden crusted bread, sliced open to display its delectable center. The small sign read *Filled with Parmesan cheese, green peppers, and onion*. I stared numbly, nose running, feeling feverish. Where had I seen that before?

I began to laugh. Dinner with Trish. Her cherished old family recipe.

The aproned woman behind the counter regarded me sternly as I blew my nose, still snickering into my tissue. "You have to take a number," she instructed.

"Never mind," I said lightly, wheeling my cart off to the deli section. I spotted them right away. Perfectly poached Bosc pears, buttery and elegant on pink paper doilies, not far from the wonderful chickens and little roasted potatoes.

I shook my head, grinning all the way into the parking lot. How many other lies had Trish told? I wondered.

I thought about it as I sipped my soup, washed it down with a cup of brandy-laced hot tea, and went to bed early.

Feeling much better in the morning, I began to make calls.

Miguel Rosado's condition had been upgraded from critical to fair. That was the good news. The bad was that he was charged with first-degree murder. He might even recover enough to serve life in prison—or take a seat in the electric chair, though the latter was unlikely in a case where his victim was a relative who was shooting back at the time.

I asked Patton, the homicide detective on the case, how Miguel was doing. "Fine," he said, "except now he has a new place to go to the bathroom from."

I winced, deciding not to ask specifics of the surgery. "Think I could talk to him?"

"Have to ask his lawyer. They're probably not thrilled that one of your reporters taped him wasting his stepson."

"Every story has two sides," I said.

A uniformed security guard guarded the prison ward. Smiling, I nodded and breezed on by. My photo ID was dangling from my belt. I was wearing my beeper and carried my portable police scanner. The problem would be the cop stationed outside the door. But he was halfway down the hall, hobnobbing with the nurses.

Miguel's ankle was shackled to his hospital bed. He did not appear capable of running even if it hadn't been. His skin was an unearthly shade of gray in contrast to the bleached white of his skimpy hospital gown and rumpled sheets. Tubes ran everywhere: draining fluids out, pumping fluids in, attaching him to hissing, whirring machines. His lips looked dry and parched. I held the water glass as he sucked weakly through a plastic straw.

"Miss Tierney? She's not coming?"

"She's out of town at the moment."

He nodded. "Ernesto is dead," he whispered.

"Yes, you did a good job on him," I said.

"He would have killed me."

"Are you saying it was self-defense?"

"You know he planned to kill me."

"How would I know that?"

"Miss Tierney. Trish. She knew. She warned me, told me he bought the gun, that he planned to kill me. Because of his mother. She said he blamed me. But I loved her."

"She told you he bought a gun?"

He swallowed, then coughed weakly. I brought the glass up and positioned the straw between his lips. After several swallows I took it away and picked up my pen again.

"That," he said, voice raspy, "was why I bought a gun too. To protect myself. She said he was looking for me."

"Why did you go to the cemetery, knowing he'd be there?"

He looked bewildered, squinting up at me as though the overhead light was too bright for his eyes. "He wasn't supposed to be there. She called me at work to warn me. She was in danger and so was I. He was crazy, threatening both of us, she said. A powder keg ready to explode. Those were her words. She said she told the police, but they wouldn't help us. She asked me to meet her at the cemetery. She was scared and wanted me to bring a gun. We were both in danger."

I held my breath, heart pounding in my ears. "What happened when you got there?"

"He was there, kneeling, with some flowers. I didn't see him until I got out of my car. She looked frightened. She yelled, 'Oh, no! He's got a gun!' and then hit the ground behind the big tree. I didn't see her again. I pulled out my gun. So did he. We were yelling at each other. He started shooting." He closed his eyes and gasped for breath. "So did I."

"Who do you think she called out to warn?"

"I thought it was me, at first."

"What do you think now?"

"It all happened so fast, too fast to stop. But now, I keep seeing his eyes, the way they looked. He was scared. He was scared of me. I think she had called him and told him the same things she told me."

"You mean that she warned him about you? That you were both set up?"

He nodded. The question burned in his eyes. "Why?" he asked me. "Why?"

"I'm not sure."

"Hey! Britt Montero! Who gave you permission? What the hell you doing in here?" The cop had returned. His face was red.

"I was just leaving."

"Damn right, you're leaving." He turned on the security guard. "You dumb son of a bitch! How the hell did she get in here?"

"She walked right in to talk to your prisoner." The guard shrugged. "I figured she was authorized. You're supposed to be watching him."

I sat in Fred Douglas's office and told him about my visit with Miguel.

"What are you saying, Britt?"

"That there's a possibility that Trish manipulated those men into violence. Victims, anguished survivors, the grieving, the bereaved, they're vulnerable and easy to set off. I suspect it was no accident that they both showed up at the cemetery with guns, ready to use them."

"That would be an incredibly dangerous and foolhardy stunt to pull." He shook his head, incredulous, disbelieving. "She could have been killed herself—almost was."

"Miguel says she dove for cover the moment he arrived."

He turned his back to me and faced the window, gazing off into the distance. After a long moment, he returned and sat at his desk, face stern.

"Have you mentioned this to anyone else?"

"No. I thought I should talk to you first."

"Good, because I don't want this bandied about. I've seen cases of newsroom rivalry and petty jealousy before, Britt, but this"—he shook his head again—"this is totally out of hand." He shook a warning finger at me. "I don't want you starting rumors or suggesting something this preposterous to anyone."

"I didn't. Miguel himself is saying this."

"Of course, what else is he going to say?" His voice was hard. "He's certainly not going to stand up in court and say that he stalked his stepson to the cemetery and pulled a gun, intending to murder him in cold blood along with anybody else who stood in his way. Nonsense. He and his attorney are going to concoct a defense, an excuse for his crime, and the way to do that is to blame someone else. It's always somebody else's fault."

I opened my mouth, and he held up his hand to stay my protest.

"That family was on record, in police reports, long before either Trish Tierney or you knew they existed. Those two men bought guns intending to use them, and they did. I will not have the integrity of one of my reporters and this newspaper impugned, especially from within."

I nodded, swallowed the lump in my throat, and walked back out into the newsroom.

I called Marty in Chicago and left a message on his machine. "I need your help," I said. "Call me."

I was fighting for both job and reputation now. The only way to win is to know the enemy.

Scattered applause rippled across the newsroom. It had actually come from jaded newshounds, acknowledging Trish's buoyant entrance. She blushed modestly and settled in at her desk. The woman had become a media heroine. There was talk of a book contract, and according to the newsroom grapevine she had met with a New York literary agent. Gretchen trotted back to Trish's desk, and I saw them laughing and chatting.

Marty returned my call and I filled him in, speaking softly so no one would hear. Mercifully, Ryan had wandered back to where half a dozen people ringed Trish's desk, probably gossiping about the celebrities she had met in the greenroom.

"Sounds like you're hip deep in shit," Marty said.

"I've stepped in it this time," I acknowledged. "I need all the help I can get. What else do you remember about her? How the hell did she get this way? Did she pull the wings off flies as a child? What did she do then, step on 'em? What can you tell me?"

"Actually, no more than what I mentioned at dinner. Let me think about it, make a couple of calls, and see what I can find out."

"Bless you, Marty."

I escaped the office then and headed over to Miami Beach police headquarters to check out some missing persons cases for a project I had in mind.

Fluffy mountains of clouds drifted lazily across a bright and beautiful sky. There is a fall and a winter in South Florida. The light becomes less harsh, more subtle, the greens less vivid. The sky is softer, the sunsets earlier, the dawns more misty. The temperature was a comfortable 72 as I drove across the causeway, windows down, enjoying the strong, frolicking breeze that stirred up whitecaps on the bright blue bay.

The high-pitched emergency tone on my police scanner jolted me back to reality. That shrill sound signals pain, open wounds, and broken hearts, alerting the street fighters assigned to hold back the tide of crime, death, and disorder. So often it comes too late.

This was the one everybody dreads. "Three-fifteen. Shots fired. Officer down, at Northwest Second Avenue and Twenty-fifth Street."

My fingers spasmed around the steering wheel. Shit, a cop shot. I wheeled into a U-turn, hit the gas, and pushed a button to lock in the frequency on my dashboard scanner. Reports came fast and furious, a cool voice, controlled hysteria.

"A second victim."

"Rescue dispatched on a three."

"At least four subjects fleeing west in two vehicles."

"The officer involved is city, off duty."

My mind's eye saw the complaint-room personnel clustering around the dispatcher listening. A van loaded with sightseeing tourists ambled along in front of me at a maddening twenty-five miles an hour. I swerved around it, passing on the wrong side. No policeman would stop me on traffic charges. Every cop in town was either on the way or glued to a radio, waiting to hear every bit and piece of information: the condition of the officer, the description of the suspects, and which way they had headed.

"Two subject vehicles fleeing west in a blue van and a white Ford Taurus taken from the civilian victim."

"Subjects armed with an automatic weapon. Appeared to be a nine-millimeter Beretta, fifteen-shot. Use caution. A second subject is armed with a short-barreled shotgun. The officer's service revolver is also believed taken."

"Where's rescue?" shouted the young voice of an officer, possibly first at the scene. His anguish and panic chilled my bones. This was no false alarm. Communications from officers arriving were fragmented and stress-filled. They never sound rattled or emotional on the air—unless a cop is shot. I wondered if it was someone I knew. I thought of Kendall McDonald.

"The officer involved was off duty in his personal vehicle."

Somebody breathing hard, trying to piece chaos together, reported: "Apparently he had left the station and came upon a carjacking in progress.

"Subject number one is described as a white Latin male, approximately seventeen to eighteen years of age, black hair shaved straight across around the ears with a ducktail at the bottom, approximately five feet four inches, one hundred twenty-five pounds, wearing baggy black jeans low on his hips, boxer shorts showing underneath, an oversize plaid shirt, high-top sneakers, and a Raiders cap. He is armed with an automatic handgun.''

Away from the mike, you could hear his rapid questions to witnesses providing the descriptions he fed into the radio.

''Reference the officer shot: subject number one is the shooter. He is driving a vehicle described as a late-model white Ford Taurus, partial Florida tag E echo, D delta, last seen proceeding west on Northwest Two-six Street from Second Avenue. This vehicle was taken from the civilian victim who—uh—looks to be a Forty-five at this point.''

Forty-five means dead. I tried to scribble notes with my right hand, the left on the wheel as 11th, 12th, 13th streets flashed by.

''Subject number two is described as a white male, late teens, possibly Latin, five feet nine inches, a hundred and fifty pounds, black baseball cap, oversize dark pants, black T-shirt with large white letters, DON'T ASK ME FOR SHIT, black high-top sneakers. This subject is armed with what appeared to be a sawed-off pump shotgun with a homemade pistol grip. Driving a blue Dodge van, last seen westbound on Northwest Two-seven Street from Second Avenue.''

''Subject number three: black male, five feet ten inches, skinny, approximately one forty pounds, jeans, wearing a dark T-shirt with some sort of design or logo on the front. He is the right front passenger in the blue van driven by the subject armed with the shotgun.''

''Subject number four, a black Latin male, five seven, one-eighty pounds. Dark pants and black Malcolm X shirt. . . .''

Suddenly gripped by a growing dread, I knew who they probably were. ''Howie, don't be with them,'' I breathed, my eyes searching side streets as much for them as for oncoming traffic.

''I think I have an ID on the subjects.''

It was Rakestraw's voice on the radio.

''The shooter is believed to be the same subject involved in numerous carjackings, ram-and-robs, and smash-and-grabs. He is armed and considered extremely dangerous. The subject is Gilberto Sanchez, d.o.b. October fourteen, 1976. Last known address, Twenty-four seventy-five Northwest Twenty-seventh Avenue. Current wants on felony murder, numerous charges of aggravated assault, armed robbery, burglary, and sexual assault.''

I didn't even know about that last one.

The scene was alive with sirens, medics, cops, and a growing number of bystanders.

As I pulled up a policeman ran toward my car, screaming at me to move it. I did. At times like this, you don't argue with the cops. I parked a short block away and trotted back on foot.

The officer lay sprawled on his back next to a red Mustang standing with the driver's door open in a traffic lane. Arms flung out at his sides, he wasn't moving, but he was the center of furious activity by medics.

His skin looked dusky. A paramedic frantically squeezed a vinyl bag, forcing fluid to flow faster through an IV into his body. An endotracheal tube had been inserted down his throat to push oxygen into his lungs.

Across the intersection a man lay in a gigantic sea of blood that had gushed into the gutter and down the street for half a block.

The scene looked like a battlefield, on a beautiful sunlit Miami morning.

Lieutenant Kendall McDonald was already there, conferring with other arriving brass. I saw Rakestraw too. I knew what he was thinking.

"Can you tell me anything, McDonald?"

He stepped briefly away from the others. "We don't know much yet."

"What happened?"

"The officer is a rookie, worked the midnight shift, got off this morning, and was running a few errands on his way home. Drove up on one in progress. The victim was struggling with the carjacker. Apparently he tried to intervene and they shot him."

"Where is he hit?"

"In the chest."

"Was he wearing his vest?"

McDonald shook his head.

"It was lying on the front seat, next to him. He was still wearing his uniform pants and a T-shirt."

I read the irony in his eyes. After a midnight tour of duty in this violent city, a cop takes off his bulletproof vest to drive home on a beautiful day and meets a kid with a gun.

"Who is he?"

"The officer's identity can't be released until his family is notified." He dropped his voice. "It's McCoy, first name Dana. A rookie. Don't print it until we give you the go-ahead."

"Right. Wasn't he the hero in that fire a couple of months ago?"

"That's him."

I nodded. "We have his picture." I remembered the youthful grin. On routine patrol, McCoy had spotted a predawn fire, rescued the occupants of a second-floor apartment, then saved the owner of a ground-floor store who had dashed inside for his business records.

"Married? Children?"

"Don't think so. Better check with PIO, they'll pull his jacket."

"Age?"

"Twenty-three. Top man in his academy class last year."

"Who called it in?"

"He had his radio and hit the emergency button. Said he'd been hit and gave the address, but it was garbled, sounded like Forty-fifth instead of Twenty-fifth. The dispatcher couldn't raise him again. A couple minutes later a civilian called it in."

"What happened to the other victim? Where was he hit?"

"The leg. We think it's the subject who's been kneecapping drivers and taking their cars."

"A fatal leg wound?"

"Hit the major artery in his thigh, the femoral artery. He was struggling; then he ran, bled to death in a couple of minutes. By the time anybody got here, it was too late."

"Any suspects in custody?"

"No. But we will." His voice had the bitter ring of certainty.

McDonald radioed orders to clear intersections in the path of the rescue van carrying the wounded officer to the trauma center, and I started looking for witnesses.

"It was pretty wild when the shooting started," said a young shoe salesman, who had been on his way to work. "It sounded pretty much like the shootings on TV, but a lot louder."

As the wounded motorist struggled for possession of his Taurus, the officer had ordered FMJ, if he was indeed the shooter, to drop his weapon. McCoy had apparently held his fire because of innocent bystanders. When FMJ started shooting at the officer, the bleeding motorist ran and passersby scattered. The officer did manage to squeeze off a couple of rounds before being hit.

When he went down, another suspect ran to snatch up the cop's gun. Then both cars took off.

"I saw the guns and told everybody to take cover," said a grandmotherly school crossing guard with a curly perm. "There were people waiting for a bus, people walking down the street, business people on the way to work.

"They just stood there and looked at me. I had to scream at them. I yelled and blew my whistle. Finally I had to run toward them—into the line of fire—to get them to move." Trembling, she seemed more shaken by the public's indifference than by her own close call.

She and other witnesses had heard McCoy shout, identifying himself as a police officer. FMJ knew he was shooting a cop.

Police were stringing yellow crime-scene tape, forcing me and other reporters back down the street in the general direction of my car. "You know who it was," muttered Rakestraw, after shepherding several witnesses to a car to take to the station. "And who was with 'em."

"You think it was Howie." I hated saying it out loud.

"Without a doubt."

"No way to be sure."

"It's over for him now. Any dream he had of cutting a deal is down the toilet. Nobody's gonna give him a break."

"He was coerced into running from the Crossing. They threatened Miss Mayberry. If he was with them today, a big if, he was coerced. We don't even know—"

"We'll know pretty quick. Once we start showing mug shots to the witnesses." He walked away.

I called the office. Gretchen wanted to know if I needed help, if she should assign someone. I told her no, I could handle it. Then I went to the hospital, arriving in time to speak to the doctor. He was brief.

"The bullet struck his heart. When fellow officers and paramedics arrived he was beyond all help, but they tried. At the trauma center we immediately opened his chest and tried to clamp the aorta, but when we did, we found that the bullet had demolished the coronary artery and left a large hole in the myocardium. Every time his heart beat, blood pumped into his chest. It was very apparent there was nothing that could be done."

If Howie *was* there, I thought numbly, his life is finished too.

Chapter Fifteen

McCoy was a rookie, a youthful hero who had not lived long enough to make mistakes, to burn out, to become jaded or calloused or bitter. He had never let anybody down. Maybe he never would have. The promise was gone. Emotions ran high. When a cop gets shot, they all take it personally. More than a hundred officers from other departments joined the manhunt. Wearing strips of black mourning tape across their badges, they searched buildings and fields with helicopters and dogs, stopping scores of suspects. All-points bulletins were issued for FMJ, positively identified by eyewitnesses as the killer.

"He's in a frenzy, like a shark," Rakestraw said, as I took notes, for attribution. "We need to get him off the street. Right now. He's extremely dangerous."

Not for attribution was his answer to my question about the sexual-assault charges.

"His sister."

"The pregnant one? Is he the . . ."

He nodded.

Was there any crime FMJ had not committed? Police set up a tip line urging the public to call. Rewards were offered. There were rumors that FMJ had been seen in Ocala, on I-95 headed for Georgia, at the downtown Greyhound bus station, and at the Port of Miami, and one sighting reported him at the airport wearing a suit and carrying a briefcase.

Witnesses were pretty sure that J-Boy was the one with the shotgun.

They were not so definite about Howie, but Rakestraw was convinced. Bulletins were issued for both, "wanted for questioning."

FMJ's mother publicly urged his surrender. Her listless performance on TV didn't reflect much hope that he would heed her words. Why would he start now?

I prayed Howie would call. He must be so scared, I thought. If the cops found him first he could be killed, especially if he was still with the others, known to be heavily armed. I focused, concentrated, willing him not to stay with them. I went by Miss Mayberry's house twice. Once Rakestraw's car was outside; another time a patrol unit was parked in front. I didn't intrude. Besides, I didn't look forward to explaining to that good woman how our high hopes had gone so wrong.

Edgy days went by with no news. The perimeters of the manhunt spread, all the way up the eastern seaboard to Union City, New Jersey. My gut feeling was that they were still in Dade County. They were Miami street kids; they knew no other place. This was their turf. FMJ's business must be shot to hell, I thought. No chop shop would deal with him now.

Several times that week Trish offered to help in the continuing coverage, but I politely declined. This was one story she wasn't going to muscle in on.

Gradually, with no new developments, the coverage began to wind down. I took a day of comp time, preferred by the newspaper's bean counters in lieu of overtime, then came in late the following day.

"You had a visitor," said Gloria, the city desk clerk. "She was here several times yesterday and again this morning." She shrugged. "Nobody told me you were taking comp time and I thought you'd be in."

"I left a note. Who was it?"

"An old lady." She riffled impatiently through the pink message slips on her desk.

"Did she say what she wanted?"

"No," Gloria frowned. "I can't find it. Trish must know. She was talking to her, about an hour ago." We both scanned the newsroom for Trish. She wasn't there.

"What did she look like?"

"You know the woman, what the heck is her name?" She shook the pencil in her hand as if the motion would stimulate her memory. "You know, lives over there in that little house by the Edgewater."

"Miss Mayberry?" Chills rippled along my spinal column.

"That's her, yeah. The one who wouldn't sell out." She picked up a flashing line.

"What was Trish doing with her?"

She shrugged, then put her hand over the mouthpiece. "She felt sorry for the old lady, who kept asking for you, and offered to help if there was anything she could do." Gloria returned to her phone conversation.

I literally ran to the elevator. I'd been a fool for not staying in closer contact with Margaret Mayberry. What had Howie said? That we were his only friends. Then I had let him down. He had only one friend left in the world.

No police car outside now. The shades were all down.

Miss Mayberry took a long time to answer. "Your friend is already here." She spoke through the screen, new worry lines creasing her worn face. I nearly pushed my way through the door.

Howie and Trish sat facing each other across the wooden dining room table. Both looked startled. He still wore his Star Trek T-shirt, though it looked freshly laundered.

"Howie!" I felt weak with relief, then had the urge to shake him until his teeth rattled. "Where have you been?" I walked over and gave him an awkward hug. He felt tense in my arms, then hugged me back, hard. "I was so worried."

"Britt," he said, eyes filling.

I turned on Trish. "What the hell are you doing here?"

"I know what you're trying to accomplish, Britt. You want to help this boy, and so do I." Her voice was warm, her face sincere.

Miss Mayberry and Howie looked at her, then me, not sure what was happening.

"I'm scared," Howie told me. "That's why I been trying to reach you. I know the police'll shoot me on sight. Will you help me surrender?"

"It's the only way," Miss Mayberry said, her jaw firm.

I nodded, then turned to Trish. "We really don't need you involved. We can handle this."

"Britt," she said persuasively. "What you're doing is admirable.

Absolutely noble. You're trying to save this"—she smiled gently at Howie—"young man. I'm on your side. That's why I came."

"Butt out, Trish. Bad things happen to people you try to help. Forget you were ever here, go back to the office, and let us work this thing out."

She searched each face and saw no encouragement.

"If that's the way you want it, I'll go. But I'd still like to help."

"We're okay," I said.

She stood and walked to the door, no longer smiling. Little trouper that she was, she gave it one last shot. "You're making a mistake."

"She's trouble," I explained, after she had gone. "We have trouble enough."

I took the chair Trish had occupied, directly across from Howie. I leaned forward. "You *were* there."

He nodded silently. Miss Mayberry stood in a supportive position directly behind his chair, her hands on his shoulders.

"Who did the shooting?"

"FMJ," he mumbled. "He smoked the dude and the cop. I never had no gun." He looked startled. "You didn't think it was me!"

"No," I said reassuringly. "Never did. I just wanted to hear it from you. What were you doing with them?"

"They wanted me to help 'em get some cars. We was going to the shopping center to find a Taurus. Then one passed in traffic and FMJ say, 'Let's take that one.' I said, 'No, man. Let's find one parked. Plenty out there.' But he wanted that one. I said, 'Don' shoot the gun, man. I don' want any trouble.' He laughed. He don't listen. Then that cop showed up. Everybody flashing iron. I seen the bullets flying by. Didn't know whether to jump out and run or stay in the van. If I stay, I get shot. If I run, I get shot. Scared to do it, scared not to do it. I just froze. I wanted to get outa there."

"Where are they?"

"I don' know, man." He was wringing his hands. "I don' want to know. Last time I seen 'em was in Hialeah. I took off. I shoulda stayed at the Crossing. I wanted to be there, to go to school. But I hadda leave."

His eyes flicked up at Miss Mayberry, who appeared unaware of his reason for running.

"Now they gonna kill me." His eyes were pleading. "I know the cops are gonna kill me."

"No, they won't," I said. "I'm not sure how we should do this. Maybe we should have a lawyer surrender you. I could go out and call one, maybe a public defender, and ask him to meet us here."

"Or you could jus' take me in there like last time. They all know you. . . ."

"They wouldn't hurt him in front of a newspaper reporter," Miss Mayberry said.

"I'm just concerned about getting stopped on the way. They might not believe we were coming in." It didn't seem quite kosher after the gigantic manhunt to simply drive him to headquarters and stroll up to the desk sergeant. We probably wouldn't get that far. They all had his picture. Maybe it would be better to approach a traffic cop on the street and quietly ask him to take Howie in. Or . . .

"I know a cop we can trust."

Howie shot me a quick look, probably thinking of Rakestraw.

"Not him. A lieutenant in homicide. His name is McDonald. I'll call him and ask the safest way for us to do this."

"I don't have a phone," Margaret Mayberry reminded me.

"Where's the nearest pay phone?"

"Next door, on the second level of the parking garage."

"Okay," I said, fumbling in my purse for change. "I'll run over there. If he's not in, I'll call the public defender's office. In fact, the more I think about it, maybe I should call and talk to them first." I pushed back my chair.

"SEND OUT THE HOSTAGE. RELEASE MARGARET MAY-BERRY. SEND HER OUT NOW." The booming voice seemed to be all around us, like the voice of God in that Moses movie.

We stared at one another. "It's them!" Howie leaped to his feet.

I dashed to the window and peeked from behind the shade.

"Oh, shit!" I said. It was the goddamn police SWAT team. "Well, now we don't have to worry about how to go to them," I said, hoping I sounded confident. "They've come to us."

Miss Mayberry's hand was over her heart. I hoped she wouldn't have a stroke.

"Trish!" I said. "Goddamn, I'd like to slap the spit out of her. Nobody else knew Howie was here, right?"

"Nobody," Miss Mayberry said.

"SEND THE HOSTAGE OUT NOW!"

Good grief. "They must think you're being held hostage," I said.

"Humph. That's ridiculous." She snorted.

"Wish you had a phone," I said, "we could dial Nine-one-one and explain. In fact, if you had one, they would have called us by now, to negotiate."

"INSIDE, SEND OUT THE HOSTAGE. SEND OUT THE WOMAN NOW!"

I peeked out again. Cops in SWAT fatigues were all over the place. The street was barricaded and the entrance to the parking garage closed. Nothing but cops scurrying in crouched positions carrying M-16s, armed for bear.

Now I knew the same sinking feeling the James boys felt, and Butch and Sundance in Bolivia, and O.J. in his Bronco. Maybe I have no sense of adventure, but I didn't like it one bit.

The little reading lamp on Miss Mayberry's desk went out. So did the dining room light overhead.

She and Howie looked startled. The room was shadowy with no lights and the shades drawn.

"They cut off the electricity. They always do that. I'm not sure why."

"They gonna kill us all!" Howie said, terrified.

"This is ridiculous," Miss Mayberry snapped. "I'll take care of them." Her dander up, she marched to the front door, threw it open, and stepped out on the porch, ramrod straight, an imposing figure in her flowered housedress.

"You—" She got no further.

The wind was knocked out of her before she could utter another word. Two SWAT members rushed the porch, grabbed her from either side, and hustled her away, out of the line of fire.

There was no time to think. Glass shattered with a blinding flash and an earsplitting explosion. All I could think of was Hiroshima. I hit the pine floor, curling instinctively into a fetal position, hands over my eyes. I heard Howie screaming. Or maybe the screams were mine. My ears rang, I opened my eyes but couldn't see, and I smelled smoke.

My mind raced. It had to be a stun grenade, used to disorient barricaded bad guys. But another sound rapidly followed, a gunshot, from behind the house, then a thunderous barrage from all sides. Glass broke and bits of furniture and debris fell around us. Howie was right. They were trying to kill us!

Still blinded, as though by a thousand flashbulbs exploding in my face, I crawled, trying to inch my way in the general direction of the kitchen as china crashed and pictures flew off the walls. I felt the slick linoleum under my hands and knees, bumped into a cabinet, opened it, and scooted inside among the bottles of furniture polish and boxes of soap power. I pulled the door closed behind me. There was a metal pipe in the middle and I clung to it, eyes closed. I was cringing under the sink like a palmetto bug fleeing the exterminator.

Overhead, dishes and flowerpots crashed into the sink and to the floor around me. It seemed to go on forever.

Trish, I thought bitterly. Trish is responsible. Lord knows what she told them. The barrage suddenly stopped. The silence was deafening.

"Howie?" I muttered, and tentatively pushed the cabinet door open a few inches, afraid they'd begin firing again. I heard shouts outside. I thought I heard Miss Mayberry screaming.

I crawled out and sat whimpering on the kitchen floor. A broken ceramic figurine that looked like a duck lay shattered beside me.

I picked up the head and began to sob. I knew I had to go back into the other room. I was afraid of what I would find. They were shouting now, to come out. Those bastards, I thought. Those bastards.

My eyes burned and stung from the smoke. I crawled to the doorway. Amid the smoke and shadows, I saw Howie where he had fallen, his head and shoulders propped against the bullet-riddled couch. His arms were bent at the elbows and I saw his left hand jerk.

"Howie, Howie, Howie," I crooned, scrambling, half crawling, to his side. His Star Trek shirt was torn and bloodied. I couldn't tell how many times he'd been hit. His eyes had that lonely look I had seen the first time I visited his rooftop home. The mischievous glint was gone.

Dammit, I thought, weeping. It's not fair. He's been alone all his life.

He sure as hell was not going to die alone. "I'm here, sweet boy," I said. I gathered him into my arms and held him.

That was how they found us.

Chapter Sixteen

They pieced the scenario together quickly. When the stun grenade was hurled, a SWAT sergeant in cumbersome gear was clambering over the chain-link fence that separated the Edgewater property from the back of Miss Mayberry's. Startled by the flash and explosion, he lost his footing and squeezed the trigger of his nine-millimeter Glock. A single silver-tipped slug slammed into the ground. The edgy troops poised out front assumed somebody had shot at them and returned fire en masse.

It happens.

Miss Mayberry's long-dead pioneer father had saved my life by building his house of solid Dade County pine in which the resin was allowed to harden, making the wood impervious to fire, termites, and bullets. The only slugs that had invaded the interior of the house had smashed through windows and the screen door.

By the time they burst in Howie was dead in my arms and I was just—resting, too exhausted to lift my head.

Rescue checked me out. Only minor cuts and scratches. I had to give a statement at police headquarters.

"How could you?" raged the captain, a huge former motorman whose gut now obscured his belt buckle. McDonald, Rakestraw, the SWAT lieutenant, and two other detectives were there. "You know better!"

"I was doing my job," I retorted. "There were no weapons. He was a scared juvenile. He trusted you." I glared at Rakestraw. "He trusted us. He was mishandled the first time he tried to come in and work within the system. I didn't know where he was today until I got there myself. He wanted to surrender and we were trying to figure the safest way to do it when you . . . you killed him." I fought to keep my composure. My ears were still ringing, and I ached to get my hands on Trish.

"You seem to forget," the captain snarled. "A good police officer was killed."

"But not by him," I said.

"Did he say where they were?" He pushed his thick, beery face close to mine.

"Why don't you ask him?" I said bitterly.

"A lot of mistakes have been made on both sides," McDonald said gently. "But we're on the same side, Britt. You want them off the street as much as we do."

I bit my lip to keep it from trembling. I'd be damned if I'd let them see me cry. "Howie said he last saw them in Hialeah. He didn't say exactly when or the address. You didn't give him the chance."

The SWAT lieutenant grew red in the face but said nothing.

"Is Miss Mayberry all right?"

"She's fine," Rakestraw said. "She's giving her statement now."

"You sure messed up her house."

Before leaving I told them, "I know who called it in to you. Trish Tierney is directly responsible for Howie's death. And she nearly got me killed too."

They exchanged puzzled looks.

"It was her, wasn't it?"

"Who?" said the captain.

"Don't give me that," I said angrily. "I know what Trish did."

Back at the office I told my bosses what she had done, how she had tipped the police with the lie that Miss Mayberry was being held hostage and failed to mention my presence, obviously hoping to see me blown away along with Howie.

"Those are serious accusations, Britt." Fred Douglas and John Murphy, the managing editor, were clearly uncomfortable.

They summoned Trish, who waltzed in prim and proper, lying through her teeth as I glared. She appeared shocked at the suggestion. "I consider Britt a mentor. I would never, ever do such a thing." She had returned to the paper, she swore, and had spoken to no one about the Mayberry house.

"I knew Britt was inside," she concluded. "She asked me to keep a confidence and I respected her wishes."

Before leaving Murphy's office she stopped in front of the chair where I sat, put her arms around my shoulders, and gave a gentle squeeze. "I'm so sorry. You must be very upset. Poor Britt," she murmured. I wanted to scream and shake the truth out of her. Instead I remained rigid.

Speechless, I saw the look in their eyes. They believed her. Were they blind?

"Ask the police," I blurted, voice quaking. Probably more to pacify me than to seek the truth, Murphy put a call in to the chief. We waited in uncomfortable silence. The chief called back with an answer in less than ten minutes.

I scarcely breathed while they spoke briefly. Murphy thanked him profusely, apologizing for the trouble, and cradled the phone.

"You are mistaken, Britt. Trish was not responsible. I think we all owe her an apology."

"What do you mean? Incoming calls are taped; they must have her voice on tape."

He shook his head. "There is no tape. The call that led the SWAT team to the Mayberry place came into the complaint room from inside police headquarters."

"That's impossible."

"The chief has investigated. The number called was a line used only by police officers. The caller was a male, obviously a policeman, using police terminology."

"Who? What policeman?"

"They don't have a name. It's possible they won't. All the complaint-room clerk can recall is that the officer reported that the suspect in the McCoy murder had broken into the Mayberry house and was holding the owner hostage. He said SWAT should be mobilized; then he either hung up or was cut off.

"They acted on it, since the information came from within and a check with the lead investigator confirmed that the woman knew the suspects. It was just presumed that the caller himself was en route to the scene. A radio car went by, saw the shades drawn, which was unusual according to the investigator, and they mobilized."

"I don't believe it," I murmured, confused.

"This professional rivalry—this cat fight—has got to stop." Fred looked exasperated. "Britt, why don't you take some time off?"

"You may be right." I got to my feet, smiling sheepishly. "Maybe I misjudged, jumped to conclusions. I don't need time off. I just need to get back to work." I excused myself and stepped out into the newsroom.

Why argue? Without proof, I'd only succeed in convincing them that I was crazy or obsessed. Maybe I was.

As I passed her desk on the way back to mine, Trish looked up and smiled. I smiled back, my heart hollow.

I couldn't shake the feeling that my world was on a collision course with disaster.

"A reporter touches lives," I told Marty, as I fought tears. "It's not supposed to be fatal."

"You did the best you could for him, Britt. At least you cared. Nobody else did. We both know the system sucks, and you're not to blame for that."

"She manipulated it, Marty, the way she did the Rosado family."

"Speaking of Trish," he said, "I haven't been able to come up with much yet. The guy I know at her last paper is out of town on vacation. I'm still trying to reach him. Ran her job, credit, and college applications, and checked her hometown newspaper and cop shop for basic bio. Trish N., born November 23, 1968, oldest of two, dad a furniture manufacturer, mom dabbles in real estate until the kid brother is born, when Trish is about six. Baby brother is sick from day one, not expected to make it. Congenital heart defect, has surgery three times by the time he's four years old.

"He and the parents do a lot of traveling back and forth to a New York hospital, where he has two of the operations. Big sister is sort of shuffled around, sent away to school at about fourteen. Then on to a college dorm, good grades in J-school, lands her first job, and is off and running."

"What happened to her father?"

"Whatdya mean?"

"She grew up without a father, like me. At least that's what she said. I assumed he was dead, divorced, or a runaway."

"Nope, still very much alive. Married thirty years. Still operates his company. Church deacon, Kiwanis, Rotary, drives a Beemer, all that good stuff.''

"You're sure?" Was there *anything* she didn't lie about?

"As shooting. All alive, if not so well."

"The brother?"

"Mark, born June 3, 1974, still lives at home. Missed a lot of school because of his health. So far just has a semester in at the local junior college. Oh, yeah, one other item. Your girl got a plaque and a little write-up in the local fish wrapper when she was twelve. Could be what drew her to journalism as a career.''

"What was it for?"

"Lifesaver, good citizen, all that shit."

"What'd she do?"

"Neighbor kid disappears, midsummer, major search ensues, the whole town involved. Trish finds him trapped, curled up in a discarded refrigerator. Guess somebody forgot to remove the door as required by law. She pulls him out. Nobody's around and the kid's not breathing. She gives him mouth-to-mouth, which she recently learned in a Junior Red Cross class, and saves his life.''

"How old was the child?"

"Three."

"Unable to explain what happened, just like an advanced Alzheimer's patient.''

"Say again?"

"Marty." Fear and excitement collided in my voice. "She rescued an elderly neighbor, a woman curled up in a storage locker in the building where she lives. Gave her mouth-to-mouth. Around the time she came to work here. She was a hero. Told me she'd never done it before.''

"That first incident happened a long time ago, back in 'eighty.''

"You don't forget something like that." I knew Marty understood and was simply playing devil's advocate. "This could be a pattern. Doesn't it strike you as interesting that both victims were helpless, incapable of talking coherently about it after being resuscitated?'' I remembered Trish saying that Alzheimer's patients were like little children. In more ways than I had imagined at the time.

He gave a long low whistle and promised to get back to me with anything else he learned.

"Oh, yeah," I said. "I remembered the name of the stalker, a Clayton Daniels, supposedly influentially connected.''

"Atta girl," he said. "I'll see what I can find out."

"You're great."

" 'Bout time you realized it."

On the way home I drove by the parking garage where Magdaly Rosado leaped to her death.

I hadn't been there before. The apartment house where she had lived stood across the street. It was an older two-story building, longer than it was wide, with crank windows and a small tiled front patio that bespoke better days. None of the room air conditioners were in use, and all the windows were open. A vacancy sign swung in the breeze outside. Not surprising. They obviously had at least one, with Magdaly and Ernesto dead and Miguel in the hospital facing a murder charge.

I knocked on a few doors but no one at home remembered much about that day, except for seeing Magdaly dead in the street. The general consensus was a surface sadness at what had happened to the family, with an undercurrent of unspoken relief that they were gone.

The municipal parking garage looked like an explosion in a paint store. In a failed attempt to disguise its utilitarian use the city had painted it in a myriad of Art Deco colors: turquoise, peach, sea blue, and pale pink. The open stairwell had purple railings. And windblown rainwater had trickled in, staining the peach-color walls with streaks of mossy green.

This modern city garage had numbered spaces. Drivers punch in their number, buying time from a computerized device on each level. It spits out receipts bearing the space number, the amount paid, and the expiration time. Meter maids run computer tapes that tell them which spaces are paid for. The system eliminates the need for attendants, cashiers, and the possibility that some deserving motorist might find a meter with time left on it.

I drove around and around, up the sloped ascent. The low ceilings in parking garages always make me claustrophobic. It was a relief to emerge from the dimly lit bowels of the garage into the expanse of open sky on the roof. It was empty. It reminded me of the Edgewater rooftop, which I quickly forced from my thoughts. There were domed streetlights for nighttime illumination. I couldn't imagine when they would be necessary, unless motorists were urged to park in garages and ride shuttles to special events. Concrete supports about eighteen inches wide and two-and-a-half feet tall were spaced every twelve feet along the perimeter of the rooftop parking. Those were the lowest places, where someone could easily throw one leg over. Connecting the supports were stretches of chain-link fencing about eighteen inches higher.

I looked down, but I have never liked heights and hate the unpleasant tingling in my lower extremities when I approach the edge. Some primal warning against the urge to leap and fly.

I climbed back in the car and began to cruise slowly down the way I had come. Three levels were empty. A few scattered cars were parked on the fourth, along with a three-wheeler ridden by a middle-aged man wearing a dark blue security uniform. He seemed startled to see me with all those empty spaces in my wake. I stopped and backed up to where he sat. He wore reading glasses low on his nose and had been filling out some sort of a time sheet. A thick ballpoint pen was clenched awkwardly between his thumb and index finger, as though hampered by an arthritic condition or old injury.

He put down the pen and gingerly stepped down from the three-wheeler. He was short and stocky, and his too-long uniform trousers draped over the tops of his scuffed black shoes.

"Hi," I said. "I didn't know they had security here. Is this something new?"

He waggled his head no. "The last six months we've had patrols running between here and the other garages around the clock. We got vandalism, graffiti, stolen cars," he said in a singsong voice, ticking off the transgressions on oddly gnarled fingers.

I shook my head, as though wondering what the world would come to next. "You must have been here, then, the day the woman fell off the roof."

He surprised me by nodding. "Yeah, coulda done without that. Her form was good but her landing was lousy. What a mess. Lived right over there." He pointed a curled paw in the direction of the apartment house.

"I saw the story in the paper."

"What a crock." He shrugged in disdain. "Don't believe half of what you read, and take the other half with a grain of salt."

I raised my eyebrows. "They got it wrong?"

"As usual," he said. "They just write what they want. All that crap about the reporter who followed her up there, tried to talk her out of it, tried to stop her." He looked knowingly at me. "All bullshit."

"How so?" I affected my best puzzled expression.

"I seen 'em come outa the building together, arm in arm, walk across the street, get on the elevator. I figured they was going for a car, but the elevator went straight to the top. Nobody parks way up there. I thought maybe the elevator was malfunctioning again. I started up, but before I could even check, here she comes over the side. *Whap!*"

I winced as his palms came together, simulating the sound of flesh meeting pavement.

"The other one, the reporter I guess, steps off the elevator a minute later, dainty as you please. I can tell you, they didn't have no big discussion like that stuff on the front page. Bullshit. They wasn't up there thirty seconds before she broke the law of gravity. Or proved it."

"I thought the reporter said she ran down the stairs."

"Guess that looked better in print."

"Was she upset when she got off the elevator?"

"Nah. Looked around, cool as a cucumber. Took her time strolling to that pay phone right over there."

"Did she see you?"

"Evidently not, judging from what she wrote."

"Did you give a statement to the police?"

"Nah." He looked sheepish. "I hadda go down to the garage on Tenth Street. You gotta check in, punch a clock at every building on schedule. You get involved with the police, you screw up the whole shift, hafta write reports. It ain't worth it. I got trouble enough trying to write these time sheets. Got rheumatoid arthritis. That's why I hadda give up a better job to move down here."

He must have seen reproach in my eyes.

"If it woulda done her any good, I'da stayed. But it wouldn't've brought her back to life."

"What do you think really happened up there?"

He shrugged. "Musta took a running leap soon as they got there."

"Think it could have been foul play? That she was pushed?"

He looked shocked, totally taken aback at the suggestion. And the man's chosen profession is security, I thought.

"Why would somebody do that? Only one up there was the reporter. Cute little thing, she wouldn't be capable. . . . Why would she do that?"

I wrote down his badge number and the name off the metal plate pinned to his pocket.

There was no place else to go, then, but home. I dreaded it but found two surprises waiting: Lottie and Onnie, sharing a cup of tea with Mrs. Goldstein in her apartment. They opened the door and called when they saw me inserting my key in the lock.

"Where the hell were you?" Lottie hugged my neck.

Onnie did too. "You okay?" she murmured. "Sorry about Howie."

"Me too," I gasped, and began to weep, big choking sobs. I had wanted to be alone, but warm, caring friends were a comfort.

The concern in their faces touched me. Mrs. Goldstein, pushing eighty and born in the Ukraine. Onnie, a thirty-year-old Miami-born black woman, tall and angular with skin the color of burned toast. Lottie, tough and Texas born, with her cowboy boots and frizzy red hair. And me, of course, the daughter of a martyred Cuban freedom fighter or executed political terrorist, depending on where you stand. What a group we are, I thought. Friends are the family we choose for ourselves. I'm lucky to have them.

They had brought pizza, a fragrant pie stashed in Mrs. Goldstein's oven. "We got your favorite, extra tomatoes and fresh mushrooms," Lottie said.

My stomach churned. No way could I eat anything, but I was glad they were there.

We trouped to my apartment, Lottie carrying the pizza. Mrs. Goldstein stayed behind to wait for her husband, who was off on an errand.

It didn't help my remorseful state of mind to see Howie's possessions still in cardboard boxes in my living room.

"Want me to get rid of those for you?" Lottie said quietly.

"No!" I said, indignant. "Those are all his belongings."

"I was there, Britt. I helped you pack 'em. There's nothing of value."

"I'll think about it later."

I numbly sipped coffee while they ate the pizza and drank lite beers. Lottie swigged hers from the bottle while Onnie sipped primly from a glass. "I know you'll think I'm crazy," I began. "And if you repeat any of this, I'll be fired." Then I told them everything.

They exchanged dubious glances several times.

Maybe they didn't believe me, but hopefully they gave me the benefit of the doubt. I saved the security guard and Miguel for last.

"They could be lying," Lottie said. "Miguel to save himself and the guard just to hear himself talk. If he saw a phony story in the newspaper, why didn't he call and ask for an editor?"

"He doesn't have a clue about journalistic ethics or how a newspaper operates."

"If all you suspect is true," Lottie said slowly, "then Trish has been monitoring and erasing your messages."

"How could she? The system's pretty tight," Onnie said.

"Unless you made your four-digit code something real easy to guess, your date of birth, your phone number, or your address," Lottie said. "A lotta people make the mistake of doing that 'cause it's easier to remember." They both watched me expectantly.

"Worse than that," I said. "I was never careful. Hell, she sat next to me, hanging over my shoulder half the time. I trusted her. I think I even asked her to retrieve messages for me a couple of times when I was on deadline."

They groaned.

"Who'd have thought," I said.

"You've changed it?" Lottie said.

"Yeah."

"Change it again," she said. "To think," she added, "I was mad as a yard dog for a while, wanted to bite myself, 'cause you and Trish were so thick. Thought I'd lost a friend."

"I'm not that easy to lose." I remembered how bitchy she'd been.

"I thought I had a choice piece of gossip," Onnie said, eyeing the last piece of pizza, "but you're a hard act to follow."

"Tell us," Lottie demanded.

"It's said that Trish slept with Abel Fellows to land the newsroom job."

"What? I warned her about him! Told her he'd come on to her if he had the chance."

"Maybe she used that information to her advantage. He apparently boasted to a buddy about it." She looked coyly from Lottie to me. "Sheila, from personnel, confirmed that he's the one who recommended her hiring."

"I thought it was me, pushing her to Fred Douglas."

"Either way," Onnie said wryly, "you helped her into the newsroom."

"And look what she's done," I said, thinking of Howie. "That bitch."

"May her bones be broken more than the Ten Commandments," Onnie said, and lifted her glass.

"Proves what I always say," Lottie muttered. "No good deed goes unpunished."

She excused herself to visit the bathroom and returned swinging a shimmery silver chain. "Where'd you git this, Britt? Found it on your bureau."

"What is it?" Onnie turned from the microwave, where she was zapping the last slice of pizza.

I sighed. "Toss it in the garbage. It's supposed to be a dream catcher. My life's been a nightmare since I got it. A Comanche friend of Trish's made it for her." I caught the circular pendant with its silver feather, then passed it over for Onnie to examine. "She gave to me when she got hired. It's one of a kind."

"Hell, no, it ain't!" Lottie said. "I just wondered when you started shopping by mail too." She is addicted. "I see these in them New Age catalogs all the time, from two or three different mail-order houses. Sell 'em by the thousands. But it ain't Comanche. It's Ojibway. Hell, she didn't even get the tribe right."

I watched them as they left, wondering what they would say about me on the way home. My best friends in the world. Did they believe me, or were they measuring me for a rubber room?

Chapter Seventeen

I called Officer Annalee Watson from home next morning. She was not in, but she got back to me in a few minutes.

"How can I help you?" Her tone was distant and not at all helpful.

"I wondered how the twins were doing."

"Fine. HRS has left them in the custody of the mother and grandmother, but they're under the supervision of a social worker and Janice has to attend parenting classes. Don't know how much she'll retain. She may have her tubes tied."

"Makes sense to me."

"Is that all?" She sounded decidedly cool.

"No, actually it isn't. I wanted to ask why you didn't call me when the twins were found."

"I did," she shot back, annoyed and defensive. "I was surprised you weren't interested. The day before it seemed like you were."

"I was. What gave you the impression that I wasn't?"

"I called you, left a message, and was about to dial your beeper number when the other reporter, Trish, returned the call. She said you were too busy on another assignment and had asked her to handle it."

"That wasn't true. You're sure you called my number?"

"The one on the card you gave me," she said impatiently.

"Didn't you find it odd that somebody else returned the message?" My messages obviously had been monitored.

"No," she snapped, "you both work for the same paper. Look." She lowered her voice. "I shouldn't even be talking to you."

"Why not?"

"You wouldn't win any popularity contests around here at the moment, if you catch my drift."

"I don't."

"I mean, I'm gonna take a lotta crap, anybody hears me talking to you. Your little escapade, trying to help a cop killer get away. Everybody's talking about it."

"What?"

"Doesn't enhance your reputation as a reporter."

"Officer Watson, the kid was a passenger in the car that day and never had a gun. He wanted me help him surrender. That's what I was doing when somebody, probably the same person who's been sliming me, dropped a dime and we were surrounded. He was a valuable witness who could have helped put the cop killer in the electric chair."

"Well, the word is out that a cop jilted you and now you're a woman scorned with a hard-on for law enforcement."

"Good grief! I used to see a police officer, sure. The conflict in our jobs is what keeps us apart. We're still good friends. Before you form any opinion, please ask some police officers who know me, who've dealt with me in the past." I took a deep breath. "I don't think you really believe these rumors or you wouldn't have tipped me off about them. Thanks for being up front with me."

She paused. "I know what it's like," she said quietly, "working in a male-run organization. And there's no busier gossip mill than a police department. I've been a target myself. When they can't attack a woman any other way, they attack her sex life. Hang in there. I've gotta go."

Not only had my messages been monitored, erased, and returned without my knowledge, some might have been added. What about the unusual number of false leads and wild goose chases I had been wasting my time on lately?

I thought about skipping the rounds on my beat for a few days or so, to let things blow over, but nasty gossip, like a virulent weed, spreads like wildfire if ignored. The most effective damage control would be to act natural, show my face, and go on as usual. Hiding out, running for cover, makes you look guilty as hell.

At least, thanks to Annalee Watson, I knew what was being said about me. I put on my favorite blouse, peach-colored with tiny matching pearl buttons, and even applied some eyebrow pencil and mascara, unusual for me to wear to work. Nothing like cosmetics to build a little confidence—armor painted on to deflect the meanness in the world. Like a good soldier on the way to the front, I drove to Miami police headquarters.

As usual, all but the handicapped slots were taken. I circled the T-Bird like a vulture until somebody backed out, then zoomed into the space.

Rakestraw was in the lobby. He spun around and headed my way when he saw me. He looked sharp and eager. "Britt, I was just thinking about calling you. Hopefully we'll get a break today."

"FMJ?"

"We're hoping. It's a long shot."

"You know where they are?"

"Not exactly, but word on the street is that they need money to get out of town. A CI we've got in a chop shop is cooperating. Ain't too many 'ninety-one Allantes around."

"True, I guess."

"Well, they put out word they need one pronto, and there's a bonus for whoever comes up with one first."

"So?"

"We got us three of 'em. We're parking 'em in plain view in areas where they hang out, where we hear they've been seen."

"Staking them out?"

"Yeah, but just in case, we've got us a brand-new toy, a monitoring device."

"Like the Lojack?"

"Only more so. It's a silent system that will track them down without fail. We've got one, plus a hidden antenna, in each car. Every three hours or so, we move 'em to a different spot, hoping to catch their eye."

I had doubts about this part. "What if FMJ passes by, spots one on the move, and decides to take it then?"

Even his mustache hairs seemed to bristle. "Don't jinx us, Britt. They're under surveillance while they're moving, and Metro undercover detectives are the drivers."

"How come they're involved?"

"These kids are street-smart; they know too many of our people." He looked worried. "FMJ can smell trouble, so we have to be careful not to hang in too close on the surveillance."

Sounded dangerous to me. "How does the device work?"

"Land-based tracking system."

We were interrupted by Artie Gregg, an auto-theft detective wearing jeans and a striped pullover. "Bill, we got one on the move!"

"Damn!" Rakestraw said. "Come on."

The three of us stampeded back to auto theft. Rakestraw high-fived a pudgy detective in front of a PC that was backed up to a printer. On the screen in front of him was a detailed road map outlined in red.

"Which one'd they get?" said Rakestraw.

"The one parked at Northside Shopping Center. Started moving four minutes ago. The team in the van on the other side is watching with binoculars, said the takers are two teenagers, possibly Latin males; they fit the descriptions. They walked up on foot. Didn't see the vehicle they got out of."

"The chopper is up and has made visual contact," a dispatcher reported in stereo on the detectives' walkies. They weren't taking any chances.

Rakestraw and I exchanged tense glances. "Let it be them!" I begged softly, thinking of Jennifer and little Jason Carey; McCoy, the young cop; and Howie. "Let it be them!"

"Look at this," said the detective at the monitor. He hit a key and the road map on the screen zoomed down to a one-square-mile area, showing streets, intersections, and waterways. A moving green dot was the Allante we were tracking.

"It works through a mainframe in Fort Lauderdale," said Rakestraw. "Prints out every eight seconds, showing where the car is at, what street, what intersection."

"I didn't know you had anything like this."

The pudgy detective at the monitor spoke without taking his eyes off the screen. "The vehicle locator box can be installed in a car, a truck, a boat. It's a little bigger than a beeper. Broadcasts on the nine-hundred-megahertz frequency band to a central computer through radio towers from Palm Beach to Key West. Covers every street and twenty miles out to sea.

"The primary purpose is fleet management, so a plumbing company can keep track of its trucks, for instance. The radio waves travel at a speed of a hundred and eighty-six thousand miles a second, and the computer measures the exact location plus speed and direction. Takes about two seconds."

"Where's the car headed?" Rakestraw said.

"North, at thirty-five miles an hour." The man at the keyboard frowned. The green dot moved with the car, miles away. I watched the three detectives glued to the screen. This, I thought, is the police work of the future. No pounding pavements or knocking on doors in the hot sun; they'll be sitting in air-conditioned offices instead, tracking suspects by computer. I loved it. What a way to monitor wandering husbands, errant boyfriends, and joy-riding teenagers.

The green dot moved north on Northwest Second Avenue, crossing Northwest 108th Street, 108th Terrace, 109th Street, 109th Lane.

"The chop shop is south," somebody said.

"Maybe they're headed for the expressway."

"We better take 'em before they get on." Rakestraw raised the dispatcher on his two-way. "Is North Miami advised?"

"Affirmative," she said. "The county and North Miami Beach also have units in the area."

The detectives in the van reported that they were following, three cars behind the convertible. "Visual ID looks good. Looks like our suspects," said a deep, calm voice.

"Everybody in position?" Rakestraw said. "Use caution. These guys are armed."

Everybody responded with a QSL, which means okay.

"Go get 'em," said Rakestraw. "Take 'em whenever you're ready."

"Let's do it!" said a unit at the scene.

The green dot on the screen continued north on Northwest Second Avenue, passed Northwest 123rd Street, then Northwest 124th Terrace. Then it stopped. The operator hit a key and an address appeared on the screen next to the green dot: 12450 Northwest Second Avenue. Eight seconds later: 12450 Northwest Second Avenue. Eight seconds later: 12450 Northwest Second Avenue.

"They're not just stopped at a traffic light," somebody muttered. "Come on, come on!"

I wondered what would happen if they ran or tried to shoot it out.

"Two in custody!" somebody shouted at the scene.

"Way to go!" Rakestraw shouted. I studied their jubilant faces, wondering wistfully if any woman could ever make any of these men as happy. I doubted it.

The stolen Allante had been pulled over within sight of the expressway. Surrounded by uniform cars, with the police helicopter hovering overhead, the occupants surrendered. A handgun was taken from the waistband of the driver.

Our elated little group was still celebrating, clinking Pepsi cans, when we got the news. The suspects, in separate cage cars on the way to the station, had been identified as J-Boy and Little Willie.

I heard curse words new to me as Rakestraw punched the wall so hard I thought he had broken his hand.

What hurt most was the unspoken realization that, had they not been stopped, they probably would have led the cops to FMJ. But nobody was hurt and two out of three ain't bad. Maybe J-Boy and Little Willie, the latter fresh out of Youth Hall, would rat on FMJ. Maybe.

FMJ seemed to lead a charmed life, but his luck had to run out soon. Since I was on a street deadline, I wrote my story on an old electric typewriter provided for the press in the PIO office, then faxed it to the newsroom on the machine police flacks use to distribute their press releases.

How primitive, I thought, feeding the paper into the facsimile machine, hoping it was not being received in every competing newsroom in Miami.

Dazzled by the recent display of police technology, I resolved to begin using a modem-equipped portable laptop computer that would zap my stories right into the *News* computer system from out in the field. If FMJ used one, why not me? Why stall in the slow lane of the new information superhighway? In reality, I was having difficulty with something as basic as voice mail. But of course I knew why. Trish was the reason. How did a simple favor, extending the hand of friendship to another woman, evolve into something so sinister and ugly? How could she? What sort of person was this?

I stayed around for a while, but the word was not promising. J-Boy demanded his lawyer and Little Willie was crying for his mommy. Before clamming up, both denied knowing any Gilberto Sanchez, aka Peanut, aka FMJ.

Beating everybody else, filing my story for the street, made me feel back on track. I pushed through the station's double doors and was trudging through the parking lot, past the grassy course where K-9 officers train their dogs, when I saw her. It was Trish. She had just parked. She wore a pink knit dress, nipped in at the waist, and was laughing at something one of two cops walking near her had said. The officers veered off to the left, to the training area. Trish kept coming my way. What was she doing here?

She saw me and smiled. "Hi, Britt," she said, apparently intending to walk on by and into the station.

"Trish," I said coolly, stepping directly in front of her. "What a coincidence. What are you doing here again, on my beat?" I spoke as though confronting a naughty child in the act.

She reacted in kind, with a sheepish but engaging grin, as though caught raiding the cookie jar. She pushed her big sunglasses up on her tilted nose. "Heard about J-Boy. Didn't think you'd spend much time here today after everything that happened."

Her skin glowed golden; she'd been getting some sun. I wondered how she found the time. She shrugged gracefully, shifting her weight like a racehorse eager to run. "Somebody has to stay on top of the story."

"That's my job," I said mildly.

"Actually, J-Boy's mother has already hired an attorney. He said I can talk to his client." Her soft dark hair formed a cloud around her face. She looked stunning.

"No way," I said. "You have no business—"

"I'm the only reporter he'll allow access to his client. No one else gets to talk to him." She smiled again, so poised, so arrogant, that I could not resist.

"Wonder how you did that," I said sarcastically. "Actually, you have more important things to think about," I told her, maintaining our tone of feigned sweetness. "I spoke to someone who was there when Magdaly Rosado died, who saw the whole thing."

She never changed expression, just stared from behind her designer shades.

"And I visited poor Miguel."

"He's not allowed visitors," she said smugly, as though relieved to catch me in a lie.

"Good reporters don't ask permission. They walk in, do what they have to do, and get out. You should know that, Trish."

Her smile faded. "Don't embarrass yourself, Britt. At least no more than you've already done. Your credibility factor in this town is about the same as Miguel's. Zilch."

Her voice was calm, innocent, as though inviting me to tea, her expression angelic.

"This is my hometown. I'll be here long after you're gone."

She laughed and I saw red.

"You killed Howie, Trish, and nearly got me killed. Maybe nobody believes that now, but they will. Lord knows how much other shit you've staged, how many innocent people you've hurt, but I'm making it my business to find out.

"In the meantime, forget J-Boy and his lawyer," I said, picking up steam, stepping closer, in her face. "I've been chasing these kids all over this fucking town! You are not stealing this story out from under me."

She never flinched. "His attorney granted me permission. Me alone. You will not have access. J-Boy is probably going to tell me that Howie killed the cop, McCoy, and that you and the old woman shielded him, knowing it."

I slapped her, hard. The blow knocked her sunglasses askew. Her smooth skin reddened into a facsimile of my handprint. I stood there, more shocked at how good it felt than at how badly I had behaved.

To my surprise she swung back. I caught her arm as her other hand clawed at my face. She was surprisingly strong. As I shoved her away, she grabbed the front of my blouse, tearing off buttons as we scuffled.

There were people in the parking lot, and we were in full view of half the windows at the station.

Shouts of "Hey! Hey!" and raucous laughter came from a few cops near their cars about a hundred feet away.

"Let 'em go, let 'em go!" somebody yelled. "This is better than mud wrestling!"

Trish swung wildly, teeth clenched, catching a fistful of my hair. Fire flared in me, fed by pain and anger. Slapping her again, I clutched her wrist as she lunged toward me, tearing at my face. I wanted to knock her right into tomorrow, knowing I would regret it. We could even be arrested for this violent little dance in front of any number of sworn law officers.

"You crazy bitch," she panted, as we broke apart.

"I'll kick your ass," I muttered. "Cross me again, Trish, and I'll do it. There's not enough room for us both at the same newspaper. It's you or me."

Her face was crimson as she explored the inside of her cheek with her tongue. "Which do you think it will be, Britt?" Her sneer displayed a tiny trickle of blood at the corner of her mouth.

"I've been there for seven years," I began, lowering my voice so the two cops bearing down on us wouldn't hear, realizing how I must look, how hot and sweaty I felt.

"Who's had the most stories, the most front-page bylines recently?" she crowed. "I've already been told that your job is mine."

"By whom?"

Her answer was a smirk. She had dropped her purse and I kicked it like a football.

"Whoa! Whoa!" warned a laconic middle-aged cop named Gravengood.

"I could wring your neck," I told her.

"Ladies, ladies. What's your problem? What's wrong with you two?" He reached out as though to separate us further.

"Watch it, Al." His husky partner hung back, wary. "I been shot at and stabbed, but I hate it the most when women start the ripping and the scratching and the yelling and the screaming and the clunking with high heels."

Gravengood ignored him. "Anybody here interested in pressing charges?"

We stared at each other, both breathing hard. "Thank you, officer." Trish turned to him, suddenly tearful and trembling. "I don't think it's necessary, but since she did attack me, would you see that I get safely to my car?"

"Sure," he said kindly. "Go on now." Then he focused on me. "Britt, what in blue blazes is going on? You crazy?"

"I'm sorry." Humiliation overwhelmed me. "I can't believe this happened. She's unbelievable. You have no idea what that woman is capable of."

"Well, I sure seen you get in a few good licks. This is a police station, for God's sake." He turned to walk away as Trish's car pulled out. "Better fix your blouse," he suggested over his shoulder.

Tears stung my eyes as I walked shakily to my car. I sat there for several minutes, trembling, trying to calm down. I hadn't struck another human being in anger since the first grade. I wouldn't have now, had it not been for what she said about Howie. Of course J-Boy and FMJ would try to shift the blame to him, I thought, after being prompted by Trish and their defense attorneys. It's convenient to blame somebody who's no longer alive to defend himself. A jury might even buy it.

I should not have lost my temper. Our fight would be the talk of the newsroom. The men would love it, embracing all the stereotypes about women being unable to work together, unable to get along.

I remembered the night I first saw Trish. That eager young woman had reminded me of myself. What went wrong?

My scalp ached where she had yanked my hair. I rummaged in my purse for a safety pin and fastened the front of my blouse. The top two buttons were gone.

I was tempted to go back to find the missing peach-colored pearl buttons but felt too embarrassed. I sniffled and checked to see if my nose was bleeding. One nostril was a little swollen, and a ragged scratch ran along the line of my jaw. It had bled, staining my collar.

Most important now was to 'fess up, I thought. I needed to explain my side to Fred Douglas before her version got me fired. But I obviously couldn't walk into the newsroom like this. What if Fred didn't believe me? He hadn't been receptive before. Why should he be now? Weary and confused, I needed time to think.

I took a ramp onto southbound I-95, drove its length, then turned around and headed north, the sun glinting off spectacular skyline and the far-off sea. I fought an urge to keep going—to keep driving, out of town, out of this mess, listening to mindless music, until I ran out of road or gas. Not so long ago I didn't know Trish. She wasn't even in the picture. I remembered the afternoon I picked up Lottie and we drove off, lighthearted and giddy, in my new car. That's the way it is, I thought. Whenever you think your life is going great, watch out! Here comes the pie.

Reluctantly, I swung off an exit ramp and turned back south, toward the paper. Traffic was jammed. The scanner reported that an overturned truck had dumped its load of tar on the roadway. Inching along, stop and go, bumper to bumper, gave me plenty of time to rethink my predicament. Unless they believed me this time, our bosses would most likely insist that Trish and I meet for counseling, the goal being for us to shake hands and agree to act like professionals. That was the best-case scenario. I didn't want to entertain the worst.

Another look in the mirror told me I should go home and change, but there was no time now. I should have done that first. She was probably already in the newsroom, telling some outlandish story. At long last I reached the downtown exit, drove to the *News,* parked in my slot under the building, and skulked up the escalator, head down, hoping not to meet anyone. First stop was the ladies' room. I washed my face, did a neater job of pinning the front of my blouse together, then tried to scrub the stain off the collar. My nose oozed blood and a dark bruise was emerging on my cheekbone. My right arm was also scratched. I dabbed on peroxide from the first-aid kit in my locker.

I stepped into the newsroom, half expecting bells and whistles to go off, sounding an alarm. Everyone looked busy, as usual. To my relief, Trish was not at her desk. Perhaps she hadn't come right back to the paper. Maybe it was my move. Dread in my heart, I went to Fred's office. It was empty.

That was when I saw them gathered in the managing editor's office. The afternoon news meeting. Shit, I thought, frustrated and eager to confess. It was that time already. They had just started, and the damn things often lasted an hour or more.

I certainly wasn't going to intrude, bouncing in there as they evaluated the world news of the day, with my bulletin that two of their reporters had just made spectacles of themselves by smacking each other around in front of half the police department, an organization whose morale and professional behavior we constantly monitor and criticize.

I had to corner Fred privately after the meeting broke.

Hands trembling, I sat at my desk trying to look busy as I watched for Trish and stayed poised to catch Fred when he emerged. Time moves so fast on deadline, yet now it dragged.

"Britt, what happened to you?" Ryan froze in his tracks.

"Shut up and sit down," I muttered.

"Did you get mugged?"

"In a manner of speaking," I said cryptically, keeping my voice low. "Say nothing. I'll fill you in later."

Last thing I needed was a bunch of nosy reporters crowding around my desk demanding details before I had covered my ass with the boss. Where was Trish? I wondered. She might have beaten me to Fred by phone.

Budgets and notebooks in hand, editors began to drift out. But Fred was still in there. The managing editor was on the phone, then he handed it to Fred. He showed no sign of coming out. Deep in discussion, they signaled the city editor to join them. All three glanced out into the newsroom several times, but I couldn't discern if they were looking at me or not.

Minutes later Mark Seybold, the paper's in-house lawyer, hurried into the newsroom, joining them. There seemed to be a flurry of excitement as the publisher also appeared. Murphy's secretary, Estelle, was summoned to the door, then emerged, an odd expression on her face.

My phone rang and I snatched it up impatiently. It was Estelle. "They want to see you in the managing editor's office, right now."

"Did they say what it's in reference to?" I asked, feigning innocence.

"You'd better get in there," she said, and hung up.

I dabbed at my still-oozing nose, stuffed some extra tissues in my pocket, and got to my feet. Face flaming, feeling as though all eyes were focused on my disheveled person, I walked into the office.

Grim faces told me I was about to be fired.

No one spoke. The managing editor motioned to an empty chair in front of his desk. The others were sitting and standing on either side of me.

I had wanted to speak only to Fred, in private. I was so ashamed. I never intended to embarrass the paper.

I took a deep breath. "I wanted to tell you first," I said, directing my remarks to Fred, who sat in a leather-covered chair to my right, his back to the picture window. Late-afternoon sun shone blood red on the water behind him. A pelican soared by, precariously close to the face of the building.

Primly I arranged my skirt over my knees.

"I assume this concerns what happened with Trish." Their eyes were grave. "All I can say is that I never intended for it to happen. I'm really sorry. She provoked me beyond belief."

This is worse than I expected, I thought, studying their faces. What the hell had she told them? Mark Seybold, wearing his navy tie covered with little locomotives, held up one hand like a traffic cop.

"Britt, I don't think you should say any more. The police are downstairs and want to talk to you. I would advise you to retain counsel. I can't represent you."

I cocked my head to one side as though I hadn't heard right. "What are you talking about?"

"Trish's death," he said. "The police say it's murder."

Chapter Eighteen

Trish's death left me speechless. Detectives David Ojeda and Charlie Simmons from homicide asked me to accompany them back to their office to "help us piece this whole thing together."

"What happened? Is it a whodunit?" I asked. They seemed to be thinking that over. "Do you have anyone in custody?"

Simmons glanced at his partner and shook his head.

I stared at the floor, avoiding the prying eyes of my colleagues as we walked across the newsroom toward the small lobby where the elevators are located.

We all looked up at the sound of someone running. Lottie came dashing full tilt down the hall that stretches the length of the building. She hit the brakes when she saw us. The news had spread with the speed of light. The expression in her honest brown eyes made me painfully aware of how all this must look.

"Britt!" Breathless, she focused on me, ignoring them. "What do you need me to do?"

"No sweat. It's okay."

"Should I call anybody?"

Who to call? I wondered. My mother was the only person I could think of, and I certainly didn't want her upset.

"No, thanks, Lottie. I'll call you later."

Ojeda was waiting, impatiently holding the elevator. We left her standing there, right hand outstretched, biting her lip, poised for action, uncertain what it should be. As the doors slid shut I glimpsed Onnie, her face frightened.

This entire situation, which could be cleared up easily, had unnecessarily upset my friends, I thought, annoyed.

The detectives' unmarked waited on the ramp in front of the building.

"Shouldn't I take my own car so I have a ride back?"

"We'll see that you get back," Simmons said casually.

What frustrated me most during the ride was their innocuous small talk. I had no interest in the state of some quarterback's shoulder or the retirement plans of a coach. I wanted to know about the case, to quiz them about what had happened, fill them in on Trish's background, and speculate on who did it. If anyone had. Could she really be dead? Murdered? It strained belief, as though the past few days were a demented dream.

Trish invaded our thinking, was paramount in our minds, yet they refused to mention her. When I asked direct questions, they were evasive, saying only that we could discuss it later, at their office.

We settled in a drab interrogation room located just off the fifth-floor homicide bureau. No hanging posters or bright tablecloth like they had for Howie, I thought.

I sat at a wooden table, my back to the wall. Ojeda leaned against the door. Simmons occupied the chair opposite me. I knew them both, had written stories about a number of their cases. Ojeda, mercurial and clever, was inclined to make snap decisions and was often too quick to make assumptions. His loud ties seemed out of character for a man in his line of work. His hairline was receding, his mustache fierce, his smile knowing.

Simmons stayed in good shape, looked and acted younger than his late forties, and had an uncertain marital status. Sometimes he appeared domesticated and wore a wedding band. Other times he did not. I had never been curious enough to ask if he was often between wives or involved in a single stormy on-and-off-again marriage.

At the moment Simmons wore a wedding band and a veiled expression I had never seen before.

"You know we want to talk to you, Britt, but we have to advise you of your rights."

Yikes, I thought, what is wrong with these guys? Are they in the wrong ballpark on this one!

He gingerly slid a sheet of paper from a manila folder. "I have the standard form right here."

"Charlie," I said, my smile impatient, "all that's not necessary. We've known each other for years; we can talk."

Ojeda stirred but said nothing.

Charlie grinned casually and tossed up his hands. "You know how it is, Britt. Procedure."

I sighed, running my fingers through my hair. "Okay, okay, I know my rights."

"Well, now." He shrugged, like a man being nibbled to death by minutiae. "I have to go through this whole damn thing line by line."

He read them, explaining every facet in excruciating detail, as though to a first-grader, enunciating the fact that I had the right to remain silent, that everything I said could and would be used against me in a court of law, that I had the right to have an attorney present.

"I've been advised to get an attorney," I commented.

He sighed. "If you think you need one."

"I don't," I said.

"So you want to sign the waiver and talk to us?"

"Sure, if that's what it takes to clear this up."

"If, at any point, you think you need an attorney, I am obliged to stop everything and accommodate you. You need not make any statement if you do not wish to do so."

Why did I get the feeling that all this was recitation by rote, like a little poem learned for Sunday school?

"Come on, come on!" I said. "Let's do it and get it over with." A moment of hesitation nagged as I signed. Was this the right thing to do? A lawyer would certainly advise against it, but that was for the guilty, those with something to hide. Not me.

I checked the NO box next to the question: Do you wish an attorney? And YES after: Are you now willing to answer questions without an attorney present?

Ojeda placed a wooden chair near the door and took a seat. Charlie remained directly across from me.

"You using any drugs?" Ojeda asked.

"Me?" I yelped. "No way. You know better."

"Under any medication? Pills?"

"The only pills I take are vitamins," I snapped.

"A lot's been going on in your life recently," Charlie began sincerely. He sounded like a shrink or somebody's pastor.

"Yeah, everybody's been talking about your escapade over at the Mayberry house," Ojeda said with a smirk.

Oh, God, I thought. "Come on, guys, don't go into the good-cop bad-cop routine. I know that act too well. This whole thing is ridiculous! By the way," I added, "that was not 'my escapade.' It went down the way it did because of Trish."

"It was her fault?" Simmons said sympathetically.

In retrospect I realized how that sounded.

"What led up to this beef between you two?" Ojeda asked.

"You have to understand the sort of person she was."

"Tell us." Charlie looked deeply interested.

I knew better. But when in doubt, tell the truth. So I told them the whole thing, left nothing out.

Ojeda nodded, leaning back in his chair, hands behind his head, armpit stains exposed. "So you been having your friend, an investigative reporter in Chicago, check her out?"

"To learn what made her tick, what there was in her background, so I could figure out how to deal with her."

"So you two weren't friends?" Charlie asked.

"No," I said quickly.

"Ever been to her home?"

"Once," I said reluctantly. "An oceanfront condo on the Beach. But I'm not sure if she was still living there. She may have moved. She was house-sitting. We had dinner."

Charlie nodded solemnly. "So you were friends but had a little falling out?"

"We never got to be really close friends."

"And you believed she was after your job?"

"That was obvious."

"And it upset you that she was winning a lot of attention, making a big splash, so to speak."

"At the expense of others, she was preying on vulnerable people. That's what I objected to." I swiveled in my chair, directing questions at Ojeda, hoping he'd say more than Charlie. "How was Trish killed? What happened? Where was she found?"

He sniffed noisily and deferred, gesturing to Charlie, who said, "We're getting to that, Britt. But first we want to know everything you did today."

I sighed. "I was here for several hours at the station, down in auto theft, on that arrest in the McCoy case. I met Trish on the way out."

"Tell us what happened."

I told them.

"Who was there at the time?"

"I saw Officer Gravengood and his partner, Hancock. There were a few K-9 officers, motorists driving by, and Lord knows who else watching out the windows of the station. I think I saw a few detectives going in the back door. From the public integrity squad, I believe."

"What did you do afterward?" Charlie said.

"Sat in my car for a few minutes, embarrassed as hell. Then drove around for a while. Probably close to an hour or so. Then I went back to the *News*. I wanted to talk to my editor. Tell him my side of the story."

"But you didn't?"

"They were tied up in a news meeting."

"You didn't think this was important enough to interrupt or send in a message?"

"You don't interrupt the news meeting—unless somebody shoots the president, the Space Shuttle blows up, or World War Three breaks out."

Ojeda pursed his lips and raised an eyebrow, looking duly impressed. "Anybody you know see you doing all that driving around?"

"Not that I noticed."

"When did you see Trish Tierney again after the altercation in the parking lot?"

"I didn't," I said. "That's what I've been telling you."

"I see."

The detectives swapped glances, and Ojeda jerked his head toward the door. They stepped outside to confer while I tapped my foot impatiently.

"Would you do us a favor, Britt?" Charlie stuck his head back into the little room.

"Sure," I said eagerly.

"We'd like to take the clothes you're wearing."

"What?"

"A formality. Just to be on the safe side."

"How?" I pictured myself huddled in that chilly little room in a bra and panties.

"One of us will drive you home, a policewoman will go inside with you, and you can change."

"Fine." By that time I was eager for anything to escape that little room, get them off my neck, and have them acknowledge that they had been barking up the wrong tree.

Before we left, Ojeda wanted something else. "One more thing, Britt. Did you—uh, wash up after your altercation this afternoon? We want to take a scraping from under your fingernails and a few pictures of your injuries."

Oh, God, I thought. They're wasting precious time while the killer gets away. But I'd gone too far to say no now. If I did, it would look as though I had something to hide. I described my visit to the rest room, when I had arrived back at the paper, but agreed to whatever they asked.

A crime-scene tech came up with a camera, took the scrapings, and snapped pictures of my scratches and bruises. I felt so stupid. Like the two detectives looked. Unless they got out and went to work, the killer's trail would be cold.

Charlie waited in the car while a black detective named Marcia Anders and I went into my apartment. I was glad that Mrs. Goldstein didn't seem to be home. I took Bitsy out for a few minutes and quickly changed into a gray sweat suit and Reeboks as the detective, a star pitcher on the policewomen's softball team, watched from the doorway. How like Trish to cause me this humiliation. I also felt an odd sense of regret. She was too young to die, too beautiful and talented. The mystery of who she was and why might never be solved now, even if her murderer was caught. As Anders grew impatient, I fed the animals; there was no telling how late I'd be.

The detective had placed the garments in large separate paper bags and was filling out labels.

I took a burger from the freezer and put it in the fridge to thaw for later.

We returned to headquarters and our former positions in the little room.

Charlie licked his lips and slid another paper from his folder. "Now, according to this incident report, you are quoted as telling Ms. Tierney, "I could wring your neck.""

Both watched me expectantly.

I thought carefully. "As I recall, I said something to that effect. I was provoked, big-time." My stomach churned uneasily. "I didn't know an incident report had been made." Actually, it was not surprising. Reporters constantly scrutinize cops. I could see where a cop would take joy in making a report on fisticuffs between two reporters.

"Gravengood thought it behooved him to do so," Ojeda said. He chewed the inside of his cheek. "You familiar with Commodore Park, over on the Miami River?"

"Sure. The lover's lane where those two kids got shot back in 'eighty-one." Teenage sweethearts attacked by some weirdo. The boy died, the girl survived, the weirdo got life.

"Precisely," Ojeda said. "Did you have occasion to see Ms. Tierney there after assaulting her in the parking lot?"

"No! Is that where you found her?"

He nodded.

"Look," I said, annoyed. "I've cooperated fully. You're wasting time, blowing the investigation and letting the real killer get away!"

"So you say you're familiar with the park?"

"Of course! I grew up in Miami."

"So you didn't follow Ms. Tierney there and 'wring her neck,' as you put it?"

"Of course not!"

"So if a witness told me he saw you there today, he would be lying?"

"Yes!"

Charlie met my eyes and looked down, almost embarrassed, then brightened with an idea.

"Maybe it was self-defense," he offered.

"You don't believe me, Charlie!" I half shouted. "I want to talk to a lawyer!"

"Sure," he said smoothly. "You need a phone book?"

He stepped out and took the Yellow Pages off a nearby desk. Ojeda brought in a phone on a long cord.

Hand shaking, I dialed Jake Lassiter's number.

Jake is a former Dolphin linebacker with bad knees, a law practice, and a rakish charm. We had a date once for a stone crab dinner, but I wound up covering a three-alarm fire instead.

Seething with indignation, I couldn't wait to sic him on these guys.

Cindy, his secretary, answered. "I need to talk to Jake," I said urgently.

"Skiing in Colorado." She sounded nonchalant. I could practically hear her filing her nails. "Be back a week from next Monday."

Who else? I wondered in desperation. Jeremiah Tannen! Jerry Tannen had recently left the public defender's office after an unprecedented winning streak. The twenty-seven-year-old boy wonder had
won his last fifteen jury trials—in less than two months. An average
lawyer in private practice might try two major cases a year. The public
defender's office is a baptism by fire. J.T. thrived on combat, a street
fighter who didn't hesitate to hit below the belt. Exactly what I wanted
to see happen to Simmons and Ojeda at this point.

Both detectives reacted as though slapped when they heard me ask
the information operator for Tannen's number. Ojeda muttered what
sounded like a curse, and Charlie pushed back his chair and walked
out.

Tannen answered his own phone.

"I'm glad you're there, J.T.," I said, dismayed at the quiver in my
voice. I began to tell him my situation.

He interrupted. "How much have you told them?"

"I've answered all their questions, done whatever they asked—"

He went ballistic. "Don't talk! Don't do anything! Don't say another word to anybody! I'll be right down."

The cavalry was on the way. But it was small comfort, because I
knew now what I had been denying to myself all along. I was in serious trouble. I was about to be arrested on a murder charge.

I sat alone in the little room while they did the paperwork. I thought I
heard J.T.'s indignant voice a short time later but could not make out
the words.

He was there when they asked me to step out.

I felt like a drowning person with my only hope for rescue this tall,
pale, boyish lawyer. His eyes were intelligent and intense behind the
lenses of his rimless glasses.

He rested his hands on my shoulders.

"I'm sorry you have to go through this, Britt. They're arresting
you."

"This is crazy, J.T."

"I know, I know. And I'll get you out of jail because this is all
bullshit." His last remark seemed directed at the detectives pointedly
doing busywork at their nearby desks, pretending not to listen.

"Don't talk to anybody unless I'm present." J.T. lowered his voice.
"You've probably said too much already. Now, here is what you can

reasonably expect. You will be patted down and processed here at headquarters. Their regulations require that you be handcuffed when they transport you to the jail in a car.''

He read my rising panic.

"I know, I know. It won't get any better. At the jail you will have to remove all your clothing in the presence of a woman matron and assume various positions so they can search to make sure you're not seeking to smuggle in any contraband or weapons. I will not be able to see you until after the booking process. I'll probably have a bondsman talk to you even though you're not entitled to a bond.''

I gasped in protest.

"I know. You're a decent person, you've lived here a long time, you've never been charged with a crime, but that doesn't help. First-degree murder is not a bondable offense. I'm gonna have a bail bondsman come and see you, not because he will be able to write you a bond but because they can get in faster than lawyers can. He'll be able to get in real quick to see you and find out what the story is.

"I'll talk to the detectives, learn what I can about the case, and talk to the state attorney.''

Even at this numbing moment I viewed my situation from an oddly distant perspective. I know something about the system and how it operates. How terrifying this all must be, I thought, for a citizen who suddenly finds himself in trouble with no idea what to expect or who to call.

"Thanks for getting here so fast, J.T. I really need help. I didn't do it. I can't believe they even think me capable of such a thing.''

"Hang tight, Britt. I'll be doing everything that can be done.''

Ojeda walked me down to prisoner processing, where I was fingerprinted and had my mug shot taken.

Lieutenant Kendall McDonald was nowhere in sight, to my relief. The cuffs were plastic flex-cuffs, first used as a cost-cutting measure for crowds of prisoners rounded up at demonstrations, concerts, and civil disturbances. Luckily the women's jail was just blocks way, the ride in the back of a cage car short enough that I could block my feelings of claustrophobia.

The officer carefully radioed his mileage to dispatch before we started and again on arrival: protection against women prisoners who might claim sexual abuse during unauthorized detours.

The four-story brick building stands in the shadow of the expressway on the fringe of Overtown. Before we rolled in through the sally port, my driver stopped and locked his sidearm in the trunk. Then he opened my cage and marched me through the double doors.

I had never really paid much attention to the sign above the booking desk: ALL NEWS PERSONS MUST CHECK WITH THE COMMANDING OFFICER.

"Guess what?" The officer escorting me grinned at the middle-aged sergeant. "Better get the commanding officer down here. We got us a news person."

"I don't think we need to bother the commander," the sergeant said good-humoredly. She wore a drab green skirt and a gray uniform shirt. "That's for when they come in the other side, the public entrance. She's coming in the criminal entrance."

I came here often during my appointed rounds. This was my first arrival in handcuffs.

"Hi, Jewel," I said.

"What happened, Britt?" She looked sympathetic. "Step across that police line once too often?" She picked up the paperwork. Her smile faded and her eyebrows lifted.

"It's a mistake," I told her.

The look in her eyes told me that's what they all say.

The Dade County Women's Jail houses prisoners with sentences of a year or less and those awaiting trial. Everything played out the way J.T. had said it would.

I was glad I had worn my sweat suit. It felt soft and comforting. Jail is a cold place in more ways than one. They confiscated the shoelaces from my Reeboks, apparently to protect me from myself, so I had to shuffle into the "pod." In this modern jail they eschew such terms as cell blocks.

Each pod has a dozen little open cells surrounding a small living room dominated by a television set. This one was tuned to some tabloid show. At the back was a toilet and an open shower without curtains. The door closed behind me with a metallic clank that stunned my soul and echoed in the pit of my stomach.

I seemed to be the only non-black or Hispanic person in my pod. "¡Hola!" I said to my new roommates. "¿Qué tal?"

They must be hard-core offenders, I thought, as they stared idly. A dangerous murder suspect like me wouldn't be locked up with small-time shoplifters and drunk drivers. I thought ironically of the times I

had wanted to interview jail inmates and been turned away. Now I had
them all to myself. My welcoming committee lunged to her feet, creating a fearful flutter in my stomach. Built like a linebacker, she
weighed 350 pounds, minimum. Her skin had the blue-black sheen of
anthracite, her overtaxed stretch pants were red, and her tent-size
white T-shirt said IF MOMMA AIN'T HAPPY, AIN'T NOBODY HAPPY.

Her blue scuffs flapped like wounded birds against the soles of her
feet as she approached.

"Here's your bed, honey," she said, in an unexpectedly high-
pitched, childlike voice. "My name is Winsome. We just got us a new
vacancy. Somebody left. An officer will be around in a minute. I'll go
to the laundry room for your blanket. I'm a trusty."

"Thank you," I said. "I'm Britt."

Her mention of the vacancy had evoked a chorus of snorts and
laughs.

"Where did she go?" I asked, gingerly trying out the bunk and
hoping its last occupant did not depart feet first.

"For pizza." Somebody tittered.

I looked around.

"Linelle," somebody said. "She gone again."

"Linelle Early?" My mouth dropped open. I had covered her es-
capades. She packed a .44-caliber Magnum and an attitude. Voluptu-
ous and affable, she was a one-woman crime wave, a Bonnie without a
Clyde. She managed quite well on her own, thank you. After her last
escape she had robbed four banks, a Wal-Mart, and an International
House of Pancakes.

"You know Linelle?" Winsome asked, in a baby-bird-like trill.

"I know *of* her."

"Everybody know Linelle," snickered a skinny woman in a striped
blouse.

"Escape? How?"

She had been checked out by a corrections officer who had obligingly stopped for a pizza on the way back to the jail. He got out to pick
up the pie, leaving his gun and his keys in the car. He wound up on a
street corner holding nothing but a warm pizza. His prisoner, his car,
and his gun were gone. Likewise his career.

"What did he have her checked out for?"

"That's what they asking him now," said a woman wearing her
hair in cornrows. She was positively gleeful.

"His ass in a sling," Winsome said, nodding brightly.

I looked around for a phone. My instinct was to call in the tip to the city desk, while common sense told me that if I did get my hands on a phone that wasn't who I should be calling.

A woman with graying hair was seated in one of the open cells, forehead on her knees, arms wrapped around her head, rocking from side to side, mumbling something indiscernible. I felt her utter hopelessness, totally out of control of my life. My heart ached for my mother. What about my car, parked at the paper? My pets at home? My job? My salary? How much would J.T. charge me?

"Ain't you Britt Montero from the *News*?" The skinny woman had sprung up from her bunk, consternation on her face.

I said I was.

"Well, hell, how you gonna help git me outa here now?" she demanded, slapping the wall, dancing in frustration on the balls of her feet. "I wrote you!"

I studied her. "You're the Singer! I read your letters."

Her dance slowed to a little strut. Famous and feared among the swank South Beach sidewalk cafés crowded with happily chatting diners, she roamed the tables belting out Patti LaBelle tunes at the top of her lungs. If her audience didn't tip, she would spit in their tricolor tortellini pesto salads.

"Don't git her started," peeped Winsome.

"I remember. You wrote that you were harassed by police officers who planted a knife on you and made up an assault charge."

"That's it!" Scathing, she looked me up and down. "Look at you!" she gestured in disgust, voice rising. "What good you gonna do me now? Why didn't you answer my letters?"

"Sorry," I said. "I've been having a bad time lately."

"Ain't we all." A solidly built brunette tossed aside the paperback romance she'd been reading and leaned forward. Her elaborately decorated fingernails were long and fake, some painted bright green. One was black, with a white moon and stars. The only time I ever had a fingernail that color was when I slammed it in the door of my old T-Bird right on deadline. Her left thumbnail was shiny green with a little palm tree and a full moon. She stared down the Singer, who stalked off, scowling over her shoulder. "Boyfriend or drugs?" the brunette asked confidentially.

"Neither," I said wanly. "It's a long story."

. . .

True to his word, J.T. sent Billy the Bondsman. We sat in the visitors' section and talked into microphones, heavy plate glass between us.

I had seen Billy Marker around for years, never holding him in especially high esteem, maybe just a step above a repo man. Billy is fifty pounds overweight, sweats too much, and wears too much gold. He was carrying a briefcase and had a pocket full of pens and dark stubble on his chin. It was amazing how glad I was to see him.

"Okay, Britt. First lemme tell ya how sorry I am to see you in this jam, but I want ya to know J.T. is doing everything he can."

That said, he got down to the meaty stuff.

Trish had been found in her car, in the park, as the cops had said. She was fully clothed, her purse and jewelry seemed intact. She had not been robbed. She had been strangled.

I shuddered at the thought. "Whoever did it has probably got scratch marks," he said, shrewd eyes lingering on my jaw.

"This is from when we had a skirmish earlier, at the station." I lightly fingered the scratch along my jawline.

He nodded. "I heard all about that, but J.T. wants you to give me a full rundown. From what we hear, the cops got physical evidence putting you in the car and an eyewitness who swears he saw you there."

"I can't believe this, Billy! What witness? It's impossible. I was never, ever, in her car and nobody saw me there because I wasn't!"

"J.T. already has an investigator working on it. He'll get a copy of the ME report as soon as the post is done. J.T. thinks the ASA was in a big rush to charge you to make sure the public didn't get the perception that the press was getting any special treatment."

I told him everything. He took notes and quizzed me about my assets—and my mother's. "For future reference," he said, "just in case J.T. can work something out. Maybe get you an Arthur hearing."

The legislature mandates that defendants be held in custody in certain serious crimes, such as first-degree murder. But the Supreme Court, concerned about fairness to the accused, created the right to a hearing that allows judges to evaluate evidence on a case-by-case basis. If the evidence seems strong enough for a conviction, no bond is permitted. If the state's case appears weak, the judge can set bond until the trial.

Billy promised to call Lottie so she could talk to my mother and my landlady and take care of Bitsy and Billy Boots. What will the poor little creatures think, I wondered, if I never come home?

I had to remain positive. At least this was a modern facility, more like a dormitory than a jail. I can get through this, I told myself, hoping I was right.

My pod mates had seen my picture on the news while I was gone, and I was greeted with more respect. I wondered what my friends and relatives thought when they saw it. I had missed dinner but wasn't hungry; in fact I felt nauseous. I sat on my bunk, head between my knees. Would my life ever be the same again? How could it?

Inez, the inmate with the ornately decorated nails, took pity.

"Scared?" she asked.

"I'm thinking about my father," I told her truthfully.

"He know you're in here yet? Maybe he can hire you a lawyer."

"He's dead."

"Bummer. Heart attack?" She looked truly concerned.

"No, he was shot."

"Cops do it?"

"In Cuba. He was in jail; then he was executed by a firing squad. Castro. When I was three."

"Don't forget to tell your lawyer." She nodded sagely. "He can use it. Childhood trauma. No papa. That's why you wound up here."

I thanked her for the legal advice and admired her manicure.

"I could do yours like this," she offered. "We have a cosmetology lab. Some of the girls are real professionals." She pulled back, studying me with a practiced eye. "You could use a good haircut."

She turned to complain to Winsome about the Singer, who was raising hell, shrieking for corrections officers, noisily demanding immediate medical attention. The woman's lungs were powerful.

"That's what happens to people in here," sighed Winsome, the unofficial manager of our pod. "Check into the Greybar Motel and all of a sudden, you get sick, sexy, and religious. The woman's had a case of the VD for a year and a half; all of a sudden she wants treatment now. Everybody in here's got the hots for somebody. And people who never saw the inside of a church all wanna carry Bibles to court."

Lights out came at eleven o'clock, though it never really grew dark. Lights burned all night outside the pod. My thoughts seemed to echo off the shadowy walls, amid the screams, cries, and whimpers.

Thoughts of my father flooded my mind. I had always identified with him. He had been wrongly accused; so was I. Now, like him, I faced a death sentence. J.T. and Billy Marker had been careful not to say it, but we all knew that first-degree murder is punishable by death in Florida's electric chair.

Chapter Nineteen

I woke up shivering in the cold and reached out half asleep for the furry warmth of Billy Boots, who usually greets me at dawn. I had forgotten where I was. I was hungry, yet could barely swallow the corn flakes, dry toast, and weak coffee. We were allowed ten minutes, no more, for breakfast.

Immediately after, I was hustled off for my arraignment, apprehensive but glad that something, anything, was happening.

We didn't travel far. This is the video era. Defendants are now arraigned on TV, so we never had to leave the building. The system saves corrections officers the trouble of transporting prisoners to and from the jail and reduces the possibility of escapes or suicide attempts along the way. About twenty of us straggled single file to the video room, where we found seats in three rows of wooden pews, fidgeting under the watchful eyes of cameras mounted high on the wall. Most of our motley crew had checked in overnight. Some were sullen, some weepy, several hung over or descending from bad trips, some in high heels and hot pants, dressed for an evening out but now wearing the dazed, rumpled look of those who have slept in their clothes. At least one wore a housecoat and bedroom slippers. A sorry group. One nodded off, but the rest of us in our wooden pews must have appeared as nervous as whores in church.

After the usual delays over at the Justice Building, the show finally got under way. The woman judge was a disembodied voice piped through speakers on either side of the room. We would be appearing on three monitors at the other end, in the Justice Building courtroom.

The largest faces the judge, like her own home-entertainment center. Smaller screens play to the gallery and the attorneys.

As the judge called out our names, each hapless defendant stepped up to a podium, on camera, center stage.

I wasn't quite sure where to look when my name was called. The camera's eye was in front of me, but the speaker was off to the side.

"How do you plead?" the voice said.

"Not guilty," I said, succeeding in appearing shifty-eyed as I averted my eyes from the speaker to the camera.

She called the next name.

"Wait a minute." I hogged the mike, loath to relinquish it to the next defendant, a blonde in a sequined sweater, who had stepped up to replace me.

"Your honor?" I said, addressing the camera. Was it on? I wondered. I would have preferred eye contact with somebody who was just and all-powerful in an impressive black robe.

"Don't say anything!" a quick male voice said sharply.

"J.T.?"

Apparently he was there in the courtroom representing my interests, but before I could confirm that I was whisked away, upstaged by the blonde in black sequins.

That was it? Somehow I had expected as much time on jail video as Trish got on the *Today* show.

I wondered how I had looked on camera. I should have tried to do something with my hair. Inez was right.

J.T. showed up at the jail that afternoon.

"Was that you in court this morning?"

"Yes. You weren't supposed to say anything."

"I wanted to ask about the Arthur hearing."

"We have to be ready first. I've got somebody looking for the witness. He's a homeless guy who lives in or around the park and collects cans for a living. Name is Carl Ashe." He looked at me as though it might ring a bell.

"I wasn't there, J.T., and I see hordes of can collectors every day. They're everywhere."

"The evidence found in the car was a little pearl button that matched the others on your blouse. There was even a bit of thread still clinging to it. Matches the thread on the remaining three buttons on the blouse you gave them."

"Is that it!" Relief washed over me. "No problem! Trish grabbed the front of my blouse in the parking lot and ripped off two buttons. I wanted to go back to look for them after I got in my car, but I was too embarrassed."

"How did one wind up in her car?"

"Probably when I kicked at her purse," I said, rueful at the recollection of my vile temper. "Some of her stuff flew out, and when she picked it up she scooped things back into it. Or maybe she just hung on to it and still had it in her hand when she left. A cop named Gravengood saw the whole thing. He even told me I should fix my blouse."

"His name again?"

I told him. "He'll remember. He's the one who made the incident report. This so-called witness has got to be just as bogus. Find him, J.T. Find out who or what he saw. It sure as hell wasn't me." Nearly overcome by frustration and fatigue, I had never felt so helpless. "I wish I was out there working on this. When can we get the hearing?"

"Look, you only get one shot. If we blow it, you're stuck. We've got to overcome the presumption of guilt. It's more important in this case that we do it right as opposed to just getting it done, which means I believe you, Britt. I believe it when you tell me you had nothing to do with the murder. Let's find the witness and see what the medical examiner's report says first."

I tried to call my mother that night, but she wasn't home. I wondered if she had disowned me. Maybe she had moved and left no forwarding address. She had always complained that I never called her. When I finally did, she wasn't home—and I was in jail. I apologized in weepy fashion to her answering machine.

By day four, I had a new haircut from the jail beauty salon, a good one, and was seriously considering green and black fake nails, though I stopped short of taking the plunge. Any variation in daily routine was a blessing. The absolute loss of privacy and dignity, under the control of strangers with never before dreamed-of schedules, rules, and regulations, was numbing.

Where was everybody from the world I had left? Lottie had delivered some clothes and some books, but I kept missing her when it was my turn at the phone. Of course in the bad light, with the blaring TV and my pod mates' constant battles over its control, it was impossible to concentrate enough to read.

I thought a lot about Howie and reached the conclusion that my current situation was what I deserved, not for Trish's murder but for his death. Nothing is sadder than when the dream dies with the dreamer. His life need not have been wasted. Had I wasted my own, in the naive pursuit of worthless goals? My job had always taken precedence, at the expense of family and personal life. Did the *News* matter now? How many of my friends believed me guilty? My editors had seemed so eager to replace me with Trish. Was any of it worth it? The *News* would publish every day without either of us. She is dead, I thought, and I am gone. We will not be missed.

Freedom was all that mattered now. My life and my priorities would change forever, I swore, if I survived this crisis and walked free again.

J.T. had been right. He was jubilant on his next visit. "I filed for the hearing," he said, sitting down. "Here's what we've got. The ME says Trish was strangled with so much force that her larynx was crushed into her spinal cord. It's very unusual for women to be stranglers. It's mostly guys because it's a power thing. The ME seems to think it improbable that somebody your size, what is it?"—he scrutinized a copy of my booking card—"five feet four inches, one hundred fourteen pounds, would be able to exert that amount of pressure. The killer is most likely taller, stronger, heavier.

"I went to the station myself, with my investigator, to search for the other button. Locating it there would bolster your story, but it hasn't turned up. Gravengood is on vacation but should be back tomorrow. And"—he looked pleased—"I hear their witness may not be credible, *if* they can find him."

"What have I been telling you?"

"Now," he said. "Here's what you can expect."

J.T. was big on telling me what to expect, and I loved him for it. He had become my one ray of hope throughout this entire ordeal.

"You will be transported to the Justice Building, but you won't walk in the way you used to. You will be brought in through the prisoner walk-through and lodged in a holding cell at the rear of the courtroom. Eventually you'll be brought in and they will handcuff you to a chair in the jury box, which is where the prisoners are kept."

He saw my face. Handcuffs make a poor first impression. I wanted this judge to believe me trustworthy, someone who could be counted on to show up in court when expected.

"They're very security-conscious right now. They've had some breaks recently," he said.

Thank you very much, Linelle.

"And the judges are very nervous, frankly, since the shooting in that Broward courtroom."

It never helps your case to shoot the judge, I thought irritably. Some defendants make it tough on all of us.

"The hearing itself will consist of three or four witnesses and a lot of arguing. It's important, Britt, that you concentrate on remaining calm. If you hear something that doesn't sound right to you, just make a little note to me. Don't try to talk to me during the hearing, because I can't listen to you and listen to the witness at the same time.

"I have no idea whether we're going to be successful," he confessed, taking off his glasses, squinting through them, then wiping them with a handkerchief. "If not, we can appeal. But let's not even talk appeal at this point. Let's talk character witnesses. Do you think anybody at the *News* would testify in your behalf?"

I wasn't sure, given all that had happened, but I gave him some names.

The Richard E. Gerstein Justice Building swarms with seething, surging masses of humanity. Apparently none of them flush, as the rest rooms are disgusting. No soap, no paper towels, no paper. I know the building well; it is a gold mine for reporters seeking stories. Today one of them was mine

The prosecutor was Audra Evans, a star in the major-crimes division. I wasn't sure if that news was good or bad. Her career was on the upswing. I had always admired her; she was sharp, eloquent, and persuasive and didn't like to lose. I hoped she was also intelligent and experienced enough to be fair.

The fifth-floor courtroom was small, with low ceilings, converted from old offices when the need for space became acute. Like the jail, the prison, the morgue, and the streets of this city—the Justice Building was overcrowded. Two small windows overlooked the city skyline, a stretch of elevated expressway, and a paved parking lot. When I had the opportunity to glance out, I could almost see the heat rising off it.

The judge had not yet made his entrance. Waiting on the bench was a black plastic nameplate: Judge Stephen McLemore presiding.

Etched on the wall behind his chair were the words WE WHO LABOR HERE SEEK ONLY TRUTH. I prayed that this time it would be true.

The courtroom began to fill up. More prisoners arrived. A husky teenager with a shaved head shuffled in wearing leg irons. Delighted relatives in front-row seats, an elderly white-haired woman, a grossly overweight middle-aged woman, and a pale, short-haired teenage girl, pointed and waved enthusiastically at their errant progeny.

"There he is! There he is!" they cried to one another, like fans spotting a rock star. No contact with prisoners was permitted, and they had to be content with mouthing messages across the room.

In the criminal justice system you see the worst people on their best behavior, unlike the civil system, where the best people behave at their worst.

From where I sat to the right of the bench I could overhear a young man in a dark suit, hunkered down in the front row of spectators next to a pouting little girl of no more than six.

"I'm a friend of your brother's," he was saying. "I'm not going to get him in trouble, so anything you tell me . . ."

There was movement at the back of the room and my heart surged as my mother, Lottie, and Onnie pushed through the double doors. My mother wore a dark suit and a somber expression. I hoped she hadn't wandered into one of the rest rooms. Her searching eyes found me and she smiled, lighting up her face. Lottie blew a kiss and Onnie did a thumbs-up. A lump grew in my throat and tears stung my eyes. Stop it, I told myself, you need to look strong.

J.T. was hunched behind them, curly-haired and intense, files under his arm. Fred Douglas followed, dignified in a suit, and took a seat toward the back. So Fred had showed up after all, I thought. Maybe they all didn't hate me at the paper. Again, I fought tears.

I wore a navy sweat suit left at the jail for me by Lottie. I didn't know where she got it. It wasn't mine, but it looked new and was my size.

The judge entered and the buzzing stopped. Tall, thin, and brusque, he was a man in a hurry, facing a logjam of a calendar he could probably never clear if he lived to be a hundred.

He was flanked by the flags of the United States and Florida. His clerk, seated directly below, was a black woman with a sweater over her shoulders and a profusion of plaited hair.

Detectives Ojeda and Simmons were present, but I didn't see our prosecutor, and that worried me. If a major player didn't show up the case would be rescheduled.

Dino Mandell, the husky teenager with the cheering section, was called first. For these hearings the defendants did not step before the judge, presumably to save time. Only the lawyers and the witnesses faced the bench, while those of us whose fates were at stake sat listening in the jury box. The accused looked sallow and sullen to me, though to be fair the courtroom lighting was not flattering to anybody, except perhaps the judge, who seemed to be in a better light, above it all. Everyone else looked drained.

The teen's hearing was abruptly canceled because of an oversight. A deposition had not been typed. "This will be reset," the judge said, without looking up. The defendant's relatives did not understand. "Thank you for coming." He abruptly dismissed them. They had been waiting for more than an hour. The oldest, apparently the mother or grandmother, craned for a glimpse of young Dino as he was led away, signaling with a cupped hand to her ear for him to call her later. At least, I thought morosely, they know where he is now, which was probably never the case when he was free to boogie and had the keys to the car.

I felt a surge of panic. Where was our prosecutor? She walked in at that moment, the enemy, the person trying to keep me behind bars. I was happy to see her.

Audra Evans had to be in her early thirties but looked younger. Her short auburn hair was cut in a smooth, casual style, and she wore a simple gray knit dress over a slim, athletic body. Unself-conscious, she seemed totally focused on her goal. Looked like a fair and reasonable woman to me.

The next defendant was a young Latino accused of robbing several jewelry stores at gunpoint and binding the elderly owners with duct tape. He and an accomplice tried to outrun police after the last robbery and were captured with loaded automatics equipped with silencers.

His "fiancée" was present to praise his good character. No more than seventeen, with long, curly strawberry-blonde hair, high heels, and a tight-fitting dress.

Does her mother know she's here? I wondered.

The defendant's mother, a cashier at Office Depot, swore that her boy was a wonderful son who got mixed up with a bad bunch after they moved from New York three years ago, when he was seventeen.

The male prosecutor asked if he had a juvenile record back in New York.

The mother considered the question for a fraction of a second too long. Time enough to recall that juvenile records are not available.

"No," she said, "nothing."

She and the young fiancée swore they would be responsible for his appearance in court and were willing to go to jail in his place. Sure, I thought, they should try talking to somebody who's been there first.

The judge denied bond. Made sense to me.

Ice skidded down my spinal column when my case was called next.

"I'm ready," said the prosecutor.

She read a brief account of the basic facts, the prosecution's version. I resisted the urge to jump up and scream "Lies! Lies! Lies!" Ojeda elaborated on his theory, that as a result of the witnessed dispute outside the station I had followed the victim, strangled her, and returned to the newspaper, where I made incriminating statements to my supervisors. He mentioned the physical evidence, the button.

J.T. stipulated that the button came from my blouse but introduced Gravengood's report. He argued that the button had obviously been carried to the murder scene by the victim and pointed out that no other physical evidence linked me to the crime.

Evans stood expectantly, hands clasped, listening to the detective, as Ojeda testified about Ashe, the eyewitness. The man had not been located to view a lineup or give a deposition, "but we hope to have him available for testimony before the grand jury, when the prosecution seeks an indictment, and later for trial."

The judge frowned. "Who is he?"

"A constant outdoorsman," Ojeda said.

The judge stopped writing on a file and glanced up for the first time.

"The politically correct term for homeless man, your honor," offered J.T. "We have been aware of the state's predicament and have succeeded in locating the witness."

Ojeda glared, eyes searching the gallery. The prosecutor objected, her graceful hands pressed together prayerfully. The judge overruled her.

Ashe shuffled forward from a back-row seat. Skinny, whiskery, and nearly toothless, he was deeply tanned. He wore saggy trousers, too big around the waist, and a T-shirt. He gave his name; his address, he said, was Miami. I could see where that might stymie a process server.

Audra Evans rested her chin on her right hand as she carefully formed her questions.

Ashe seemed to enjoy the attention almost too much. He remembered being at the park the day the body was discovered and talking to Detective Ojeda. "He ast me if I saw any blonde woman round there."

"And what did you tell him?" the prosecutor asked.

"Yeah. I saw a blonde woman."

"Do you see her in the courtroom today?"

The witness shrugged, smiled, and turned to a middle-aged blondish woman in the front row of spectators. "There's one now."

Titters erupted across the room.

"We're talking about a specific blonde woman," Evans said, looking coldly at Ojeda.

"I see blonde women everywhere. I see 'em in my dreams." He offered a toothless smile.

Ojeda buried his face in his hands.

The associate medical examiner, a mild-mannered young man in spectacles, spoke next.

Trish was strangled from behind and pulled back, still struggling, over the seat of her car. A heel mark from her shoe was found on the dashboard. She had been so self-possessed in life that I found it difficult to picture her as victim. The doctor went on about petechiae and hemorrhages around the superior horns of the thyroid cartilage. "The hyoid bone was in its normal three parts in this case," he explained. "But the connections were stressed and hemorrhagic, and the greater horns on the right and left of the hyoid bone were fractured, despite the fact that the hyoid bone had not yet fused into a single structure as they do when we get older."

Coaxed by J.T., the medical examiner testified that all this indicated that a great deal of force was used to kill Trish and it seemed an unlikely crime for a suspect of my size.

The prosecutor pointed out, however, that Trish was an even smaller woman, at a hundred and five pounds, and that rage often enables people to perform acts of strength that might otherwise seem impossible.

J.T. asked about other medical tests and drew out testimony that, though vaginal examination revealed no semen, there appeared to be a lubricant on the pubic hairs and around the vagina, which indicated that Trish had had recent sexual intercourse. It was impossible to say how close to the time of death it had occurred.

Who was that? I wondered, remembering her sly smile the night we discussed love lives.

Inventory of her purse had included a six-pack of prelubricated condoms, with one missing.

Evans objected, calling it outside the scope of the investigation.

Fred Douglas testified that although I did experience difficulties with the deceased, I appeared genuinely shocked at the news of Trish's death and that my apologies could have been construed to explain our parking lot confrontation.

Douglas said I had always done my job in "a highly commendable fashion," adding that "in fact, she was recently nominated for a statewide award. We're proud of her work."

What award? I wondered.

Lottie testified next as a character witness. J.T. had said he would probably have my mother say relatively little, since, according to him, "everybody knows that mothers will say anything."

At this point I would have hated to hear her say that I was a wonderful daughter who got mixed up with a bad bunch.

J.T. presented evidence to show that I was "a local product" who had grown up in Miami and that after college I worked, paid my taxes, and behaved responsibly.

He also pointed out that the prosecution's eyewitness, the happy "constant outdoorsman," might also be a wino and did not appear particularly credible.

He concluded by saying that my mother, a widow, was willing to mortgage her condo, her chief asset, in which she had about $50,000 in equity, as collateral for my bond.

She hadn't disowned me.

Audra Evans called the crime particularly violent and objected to bond.

"I'll set bond at seventy-five thousand dollars," the judge said. He instructed me to surrender my passport, ordered me not to leave Dade County, and called the next case.

Chapter Twenty

Now remember,'' J.T. warned, ''this doesn't mean the charges will be dismissed. All it means is that we've created a question in the judge's mind as to whether or not you are the person who committed this crime.''

I worried about the collateral, but Billy Marker said he'd take the risk—along with a mortgage on my mother's condo, of course.

The nonrefundable $7,500 premium would just about deplete my savings, already dented by the down payment on my T-Bird. But for freedom, the price was cheap.

Lottie and Onnie and, of course, my mother had all prepared to kick in. Bless them. True friends are those who really know you but love you anyway.

''Don't you-all come back again, child, ya hear?'' Winsome trilled as I waited for Marker to write the bond.

I thanked her, then hugged her and Inez. The Singer promised to write. I knew she would.

My knees shook in Lottie's car. I wanted to drink in the big, broad blue sky and savor the sweet taste of freedom. It was heaven to fill my lungs with fresh air again, to escape the sounds and smells of the pod. Lottie, my mother, and Onnie wanted to cook dinner or go out. All I wanted was to go home.

We went to my apartment, where Bitsy went berserk, running in circles yapping. Even Billy Boots forgot his usual reserve and wanted to be held. I wanted to kiss the floor. First thing I did was toss out the burger, now gray and lethal, that I had thawed for that missed meal that now seemed so long ago.

Mrs. Goldstein brought homemade coffee cake, beef brisket, and noodle pudding. We all ate at my kitchen table. I devoured the good food, relishing every wholesome morsel. "I never want to see bologna or chili with rice again," I told them.

"I think you and I ought to get away for a few days, to the Keys or Cocoa Beach," my mother said. "You need to relax."

I squeezed her hand. "Sounds wonderful. But my first priority has to be my own defense. The case goes to the grand jury in a few weeks. We have to find out who killed Trish before that happens."

"Oh, Britt." My mother looked tearful. "Can't you leave that to your lawyer and the authorities?"

"Who cares as much as I do about proving my innocence?"

"Us." Lottie raised her hand like an eager schoolgirl. "We're with you."

"I need all the help I can get," I said gratefully. "J.T. is a champ, but Lord only knows what I owe him already. What's left in my savings account has to go to him for a retainer. If I have to go to trial, do you have any idea what that would cost? I go to trial and I'm in debt the rest of my life, to say nothing of the fact that my life might be spent behind bars. You can go broke proving you're innocent."

I looked at their serious faces.

"There's only one way to get my life and my job back, and that's to find out who killed Trish."

"Count me in," Lottie said.

"Me too." Onnie nodded.

My mother closed her eyes. "You are just like—"

"I know," I whispered, placing my hand over hers. I wondered if he would always be a source of tension between us. She had never forgiven him for allowing his dream of a free Cuba to become a fatal obsession. Maybe it's because every time she sees me, she sees him.

Perhaps it was my new freedom or the fact that I knew time was short, but I felt positive and energized.

"We can do this," I said.

"Right," Lottie answered.

"What can I do?" Mrs. Goldstein asked.

"Cookies," Lottie said. "Lots of cookies, chocolate chip. We're gonna need energy for this caper."

"I'll start baking in the morning," Mrs. Goldstein said, and went home to feed her husband. My mother sat quietly, smoking a long brown cigarette. I thought she had quit again but did not mention it, afraid it was me who had driven her back to the habit.

"Let's brainstorm." I took a legal pad, the kind I like to use for sit-down interviews. "Trish was having an affair with somebody. Whoever it was probably killed her."

"Think it was Abel Fellows?" said Onnie.

"Doubt it. He's a casting-couch type, probably just an encounter she used to get what she wanted. But we should include him on our suspect list."

"Miguel Rosado certainly had a motive," Lottie said.

I wrote his name on the yellow pad. "He's probably still in the prison ward at the hospital or in jail. That'll be easy enough to check. I've had plenty of time to think about it during the last few days. I think it was a cop because—"

"Speaking of cops," my mother interrupted, "that Kendall Mc-Donald, the one you used to see, called me twice. He was so sweet. I wish you—"

"McDonald?" I stared at her.

"Called me too," said Lottie.

"He asked if I was all right and seemed so concerned," my mother said. "He wanted to know what you needed. He said he had to remain at a distance from the investigation but that behind the scenes he was doing what he could," she said. "He sounded genuinely upset."

"Why didn't you tell me?" I smiled, eyes misty. I had assumed the man had run like a thief.

"He can help us," Lottie said.

"If he did, it could cost him his career. He couldn't afford to be linked to a reporter, remember? Can you imagine a police lieutenant involved with a murder suspect? Bum career move."

"He'll call you," Lottie said laconically. "Bet on it." She sipped her tea. "Marty's been trying to reach you, and also Curt Norske, your good-looking boat captain."

"I oughta get back to Marty," I said, jotting myself a note. "Curt can wait."

"Unless we need a boat to flee the country," Lottie said. "I believe you're right about it being a cop."

"It would explain Trish's pipeline into the department, the Zachary Linwood case and the others. How she seemed to know what I was working on before my editors did. It would explain how the tip that

Howie was holed up at Margaret Mayberry's was called in by a cop, when only Trish knew. She told her lover, and he did it. Makes sense. Did the detectives ever come to the office and search through Trish's things?''

Onnie glanced at Lottie and shook her head. "Never did."

"What's wrong with them?" I said, indignant. "J.T. is right, Ojeda is a hard-nosed hot dog. He was so focused on me as a suspect he didn't even bother to look at other possibilities. I was the easy target. Wonder what's become of her address book and the stuff in her desk?'' Suspended from my job until the charges were resolved, I couldn't very well go snooping around the newsroom.

"Maybe Ojeda overlooked it, but we didn't," Lottie said. Onnie nodded.

Startled, I studied the two of them.

"The night after you were arrested, we came in at two A.M. and went through her desk. Anything that looked interesting, we copied on the Xerox machine.''

"I don't believe you guys!''

"Ryan was in on it too. He was the lookout. He's beginning to think that's his permanent job.''

"Why didn't you tell me?''

"We was getting around to it," Lottie said. "It hadda be a cop she was sleeping with. You know what she had? A copy of the goddamn police roster! A printout with the badge numbers, names, ranks, dates of service, home phone numbers, and addresses of everybody, from the chief on down to the last cop and civilian employee, listed alphabetically. More than a thousand of 'em. Big thick sucker.''

"They guard those like gold!" I said. "They print out a limited number for use at the station. When they update they shred all the old ones.''

"Hidden in the bottom drawer of her desk. Also had the call sheets they issue to cops with the home phone and beeper numbers of all the on-call assistant state attorneys and medical examiners.''

"Wow, how'd she ever get access to that stuff? You copy them all?''

"Helluva job," Onnie said. "Spent more than a hour at the copy machine looking over my shoulder.''

"Cool. They'll come in handy for us, if I ever get back to work.''

"You will," Lottie said.

"Where is her stuff now?"

"Murphy had the city desk clerk clean out Trish's desk. Two boxes stacked in the wire room."

"We ought to have J.T.'s investigator or the cops go through it before they send it to her parents or it disappears. Maybe homicide will get on the right track. What else was in there?"

"Police reports, even supplements. Stuff that could only come from inside the department. Her Daytimer, with engagement calendar, notebook, credit card receipts, canceled checks."

"You copied them?"

"Naturally."

"You guys are amazing. Where are they?"

"Got 'em in the trunk of my car with my camera equipment. Want to go through 'em now? Didn't think you'd want to get into that tonight."

"Why wait?" I was way past exhaustion.

I put on a pot of coffee while she went out to her car and brought back a cardboard accordion file.

We spread the contents out on my kitchen table. It was odd to see neat, precise notes recently handwritten by someone now dead. Trish had kept all her receipts and records in her Daytimer. She apparently kept it in the office while she worked and then carried it home with her at night. I recalled having seen her with it on her way out the door at the end of the day.

We shuffled through copies of receipts and canceled checks. "Ha," I said, noting some Epicure bills. "I know about these."

"Here's her latest rent check," Lottie said.

"Rent? I thought she was still staying at the condo on Collins."

"She was."

"I didn't think she paid rent. She told me she was house-sitting. Let's see." Sure enough, the memo said rent and listed the address. The canceled check was made out to a Clayton Daniels. Why was that name familiar?

"Clayton Daniels!" All eyes were expectant and on me. "That's the name of the man she said was stalking her! Trish said she left Oklahoma because a stalker was making her miserable. And that was his name." I turned the check over. "This was cashed locally."

There was a phone number under the endorsement on the back. I made a note to call it in the morning.

"I don't understand," said my mother. "What can that mean, Britt?"

"Means she sure as hell wasn't renting an apartment from the man who stalked her out of her last job."

"Means she was jist a damn liar," said Lottie, pushing her hair back and riffling through the police roster. "Wish it showed which a these guys are single. You'd think they'd put their marital status on here."

"Everything Trish said was a lie. God, maybe her own web is what strangled her," I said.

"More likely somebody she snared in it," Onnie said. "She sure spent a lot of money."

"On herself," said my mother, shuffling through copies of credit card receipts. "Suit from Lord and Taylor, dresses from Collection Fifty-one, shoes from Saks, the Woman's Place—"

Lottie and I looked up. "Let me see that," I said.

"What is it?" said my mother, handing over the receipt.

"An abortion clinic," we chorused.

"We know because we've covered demonstrations there," Lottie added demurely.

I checked the date on the receipt for $350 with the same date on pages copied from her engagement calendar. "Here it is," I said, "a two o'clock appointment, two weeks before the murder. She was off for the next two days.

"Her tipster, her source, her lover, her killer. Makes sense," I said.

"Why do you think he'd turn on her?" Onnie said.

"With Trish anything is possible. I keep going back to that major coup, Lottie, when you and Trish scooped the world on the Zachary Linwood arrest. Her relationship with somebody on the inside had to already be in bloom. The department claimed only a few people were privy to that investigation. If the killer was one of them, that narrows it down." Something nagged at my consciousness. I recalled the press conference. "Remember, the chief was mad as hell and ordered internal affairs to find out who had leaked the information."

"I thought he'd have a stroke," Lottie said.

"Well, whatever happened to that IA investigation? Did they ever find the leak? Who was it? What the hell happened?"

"Those probes rarely pan out," Lottie said. "Cops investigating cops. Even if it did, you know how they like to keep that stuff quiet. Maybe Kendall McDonald can help us."

"Won't hurt to ask," I said, doubtful that I'd have the opportunity to talk to him.

I felt like we had just begun, but they all looked tired and I knew they had to work the next day.

"Why don't you guys go home and get some sleep?" I told them. "Leave this stuff here and I'll keep digging."

"Yeah, I've got to pick Darryl up at the sitter." Onnie yawned.

My mother carried her cup and saucer to the sink. "Would you like me to stay here with you tonight, Britt?"

"No, I'll be all right."

"Are you sure you want to be alone?"

"Absolutely. After sleeping with four hundred other bad girls in the jail, it will be a real pleasure to sleep alone." I kissed her, hugged them all, and saw them off into the night.

It was after midnight, but I prowled the apartment restlessly. Bitsy dogged my heels, refusing to let me out of her sight. Maybe some wine would make me sleepy, I thought, folding the papers back into the file.

I took the dog outside for a few minutes and stared at the stars. The air was cool, with charcoal-colored smudges moving across a sky the color of blue steel. The wind was as smooth as silk against my skin.

Moments after we went back inside, the doorbell startled me. Was Mrs. Goldstein still up? What did Lottie forget?

Without checking, I threw open the door.

Kendall McDonald stood there. We just stared at each other for a long moment.

"I thought they'd never leave."

I fit perfectly into his arms as he folded them around me. Home at last.

"You mean you were lurking out there for hours in the dark?"

"Of course not. I was driving by every five minutes."

Our lips were smiling as we kissed.

We sank into a stuffed chair, me cuddled in his lap.

"We have to stop meeting like this," I said, recalling his last unannounced arrival on my doorstep, after my frighteningly close encounter with the Downtown Rapist.

"I can't take much more of it either. This whole thing has been a nightmare," he said, and stroked my hair.

"Tell me about it." I traced the strong jaw, the cleft chin.

"It put me in a bad position."

"Oh, and I was in fat city?"

"I didn't mean that. I mean I wanted to get involved, I wanted to help you. I owe *them;* I care about *you.*"

We held each other.

"We belong together, Britt."

"You mean you'll come see me every visiting day?"

"Jesus, Britt, I'm serious here. When I thought of you over at the jail—" Our kisses interrupted.

"Aren't you afraid to be alone with me?" I murmured.

"I'll chance it." He changed position, pulling away as he unbuckled his leather shoulder holster. He placed the gun on the floor beside our chair. "See," he said, as we reentwined, "I'm an unarmed man."

"I mean the department, if somebody finds out you're here."

"I don't care. This night is ours." He pressed me closer.

"Do you have a license to carry that, lieutenant?" I asked.

I didn't sleep alone after all.

Not only did I wake up in my own bed but there was a bonus prize. The aroma of coffee was in the air and the warm spot next to me had been left by McDonald, who was now in my kitchen. I padded barefoot to the door and watched him.

"We've gotta get some groceries in here," he said, caught peering into the cupboard. "I found some coffee cake, but what's that smell in the refrigerator?"

"A hamburger I put in there to thaw, just before I got busted." I pulled on a bathrobe and joined him.

He kissed my mouth, my forehead, my nose.

"You lost weight," he said, hands around my waist. "You need to put on a few pounds. You also did something new to your hair. I like it."

I laughed. "I must admit, you are an improvement over my last roommates."

"How bad was it? I was going nuts. I felt so helpless."

I pulled away and sat down at the table. "It certainly increases your appreciation of the little things in life. It was an eye-opening experience, one I'd rather not repeat."

He poured coffee and placed a piece of cake in front of me. I attacked it with my fork.

"You wouldn't believe how good it feels to use one of these again." I held it up and admired the tines. "It's not easy maintaining your dignity and your table manners when all you're allowed is a plastic spoon."

"My poor sweetheart."

"Spaghetti night was a trip."

Our bare feet did sexy things to each other under the table.

"Oh, I forgot to tell you," he said, wiping crumbs off the sensual mouth I suddenly hungered for more than food. "The latest on Gilberto Sanchez, aka FMJ."

"They've got him?" My foot froze in midair.

"No such luck. He stole a car."

"Oh, *that's* new?" My toes resumed stroking his instep under the table. "Stealing a car is as natural to him as living and breathing."

"But now I think we're not the only ones looking for him."

"The FBI?"

"People who may be slightly more determined and a damn sight more lethal. He hit the jackpot this time. We had a tip that he was seen in Allapattah, nearly got 'im. Found the car he was reported driving. Prints inside were his. Something must have spooked him into ditching the car. Slipped through our fingers again like soap in the shower. But here's the interesting part. The car he got away in was a Mercedes. The driver had stopped to use a pay phone and left the keys. He turns around and this kid is driving away in his Benz. The guy reports the car stolen, but he's real upset, really nervous."

"You should have told him he was lucky he didn't get shot in the leg."

"Next day we get a call from a salesman at the Jaguar dealership on Seventy-first Street. Kid fitting FMJ's description came in to buy a new sixty-two-thousand-dollar Jag, for cash. Had the money in a shopping bag. But he had no ID, no driver's license, no nothing, and they couldn't sell it to him. Broke the salesman's heart."

"He called you?"

"Nope. The kid comes back half an hour later with a homeless guy . . ."

"You mean a constant outdoorsman."

". . . who hangs in the neighborhood. The homeless guy, who has ID, buys the car, and they drive out in it."

"Then the salesman called?"

"No way. It was another salesman who was jealous. He calls and reports it. Sour grapes. We find the homeless guy drunk as a skunk, pockets stuffed with cash. The kid paid him three thousand to buy the car for him."

"Where did all the money come from?"

"We run the guy who reported the Mercedes stolen. DEA says he's a money launderer for the cartel. Must have had a suitcase full of cash stashed in the trunk. Word on the street is that it might have been as much as two million. Rakestraw is beside himself."

"With a car like that, FMJ should be easy to spot."

"Everybody was looking last night."

"God, I hope I'm back to work when *that* story breaks."

"Better hurry."

"I know how much your career means to you," I said slowly. "And I want to protect you, to keep you out of this. But I need your help. I have to know if IA found the leak in the Zachary Linwood case."

"Why?"

"I just need to know."

"How does it tie in with your case, Britt?"

"I'm trying to find the real killer. I don't want to lay it all out yet, or put you in the middle, until I can piece it together. Can you just do that for me?"

He studied me. "Sure."

"Think you can find out today?"

"I'll try, but be careful, Britt. I wish you would trust me."

"If it doesn't work out, I don't want to take you down with me."

We splashed in the shower and washed each other's hair, but my heart wasn't in it. I was preoccupied, mind racing. I was fighting the most important deadline of my life.

For the first time, I couldn't wait for McDonald to leave. "You'll call me right away?"

He nodded.

"One other thing," I said. "The detectives on my case never even bothered to take a look at the contents of Trish's desk at the office. I think it's important that they do before it disappears." He agreed.

Two minutes after he left, I was on the phone, the taste of his kiss lingering on my lips.

Clayton Daniels was eighty-eight years old and living in a retirement village in South Miami. After the death of his wife five years earlier, he had rented out their apartment. Trish, the latest tenant, had an eighteen-month lease. Distressed by the death of the lovely young woman who had lived in his apartment, he was relieved that at least it didn't happen there. Would have made it much more difficult to rent.

Miguel still languished in the prison ward, nearly well enough to be moved to the jail.

Marty was next. "Britt, thank God! Where are you?"

"Home, released on bond. Trying to find out who killed her." My voice sounded small, and surprisingly his concern made me want to sob. Was the afterglow from McDonald wearing off faster these days, or had the caffeine reached my brain, awakening me to the enormity of my problem?

"I left a message for you before I heard about Trish. You didn't kill her, right?"

That's what I always liked about Marty. Always to the point.

"Right."

"That's what I figured. The reason I called was that I learned more about Trish's departure from the *Beacon*. She was a star there for a while. Came up with great stories. Had a sixth sense, a natural reporter. Always in the right place at the right time. It's a small paper, and she won them first place from the Oklahoma State Press Association for deadline reporting. First time the paper was ever even nominated.

"Her first big story for them was about the disappearance of a two-year-old, the only child of a couple in her neighborhood. Was missing for days: search parties, cops, bloodhounds, choppers, park rangers, the whole enchilada. Starting to sound familiar?"

"You're not saying . . .?"

"Yes indeed. Trish found the missing child trapped in the storm cellar of a cabin already searched once. He was unconscious, but she revived him.

"Then she was assigned a feach on a day-care center, but while reporting it she uncovered evidence of abuse, apparently while interviewing the children. The center's operator was later convicted. This was the prizewinner. But the case was later reopened and the woman's guilt questioned. There seemed to be a possibility that the molestation stories were planted in the children's minds. Meanwhile, her editors began asking themselves, Was she always there, in the right place at the right time, because she had a street reporter's instincts or because she *made* something happen at that time and place?''

I shuddered as I listened.

"Britt, you still there?''

"Yes, go on. Please.''

"They became uncomfortable. Nothing could be proven and the consensus among some people who worked there was that nobody at the top was eager to prove anything. A scandal would have ruined the paper's credibility and tainted their big-time award. She was just quietly told to find another job.''

"So they turned her loose on us.'' I remembered how in the beginning I had warned Trish about Miami. Miami should have been warned about her.

"That's what it looks like. If push came to shove, though, with the current situation, I'm sure they would talk candidly to detectives rather than face the scrutiny of two investigative reporters from big-city newspapers in Chicago and Miami.''

"I think I love you, Marty.''

" 'Bout time you realized it.''

"What about her family? Her body was sent home for burial. From what I've heard, they didn't come here. The landlord said they've asked him to have someone pack up and ship her personal possessions and give the rest to charity. Think they'd talk?''

"One way to find out. Do I call them or do you want to do it?''

"I guess it should be me. I'd much rather knock on their door in person, but I'm not allowed to leave the county, much less the state.''

"You ever need a hideout, Britt, *mi casa es su casa.*''

I took down the phone number, fortified myself with a cup of coffee, and sat at the kitchen table with a notebook and the phone.

The mother answered.

"Mrs. Tierney. I'm calling from Miami. My name is Britt Montero, and they say I killed your daughter. I didn't, and I need your help.''

There was a pause, the connection was broken, and a dial tone followed. She had hung up.

I took several deep breaths, said a prayer, and dialed again.

"Mrs. Tierney? We were cut off. This is Britt Montero again. I need your help.''

"We just buried our daughter,'' she said, after a moment.

"I know, and I deeply regret your heartbreak, but I am charged with a crime I didn't commit. I need to find out everything I can so we can identify the real killer."

"How can you call us at a time like this?"

"Mrs. Tierney, I understand your pain. But what about *my* mother? She is a widow and I am her only child. She just mortgaged her home to help me bond out of jail. I am innocent. Please help me."

She sighed hopelessly. "We knew nothing of her life there. We haven't been very close to Trish in recent years. There isn't anything I can tell you." Her voice was flat, as though numbed by old pain.

"So you wouldn't know who she was seeing here in Miami? She didn't mention anyone?"

"We didn't even know she had moved to Miami until clippings of her stories began to arrive in the mail."

"No phone calls? No letters?"

"Just the clippings. Her bylines. I guess she wanted to show us her work, what she was doing. She was such a lovely child."

"She was a beautiful woman."

"She was. Trish had a strong need for attention, and I'm afraid it was our fault. She has a younger brother, a wonderful boy, who has been terribly ill all his life. We never knew how long he would be with us. It was touch and go so many times. Of course his needs consumed all our resources and attention. She felt neglected, I suppose. How ironic. He is still with us, and she is gone."

"When did you first realize that she had this—need for attention?"

"Looking back, I think the first time was when Markie was just a baby. We had gotten him a puppy, and one day it disappeared. Trish was only six or so, but she went out and found the dog. We were all so thrilled, we praised her to the skies.

"One day weeks later, her brother stopped breathing; she ran to tell us and we barely saved him. We thanked God she was there. Our little heroine.

"Then other things began to happen to Mark over the years. Only when he was with Trish. I didn't want to admit it, but I became afraid to leave her alone with him. Things, accidents, kept happening. When she was twelve, there was an incident with another child. We sent her away to school when she was fourteen. She hasn't lived at home since. We continued to deposit checks to her bank account every month, to assure that she would never be in need.

"She wants and needs attention and will do anything to get it—she did, that is," she said, catching herself. "Forgive me. I have not yet become accustomed to referring to my daughter in the past tense."

"I understand. You will be as honest and candid with investigators if they should contact you?"

"Of course. You read her stories, didn't you? She did have a talent, didn't she?"

"Yes, she did. A real talent."

I hung up and rested my head on my arms, on the table, suddenly very weary. Everybody, I thought, is somebody's child.

The phone rang, startling me.

"It was Tully Snow," McDonald said.

"It was Tully Snow!" I told Lottie and Onnie, who had arrived for more brainstorming and a quick lunch. They brought sandwiches from the *News* cafeteria. On a par with jail food, they still made me homesick for the paper.

"Tully Snow? I remember when we did stories about his poor little baby sick with leukemia. He was the one barking and snapping at us at the vice mayor's office that day, yelling at me not to make pictures," Lottie said.

"Ever strike you that he might have been protesting too much?"

"An Oscar-winning performance," she said, dipping into the bowl of fresh-baked chocolate chip cookies. Sinking her teeth into one, she rolled her eyes and sighed. "This is why I came, Britt. Speaking of sweet, sinful stuff, you had yourself a little company last night, didn't you?" She cut her eyes at me.

Was I that transparent?

"Thought I spotted his Cherokee turning the corner as we pulled onto Alton."

My face reddened, giving me away.

"Told you!" she said to Onnie, and they both grinned.

"He was here," I said. "He's great. Let's get back to business. According to McDonald, Snow admitted he was the leak when IA called him in. Told them it was an accident, a big mistake. That he didn't know Trish was a reporter, that she was in the office, sitting on the other side of a partition and overheard him discuss the case on the phone. He was reprimanded for not reporting it to his supervisors."

"He lied. She knew more than one side of some mythical telephone conversation. She had every detail, chapter and verse."

"True." Lottie nodded.

"What do we do?" asked Onnie.

"I called his office and left messages. Tully was in, but he isn't returning my calls."

"What would you say to him?" Onnie asked.

"I'm not even sure. I was gonna play it by ear. If only we had a physical link."

"*They* sure did. Why did they have sex in the car?" Lottie said. "The sun's already setting at that hour this time of year, but it's still risky. She had an apartment; there's motels and hotels everywhere."

"Had to be spur-of-the-moment," I said. "Maybe she called him after our fight at the station and they arranged to meet there for a few minutes. Wasn't so spur-of-the-moment that they didn't use a condom. If only they hadn't, DNA testing could have proved he's the one."

"We know they didn't at least once."

We stared at one another, all wondering the same thing.

"You think they keep specimens?" I asked aloud.

After they left I called Dr. Sandra Lowe at the medical examiner's office. She had the information I wanted. I knew then what I had to do.

My appointment with J.T. was at four o'clock. He was renting office space in the penthouse suite of a prestigious Coral Gables law firm.

It was exhilarating to be back behind the wheel, master of my fate. I wondered if the other drivers on the expressway appreciated the joys of freedom. Judging from their performance, they didn't. Most seemed bent on being locked up or engaged in a gunfight before reaching their destination. I reached for the dashboard scanner out of habit but didn't turn it on. What if I heard a great story go out? What would I do? The only story for me to focus on now was mine.

The drive took only twenty minutes. I boarded the elevator with several people and hit the penthouse button.

"Penthouse. Sounds very fancy," commented a passenger to my right, a friendly man in his fifties.

"I don't know," I murmured. "I've never been there before."

"That's where all the lawyers are," he said. "When you get the bill, you'll want to jump."

He was probably right. J.T. had to pay the rent somehow. Whatever happened to lawyers who start out modestly in little storefronts?

At least there was no waiting. His office was actually a desk, a telephone, and a filing cabinet tucked into a small windowless alcove in the spacious suite. His cheap suit didn't fit the high-end environment, but he was sure to be better dressed soon.

"J.T.," I said. "I want you to make a deal for me."

My words jolted him back in his chair, stunned.

"Not that kind of deal," I said quickly. "I think a cop killed Trish. I want you to get the state to let me wear a wire and go talk to him."

He let out his breath in a *whoosh* and shook his head. "The state would never *ever* wire a homicide defendant, especially against a police officer. No way would they agree."

"What if I took a polygraph first?"

"They're not admissible in court."

"I'm willing to sign a waiver agreeing to have the results admitted into evidence. Pass or fail. The examiner of their choice. They can choose."

"No way. Britt, this is unrealistic. The machine is only as good as the operator."

"I've been framed, J.T. It's the *only* way. I'm gonna lose this or I'm gonna win it. I'm the victim here, this is the perfect frame, and my way is the only way to prove it. You have to persuade the cops, the prosecutor, and the judge to agree to this."

Shaking his head, he waved his arms, wincing, resisting, refusing.

"Hear me out." I opened my notebook and filled him in on everything.

He sat silent for a few moments after I finished my recitation.

"It would be very risky. It's bizarre," he finally said.

"I want to do it."

"I'd have to be able to convince the prosecutor that there's more to this case than meets the eye."

"There is. You can do it."

"It's a major gamble. It's dangerous."

"It's my life."

His expression still doubtful, he called the prosecutor to arrange a meeting with the detectives and the judge.

That night I used Trish's handy-dandy personal police roster and called Tully Snow at home. "I can't talk to you, Britt," he said, and hung up.

I dialed back. He hung up again.

McDonald called to tell me the latest on FMJ. Detectives had paid a call on his mother, just to touch base. Nobody home, door unlocked. Mother and daughter gone. They seemed to have taken nothing, not even their toothbrushes. Neighbors had seen them with a baby and a diaper bag, wrestling a suspiciously heavy suitcase into a taxicab twenty-four hours earlier.

"You think they took off with FMJ and the money?"

"He's not the sharing type, and he's still around. He could have bought a lot of distance with that kind of cash."

"You think they ripped him off?"

"Sounds like. The neighbors say he showed up last night screaming and cursing. Tossed the place. Every drawer upended, every closet ripped apart."

"Why didn't they call?"

"They're all afraid of him. But maybe his luck is finally running out."

"I wouldn't count on it."

"How does Chinese sound to you? A little shrimp-fried rice. Moo Goo Gai Pan. Personal delivery, in about an hour?"

"Sounds great to me," I said. "Maybe you could just leave it outside the door. Much as I want to see you, I don't think it's a good idea right now."

He sighed. "I heard what you've offered to do," he said. "It's crazy, but I think they're going to go for it."

Yes! I thought.

"Wish we could be together tonight."

"So do I," I said. "There will be plenty of other nights, if this works."

He sounded wistful. So did I.

Chapter Twenty-One

Five pens traced my past, present, and future in shades of red, black, green, and purple. The machine, a Stoelting Ultrascribe, was state-of-the-art. The operator, Ted Gentry, a rugged former cop, went into business for himself after surviving a near-fatal shooting.

I was wired.

Fingertip attachments were fastened to my ring and forefingers to measure my galvanic skin reflexes. "Your skin is an organ," Gentry explained. "When faced with threatening situations the skin constricts, forcing moisture out of your fingertips and forehead."

I wondered if that was what made Billy the Bondsman sweat so much. Thoughts of his clients skipping town probably had his skin in a constant state of galvanic reflex.

Corrugated tubes had been molded around my upper chest and stomach, measuring muscle constrictions and changes in respiration. There was a blood-pressure cuff on my arm.

Gentry had arrived at the state attorney's office with his truth machine in a Samsonite case, then set it up in a room designed for departmental examiners and equipped with videotape and camera facilities.

The questions had been reviewed earlier by the detectives, prosecutor Audra Evans, and J.T., who all agreed they were comfortable with them; the questions were fair and covered everything.

This was it. Do or die. I sat facing away from the moving pens that recorded my responses. That enables one to focus on the questions instead of watching what the pens are doing.

Lottie had been more nervous than I was that morning. "Lordy, I could never take one-a those thangs. I can't even answer the simplest question. For instance, they would start out by asking if Lottie Dane is my name. And I would start to thinking, Well, do they mean my maiden name? My married name? What about my nickname? Lottie is short for Carlotta. So if I say yes and don't tell 'em about Carlotta, is that a lie? If I don't mention my middle name, Samantha, after my mother's first cousin, will that show up as a lie? My daddy always said I was supposed to be a boy named Clifford after his granddaddy. What the hell *is* my name? *Arrrgh.* I would flunk right then and there, and that's only the first question."

"Shut up, Lottie!" I snapped at her. "Don't tell me that. Not today. If something goes wrong and I don't pass, they're gonna grab a rope and find a tree."

"Sorry," she muttered. "But it's like a choice between shit and shit."

"It's the only way. Don't make me crazy now."

It didn't help that the first question Gentry asked was my name. I put Lottie out of my mind and answered.

He ran five charts, repeating the same questions over and over.

The homicide detectives, Audra Evans, and J.T. were watching from another room, via video.

Evans and J.T. walked in as Gentry removed the attachments. The detectives straggled behind.

I looked expectantly at Gentry. "Do you have to interpret the charts? When can we hear the results?"

"Right now." He faced the lawyers and the two detectives. "No deception indicated to any of the relevant test questions. In my opinion, she's truthful."

"Flying colors!" was how J.T. put it. My elation was tempered by the fact that the toughest task still lay ahead. I was eager to get it over with and seize back my life.

They debated the latest device, in the form of an innocent-looking beeper, versus the traditional wire. Since I wasn't working, a beeper might seem suspicious. A woman investigator from the state attorney's office fitted me with the wire. The battery pack was in the small of my back, securely taped in place; the wire ran around my waist up and under my bra; the tiny microphone was positioned between my breasts. Wired for the second time that day.

"Try to get him to turn off any radio or TV and stay away from fluorescent lights," she said. "Try not to sweat. If it gets wet it could short-circuit and give you a bad burn."

Oh, swell, I thought. Will he become suspicious if my bra begins to smolder?

Ojeda and Simmons, who still appeared dubious, J.T., and two state attorneys' investigators were coming along.

I was nervous. "He's a smart cop," I said. "Park as far down the street as you can. Around the block if possible. We don't want to tip him off. If things sound like they're going bad, I can take care of myself. Don't come charging in like gangbusters unless he's already made incriminating statements."

We tested the equipment; then I drove my T-Bird to Tully Snow's home in Cutler Ridge. The others trailed in a unmarked van from which they would monitor and record our conversation.

Instead of the fiery dusks of summer, the November sun was a sinking disk of burnished gold. My future was up to me now. Guilty cops have a tendency to break, a compulsion to confess. I had seen that many times over the years. I think it is because most became cops in order to do the right thing. It's in their nature. Then women, whiskey, or money brings them down. Once they weaken, the next time is always easier.

I was relieved to see that he was home, or someone was. A light was on inside. The house was green and white, a rambling ranch style with huge shade trees hugging the gravel driveway. A freestanding carport nearly obscured a toolshed out back.

I pulled right up into the drive.

I rang the doorbell and listened to the three-toned chime inside the quiet house.

He opened the door wearing jeans and an unbuttoned long-sleeved shirt over a T-shirt.

"We need to talk, Tully, about our futures."

His eyes swept the driveway and the street behind me.

"How'd you get my address?"

"Remember when Lynette was sick? We did an interview for a story about the fund-raisers."

The past and what it had meant to him took him by surprise.

"Those were tough times," he said slowly.

"Can I come in? We need to talk."

"Just for a minute," he said, stepping back from the door. "I'm on my way out, have to run an errand."

As I entered, he stepped out and looked up and down the street. I hoped he saw nothing suspicious.

I don't understand Miamians who decorate their homes like ski lodges with dark furniture and fabrics that make you want to huddle around a fireplace in ski boots and sweaters. The red velvet sofa was trimmed with leather and mahogany.

We seemed to be alone. I was happy to see that he did not appear to be wearing his gun.

"Where are Evie and the kids? They must be almost grown by now."

"She's been staying with her mother lately. The kids are back and forth." His hair was beginning to gray at the temples, and he looked slightly out of shape. But I didn't have to wonder what Trish saw in him. She saw information, news tips, the inside track to breaking stories.

"You didn't come to see them," he said.

"No, I didn't. I came to see you." I sat down, without being asked, on a dark armchair. "I did nothing wrong and you know it. You framed me."

"What the hell you talking about, woman?" His face reflected surprise and indignation. His eyes did not.

"Forget the performance and sit down. This is me and you. Britt to Tully. You better hire yourself a lawyer and go down to talk to the state attorney."

He picked up a pack of cigarettes from the mantel and lit one. His hands were shaking. "You've got the wrong man. You must be crazy. You've known me for years."

"You framed me. Not only do I know it, but the prosecutor knows it now, as well as the judge. I passed a polygraph today and proved what you and I already knew—that I didn't do it."

"They ain't worth shit in court."

"Right. And I might go to jail," I said brazenly, "but I didn't do it and I'll get out. I may do a year, a year and a half, if my lawyer doesn't win an acquittal in the first go-round. But I'm gonna get out. You're not.

"When you go, you'll fry because they'll know you set me up. Let me take the fall for you, and the state will crucify you in court. You're the man who sits in judgment of other police officers and public officials."

"You're implying that I had something to do with the victim?"

"I don't have to. DNA testing will do that for me."

"They've got nothing to test, from what I hear."

"Don't be so sure. You were smart enough to use a condom before you killed her. But what about the abortion? You knew she had an abortion last month."

"No, I didn't know the girl. I wasn't aware." The glitter in his eyes told me he did.

"Did you know that they retain specimens from each aborted fetus? Tissue is saved for three months. They keep slides of the products of conception forever."

"If they run DNA, they need something to match it to," he said. "A man in that situation would be crazy to give up a sample of his body fluids."

"And there's not enough probable cause, as yet, for a judge to issue an order that you do so," I agreed. "But in this case that won't be necessary."

He cocked his head to one side and looked arrogant, puffed on his cigarette, and waited, smoke veiling the expression in his eyes.

"The department will ask for a sample. Eventually they'll get it. Whether you agree or not. Remember your annual police physical? You've taken one every year now for eighteen years. It's mandatory. They take your blood and your urine. Of course they could take it even sooner, with the department's random drug testing."

His posture began to soften slightly.

"You could always quit the job," I said, "but that would give a judge probable cause to sign a search warrant to take your bodily fluids."

I wondered how the guys in the van were enjoying my monologue.

I sighed, speaking more softly. "I always admired you, Tully. I thought you were a good cop. What the hell happened?"

Here I was, I thought, doing bad-cop good-cop all by myself.

I learned forward, affecting the expression of genuine concern that I had learned the hard way from Simmons.

"You'd better go in," I said, "and try to do the best you can for yourself. You've dealt with these cases for years. You above all people should know you're dead. You're caught cold. Cut the best deal you can."

He sighed heavily, put out his cigarette, and put his head in his hands.

"The bitch," he said. "I was a good cop. I *am* a good cop. After

Lynette died, things were never the same at home. I stumbled, in a bad moment. I succumbed to human weakness which I now understand.''

''What happened?'' I whispered. ''How did you meet her?''

''I was at a low point. Things weren't going right at home. Felt sorry for myself. Met her one night in a bar over on the Beach. We had a few drinks, talked. She was good-looking, friendly. I mentioned losing Lynette and she said she had a brother who died. She understood. If I hadn't been drinking . . .''

He reached for a cigarette and lit another.

''It developed into something more serious. A guy like me. A beautiful young girl like her. It had been a long time. . . . She seemed so innocent.'' He chewed a bit of tobacco off his lip. ''She wasn't.''

He glanced up at me as if he thought I would be surprised at that news.

''I was happy for her when she got the job she wanted. But she was obsessed. She wanted more and more. What I was doing wasn't ethical. I was putting my job in jeopardy. But she wouldn't let up. Nothing was ever enough. I gave her the Linwood story. Thought that would put her in solid with the editors at your place. But she always wanted more. She wanted to beat you, Britt, she wanted to beat the world. She was starting to scare me. A sick chick. All I wanted by then was to try to work things out with Evie, get her and the kids back, be a family again. Then she got pregnant. Used the abortion to make me feel more guilty.

''I couldn't break away. She threatened my job, she threatened to go to my wife. She was hysterical, mad as hell at you that day. I caught the tail end of it, coming into the office; saw you take a swing at her— something I'd honestly been wanting to do. Walked right on by. By the time I got upstairs, she was on the phone, screaming at me to meet her. I went over there.

''Much as I hated her at that point, the woman had a way about her. She could make you melt. God, Britt, she wanted you dead.'' He smiled wryly. ''You oughta be glad I did you the favor.''

''I didn't see it that way when I was sitting in jail.''

''You know I never meant for any of it to happen. She kept goading and threatening. I just couldn't take any more and things got out of hand. After I realized she was dead, I remembered that everybody had seen you two smacking each other around outside the station. It occurred to me that you were suitable for framing, the most likely suspect. Nothing personal, Britt. I was just trying to save my own ass. She was crazy, you know.''

''She was,'' I said. ''You don't know the half of it, Tully.''

''Funny thing is,'' he said, staring past me, ''for years on my job I never could understand those other people, how they got themselves in trouble the way they did. I held them in contempt. But we're all human beings and have frailties. All of us.''

''You're right, Tully. We all do.''

''I guess I better call the FOP attorney,'' he said. He stood up slowly, as though he ached all over. ''I don't know if Evie will stand by me. I don't deserve it if she does.''

''I'm betting that she will.''

I walked out into the clear night air, embarrassed that the sounds of my weeping were recorded true and clear on the tape that would send Tully Snow to jail.

Chapter Twenty-Two

The cops picked up FMJ's mother, sister, and baby in Boston, with $750,000 in cash. They told investigators that FMJ brought it home to stash in his room while his mother was away at work. He swore his sister to secrecy. When her mother came home, she tattled. They found it and were gone.

The man with the Mercedes put in a claim for the money. The cops told him they would discuss it only in the presence of IRS agents. They haven't heard from him since. The cops earmarked the windfall to underwrite TRAP, the new undercover Tourist Robbery Abatement Patrol. A lawyer, however, has filed a claim in behalf of FMJ's mother, who says her earlier statement was a mistake: the stash was really her savings, from tips.

I have been nominated for the Green Eyeshade Award from the Southern Society of Professional Journalists, for deadline reporting on the fatal shooting of Officer Dana McCoy. Winners will be announced next month.

My first story, my first day back at work, was the homecoming of Jennifer Carey. She came home in a wheelchair, her hair almost grown back from the surgery for her head injuries. She recognized her baby daughter and cried tears of joy as little Eileen was placed in her arms and her husband pushed them into their living room.

Lottie shot pictures. "This is the happiest day of my life," Jason Carey told us, through tears, as we said goodbye.

I thought about that on the way back to the office. His young wife faces years of therapy, his little son is gone forever. Yet he considered this the happiest day of his life. How can I feel sorry for myself or bitter about what happened to me? Happiness is relative.

Waiting on my desk were a dozen red roses from Kendall McDonald and a stack of mail, much of it from the jail.

I will read each letter carefully this time. We are all human, we all have frailties.

Before I could even finish the Jennifer Carey story, my phone rang. "Guess what?" Rakestraw said. "We've got us a carjacking in the north end."

"Yeah?"

"The driver's been shot in the leg."

"Oh, no!" I snatched up a notebook. "Give me the address." I jotted it down. "I'm on the way."

ACKNOWLEDGMENTS

I am grateful to South Florida's best and bravest: Sergeant William Glaister, Detective Joe Rimondi, Sergeant Jerry Green, Lieutenant Robert Murphy, Sergeant Rick Kolodgy, Lieutenant Jack deRemer, and Miami SWAT Officer George Velez; and to Joseph Harper, the man of truth. I am indebted to my steadfast friends Renee Turolla, Kal Evans, David Thornburgh, and Ann and D. P. Hughes; and I thank Joel Hirschhorn, PA, prosecutor Lisa Kreeger, Karen McFadyen, and Doctors Joseph H. Davis, Bernard Elser, Valerie Rao, and Steve Nelson for their brilliance and generosity of spirit. Photojournalist Bill Cooke and Arnold Markowitz of the *Miami Herald* gave their usual spirited support, and Mike Baxter rescued me once again from an information superhighway disaster. I also want to thank my agent, Michael Congdon, and my talented editor, Leslie Wells. Special gratitude and affection go to Ruth Ann Cione, the best and the brightest, and to Marilyn Lane, driver of my getaway car.

Friends are all that matter.